W9-BMA-714

FORTUNES OF WAR

By the same author

ALANBROOKE
AND WE SHALL SHOCK THEM
THE CHRISTIAN WATT PAPERS
AUGUST 1988

David Fraser

FORTUNES OF WAR

W·W·NORTON & COMPANY
New York   London

277989

Athens Regional Library
Athens, Georgia

Copyright © 1985 by David Fraser
All rights reserved.
Printed in the United States of America.

This book is published in England by William Collins Sons & Co. Ltd. under the title
A Kiss for the Enemy.

Library of Congress Cataloging in Publication Data

Fraser, David.
  The fortunes of war.

  1. World War, 1939–1945—Fiction.   I. Title.
PR6056.R28645F6   1985   823′.914   84–22714

ISBN 0-393-01973-X

W. W. Norton & Company, Inc., 500 Fifth Avenue, New York, N.Y. 10110
W. W. Norton & Company Ltd., 37 Great Russell Street, London WC1B 3NU

1 2 3 4 5 6 7 8 9 0

CONTENTS

PART I

1958

'I TOLD YOU that you'd yearn for speed, itch for an autobahn, get frustrated! Narrow roads, having to remember to keep left – terrible!'

They were, indeed, driving slowly but the older man, an Englishman, joked only to relieve the tension which lay between them. His companion, younger by twenty-three years, caressed the steering wheel of the Mercedes with the tips of his fingers, unsmiling. It was a hot day, the Sussex roads certainly narrow. When the younger man spoke he took up an earlier thread of conversation, undeflected. His English was excellent, his accent that of a foreigner but agreeable, a little soft. His voice was subdued. He played an imaginary scale upon the steering wheel.

'My generation find the Nazi period hard to understand, you know. People at home, people in Germany don't much like discussing it. It's a mystery. The frightful, horrible things done – some people say they can't believe them.'

The other sighed. They drove another twisting mile or two, talking quietly, painfully about those times. Across downland and shimmering in heat haze the English Channel now and then appeared, a sliver of distant coolness beneath the afternoon sun.

'Was it just a misfortune, Uncle, that a gang of scoundrels persuaded enough Germans to let them run the country, fooled them, a disaster which might have happened anywhere? Or did German history make something like that inevitable?'

'I'm not sure.' Indeed, the older man was unsure. His mind went back twenty years to a certain street bedecked with blood-red banners. To the bullying, loud-mouthed prejudice on the one hand, the smell rather than as yet the stench of hatred and persecution. And, on the other, to the enthusiasm of the young: the absolute identity, at a certain level, of Volk and Führer. There had been intoxication at that time in

9

Germany, a sense of purpose, unity and hope, no question about it. Turn that coin over and on its other side everything repelled, was vile.

How could one explain all this without sounding like some sort of naïve apologist for a criminal régime, murderers of so many, destroyers of so much, destroyers in the end of all he'd loved?

He looked at the young man. All they'd loved.

'I'm not sure.'

But after a few more exchanges he knew that he had to bring the conversation back to their own lives, their own hearts. From the general to the very, very particular. The terrifyingly particular. Now, therefore, he began talking with a different note in his voice, asking quiet questions, nodding to the answers, talking softly, the gentle purr of the Mercedes' engine distorting his words not in the least. The young man gazed straight ahead, controlling the car with expert delicacy, absorbed, frowning a little. Suddenly he turned his head, looked full into his companion's eyes and smiled.

'Uncle–'

'For God's sake get over to the left!'

PART II

1937–1939

PART II

---◆---

1937–1939

Chapter 1

'NOTHING TO CHOOSE between them! Murdering buggers! One lot backed by bloody Bolshies, the other by bloody Huns! Shits all, Spanish shits, Iti shits . . .'

'Shut up, Freddie. You're pissed.'

It was a warm, June afternoon in The Broad, at Oxford. A gaggle of undergraduates had emerged unsteadily from Trinity, continuing into the street, it seemed, an argument about events in Spain where Civil war had erupted the previous year. It did not seem the level of discussion had been high.

'. . . Balkan shits, English shits –'

'*Shut up, Freddie! You're pissed!*' It was a pacific voice, although slurred. But Freddie – whose declamation at the top of his voice had already attracted a number of onlookers moving along the pavement from the direction of Blackwell's bookshop, curious, disapproving – was not without support.

'Dead right, Freddie!' yelled another voice, a voice afflicted with what sounded like hiccups. 'Murdering buggers, dead right! And there's a bastard at Balliol who's having a party in his rooms to get support for them.'

'Support for who?'

'Not sure.' The Hiccupper elbowed his way toward Freddie. He was a large young man, face red with drink, small ill-tempered eyes gleaming, the urge to violence plain. 'Not sure. Let's break the bloody thing up. That shit Rivers's rooms.'

'We've not got time,' said the pacific voice soothingly. 'Come on, we're due . . .'

'Of course we've got bloody time. Rivers is a Communist anyway.'

'No,' said a voice uncertainly, 'I think he's a Fascist. Bloody blackshirt or something.'

'No, I know he's a Red.'

'Well, whatever he is,' bawled Hiccuper impartially, 'let's break up his bloody tea party.'

There were eight of them and by now a dozen or so spectators; a cluster keeping its distance.

'I've got to get back. Come on Freddie, we said . . .' It was the pacific voice, fighting a losing battle.

'More money than sense,' a man called angrily from the edge of what was now a small crowd. The man did not look as if connected to the University. He addressed nobody in particular. Heads turned.

'Balliol, boys!' shouted Freddie, suddenly clutching at Hiccupper for support in what appeared an attack of vertigo.

'More money than sense, that's you!' the same man called offensively. Several voices said,

'That's right,' not very loudly.

The man's words penetrated the fuddled brain of Freddie.

'What bastard thinks I've no sense?' Very unsteadily, challenged, he broke away from restraining hands. This was bound to be a row. This was bound to be fun.

'This way to Balliol, Freddie!'

'This bugger to settle first,' Hiccupper called encouragingly, joining his shoulder to Freddie's to shove through the little knot of people towards the man who had shouted at them. The latter now said, less loudly and with a nervous note in his voice –

'Come on, then!'

Anthony Marvell was making his way along The Broad towards the Sheldonian Theatre and stopped, without particular interest, to see what was up. He recognized with no surprise the inebriated voice of Freddie Barnett, an acquaintance but certainly not a close friend, a generous and unstable youth given to this sort of thing, one whose money attracted sycophants. Anthony stayed well clear of the knot of people enclosing the actors in this little scene and spilling over from pavement to roadway. Traffic was light, but Freddie's voice and antics would at some time attract the notice of police or proctors. Anthony had no wish to be caught up in the absurdity of a Freddie Barnett brawl.

'So you think I've no sense,' yelled the Barnett voice. 'Hey, where is he?' Anthony, about five yards away, saw that

14

Freddie's progress, supported by the Hiccupper, was blocked, perhaps unintentionally, by a slender form in a rather long-skirted grey coat of curious cut, his back to Anthony. It was not a back that Anthony recognized.

'You aren't the bugger who thinks I've no sense, are you?' shouted Freddie.

'No,' Hiccupper roared, 'not this one. You, get out of the way, would you?'

He was clearly in a mood to pick a quarrel with anybody in his path. Grey coat showed no signs of moving. Something in his demeanour appeared to inflame Freddie, pushing past towards his adversary. He blinked uncertainly and said,

'Who are you, anyway?'

'My name is von Arzfeld.'

'Your name is –' Freddie was now distracted from pursuit of the man who had called his intelligence into question. Hiccupper, too, stopped pushing and glared. Freddie belched and said,

'You a Hun?'

The young man in the grey coat was about twenty years of age, tall, with a handsome, intelligent face and a very serious expression. He was a dark young man, with a brown complexion and a certain air of attentive puzzlement, as if he were determined to record and comprehend every strange circumstance brought to him by life. Anthony had moved a few paces to the left to observe the stranger's face. He had never seen him before. A visitor, presumably. He found he did not want to take his eyes from that face, so gentle, so withdrawn.

'I am a German,' said the young man very calmly. 'I am residing here for one month.'

Hiccupper suddenly said, 'I don't think I like Huns.'

'Shut up,' said a new voice. 'This chap's a visitor. And for Christ's sake come on, if we're to break up that shit's party at Balliol. Freddie –'

But Freddie, who had now apparently forgotten the earlier insult he had been moving to avenge, stood his ground, swaying. He belched again, and said,

'I don't think I like Huns either. What did you say – Von Ars, von Ars –'

15

'Von Arzfeld.' The voice was still very quiet.

'Well, Mr von Arse-whatever-it-is –' At this moment Anthony, who had levered himself into the crowd and was not a yard from Freddie Barnett, stepped forward.

'Hello, Freddie,' he said pleasantly, 'I didn't know you two knew each other. This is an old friend of mine.' He took Von Arzfeld's arm with an engaging smile.

They walked up the Cornmarket. Freddie and his companions had melted away in various directions, the foray into Balliol apparently forgotten, bibulous and apologetic expressions of friendship having replaced drunken insult and suspicion, invitations to further meetings falling thick upon the summer afternoon air. Frido von Arzfeld had said nothing when Anthony first led him away, said nothing but looked at his companion, thoughtful and enquiring.

He saw a young man of about his own age, tall, pale, with hair as dark as Frido's own, but with a very fair skin. Anthony Marvell was broad shouldered and long limbed, bones delicate, mouth a shade sulky. As they walked Frido noted that Anthony always turned, swinging his body round towards him, when he had something to say, at whatever risk of cannoning into a passer-by. He was restless, too, this Anthony Marvell. It was hard to imagine him in repose. He talked fast, with a slight but attractive stutter. His eyes were brown and Frido soon noticed that when Anthony was talking to someone he gave his whole attention, fixing his companion with an unwavering, concentrated stare. This could be enchanting. It could be unnerving. 'He is serious,' thought Frido with a feeling of contentment. 'He has mind and heart.' And as they strolled, on that first of many evenings, towards Carfax, Anthony suddenly stopped dead, turned to Frido and smiled. It was a smile of great charm.

'Are people as rude and boring when drunk in Germany?'

'Worse!' said Frido, with feeling.

'Oh well, I'm sure you've found that Oxford isn't only like that.'

'I know that. I have two more weeks here. I have been very happy.' Frido was on an exchange from Marburg University.

'You're going to have lunch with me tomorrow. And often thereafter.'

They walked on, Anthony skipping now and then, turning to face Frido, sometimes walking backwards, laughing a good deal. Frido interrupted him at one point –

'I am very sorry. I did not quite understand.'

'I'm afraid I gabble terribly, talk too fast –'

'No, no. My English –'

'Your English is perfect.' Anthony gazed at him. Despite Frido's gravity there seemed a touch of the south in that swarthy colouring. Austrian or Bavarian origins might have been guessed, although this was belied by a certain stiffness rather than suppleness of gesture. In fact his family came from Lower Saxony. 'How concentrated he is!' Anthony thought. 'How much he minds about everything.' But he had already discovered that Frido, too, could smile; and that when he did so, his whole face smiled.

They reached Carfax. In front of them Tom Tower stood out against the cloudless sky. Large numbers of undergraduates drifted up St Aldate's from the river, scarved, flannelled, laughing, shouting, chatting. The great bell of Tom tolled half past five. Frido thought, curiously, that Freddie Barnett and his friends had started the serious drinking of the evening rather early. As if responding to telepathic communication Anthony said, with a chuckle –

'I think we got caught up in the end of what must have been a pretty extended and expensive lunch party!'

They stood for a moment, pausing at the four arms of Carfax.

'Come on, walk with me down The High.'

'The High,' murmured Frido, nodding happily. He was learning Oxford's language. In fifteen minutes each felt that he had known the other a long time. In an hour they would have become friends for life. They walked slowly down The High, talking, talking.

The sound of bagpipes was infrequently heard in Oxford's High Street. This now, quite suddenly, assailed them. Undergraduates habitually cultivated with success a determination to be surprised by nothing, and Anthony only raised his voice and stuttered a little more, making himself heard with difficulty above the shrill, insistent notes of the kilted piper walking slowly up and down, just clear of the pavement, a hundred yards ahead of them.

'Ah,' said Frido very seriously, 'look at this!' They were approaching the twin cupolas of Queen's. The piper, now level, wheeled majestically and marched away in front of them playing 'The Highland Wedding'. On the pavement a few yards ahead the piper's companion, a small man, a shrunken man in a threadbare coat, with only one arm and wearing dark glasses, held out a cap. His other sleeve was pinned to his side. On his chest was fastened a large piece of cardboard with an inscription.

'For King and Country. Wounded and blinded. Ypres 1918.'

They both fumbled in pockets, Anthony frowning, shame-faced, Frido watching him for guidance, uncertain, troubled. Pennies dropped into the cap and the small, shrunken man straightened himself as if to attention. The piper wheeled once again, countermarching.

'Plenty of those still,' said Anthony softly. It was 1937. 'They're largely bogus,' people often said, comfortably, 'especially the ones who pretend to be blind. They're run by crooks, put out on the beat like tarts, it's mostly a racket!' They walked on towards Magdalen, no particular destination in mind, simply delighting in the discovery of each other's company. Anthony suddenly checked, and touched the other's arm.

'Hang on here a moment.' He darted back, weaving through the not inconsiderable number of people strolling at that hour through Oxford's streets on a fine afternoon. A moment later he had reached the small, shrunken man, wearer of the placard, 'For King and Country'. He found a half-crown in his pocket and dropped it into the still outstretched cap.

'Thanks, sir,' said the man without particular emphasis.

'Well, good luck,' said Anthony awkwardly. To his embarrassment he found that Frido von Arzfeld, too, had retraced his steps. Frido said nothing, but simply nodded, as if understanding perfectly. He, too, put a silver coin in the cap. They resumed their walk, silent for a little. Anthony took his companion's arm, as he had when first befriending him in the middle of a hostile, drunken group, a half-hour before. He felt a current of sympathy pass between them.

18

'We never want anything like that again. I hate seeing them.'

'My father,' said Frido quietly, 'also lost his arm.'

'Well, never again! War, killing, destruction – it's madness, evil madness! Of course there are things like this wretched business in Spain. But between European nations – like last time – My God, No!'

'I agree.'

'So-called patriotic emotion – it's often tribal, animal emotion. Intolerance. The wolf-pack. Like those drunken fools this evening. As for war – well in spite of – oh, everything – I think that's something most people are determined not to repeat. Never again.'

'Indeed,' said Frido. 'Indeed. Never, never again.'

Chapter 2

———————◆———————

JOHN MARVELL stopped his large black Packard in the middle of Flintdown High Street, switched off the engine and climbed stiffly from it, one leg as ever aching somewhat. The driver of the baker's van behind him followed suit. The owners of two parked cars at the curb, returning to them with business in the little market town completed, paused and looked at their watches. A number of people came to shop doors and stood quietly. Flintdown church clock started to strike eleven. Unreliable, despite the ministrations of the verger, it was always corrected to within seconds of 'the wireless' before this occasion. That November morning in 1937 was cold and sunny, 'Not unlike,' thought Marvell, 'that other morning, years ago. *Our* eleventh of November.'

Flintdown was now silent. The whole of England was silent. At this hour, on this day, 'Eleventh hour of the eleventh day of the eleventh month,' people withdrew absolutely for two minutes from the pressure of daily living, of getting and spending and chatter. Work stopped. Machines were still. Travel was checked. All stood bareheaded – in church, in the street, at their place of work, in their homes. The old remembered sons. The middle-aged – John Marvell was forty-seven, his wife forty-three – remembered brothers, lovers, husbands: above all, comrades. The young – those under the age of thirty – recalled parents. And the children, who recollected nothing directly, had grown up beneath the shadows of a great melancholy, a corporate sadness.

The notes of the church clock continued to reverberate through Flintdown, echoing, measured, relentless. It took thirty-five seconds for the hour to strike. After the last note, two minutes would elapse – nobody needed a signal to mark the end of this extraordinary, united act of homage. So it had been decreed from the first year of victory. England could have accepted no less dignified an annual gesture. After two minutes folk would begin to walk quietly on, talking little. The first car door would close without fuss, the first engine apologetically start. Traffic would move again, commerce be resumed. Few people would refer directly to the experience just shared. There would be an occasional comment, understated, a relief of feelings:

'My husband just has to stay at home, he has to listen to it on the wireless, from the Cenotaph –'

'My sister lives near Croydon, they have the aeroplanes there, last year one came over during it – during the silence! It was all wrong, it could have waited, couldn't it! After all . . .'

'I liked it when we had the special service, the bugles and that, no matter the day of the week, there's fewer go to that now, save the Legion.'

But on the whole, Flintdown resumed its business without introspection. For two minutes there had been peace, broken by no human voice, interrupted by no sound contrived of man. For two minutes, although they certainly did not think of the matter thus, Flintdown had been at prayer, quiet, vulnerable and receptive.

John Marvell, a very private man, always felt awkward at the ritual gatherings, the bemedalled parades at which, as a wartime ex-officer, he was invited to appear. Latterly, he had excused himself –

'Mrs Marvell, you know – really we like to be quiet . . .'

His absence was regretted and by no means comprehended, but he was a respected figure in the county of Sussex, a well-liked, dutiful man and this apparent and atypical lapse in proper sentiment came to be accepted. It was now an acknowledged thing that 'Mr Marvell doesn't come'. His presence in Flintdown High Street anyway caused no remark, for his own parish church with its war memorial was several miles away.

Marvell generally tried to be at home on the morning of Armistice Day. It was inevitable that his wife Hilda, without morbidity, thought particularly at that time of her elder and

21

beloved brother, killed on the last day of March, 1918 during the final great German offensive which had seemed destined to crack the British front in Picardy. John Marvell liked being with Hilda on the morning of 11th November. She was a practical, unsentimental woman; they gave each other tranquil, undemonstrative support. And John, too, had lost an elder brother. He moved his mind away. That was a corridor off which were too many locked doors and he never walked down it far.

On this occasion, however, he had needed to go to Flintdown. A meeting with a local solicitor, a matter of some urgency concerning one of the farms, had been postponed from the previous week by the solicitor's, Christie's, attack of influenza, just over. And Christie's business had taken twice as long as forecast. Hilda was not alone – not, he thought, that it would have bothered her whether she were or not. He simply liked to be there, liked her to feel his presence, unobtrusive, comprehending, not only husband but contemporary. Their generation had shared an experience at which their youngers could only guess, and sometimes, John knew, impatiently resented with a sense of exclusion. But Hilda was not alone at Bargate. Anthony was at home, down from Oxford for three weeks' convalescence after a disagreeable bout of jaundice.

John drove homeward through the lanes to Bargate, seven miles from Flintdown. As he turned in at the white painted gates, up the long drive of Bargate Manor, his heart returned to the scenes evoked by the silence in Flintdown High Street – to that morning nineteen years before, when an orderly had brought to Company Headquarters a pencilled message from the Adjutant, confirming what had been rumoured for forty-eight hours. German emissaries had accepted unconditionally the terms dictated to them by Marshal Foch. All fighting was to cease at eleven o'clock. Thereafter, no guns would fire.

It had made little immediate difference to John's battalion, 'resting' as they were behind the lines. But it meant that no more friends – there weren't many left – would be killed. There would be no more letters to write to mothers and wives.

'Your son was an excellent soldier, a gallant man who will be sadly missed by all his comrades in this Company. No words of mine etc. etc.'

22

No more of that. Was it really nineteen years ago, that extraordinary sense of light, of quiet, of anti-climax, no appropriate words to speak nor thoughts to think? 'It seems yesterday,' John said to himself. 'It has dominated these years so heavily.' Soon, he supposed, it would be a distant memory, a gradual emergence from a fear and a pain which later generations would be unable to imagine and would blame their elders for permitting, however young they were. He left the car by the front door and went into the house in search of Hilda.

Every house has a centre, a point where the most significant developments occur, where opinions and affections are most often formed, where the heart most memorably beats. At Bargate Manor, this centre was the inner hall. The front door opened to a flagged space, with chests, umbrella stands, shooting sticks and croquet mallets piled haphazardly, foxes' masks mounted and scrupulously marked with the date and place at which young Marvells had been honoured by successive Masters of Foxhounds. From this outer hall – echoing, functional, draughty – glass doors gave on to the inner hall. The inner hall was the heart of the house.

It was a large, low-ceilinged oak-panelled room which ran the depth of the building, so that at the far end from the outer hall, windows opened on the garden – the rose garden, with brick paths intersecting beds of musk and floribunda roses. In a huge, stone-surmounted fireplace logs burned without ceasing from early November until at least the end of March, so that although the fire seldom smoked uncomfortably there was always awareness of its scent and crackle. Tables, piled high with books and magazines, separated a large number of comfortable sofas and armchairs. There were, on one wall, a set of eighteenth-century prints of Sussex; although a few 'good' pictures hung in the drawing and dining rooms – and some undistinguished Marvell portraits in the library – the panelling of the inner hall was beautiful in its own right and needed little embellishment. It was a dark room, yet never depressing. Colour was provided by the gentle shading of the sofa covers, by crimson curtains after dark, and, in almost all seasons, by a huge bowl of flowers which were Hilda Marvell's

23

skill and delight. The inner hall never seemed empty. It was irredeemably untidy, and conveyed always a sense of companionship, of voices.

Bargate was of no great architectural distinction. The oldest section – of which the inner hall formed the main part – was built in 1625. An elegant, though not altogether congruous, wing was erected at a right angle to the Jacobean house in 1768. In this wing, reached by a passage from the inner hall, was a long drawing room with French windows opening on to a lawn, next to a small, square study invariably knee-deep in John Marvell's papers. This eighteenth-century wing also contained a very delicate, curving staircase.

Less happily, John's grandfather had, in 1860, felt an injudicious urge for grandeur on a larger scale. He had, in consequence, tacked on to the other end of the original building a library (the biggest room in the house), a billiard room, and a number of closets and washplaces which earlier generations had found unnecessary and which, although adding to comfort, were unsightly. The windows of these Victorian rooms were large, plain and disproportionate to the original (whose front they extended). Behind the library was a new dining room and extensive kitchens, also added in the Victorian era. Nevertheless, Grandfather Marvell had kept the colour tones of the house's exterior harmonious. He had used the same grey facing-stone, and the general effect was, by 1937, by no means disagreeable. Climbing creeper helped blend the work of one century with another. Like many English houses, Bargate was a hotchpotch, but a hotchpotch with some dignity and a good deal of charm.

John went into the inner hall. A man with hair now greying, clean-shaven, face weather-beaten, lined and kindly, he walked with a slight limp. It was impossible to imagine his quiet, courteous voice saying a hurtful or malicious word. Hilda Marvell smiled up at him from a chair where she was making entries in a notebook on her knee. She had, he knew, been listening to the broadcast ceremony from the Cenotaph in London.

'Did it come through all right, my love?'

'Oh yes! It was such a relief to think it was George there – everything bound to be done right. Before, one never knew.'

'Perhaps that's a little unfair, darling,' said John mildly. 'His predecessor always struck me as perhaps never happier than when among old soldiers. And I remember seeing him once, in 1917. I suspect the War was one of his best times.'

Hilda shrugged her shoulders. She had felt little sympathy with the character and the predicament of King Edward VIII. She said,

'Anthony doesn't agree with me, of course. I was unwise enough to say something of the sort to him and he snapped at me. He thinks our generation turned against someone who could have led us all towards a better future. He thinks –'

At this point, however, Anthony himself came into the inner hall.

'I hope it's not the wrong day to ask, Mummy,' he said rapidly, 'but I've just been on the telephone to a friend of mine. He rang up from London and asked if he could come down for the night tomorrow, Saturday. I told him it would be splendid.'

'Of course it's all right,' said Hilda. 'Why shouldn't it be, darling? I know we can manage one more.'

'The thing is,' said Anthony, 'he's a German. His name is F-F-Frido von Arzfeld. He was at Oxford for a month last term, on a reciprocal visit of some sort. Now he's come over to fence for his university. I told him in the summer to get in touch with us at any time. He's taken it up. He's charming.' He looked defiant. He had never mentioned Frido before.

There was a perceptible silence, momentary but definite. Hilda said,

'That will be delightful. What university is he at in Germany?'

'I think he's about to leave. Marburg.'

'Your sort of age?' asked John.

'A bit younger. He's done everything, university and all that, very young. Now he's going to start his military service, after Christmas. Of course, they've introduced universal conscription again. Everybody has to do it.'

'I know that,' said John, a little drily.

'Well, we shall look forward to seeing him tomorrow,' said Hilda. 'Marcia will be down this evening. Otherwise we're on our own. Or at least, not quite – Stephen's coming over for dinner and staying tomorrow night as well. He's on his way back from somewhere on the coast, some speaking engagement.'

Stephen Paterson, a Member of Parliament, was Hilda's younger brother by eight years. She murmured something and left the room. Adjustments would need to be made.

'Do *you* mind, Dad?'

Anthony looked dissatisfied with the tranquillity in which his initiative appeared to have drowned. He sat down on the same sofa into which his father had subsided with *The Times* and turned to him with a suspicious half-smile. John felt the challenge and went through the motions of turning the paper's pages while replying with what he hoped could be taken as nonchalant detachment.

'Mind what, old boy?'

'My asking Frido here. My entertaining a Hun, a Boche. Your words.'

'Of course not. All that was years ago.'

'But you still feel it, don't you? You still feel hostility. Mistrust.'

John tried to appear judicious. He knew, and he knew that Anthony knew, that this was indeed so. And recent events –

'I don't – at least I hope I don't – feel prejudice now. All bad on the other side, all honour with our own. I don't think I ever argued that. But at times – still, one must be patient, humble. Nobody had or has a monopoly of right. And if we can't see each other's virtues as well as vices after twenty years, it's a bad lookout for Europe.'

'You're a fair man, Dad. But what do you feel in your heart?'

'I think the thing I feel strongest of all – by far – is that I never want to see a war again. And certainly not against Germany. Nor against anyone else for that matter.'

'Well, you'll have that in common with Frido, anyway. His great obsession is that we've got to be friends. He sees England *couleur de rose*.'

John considered his son carefully. He was very proud of him. Anthony could be intolerant, hasty and short of patience. What young man of spirit could not? He would, with luck, always have the courage to challenge conventional wisdom while retaining the wit to conclude – and, perhaps, the humility to admit in due course – where he was wrong. Anthony was a fine-looking young man, John thought complacently, a strong body and an interesting, handsome face. 'Hilda's son,' his father often said to himself with love, but he felt personal satisfaction too. And what was youth but a time to flex all muscles, particularly those of the intellect, and try all adventures, not excluding those of the mind? John rejoiced in Anthony's natural elegance, in the grace of his movements, in his agility of mind and body. Now Anthony leapt to his feet, mood changed, clouds dissolved, stutter not in evidence.

'You understand things very, very clearly, Father!' John thought it untrue, but he felt warmed and grateful. He felt blessed. 'He's a kind-hearted boy,' he said to himself, inadequately.

'Yes,' said Anthony, 'Frido thinks we're marvellous. Gets us all wrong of course.' He was smiling now.

'And what,' asked John, 'does he think of his Chancellor?' The Nazis had been in power for four years.

'Of Hitler? Harder to be really sure. His family, I gather, are dead against. They're very *ancien régime*, I suspect, and for them Hitler's a nasty little upstart with a raucous voice and some undesirable friends, that sort of thing. Frido feels a good deal of that, I think. And he's a decent as well as very charming chap. You'll agree, I know. But of course he'd certainly say that they – the Nazis – have done a lot for Germany. And I think they feel that the SA – the Brownshirts – were sorted out in 1934 and the early excesses (as he'd put it) were got under control.' Anthony smiled again. He was recalling Frido.

'And what are they going to do for the rest of us, does he suppose?' said his father. He did not particularly invite an answer. The question was more comment than interrogation. Muttering how far behind he was with correspondence he moved towards his study. Anthony remained standing, gazing at a large, smouldering log that looked poised to roll forward undesirably. His mind was elsewhere. The dark room enclosed him, rustling, creaking and whispering.

Frido von Arzfeld found it almost impossible to think, during dinner, of anything except the exquisite girl sitting on his left.

27

On his right was his hostess. Opposite, at the oval table, sat his hostess's brother, Stephen Paterson. At the other end, John Marvell was between his two children, with Marcia on his right, next to Frido, and Anthony between his father and uncle. The table was set in a large bay window in the dining room, itself a part of Grandfather Marvell's improvements, panelled in not unsuccessful imitation of the inner hall.

Marcia had the same smooth, pale skin as her brother, but her hair was brown rather than black and her dark eyes shone where Anthony's more frequently smouldered. Everything about her seemed to glow. It was impossible to imagine her except smiling. She seemed never still, a creature full of dancing movement. Tall – taller than her mother – she was slender, with delicate wrists and ankles. Her voice was gentle like her father's, and rather deep.

Frido's manners were perfect. Familiar by now with English ways, he reckoned he knew which gestures were out of order. He did not raise his glass of claret to Mrs Marvell and he had got over his earlier surprise that his companions were apt to start drinking wine as soon as their glasses were filled. He had replied with easy correctness to his hostess's enquiries about the University in Marburg and felt little surprise that she clearly had never previously heard of it. He had been told that the English, unlike the French, cooked without skill and ate without discrimination. This might, he supposed, often be true, but at Oxford, more often than not, he had lunched and dined in sumptuous style. And here, certainly, the dinner was delicious.

As if reading his thoughts, the voice on his left said,

'How do you like English cooking, Frido?'

He found himself blushing. Despite practice he had not yet got used to the fact that even unmarried women of good family used first names to strangers within minutes of meeting. Or so it appeared. He had also been told that it was a mark of poor breeding to discuss food or praise it in a private house. Yet here was this divine girl tempting him to do exactly that. This, late during the meal, was the first conversational opening to his left. It unfortunately coincided with a lull in other conversation and a gentle smile towards him by his hostess who had heard the question. His answer would be listened to by all. It was of absolutely no importance but it would be listened to by all.

'It is excellent, I think. Some of our dinners that Anthony and I had at Oxford were wonderful. But nothing, Mrs Marvell,' Frido said, turning politely to Hilda, 'was better than your hospitality this evening.'

'English beef,' said Hilda, smiling. 'Unexciting, I'm afraid.'

'Unexciting.' Frido cogitated on the term. Stephen Paterson did not intend to spend the evening discussing food. A short, plump, ambitious man with a roving eye, he liked to turn every occasion, every contact, to good account, to store useful information, to cull or create impressions. He had a young German captive at his brother-in-law's table and he wanted value from the fact.

'I imagine the food situation's pretty tricky in Germany isn't it, von Arzfeld? Friend of mine was paying some sort of official visit the other day – Coblenz, I think it was – and found that your Government have decreed on one day in the week there's to be no meat served or eaten! Import-cutting and all that. Can't be very popular.' His voice was loud.

Hilda wondered for the hundredth time how wicked it was to dislike her younger brother so much – she who had loved her elder brother so extravagantly. She would have been unsurprised to learn that parallel reflections were, at the same moment, going through the minds of both her husband and her son.

'It is true,' said Frido, turning his courteous gaze on Paterson and speaking his slow and somewhat pedantic English, 'that in Germany at present there is, in every week, a day without meat in the restaurants and so forth. Vegetables are served on those days. The reason for it was explained by our Government. I do not think it is very unpopular. There are some shortages in Germany, yes. It is a question of making our economic position strong and independent. That is what we are told.'

Stephen Paterson helped himself to some fruit.

'Your economic position might be stronger if you didn't spend so much money on expanding your Army, your Navy and your Air Force. Isn't that true?'

John Marvell felt uneasy. This young man was Anthony's

29

friend. John couldn't let him be hectored about his own country's policies when in a foreign land.

'Well –' he said. But Frido showed no sign of embarrassment or discomfiture.

'I believe that is so. Although it is also true, I think, that all the work and the manufactures have meant more people active and earning and spending money. For a little.'

'For a very little,' said Stephen, 'until the day of reckoning comes. We all have to trade. We all have to make things to sell to other people. Not guns for soldiers to carry on their shoulders in those big parades of yours.' His tone was intentionally goading.

'But I think,' said Frido, 'that very many German people want to see our soldiers with guns on their shoulders – in those big parades of ours.' He smiled as he said it. The silence at the table became more pressing. The conversation had assumed a new dimension.

John Marvell had pushed a decanter of port to his left hand. Anthony, in the aftermath of jaundice, was drinking nothing. Stephen helped himself. Hilda disliked the talk's turn and tried to catch Marcia's eye, to draw her from the table. Then she would be able to say, 'Coffee in the drawing room tonight, John. Please don't be too long.' But Marcia was looking at Anthony. Hilda intercepted a grimace.

'Well,' said Stephen, 'you've spent some time at Oxford. You know by now, if you didn't know before, that Herr Hitler's got people very worried. Very worried indeed.'

Frido looked attentive. At moments like this he found himself, quite inappropriately, thinking of his own family and home. There his father, who had lost an arm in that same '*Kaiserschlacht*' in which Hilda's brother had died, lived the life of a recluse, conscientiously tending the woods he loved, his family's inheritance. The older von Arzfeld took part in neither social nor public life, an old soldier ten years John Marvell's senior, contemptuous of demagogy, mistrustful of politicians all. 'They would get on with each other, those two,' thought Frido. Frido had lost his mother in 1920, in the hungry years when his sister, Lise, was born. His elder brother, Werner, had been six years old. A withdrawn, brooding father and a house empty of their mother had given to the children

30

an austere childhood, distinguished by their love for each other and for Arzfeld, its woods and meadows, small streams and ancient house walls.

Frido looked at Stephen. 'I will not,' he thought, 'attack the Nazis here, among these people. I will listen, and say as little as I can. Some things I must, perhaps, say.'

Stephen showed no sign of abandoning his theme. Hilda had managed to carry Marcia away to the inner hall.

'People here are ready to try to understand Hitler's point of view, you know. The Prime Minister in particular. I see a good deal of his Parliamentary Private Secretary, as it happens. There's a general feeling that Versailles shouldn't be the last words on a European settlement. But your emphasis on military build-up – that gives everyone the feeling that you don't want to talk, you want to march!'

Frido spoke with deliberation. 'As you know, Mr Paterson, Germany's armed forces were restricted by the Treaty to a very small number. A number which could not possibly defend the frontiers of the Reich –'

'And you've broken that restriction, that Treaty –'

'It made our Country,' Frido continued, 'without defence, at the mercy of all. We could see our land occupied at any time by others who said they had claims against us, just as the French African troops occupied the Ruhr some years ago, because –'

'Yes, we know all about that,' interrupted Stephen brusquely, 'the French behaved badly, we know that. But that's over. And after all, you'd fought on their soil for years. Don't forget that.'

'That was war, Mr Paterson. To protect itself in a war on two fronts, east and west, Germany has to seek a decision by –'

'Of course it was war. But who started it?'

John Marvell intervened.

'Don't let's refight the war, Stephen. It's over.' He could not resist adding, 'And as the only one in the room with direct experience of it, I don't want a re-play! Anyway, it's too late for these historical arguments. We ought to join Hilda and Marcia. Pass the port.' They were not historical arguments, and he knew it.

31

Stephen refilled his glass and pushed the decanter towards Frido. He was not prepared to be deflected.

'What I'm saying to our young friend here is that Germany's attitudes are getting Europe thoroughly alarmed. Austria, Czechoslovakia, Poland –'

'Each of those countries,' said Frido, 'has a difficulty in the relationship with Germany. Austria was left in a completely uneconomic situation by the Peace Settlement, by the creation of separate states out of the former Empire. This left Austria starving and without a future. Her people are German.'

'They may be German by race. They certainly don't want to be German by nationality.'

'I think many do,' said Frido calmly. 'Then there is Czechoslovakia. There are many Germans there, in the western part. They do not wish to belong to a state in which they feel they have no part.'

'I don't believe it.'

'I think it is so. In Poland, too,' said Frido, 'it is the same. And in Poland part of our country, the ancient Prussia, is divided from the rest by a corridor, created as part of Poland but really part of Germany.'

'It used to be Poland. And without it, Poland would have had no seaport.'

'Not all countries,' Frido remarked, 'have a seaport.'

John saw a chance to steer the conversation towards some sort of anodyne consensus. Somewhat to his surprise he had found himself liking Frido. He liked his looks, his self-control, his reasonable tone.

'We must be going. Joining the ladies. I think a lot of people appreciate there are some tricky questions in Europe. The great thing is to talk about them, not fight about them.'

'I agree with my whole heart,' said Frido.

John put his hands on the table and made to rise. But Stephen was dissatisfied. On a political question he could be presumed to have superior understanding to his brother-in-law and he had been cheated of the last word. He looked at Frido without rising, drained his glass of port and looked at him again.

'So you're on Hitler's side, are you?'

'Herr Hitler,' said Frido, with extreme care, 'has done some very successful things, I think. We have now no unemployment. People are happy, again, to be German. For long they were told they must be ashamed. Now they are told to be proud. For all that Herr Hitler is praised. By many people.'

'And his Nazi thugs,' said Stephen. 'His private army? His grabbing of personal power after Hindenburg's death? His murder of his own friends, let alone opponents, three years ago? Is that praised, too?'

'Perhaps not. Our country had been in a difficult, violent situation. But those things are over now.' Frido's mind went back vividly to his father's furious outbursts in the summer of 1934. *'Mördere! Abschaum!'*

'Some things were not good,' he ended lamely.

Stephen felt his advantage.

'The trouble with you Germans,' he said, 'is that you can't find a middle way. You're either asking for pity because your own arrogant folly has led you to disaster, or you're frightening people into fits because you're strong again.' His voice was quiet. Frido flushed. He wished his English, fluent though it was, were more adequate to express his feelings.

'Perhaps, Mr Paterson,' he said, 'it is right, much of what you say. But it is not simple. And I think if people have ever had to ask for pity, as you said, it makes them very hard, determined not to – not to be like that again. And people, especially young people, need to hope the future will be better, and that they can be free and proud and strong.' He wanted to tell the Marvells that it was all a great deal more complicated than they supposed. He wanted them to understand the background of fear and resentment, the memories of hunger, deprivation and ruin, which Hitler had been able so unerringly to exploit. He wanted to say that of course many decent people were deeply uneasy, but that their uneasiness was offset by a sudden, extraordinary revival of national morale, and that both aspects had to be comprehended. He found himself wanting, above all, that they should know people like his father, a grim, silent, moral man, a patriot to his fingertips yet repelled by what he learned of the excesses of the régime. He sighed.

'It is not simple,' he repeated.

Stephen Paterson had drunk enough port to make him bellicose.

33

'Well,' he said, 'just watch out, my boy. Just watch out – or you'll get a hiding like you did last time. You tell that to your friends in Germany.'

'Come along,' said John, getting to his feet, inwardly fuming. 'No war talk! Come along!' He blew out the four candles on the table. They were all standing. Frido looked at Stephen.

'I think, Mr Paterson,' he said, 'I will not tell that to my friends in Germany. It is not a good sort of message. They want friends with England.' His fluency was leaving him and his voice was uneven as his temper rose. Stephen looked at him with a hard smile, content with the end of the exchange. With exaggerated politeness he gestured to Frido to precede him from the room.

'Was Uncle Stephen rude to you?'

To Frido's relief Anthony had managed to form a group, away from their elders, of Marcia, Frido and himself. Marcia smiled up at Frido.

'He can be very rude. It's the way of all politicians! They have to shout at each other so they shout at the rest of us. It doesn't mean anything.' Anthony had murmured a furious word to her as the men had returned from the dining room.

Frido was still trembling. He tried to speak judiciously.

'No, your uncle was right in many things. But we must talk of better things than boring politics.'

Anthony had been appalled at the exchange in the dining room. He had been about to break in with some vigorous rejoinder to his uncle but had never caught an opportunity. He had not wished to pre-empt Frido. He was anxious to erase the scene, as far as he could, from Frido's mind. Now he said, stuttering, 'M-M-Marcia and I are planning a little European tour in the spring. I'm working with my mother to persuade her that I'm an adequate chaperone for my sister. Perhaps we can come and see you?'

'Of course,' said Frido, bowing. His head spun.

'Can we really?' Marcia opened her eyes wide. Frido began telling them about the country around Arzfeld, speaking of a landscape through which, in imagination, he was strolling with this superb, silk-skinned girl. And Marcia, half-listening to

34

him, wished that he was not leaving Bargate in the morning. She found herself wishing this very much indeed. She had hardly talked to Frido. He had been monopolized by her mother and by the men. She smiled at him again and held his eyes with her own. Across the room she sensed that her mother murmured something to John Marvell. Marcia said,

'It would help my German. It's not bad, but I really want to improve it because there's an idea I might go to cousins in Vienna and study art there, next year some time. Mummy's got a cousin in our Embassy.'

'You will, I hope, nevertheless improve your German, not your Austrian,' said Frido smiling. 'They speak rather differently you know.'

'Come on, Marcia!' Stephen was calling from the fireplace. 'Last time I was here you beat me at billiards! You promised me revenge! Quite true,' he said to John. 'She's a female prodigy your daughter. Let's have fifty up, Marcia,' he bellowed.

'All right, Uncle Stephen. It shouldn't,' she said to the others with an impertinent smile, 'take me long.' They left the room and Anthony held Frido firmly to their corner.

'Do you really mean Marcia and I could visit you in the spring? Could we come for a day or two to Arzfeld?'

'It would,' said Frido with feeling, 'make me very happy. I hope for more than a day or two. But I must explain. It is not like here. My father lives by himself, as you know. Very simply. It is not –' he felt for words.

'Not very feminine, perhaps?'

'That is correct,' said Frido, relieved at the comprehension. 'Not feminine at all. My father does much work in the woods. There are many dogs and horses. It is quite rough – hard –'

'And no ladies.'

'Except my sister, Lise. She is eighteen.'

'Only a year younger than Marcia.'

'She seems more, I think. More young, I mean.'

Frido simply could not envisage the Marvells at his home. Nor could he imagine his father's reaction to the arrival of two such guests. As long as Frido remembered, nobody outside the immediate family and their servants had slept at Arzfeld. He thought of the whitewashed, stone-floored, shuttered

35

house, beautiful, functional and austere, of the silent woods on every side, the peace of the place. He thought of the ubiquitous harness and whips, the hunting trophies, the sense of unity between forest, farm, stable and house, the regular prayers. How would the Marvells, from this house full of flowers, carpets, chatter, candles – how would they adjust to a setting so tranquil and so primitive?

'I'm looking forward to it already!' said Anthony. 'Of course we will come!' They talked of roads and travel. Their intimacy from Oxford days was entirely re-established.

'Do you play billiards, Frido? No? Well, let's go and see how Marcia and Uncle Stephen are getting on. She should have beaten him by now. She's pretty good and he's rotten. He hates losing of course!'

Laughing, he led Frido toward the billiard room, his good humour restored. 'It's that door at the end of the passage,' he pointed, 'I'll be with you in a minute.'

'You little devil!'

Marcia had brought off a skilful long range pot of the red ball to take her score to fifty-one. Stephen, who had struggled to thirty with shouts of indignation at his ill-fortune, put down his cue on the corner cushions and held out his hand with mock good sportsmanship.

'Well done, little Marcia! You're quite a girl aren't you!'

He put an affectionate arm round her. Marcia laughed into his face. The house was warm in spite of the autumn weather and her neck and shoulders were bare above a dress of flame-coloured silk.

'Quite a girl!' Stephen breathed heavily, 'and a lovely girl too!' He kept his arm firmly round her waist and started to stroke her bare arm with his other hand.

'What are you going to do with your life, Marcia? You'll lead a lot of men by the nose, I'm sure of that!' Stephen's hand was active. He began caressing arm, neck and shoulders.

'Uncle Stephen,' said Marcia very coolly, 'I think we'd better go back to the drawing room.'

'In one minute, my poppet,' muttered Stephen. He dropped his face to where her dress divided above two small breasts, and buried it in her flesh. Marcia pushed him away hard, starting to laugh again. Stephen, thoroughly excited, panted 'Oh, you little darling!' and grabbed at her. Marcia sidestepped, and ran round the billiard table. Stephen pursued. Marcia said, very loudly, '*No*, Uncle Stephen. That's enough!' Stephen took three very fast steps and managed to catch her wrist, lust lending him agility. As she turned, trying to break free, he caught her from behind, pressed his mouth against the back of her neck and ran his hand up beneath her dress. There was a sound of ripping material.

'Stop it, Uncle Stephen!' shouted Marcia at the top of her voice. 'You're drunk, you're disgusting, and you're tearing my clothes!' She jerked herself free. One shoulder-strap was torn. A stocking was beginning to come down. Marcia was flushed, her eyes more brilliant than ever.

Stephen's billiard cue was lying on the corner of the table. Snatching it, Marcia brought the butt end against his shirt front with all her strength as he again started towards her. Stephen grunted. Marcia took it back ready for another blow. At that moment the door opened and Frido walked into the room.

Chapter 3

———————————•———————————

'ANT –'

'Why the hell do you have to call me "Ant"?'

'Don't be pompous. Nobody with a three syllable name can expect it to be used, and you always banned "Tony".'

'Hasn't Marcia got three syllables? What about "Mar" in future?'

'Perhaps you'd rather "Anton"?'

'I think I would, Marse.'

It was good-tempered, nursery wrangling. Anthony found Marcia, separated from him in age by under three years, a perfectly ageeable companion. They had crossed France, driven into Germany via Belfort and wandered eastward through the Palatinate in high good humour. Anthony's car, an elderly Morris, a source of pride but with an erratic reputation, had behaved with stolid docility. Except for the rich, and the Marvells would have been astonished to be so classified, foreign travel was a comparatively rare experience for Anthony's and Marcia's generation. At least when young.

It was near the end of April, 1938, a clear fortnight before Anthony was due to return to Oxford. The elder Marvells had attempted to place an embargo on the venture, appalled by the German invasion of Austria one dramatic March weekend. It had all appeared peaceable, with German columns photographed amidst ecstatic Austrian crowds, tanks decorated with evergreen branches rather than braced for war. But all Europe had shuddered, and it was fortunate from the younger Marvells' point of view that the opinion of Cousin Francis Carr in Vienna had been sought. He had written an encouraging letter. Everything, in both Austria and Germany, appeared perfectly calm. Although not welcoming the 'Anschluss' he doubted whether the peaceful assimilation to the Reich of a friendly, German-speaking Austria, itself in a parlous economic condition, betokened the imminence of a European war. In great spirits, Anthony and Marcia had crossed the Channel.

'Ant, what's the name of the place we thought of reaching tonight?'

'"Anton" if you must, damn you! Herzenburg. Look east from Stuttgart on the map.'

'What's east?'

'Right, you half-wit! Move your finger several inches to the right.'

He drove on.

'I don't think it's marked.'

'God, women!' said Anthony, happily. It was a beautiful spring day. It was agreeable to be driving this doubtful machine across Europe, with as pretty a girl as Marcia beside him, even though she was his sister. The country was green, the dark red roof tiles of the small towns and villages harmonious. Anthony was astonished at the sheer beauty of Germany. He had expected dourness, a grey, Teutonic face, a land with a scowl. Instead there was on all sides colour, vivid enchantment, a fairy-tale quality. The half-timbered painted houses, the sharply etched peaks of wooded hills, the enclosed valleys, somehow conveyed a different, an older, a half-mysterious world. They had been driving in this country for only two days, and had spent but one night in it, at a small, clean *Gasthof* near the Rhine. Nowhere, yet, had either felt any sense of menace – menace which, they had half-imagined, would strike them immediately the frontier was passed.

They rounded a corner. Their way ran through woods of birch and larch.

'I've found Herzenburg,' said Marcia contentedly. She sat well back in her seat and tilted a large straw hat forward to shield her eyes fom the April sun. The weather, she thought, was remarkable. It was a summer hat.

'This,' said Anthony, 'is going to take some time.' He braked and reduced speed to a crawl. He noticed that the petrol gauge showed low.

Ahead of them was a moving column of bicycles. The dusty road twisted through the trees but at least a dozen were visible. Each was ridden by a boy of about fourteen, and each boy wore a khaki-coloured shirt and pair of shorts identical with those of his companions. This was an organized, a disciplined expedition. Anthony began slowly to pass. As he did so, most boys smiled broadly, raising right hand from handlebar in a wave of salutation. Eventually, they reached the head of the column, where the leading bicyclist was riding a machine adorned by a small, triangular pendant. It was red, with a white circle. On the circle was embroidered the swastika: the '*Hakenkreuz*'.

The Marvells drove on in silence. There was little traffic on the road.

'They look happy.'

'Oh, *they're* happy! They're children. What do *they* understand?'

Anthony felt older, experienced and yet confused.

'Hitler's put a spell on a whole generation. And on enough of their elders who should know better.'

'Let's keep an open mind,' said Marcia. 'We said we'd try.'

They pulled into a filling station. There were tourist vouchers to be used: pre-paid, privileged. An attendant moved towards the car. He looked surly.

'*Grüss Gott*,' said Marcia, an Austrian ski-ing holiday well remembered. The German of both brother and sister was fluent but haphazard as to grammar and correctitude. She gave the man a smile. Few failed to respond to Marcia's smile. This particular Swabian was one of the few. He looked at her suspiciously. *Ausländere*! and trying their idiotic Bavarian on him! He fiddled with the petrol cap.

'*Guten Tag*,' said Anthony.

'*Tag –*'

Petrol began grudgingly to flow.

'We've come from England,' said Anthony. 'It's our first visit to Germany.'

'England!' said the man in neutral tones. Anthony saw for the first time that he had a wooden stump instead of an ankle protruding from the left trouser leg.

'I expect you were in the War. When we were enemies.' Anthony smiled as he said it and the man nodded with something like an answering smile. He finished filling the tank of the Morris and moved to Anthony's window to inspect the coupons.

'Mein Herr, you are too young to remember! I left my leg in Belgium fighting you!'

'My father,' said Anthony, 'was also a soldier. He also carries wounds and always will. And he was in Belgium. Ypern.'

'Ach!' said the other, with feeling, 'Ypern! It was the worst place! They talked about Douaumont, about Champagne. But Ypern! We were never dry. British shells, mud, hunger, never dry! It was the worst place!' How curious it is, thought Anthony, that he gets visibly friendlier as he recalls those hostilities, those sufferings.

'Mein Herr, we never want that again.'

'We certainly don't! My father would agree with you, *vom ganzen Herzen*.'

The man accepted a fifty pfennig piece with a nod of something like goodwill. At that moment, the column of bicyclists appeared. They were singing. Despite the effort of pedalling and the extended column, the harmony of at least the first half dozen was admirable.

> *Ein schifflein sah ich fahren,*
> *Käpitan und Leutenant,*
> *Und drinnen waren geladen*
> *Drei ganzen kompanien Soldaten –'*

They waved another cheerful greeting to Anthony and Marcia without slackening pace or rhythm –

> *Käpitan, Leutenant,*
> *Fahnerich, Serjeant,*
> *Nimmt das Mädel . . .'*

The petrol attendant had appeared to take no notice of them and had busied himself finding a sponge and paying some perfunctory attention to the windscreen of the Morris.

'*Nimmt das Mädel bei der Hand!*' he muttered. 'That's all they're good for.'

'They seem happy youngsters! *Sorgenlos!*'

'*Ach, ja, Sorgenlos,*' grunted the man. He grimaced and turned away.

'I think Herzenburg is about two kilometres, Anton. If we are where I think we are.'

'Then I don't think we are, darling sister. We've just passed the "Herzenburg" town sign. We must be coming into it now.'

'How odd!' Then they were both silent. Ahead of them, five hundred yards away, high walls extended each side of a tall brick gatehouse. The walls, also of dark red brick, were crowned with tiles along ancient ramparts. The gatehouse was built over a narrow way, penetrable by only one car at a time and regulated by an incongruous traffic light. A few modern houses had been built outside the walls of Herzenburg. Within, under the sharp but fading light of late afternoon, the place held promise – or threat – of entry to an earlier, an enchanted age. Behind those walls, which the Marvells' guidebook assured them still entirely surrounded the mediaeval town, surely anything might happen.

'I want a photograph of this before the light goes.'

There was space to park in front of the great gate, and Anthony dismounted with Leica camera and walked away from the walls to compose a shot. Marcia strolled to the gatehouse itself and inspected it. Its barrel roofing extended to a surprising depth. These were formidable walls, massive, serious. The town might have prettiness, *gemütlichkeit* within. Through the gateway Marcia could glimpse a narrow street, steep gables, brilliant window boxes and gaily painted shutters. But the place had been built to withstand war.

Her attention was caught by something on the outer wall itself.

'Anton, come and look at this.'

Nailed to the wall, about seven feet from the ground and distanced some five yards from the gateway so that it could not fail to catch the eye of every traveller entering Herzenburg whether by car, bicycle or on foot, was a rectangular wooden board some three feet tall. It was varnished to withstand weather. In the centre of the board was painted, with some skill, a bearded face. The face, surmounted by black ringlets, was dominated by a huge, hooked nose and adorned by a grinning mouth and hooded eyes. Within the limits imposed by his crude medium the artist had conveyed, with a good deal

42

of ingenuity, a countenance of avarice, lechery and cunning. It was a horrible face.

'What a ghastly thing!' said Marcia, laughing uncertainly. 'Who's it meant to be? What's it advertising against? I can't ever read that writing of theirs.' For beneath the caricature were lines in heavy Gothic script. Anthony translated them slowly aloud.

'I am a Jew.
I suck the blood of Christian merchants.
I exploit German workers.
I *verderbe* German maidens. ("What's that?" said Marcia. Anthony was not sure – " 'Corrupt' I think. I'll check.")
'I make my home, like a maggot in the flesh, in the German State,
In order to destroy it.'

'Charming,' said Marcia, shakily. 'Do you suppose the City Fathers put that up?'

'The Party, I expect,' said Anthony. It was the most disturbing phenomenon they had yet seen and it revolted them both.

'I'm going to photograph it.' It was already getting dark but Anthony was skilled with camera and the photograph was to come out all right.

Next morning they explored Herzenburg. The previous evening had been highly enjoyable. Lamps set in fantastically wrought iron brackets had lit the narrow streets from one *Bierstube* to another. In each there had been singing, the music of the accordion, stamping of feet, an atmosphere of exuberant welcome. Marcia's face had sparked instant but generally good mannered attention, and their adequate command of German had quickly brought brother and sister on easy terms with the large number of young people celebrating the evening.

'Is it always like this?'

'No, they told me at that last place. It's some sort of special jamboree – a traditional thing, an anniversary of the town's liberation from somebody or other in the seventeenth century. In the Thirty Years' War, I imagine. Or from the French, perhaps.'

'Well, at least that's a long way away from the Party, and all that,' said Marcia. They almost succeeded in forgetting the old Jew hanging outside the town wall as they moved to yet another cheerful, musical crowd of handsome young.

As next morning they walked out into the town's main street Marcia stopped with a sense of shock.

'Was it like this when we drove in?'

'Of course not. They've been busy overnight.'

From one end of the street to the other, from tall ceremonial poles, blood-red banners were suspended. The poles were placed at intervals of about twenty metres so that the impression looking up the street was of a continuous riot of crimson colour on either side. In the centre of each banner was a white circle, and in the circle was the swastika. The effect was dramatic and dominating.

Anthony recalled a verse of the *Horst Wessel Lied*, so often heard on the wireless and sung more than once the evening before –

> *'Wann wehen die Hitler Fahnen*
> *Über allen Strassen*
> *Dann bricht der Tag*
> *Der Deutschen Freiheit an –'*

He gave a snort and spoke rather loudly.

'The Nazis seem to have taken over the triumphs of the Thirty Years' War.'

A group of four young men were passing at that moment. They wore khaki shirts and ties, peaked caps with strap beneath the chin, brown breeches and high brown boots. Their leader looked sharply at Anthony and gestured to his companions to halt. He had heard the remark. He approached Anthony and stood in front of him with a polite smile. His right hand shot up.

'Heil Hitler!'

'Heil Hitler!' said Anthony with a deprecatory grin.

'You are English?' said the young man, in English.

'We are. I can see,' Anthony said in German, 'that you speak excellent English but I need to practise German. It is our first visit to your country.'

'And do you like it?'

'It is beautiful.

'We are making all things new,' said the young German. 'We are rebuilding our country. We are doing it all together, the men, the women, the rich, the poor, the old, the young. Especially the young. We are all working, all helping each other, making a new, happy Germany.'

'How admirable.'

'This is being done under the guidance of the National Socialist Party. It is a party of all the people.'

'And the celebration today – it is an historical event, is it not?'

'Yes, it is the celebration of the liberation of the town from their enemy, from the French. The National Socialists have brought a new era but they also believe Germans should know and value their own history. That is very important. So every traditional event of this kind is supported and encouraged by our Party. You may like, perhaps, to contribute to our funds? It is to help old Party workers who can no longer help themselves. Maybe they are sick.' He extended a tin and Anthony put a mark in it.

'*Vielen Dank!* Tell your friends in England what we are doing.'

'I will,' said Anthony, 'I will indeed.'

With a further 'Heil Hitler' and a bow to Marcia imitated by all three companions, the young man took his little group on their way. Brother and sister walked on in silence.

Marcia pointed to a shop window.

'Look, Anton!'

In the window – repeated in a number of alternative wordings to the same effect by more than half the shops in the street – was a large notice.

'*Juden unerwünscht.*'

'Pretty categoric!' muttered Anthony. 'Jews not wanted!' Then, 'Who are these? We've not seen these before.'

Coming towards them on the pavement marched a knot of seven or eight young men in black uniforms, with side-caps and armbands bearing the ubiquitous swastika. Their buttons were of silvertoned metal. Swinging from the belt against the left buttock each carried a short, white rubber truncheon.

'I think these are what they call "SS". Sort of private Nazi army.'

More groups of SS men passed. All looked young, cheerful and confident. Marcia drew admiring glances. Several exchanged remarks as they passed and there was some broad laughter.

'Back to the car!' said Anthony. 'We said we'd reach Frido by this evening. We've quite a way to go and we know how slow some of these roads are.'

'Don't you think we ought to stay a bit, Anton, and see what happens here, at their celebration?' Already they could hear the insistent notes of a band, the intoxicating, rhythmic throb of a military march from what seemed to be a square, two hundred yards ahead.

'No,' said Anthony, 'I think we'll go. I think, just for now, I've had enough of Herzenburg.' They had already loaded the Morris and soon were on their way.

Anthony let his thoughts run. In these uniforms, banners and slogans, in this posturing and stridency, there was something curiously unreal, theatrical. It was as if a large part of the population had decided to put on fancy dress and enact a series of dark, mediaeval charades – and then found themselves caught up in the enactment, somehow enchanted, intoxicated, unable to break the spell and return to the more prosaic, the drabber, liberal modes of thought and life they had been bewitched into deserting.

The Shylock looks of the Jew caricature hung in his mind, as did the sneering hatred which seemed to drift like a gas from the heavy black, Gothic characters of the texts all over Herzenburg. He was reminded of other faces of exultant onlookers, at the Crucifixion or some comparable scene of cruelty and pain, as depicted by early Flemish artists – that grinning enjoyment of others suffering, that incapacity for pity which, if the painters were to be believed, must have been a hideous counterweight to the simple beauty of so much mediaeval life. Had Germany reached back, and reverted to such types? Anthony drove into a filling staton.

'We need some oil.'

The garage attendant, another elderly veteran as was clear from heavy military moustache and erect bearing, had beautiful manners, and kind, courteous eyes. To exchange the briefest of greetings with him was to feel more at peace.

Frido von Arzfeld walked back towards his home through woods bursting into leaf. Winter was surely over, he thought, although last year there had, remarkably, been a heavy fall of snow in the first week of May. He was content that the Marvells should see Arzfeld in the spring. He loved it at all seasons but spring and autumn were best. He knew Anthony and Marcia were driving north from Franconia. They might arrive at any time from mid-afternoon.

Frido thought of his last meeting with them, of Bargate. Anthony had shaken his hand and looked into his face with what was, he knew, real affection, although, with the English, one could never be absolutely sure. And Marcia – his mind's eye saw Marcia's flushed face in the billiard room, the glinting eyes of that unpleasant, ill-mannered Deputy, the uncle, Herr Paterson, clearly a man of disgusting morals. He remembered Marcia's broken shoulder-strap, her bare shoulders, her dishevelment. How lovely she had looked! Had she led that old lecher on? Had she meant it when she had said goodbye to Frido, had pressed his hand, held his eyes with hers and said, 'I can't wait until the spring, until our visit to your home, Frido'? But with English girls, too, thought Frido sadly, perhaps one could never be sure.

He heard his name called –

'Frido, Frido!'

It was Lise. Good heavens, had they come? It was past five thirty. He started to run towards the house. Lise appeared at the iron gate which connected the wood with the vegetable and fruit garden, fenced against deer and hare, which lay behind the house itself. He could see her, but two hundred metres separated them and he couldn't make out what she was calling.

There was no formal flower garden, nor lawns at Arzfeld. All appeared practical, functional, part of a way of life deeply rooted in the soil, of a culture untouched except lightly by the decoration, the elegant artificiality of the eighteenth century. The house was large and plain. It looked both farm and manor. Arzfeld had beauty, but beauty in which man's work was so harmonious with nature as almost to seem part of it. The deep red of those brick walls which were not whitewashed, the darker red of the tiles, the faded, peeling yellow paint on the shutters were all colours whose tones blended perfectly with the varied greens and browns in Arzfeld's background of tree and meadow. House, stable, farmsteading, extensive barns, dusty cart road running to the courtyard before the main entrance – all seemed as if they had been in place for ever, interlocking parts of a whole dedicated to the management of animals, crops, timber; inseparable from husbandry and the land. The atmosphere of the place was, the Marvells later decided, mediaeval. The word was expressive but inexact. Certainly, Arzfeld could be imagined at any time in German history, backdrop to any scene of peasant serfs, armoured *landsknechte*, wandering friars. But the house in its present form had been chiefly built in 1555. The von Arzfeld of those days had been touched by the inspiration of Luther. He had devotedly supported his lord in the league of Protestant princes, and an imaginative eye might deduce the fact from his building. The place was lovely but austere.

Lise was shouting something about a telephone. It seldom rang at Arzfeld.

'Who, Lise?' Frido shouted back. 'The Marvells, yes, but from where? Where are they?'

But it was not the Marvells.

'Werner has telephoned. He is arriving here this evening. He has seven days' leave, unexpectedly. Wonderful!'

Lise's eyes shone. She adored both her brothers but Werner, now twenty-five, and Frido's senior by several years, was her idol. Infrequently at home, Werner's value was enhanced by rarity. He was an officer in the Army. His cadet training had been cut short because German military expansion had led to an urgent demand for more young officers. Werner had thus been a lieutenant for nearly four years. He was stationed in a small garrison town in Bavaria, between Munich and Garmisch.

'When does Werner come, then?'

'Today. By train. I've asked Franz to fetch him from the station. He'll be here for supper.' Most trains stopped at the small town on the railway only three miles from Arzfeld. Franz,

48

elderly farm bailiff, drove a horse and trap, and picked up the infrequent visitors. Frido demurred.

'I can go in the car.' It was Frido's proudest possession.

'I thought perhaps – the Marvells –'

Frido agreed. Best see how the evening went, at what hour Anthony and Marcia would arrive. The plan could always be changed. And Franz covered the distance to the station remarkably quickly.

'Did you tell Werner we are to have visitors?'

'Of course. Friends of yours. He was surprised.'

'I hope he wasn't upset.'

'No, I'm sure he wasn't.' But Lise was not really sure. Werner must have wanted his family, his home, peace, no strangers. He'd not been to Arzfeld for months and months.

'Just as well,' said Frido, 'I know he'll like them very much.' He loved his brother. Werner's visits were occasions of joy. But now he felt a touch of cool at the heart, he could not say why.

He smiled at Lise and thought how attractive she was. They were all dark complexioned, with smooth, olive skin. In Lise's case this was unusually combined with fair hair, silkily framing a face of exceptional prettiness, with brown eyes and a small, tilted nose.

'Perhaps Anthony will fall in love with Lise,' he thought. 'That might be symmetrical. Symmetrical but difficult.' Then he thought of Marcia again. Of recent days he had thought of little else.

They walked together toward the house. By a side door a tall figure was standing. Grey breeches, black riding boots; left sleeve of a green collared jacket tucked into a pocket, pinned there, as all knew. Face lean and lined, high cheek-bones, thin mouth, a permanent limp since 1917. Kaspar von Arzfeld stood very still.

'You have heard that Werner's coming? We can hear about this Army of ours! And I want to speak to him of next season's planting plans. I have spoken of them to you, Frido. Not to Werner. It should be done.'

'Exactly so, father.'

'He will be here for supper. Perhaps we shall eat late this evening. Is that not so, Lise?'

'Yes, exactly, father.'

'At what time will the English family arrive?'

'It is not certain. They are coming by car.'

But at that moment Kaspar von Arzfeld cocked his head and said, 'I think I hear something.'

The clock in the stable block struck six. Two minutes later, Anthony's Morris came into sight round a corner of the wood, followed by a cloud of dust.

Anthony Marvell looked thoughtfully from his host to Werner von Arzfeld, the elder son. Anthony's German had improved in the last few days. He and Marcia shared a facility for languages, and enjoyed them. Despite a childhood almost entirely free from foreign travel, both were competent in French and German, the work of governesses at an early age, farsightedly employed by Hilda against the protests of the young. Their fluency owed little to formal schooling. Now Anthony felt at ease, anticipating with pleasure practice and conversation in an entirely German household. He was already talking much faster – more like his pace in English.

Kaspar von Arzfeld, however, insisted on speaking a slow, careful English. His vocabulary was sound, his grammar excellent, his grasp of pronunciation imperfect. He, too, had looked forward to a chance to practise again a tongue learned in youth at which he had once been unusually proficient.

'I was determined, Herr Marvell, that my sons should learn both French and English. Does Frido speak correctly?'

They had supped in a low-ceilinged, white-painted room, with heavy oak furniture and antlers of many stags adorning the walls. Now they sat before a huge open fire in the central hall of Arzfeld, a room not dissimilar from and serving the same purpose as the inner hall at Bargate. Chairs were more upright, but had the same comfortable shabbiness. On a long refectory table was a flat, circular bottle containing a white wine from the banks of the Main. It was new to the Marvells, a post-prandial drink, delicious.

'Frido speaks English very well indeed. Perfectly!'

'Ach! Perfectly!' Werner von Arzfeld said it softly, with a smile. His expression was both sardonic and affectionate. 'How

50

superb looking he is!' thought Marcia. 'Like Frido, but every feature stronger, more definite. Harder.' Werner had said little at table. He had held a long conversation with his father before they had gone to supper, murmuring apart while Frido and Lise chatted to the Marvells. At supper Kaspar had spoken knowledgeably about the state of agriculture in Europe, and the problems of forestry. Now and then the conversation had taken a turn leading, it seemed, to a dead end unless some essentially political issue were at least to receive acknowledgement. At such moments Kaspar pursed his lips and opened another line of talk.

Anthony was determined to extract from his host some comment, however neutral, on the European scene. The older man could not be drawn. Werner at times shot at Anthony a look with a sly smile behind the eyes. 'I know what you're after,' he seemed to be saying, 'but you won't get this old one to say much.'

Lise spoke little, now that conversation was general, but sat with a slight smile on her gentle rather submissive face. The atmosphere at Arzfeld was essentially, almost brutally, masculine. The long widowerhood of Kaspar contributed to this, but it went deeper, had persisted far longer. This was a house for the forester, the huntsman, the warrior, a place of horns and saddles and armed men.

Kaspar drew on his cigar.

'Herr Marvell, there is a famous English poet, Andrew Marvell. You are of the same family?'

The question was not uncommon.

'I believe we may come from the same origins, yes. My father says there is a connection. But we are not descended from him.'

Kaspar had prepared himself.

> '*And now the Irish are ashamed*
> *To see themselves in one year tamed –*'

He stopped suddenly, appalled. Was it not, perhaps, dangerous, delicate, insufferable manners, to speak of the Irish to this young Englishman? Was Ireland not still a rebellious province? He simply could not remember how matters stood, but felt that his choice of quotation had been boorish, inept. To his relief, however, Anthony completed the verse –

51

Athens Regional Library
Athens, Georgia

277989

> *'So much one man can do*
> *That does both act and know.'*

He stuttered slightly, as always when quoting.

Kaspar smiled at him gratefully. 'Ode to the Lord Protector,' he said. 'To your Cromwell, eh?'

Werner von Arzfeld spoke English well, though less practised than his brother, 'Ach! What was that again? So much –'

> *'So much one man can do*
> *That does both act and know!'*

'It is good that,' said Werner, 'and true, I think. Those that act, that perform deeds are often without wisdom. And those that know and are wise, too often think and talk and do nothing. Is that not so?'

Marcia had been sitting on a sofa exchanging in a soft voice desultory, smiling remarks with Lise. Lise had acknowledged them with answering smiles, but briefly and with an anxious eye for her father and brothers. It did not seem entirely appropriate to conduct a feminine *tête-à-tête* in the presence of so much masculine, worldly understanding from which, surely, one should learn. Marcia had, at the same time, been particularly conscious of Werner. She thought it about time that her voice, too, should be heard by the men and she now responded to Werner's general question.

'Perhaps people that know do nothing *because* they're wise. What's so clever about action?'

Frido looked disconcerted. Werner smiled.

'You are a soldier,' said Marcia directly to Werner. 'I suppose you're brought up, trained to think that doing is the important thing. Not meditating!'

'I was also brought up to think that action, unless directed by a well-trained, objective mind is likely to be disastrous!'

'We're some way from Cromwell,' said Anthony. He felt liberated from excessive constraint by the delightful wine and he was determined to use the evening, the presence of a German officer, for contemporary probing rather than philosophic word-play. Germans, he said to himself a little hazily, go in for heavy generalizations, so I've heard. Real issues have to be measured by particular examples.

52

'C-Cromwell,' said Anthony, as they listened attentively, 'had Marvell writing an ode in his praise. He may have tamed the Irish in a year, as the poet put it, but it didn't last and they hate his name to this day. He treated the Irish, when he caught or beat them, as being outside the pale of ordinary humanity. Men, women and children.'

There was a silence. Kaspar von Arzfeld said,

'Religious questions bring great savagery. That happened in the seventeenth century. You had your Cromwell. In Germany, we had war for thirty years. Men come to believe that their enemies are less than human, accursed by God. Then every cruel action becomes – permitted.'

Anthony felt a bond of sympathy with this old countryman with one arm, so unpretentious, so grave and so sincere. He experienced a sense of barriers coming down. It must be a time for frankness. Friendly frankness.

'Indeed, that was so in the seventeenth century, as you say, Herr von Arzfeld. And what about now?'

'Now? I do not think Catholics and Protestants wish to kill each other now! Here in this valley,' said Kaspar with a smile, 'it is true that Catholics tend to live on one bank of the river and we Protestants on the other! We do not, perhaps, make our friends very much among people of the other Church. But we do not think them accursed! We live happy together now, we are all Germans, these things are long past.'

'I was with Marcia in Herzenburg this morning,' said Anthony, 'in Franconia.'

His host nodded.

'Herzenburg. A pretty place,' said Werner.

'A beautiful place. Marcia and I were very – very surprised, to see the number of placards violently hostile to Jews: "Jews not welcome." Is that the policy of your Government? Are Jews regarded as Germans with the rights of Germans – officially?'

There was a long silence.

'It is a complicated matter,' said Kaspar steadily. None of his children looked at their father. 'Yes, it is complicated,' he continued. 'There has been much feeling against the Jews in some places. Generally for economic reasons, I think. Of course, there are also historic prejudices – in most parts of Europe, I believe. Perhaps less in Germany than elsewhere, like Poland, Russia. Herzenburg is an ancient, mediaeval town, your guidebook will have told you. Perhaps it has, also, some ancient mediaeval habits of mind.'

'Surely what we saw wasn't just the expression of individuals' dislike? And there was some sort of official celebration. Nazis in uniform everywhere.'

Von Arzfeld nodded, expressionless. Werner looked at Anthony with the same silent smile in his eyes. 'You've not got far, have you!' he thought. The men puffed at their cigars. Anthony frowned.

'How long leave have you, Werner?' asked his father.

'One whole week of peace. Arzfeld in the spring. And I hardly saw it last year.'

'I hope,' said Kaspar seriously to Anthony, 'that your sister and you will stay here as long as you wish. Frido does not return to Marburg at all. He will start his military service in June. You have heard that my son, Werner here, has a holiday. It will be good for Lise that you are with us.'

'You're very kind, sir.'

'This is a beautiful part of Germany, especially in the spring. Our beechwoods are famous. And you have a fine car. So does Frido. You can visit, if you wish, some of our Lower Saxon villages and towns. There is much to see.'

'We must not stay too long. You're too kind –'

'It is a pleasure for us. Frido and Lise see few people when they are in their old home. It is a pleasure for us.'

Lise smiled at Marcia and nodded as her father spoke. She took Marcia's hand.

'It is as my father says. There is much to see. Here it is always quiet. Not dull, but quiet. Here there is always peace.'

Chapter 4

'YOU LIKE to ride horses, Marcia?'

'Yes, Werner, I love it. I'm not very brave but I love it.'

'I know that already. I could see how it was when we were in the stables with the horses on Tuesday. I watched you and Lise. You love them. This morning we will ride. I will show you some parts of the countryside you have not seen.'

'How lovely. Anthony's never been as keen as me, but I expect he'll –'

'Anthony is taking Frido and Lise on a long expedition. They are going to Celle. It is a town north of Hanover. It was where the "Kurfürsten" had their palace. Later, they were your kings.'

'Oh, is it pretty?'

'Very beautiful. But the woods here are more beautiful still. And the day is warm, extraordinarily warm. The sky is blue. It is better to ride on a horse and smell the smells of outside than the petrol from Anthony's car, is it not? We will take something to eat in a bag with us.'

'Your father –'

'My father has business.'

'I've not got anything to ride in –'

'Lise will lend to you. You and she are the same size, I think. I have spoken to her.'

Marcia thought she had never experienced such a degree of tranquillity. The silence in the woods was like a piece of music. They had climbed some way. Now they rode between huge beeches, planted regularly but without oppressive symmetry. They trotted along broad, grassy rides, the spring sun striking through the trees to produce alternate patches of shadow and light. The woods hung from a steep hill whose contour their

55

horses followed, a hill crowned to the east by the broken rolling country in which Arzfeld lay. West, and now far below them, the river Weser flowed quietly northward in the valley, silver and serpentine.

Marcia felt very happy. All about her pleased the eye. Arzfeld, in the five days she and Anthony had spent there, had enfolded her in a friendly yet disciplined calm. She had, to her surprise, found herself enjoying the emphasis on regularity and simplicity – the sense of harmony between her host's family, their employees and their possessions. She felt witness to an unbroken rustic process. The link that bound these people to their home was primitive and potent. Marcia was seeing all things through a joyful haze. She was well aware why. Werner kicked his horse to a canter and she followed.

The evening before had been fine and promised the perfect April day which they now enjoyed. After supper Lise had sat at the piano with a shy, secret smile. After a little – the notes falling on the air, gentle, unassertive, she said something to Frido who had been humming softly.

'Aha,' said Kaspar – 'Ja, Frido – the second verse –'

Frido, without self-consciousness, put back his head without rising from his chair –

'Der Mond, der ist ihr Buhle –'

He had a gentle, true voice.

'Bravo, Frido,' said his father.

'Go on, Frido,' said Werner, 'you can't stop before the final verse. No happy endings please!'

> *'Sie blüht und glüht und leuchtet*
> *Und starret stumm in die Höh:*
> *Sie duftet und weinet und zittert*
> *Vor liebe und liebesweh*
> *Vor liebe und liebesweh!'*

Frido sang, very softly. He enunciated clearly and Marcia thought she had caught most of the words. The song was half-familiar.

She said, *'Lotosblume,* isn't it?'

'Yes. The poor *Lotosblume* – and the poor moon, her lover.'

'What's "*Zittert*",' Frido?'

'Trembles. She weeps and trembles.'

'From love and its pain,' said Werner with his usual half-smile – '"*Chagrin d'amour*" and so forth.'

'Is it Schumann?' asked Marcia, breaking a quiet that had a touch of tenseness in it.

'It is. A song by Heinrich Heine.'

'Ah,' said Anthony. '*Ein Jüde*,' he added with a smile to Kaspar.

'A charming lyric poet,' said von Arzfeld, unsmiling, and they were quiet again as Lise touched the keys.

After that first evening, neither Anthony nor she had directly raised with any of the von Arzfelds the questions which were so profoundly disturbing the mind of Europe – the character, the obsessions, the brutality of Germany's young régime. Marcia would have described herself as not particularly interested in politics, but these things were frequently headlined in the British press and the sort of vindictiveness which she and Anthony had witnessed in Herzenburg had little to do with politics and everything, surely, to do with common humanity. It erected a barrier, created a gulf filled by unspoken, distressing ideas, between, she thought, them and us.

But this shadow in the background, which she would have liked some open discussion to acknowledge and perhaps to lift – this had certainly not darkened her increasingly radiant perception of Werner von Arzfeld. She found that she had never experienced so disturbing a personality. 'He is so different to his brother,' she thought. 'Frido is charming, gentle, articulate.' Werner said little. He appeared, at times, almost surly in his silences; his quick, decisive movements, made as if impatient with the delay which consideration of others might impose. Yet Werner's smile was enchanting, and his eyes caressing and hypnotic. As Marcia rode from sunlight to shade and on again, she felt Werner's presence all about her, both exciting and alarming.

Werner checked his horse to a walk and Marcia drew level. She looked into his face. Her cheeks were flushed from the exercise. She wore a borrowed riding cap and a pair of Lise's jodhpurs and was warm enough with only her cardigan over a short-sleeved yellow shirt.

57

'Werner, you know that question we were talking about on our first evening – the way Jews are being treated –'

Werner appeared not to hear. He did not turn his head. They were riding stirrup to stirrup.

'We've not talked about it since, but –'

Werner suddenly reined in. He said,

'This way,' and cantered fifty yards to his left down a small crossing ride, leading to a circle of grass surrounded by young evergreens. Plantations of the latter were interspersed with the great beech colonies in a pattern of contrasting colour and texture. Marcia followed. Werner dismounted and took her horse's bridle.

'We will eat here. It is warm and dry. And through the trees, there, one looks west across the valley. It is beautiful is it not?' He smiled into her eyes as she slipped from the saddle, took off her cap and shook her hair from her face.

It was indeeed a beautiful place. The dark shapes of hills rose sharply west of the Weser, etched against the sky. Small, red-roofed villages were perceptible in their folds. Werner looped the reins of both horses over the stump of a dead tree and produced a blanket from in front of his saddle. Unfolding it on the grass he took bread, smoked sausage and apples from a saddle bag.

'The grass is already dry but this will be better.' He gestured to Marcia to sit down. She took off her cardigan and felt the spring sun hot on her bare arms. Really, it was remarkable weather! Werner, sitting beside her, started cutting the sausage with a pocket knife.

As he did so, he said softly, in his exact, slightly pedantic-sounding way, not looking at her,

'You and your brother always want to talk about Jews. There are many other things to talk about. Many other things I would like to talk to you about, Marcia.'

'Werner, you can't say we "always" want to talk about the Jews! We – Anthony – mentioned them once, our first evening. Not since. And isn't it important? If one lot of people are being bullied, hounded –'

'Hounded?'

'Yes. Hunted. *Gehetzt*, isn't that it? And if that's happening,

58

isn't it both wrong and important? And it's getting you all a very bad name.'

Werner had finished preparing the sausage. He folded the knife, put it away and seemed to be considering. He said,

'Yes, I think it is important. And there are other things important also. Just now the most important thing for me is this.'

Next moment Marcia found herself held tightly in his arms, his mouth seeking and finding hers.

'Marcia, you are delicious, you are as beautiful as the morning, you are soft, you are smooth –'

'I feel terribly wicked. But terribly happy. It was all right in the end, wasn't it? But, oh dear, Werner, I'm really a very carefully brought up young lady, you know.'

'I am sure of it. And I am a very polite, responsible officer.'

'You! You're a fiend! Look me in the eyes again! What are we going to do?'

'Perhaps we shall stay here for ever. The horses are happy. They are warm and lazy and there is some grass. And a stream at the foot of the little hill. You too. Are you warm and lazy?'

'Very warm.'

'And lazy?'

'And lazy. I think I'd like to go to sleep. How long have we been here?'

'About an hour. One marvellous hour. Everything will be all right. You must trust me.'

'I do. But Werner, you must think terrible things of me. To let you –'

'I think only wonderful things of you. You enchant me.'

'Werner, are you *sure* –'

'I am sure. Everything will be all right. And all that matters is when I see you again. I have to return to my regiment tomorrow. You will soon be going to England. All that time I shall want you. I shall dream of you in my arms. My eyes will see you when I close them, my hands and limbs will be hungry to touch you. When –'

'Werner, my father and mother have talked about sending

59

me to Vienna this summer to study art which I want to do. We've got cousins there.'

'Austrian cousins?'

'No, Cousin Francis Carr is very British, he's my father's cousin and he was at the Embassy. Now, of course –'

'Of course. No Embassy. There has been a union between Germany and Austria.'

'Well, Cousin Francis is still there, with his family. I think there's a British Consulate-General or something. Would you be able –'

'Vienna is not a long way from where my regiment is in Bavaria.

'You are really warm enough?'

'Well, I think I ought to put on *something* –'

'In a little while.'

'Werner! Oh! . . .'

'In a little while. Not quite yet.'

It was at about six o'clock that Anthony's car began to make disquieting noises.

In the morning Frido had been an excellent guide to Celle. Anthony had insisted on giving him and Lise lunch at a small *Gasthof* in the country five miles east of the town. The afternoon was spent in leisurely exploration north-eastward.

'There is a cousin of my father who lives not far from Celle,' said Frido. 'She married an officer in the Luftwaffe called Langenbach. She's part English. Very charming. She has an English grandmother.'

'I didn't know you had English relations, Frido.'

'It is not so. My cousin, Anna, is born von Arzfeld but the grandmother who is English is not our grandmother. Anna's grandfather and our grandfather were brothers. Anna's grandfather married an English lady. Both Anna's own parents are dead.'

'Is her husband's airforce station near here, then?'

'No, she is living with his parents. He is away. He is in Spain.' Frido's voice was surprisingly cold.

Anthony digested this. From the start, the civil war which had broken out in 1936 in Spain had aroused strong emotions in Britain. It was peculiar to hear, in so matter of fact a way, of a German officer serving there, presumably flying. A good many of his acquaintances at Oxford believed with furious indignation that the Spanish Republic was victim of an appalling conspiracy of evil; that democracy and decency were ranged against brutality and oppression; that right was self-evidently on one side. There had been countless demonstrations and fund raising occasions. Trains packed with volunteers had steamed out of Glasgow amid cheering crowds and a good deal of confusion.

'Communist organized, all this, of course,' John Marvell had observed. 'Wonderful chance for them to show themselves on the side of the angels.'

On the other side of the coin he recalled a lunch in a friend's rooms at Magdalen. A fellow guest, aged about thirty, was introduced to him as a Norwegian: a stolid, dependable-seeming man, a little dour. Anthony learned that the Norwegian worked in a family timber business, with an office in Spain.

'But no longer, unfortunately. We had to get out.'

'And whose side are you for?' asked Anthony.

'Me?' said the Norwegian, looking astonished at the question, 'Why, for Franco – and civilization. It had broken down completely. There was anarchy. Butchery. He, or somebody, had to come.'

And whatever the rights and wrongs of it, a good many people took small interest in what they regarded as the incomprehensible quarrels of a bunch of Dagoes. Anthony's mind went back to drunken shouts in The Broad at Oxford, to Freddie Barnett's high-pitched yells, to Frido's grave face.

Now Frido was talking again.

'Langenbach is quite well known as a brilliant flying man, I believe. He's a lot older than my cousin, Anna. He is clever, too. Now he is away, she lives with his parents. I would like you to meet them. They are nice people. Rather strict but nice.'

'Is it on our way?'

'No. It is eastward. I should have planned earlier perhaps.'

He sounded regretful. Anthony was not sure whether Frido was tacitly suggesting an unannounced descent upon the Langenbachs. Nothing, in fact, was further from Frido's mind.

Such things were not for hasty improvisation. The Langenbachs, staid and formidable, were not of the kind to welcome 'dropping in' by a young trio, whether or not they claimed cousin-ship with their daughter-in-law Anna.

'When you come again we will arrange something,' said Frido. 'Next time. Next time will be soon, please. I would like you to see the house, it is rather famous, it is old, older than Arzfeld. And our cousin is charming.'

'Charming!' said Lise, fervently.

Eventually they decided to head south, toward home.

'It's been a lovely day,' said Anthony with sincerity. He turned his face full to Frido and smiled, in the way Frido recognized from their strolls through Oxford side by side, Anthony careless of whom he bumped. Frido found himself wishing that this habit was confined to pedestrian rather than motoring progression.

'How far to home, Frido?' They had been wandering with little sense of time or distance.

'About sixty-five miles, maybe.'

Anthony whistled. 'That's going to take a bit of time! As we know, the roads aren't exactly fast.' Soon it would be dark and he had discovered, rather surprisingly, that Frido's skill at map reading was less than perfect.

'Damn!'

The striped pole of a level crossing descended before them. Anthony wound down the window.

'I can't even hear the train!'

'It will come,' said Frido lamely. Kaspar von Arzfeld liked regularity. Uncovenanted lateness for meals was to be deplored. Lise was additionally nervous because her attentions were needed for the preparation of supper, but she said nothing.

Anthony switched the engine off. After what seemed an eternity a slow freight train rumbled past. It consisted of flats: on each flat was a large shape covered by tarpaulins, each shape exactly similar. Anthony's inexperienced eye took in what appeared to be caterpillar tracks, visible below each tarpaulin.

'Do you suppose those are tanks, Frido?'

'Well maybe, I don't know,' said Frido.

'Hell of a lot of them.' Anthony looked at his watch. Nearly six o'clock.

Eventually the train passed and the barrier lifted. It was three minutes after they started again that the sounds beneath the bonnet of the Morris became insistent and menacing. Neither Anthony nor Frido was a skilled or even primitively instructed mechanic. They looked at each other. It was a regular, rapping sound. Anthony made a face and drove on faster. The sound grew louder.

'I think you have trouble,' said Frido, very seriously. At that moment steam began to float back over the windscreen. The rapping noise was now louder than the engine.

'Better have a look,' said Anthony. He had no idea what to look for. He stopped the car on a grass verge, and dismounted to fiddle with the catches securing the bonnet. The others climbed out.

'Have you a torch in the car, Anthony?' There was no torch. The light was fading. A cloud of steam hit them as the bonnet flap was raised. There was a hissing sound. A great deal of oil appeared everywhere.

'Anthony, perhaps it would be better to return to the village we just went through. We can borrow a torch. We can inspect.'

'I don't think inspection will help us much. But I agree. Let's go back there.'

They climbed into the car. Anthony pressed the self-starter. No response. This happened several times.

'I'll swing it.'

But efforts with the starting handle also proved futile.

'Do we know what the village was called? We'd better walk back to it and see if we can organize help.'

'I saw the name,' said Lise, 'I don't think I have been to it before. It said Kranenberg.'

Frido had a cigarette lighter and they inspected the map.

'I can't see it. This is our road south isn't it, Frido? And we've just crossed the railway.'

Frido was peering intently at the map, frowning. He sighed. He had found Kranenberg.

'Anthony, we are on the wrong road. We have been going east. Not south but east. South-east.'

They digested this.

'Well,' said Anthony, 'we're broken down, wherever we are. And I think we'd better set out in search of rescuers. Do you suppose there's such a thing as a telephone in Kranenberg?'

Frido was still bent over the map.

'We are very near the Langenbachs. The family I told you about. Where Anna von Arzfeld lives. Anna Langenbach.'

'How near?'

'Maybe two miles. This is what I will do. I will walk back to Kranenberg. I will telephone from there to Anna and explain. I will ask her to organize help. She – the Langenbachs – will know where the nearest repair garage is, someone who can tow the car in. I will ask Anna to speak to them. She will advise us.'

'If she's there.'

'I expect she is there. It is very quiet. She does not go away. It will be easier if I speak to Anna. If she is not there I will explain to Herr Langenbach.' Frido sounded dubious and disappeared into the gathering darkness.

About two hours later Anthony looked about him and marvelled at how swiftly life's minor disasters can become instead delightful adventures. A broken-down car on the wrong road in a strange country, dark falling and companions as mechanically unskilled as he was, had promised tedium and discomfort – to say nothing of the displeasure likely to be felt by Kaspar von Arzfeld. Now, Anthony reflected, it was turning into one of the most enjoyable evenings he had experienced in Germany.

Frido had returned to the car with a lighter step and brighter voice. Their cousin Anna Langenbach had been at home. Yes, she knew an excellent garage, but it was fifteen kilometres away. Meanwhile, she proposed immediately to come in a car and consult at the scene of the disaster. Thus, a few minutes after Frido's return, a car drew up on the quiet road followed by some sort of farm truck. Torches flashed. Anthony could get little impression of who was who. There appeared to be a woman in the car, accompanied by a man, and there was the driver of the truck.

Anna had brought the farm bailiff and an employee described as a 'clever mechanic' with a vehicle, well able to tow the

Morris to some place of shelter and inspection. In what seemed no time at all Anthony found himself steering the Morris towed behind the truck, the bailiff sitting beside him while Lise and Frido drove with their cousin. He had thankfully acquiesced in the proposal of the clearly competent bailiff, that the 'clever mechanic' should see what he could find under the bonnet. Only after this preliminary diagnosis would steps be taken, if necessary, to summon the garage repair service from fifteen kilometres away. Meanwhile –

'Meanwhile,' Anna Langenbach had said, 'you will all have supper with us. My parents-in-law will be delighted. It is a surprise of the nicest kind.' Her command of English was that of one who had spoken it from birth – which, on and off, Anna had done. And Anthony thought he had never heard so charming an accent, a mere touch, an inflexion, a lilt which betrayed one knowing a tongue perfectly but still more at home in another.

After presentation to Herr and Frau Langenbach and an exchange of comments on the general unreliability of machines, Frido had asked permission to telephone Arzfeld.

'Of course,' said Herr Langenbach. 'You will wish now to tell your father of your mishap. But I must inform you that it is most unlikely that your vehicle will be repaired tonight, unless the problem is an easy one. It may be best to telephone again after they have looked more carefully at the engine. I do not understand these things but I am sure you will not be able to continue your journey if the trouble is serious.'

And so it proved. The bailiff reported at eight o'clock. The 'clever mechanic' had had little difficulty in his preliminary diagnosis. It appeared most likely that a new engine would be required, or major surgery at least. The bailiff spoke exactly and pessimistically. Anthony listened with mounting consternation.

'A new Morris engine! Here in Lower Saxony!'

'There may be something the garage can do tomorrow. They are very good people,' said Anna soothingly. She radiated competence and composure.

'And now Frido,' she added, 'you must telephone Cousin Kaspar and tell him that you will all spend the night here. And he need not worry. If the garage cannot put the car right tomorrow I will drive you to Arzfeld with pleasure. I should enjoy it. And you are welcome here as long as you like.'

Both Langenbachs had bowed their agreement. Anna's father-in-law was not unlike Kaspar von Arzfeld, Anthony decided. He had the same withdrawn serene authority although he had not the air, like Kaspar, of a military man. Instead, he gave the impression of an academic, and this was near the truth, for although Gottfried Langenbach had done little in life except care for his fields, his possessions, his remarkable house, he was, by taste, a scholar and he was happier in his extensive library than anywhere else. He looked delicate, and Anthony later learned, without surprise, that chronic asthma had preserved him, no doubt protesting, from military service in 1914. His wife was tall, gaunt and somewhat forbidding, with iron grey hair, high cheekbones and a figure like a ramrod. It must, thought Anthony, be remarkably tedious for Anna, in her husband's absence, living with this no doubt generous but certainly austere couple.

It had been light enough to gain an impression of the house as they arrived. Schloss Langenbach was a long, low building, with tall, curiously-shaped chimney stacks, all dissimilar; with wooden shutters, each painted a faded red and white, on each of its many windows; and with two towers, taller than the rest of the building and culminating in squat, onion-shaped steeples, straddling a gateway into the small courtyard round which the house was built. Although of no enormous size, Schloss Langenbach gave the sense of having housed a little local court, of a master, in periwig and lace, dispensing patronage and justice to the immediate neighbourhood. Arzfeld, Anthony decided, had to do with husbandry, forests – and, at times perhaps, with war. Langenbach held a whiff of scent and patches and powder, a small echo of Haydn or Mozart, despite its more ancient origins and undeniably heavy interior. Unlike Arzfeld, Langenbach seemed to impose a certain graceful formality.

Yet Anna herself was radiant. She showed no sign of being overwhelmed by the atmosphere of Schloss Langenbach. The house was dark, with a profusion of carving – as far as Anthony could judge, carving of high quality of a kind more familiar in mediaeval choir stalls than in a private house, however august. Old Frau Langenbach guessed his thoughts.

66

'My husband's ancestors were benefactors of the church in Kranenberg, which was a more important place in the seventeenth century than it is today. They employed craftsmen who went on and on – first the church, then this house – sometimes one can forget which one is in! Do you find it oppressive? I did, when I first married and came to live here. It felt so like a museum. But one changes. Our son, Kurt, thinks of nothing but aeroplanes. He becomes impatient here. My daughter-in-law, Anna here, is an expert on both house and church. She has become a great friend of the pastor.'

Anthony could imagine. 'Your son – and – and your daughter-in-law – live here always, when he is not away on duty?'

'No, at first they lived in Berlin. My son was in the Ministry.'

Anna was sitting on Anthony's other side. She smiled at him, joining in a conversation which had turned to herself as subject.

'You know Berlin, Herr Anthony?'

'No,' Anthony said, adding – 'It's kind of you to speak German to me when your English is so perfect.'

'Not kind. My mother-in-law does not speak English.'

Anthony felt abashed. Of course that was the reason! But Anna's smile made of any remark a gentle benediction. He felt warmed by it. She had, he decided, an extraordinary personality. She exuded efficiency and energy, complete self-possession, so that she seemed naturally to dominate her surroundings. Yet she was also feminine, and so gentle and smiling that 'domination' was the last word that could be associated with her.

In appearance Anna Langenbach had, certainly, a strong resemblance to the von Arzfelds, her cousins. She had Lise's fair hair, with darker lights in it. Her skin, although it was of the fortunate kind that could brown in the sun without burning, was fairer than Lise's – a cream and roses complexion, and with eyes blue instead of brown. But her face was very strong. Compared to Lise or even to Frido she was immensely positive. This was a woman who would always have ideas, take initiatives, lead not follow. It was clear that Frido was proud of this relation; and that Lise worshipped her.

67

Anthony looked hard at Anna. They were supping simply but well.

'You must be well informed on what's going on in Spain.'

She shrugged, 'My husband doesn't write much of the situation.'

'Has he been there long?'

'For six months. He is due for some leave, for a holiday, in July. And after that he doesn't know. Maybe again in the New Year, something like that.'

'Will the war go on as long as that?'

She considered that, and answered it directly.

'Yes, I think so. But not after next year.' Anna showed signs of preferring some other topic. 'Did Frido tell you I have English blood?'

'He did. And do you know England well?'

'My grandmother lives in London. I used to see her often once. Now it is more difficult. I am very fond of my grandmother. Maybe I will visit her in the summer – after my husband's leave.'

'You should persuade your husband to spend some of his leave bringing you to England.'

'Not likely, I think. More likely I come afterwards. In September perhaps. This September, 1938. I will not have seen my grandmother for nearly three years. It is too long.'

'I hope,' said Anthony, 'that you will find time to visit my parents' home. We'd love that. They're very friendly, easy people I promise you. Frido will tell you!'

'I am sure of it,' said Anna Langenbach. 'But if I go to England I shall, I expect, be with my grandmother all the time.' Her smile was cool and somewhat dismissive as she turned to talk to Herr Langenbach who, with Lise on his right, had abandoned himself to prolonged silences. The old man's eyes lit up as his daughter-in-law made some laughing remark.

'Ach! Anna!' he said, and took her right hand in his.

After dinner they moved into a long gallery, a place of dark portraits and many windows in the wall which faced them. Anthony manoeuvred himself into a talk à deux with Anna Langenbach. He asked about a particular picture at the other end of the gallery. She beckoned him to look closer and began explaining it.

'It was a Langenbach in the eighteenth century – very early, just after the Elector became your King. You see the boundaries are rather hard to explain quickly; Germany was a patchwork, but these lands were subject to the Elector of Hanover.'

'Our George I. Who imprisoned his wife until she died because she was unfaithful, is that right? We visited their palace at Celle this afternoon.'

'Yes, poor Sophia Dorothea. She had rather a terrible life. She fell in love, you see. She had been married to the Elector and then she fell in love with Count Königsmarck. The Elector's officers killed him.'

'The guide told us about it.'

'He may not have told you that as Sophia Dorothea was dying after all those years of lonely captivity, the story is that she said one thing – she said, "Summon my husband to meet me at the judgement seat." Did they tell you that?'

'No. They didn't tell us that.'

'And he – her husband, your King – was travelling in a coach from England to visit Hanover. And at that moment he died. It is a good story.'

'It is a very good story.'

'And was she justified to call him so?'

'Absolutely justified, don't you think?'

'I suppose so,' said Anna with a shrug. 'Love – well, it's a difficult enough emotion for anybody to manage, and for a young girl, married to a prince, friendless, at her husband's mercy – it must have been hard.'

They wandered to another picture. Anthony heard himself saying softly,

'I m-must say again how much I hope it will be possible to see you when you visit England, visit your grandmother.' He tried to keep his voice normal, unemphatic, but he found himself a little short of breath. The connection to their last exchange, to the sad story of the little Electress, was obtrusive. Anna suddenly turned and looked full at him.

'You say that rather insistently!'

'I intend to.' Anthony did not take refuge in a light laugh, a disclaimer. He stood his ground. He knew that his expression was painfully serious. He held Anna Langenbach's eyes. She, too, looked grave.

'We have never met before. I doubt if you or your family would find me – find us – particularly interesting.'

'I am not speaking of my family.' Anthony supposed he had drunk too many glasses of a delicious Mosel at dinner. He, stuttering Anthony Marvell, was meeting this young, married woman for the first time and was pressing her for another meeting, pressing her in a tone of voice which he knew was most improperly sincere.

Anna spoke quietly. 'You are a person of strong impulses, Mr Marvell!'

'Anthony. Of strong feelings, perhaps. And you?'

She disregarded this. 'When I first saw you, I thought, "He's got an uncertain temper, he is unpredictable." Is that true?'

So she had, immediately, considered him! 'Well, I can be impatient,' Anthony said softly, 'I can be intolerant. But I think I have it in me to be –' He fumbled for a word and sighed.

They had moved from picture to picture hanging on that long wall, both tacitly joining in the pretence that they were merely examining them together, Anna explaining Langenbach ancestors, Anthony trying to ask intelligent historic or artistic questions, in an unsteady voice.

'And if my car is not repaired, can you really drive us to Arzfeld?'

'Of course I can,' she said in a conversational voice. 'I love any excuse to go there.'

'You must not bore Herr Marvell with our family,' called out old Langenbach with a chuckle from the other end of the room where Lise was entertaining the older people and Frido stood smiling quietly. 'They were a dull lot.'

'A most interesting lot, sir!' Anthony rejoined with a smile as he followed Anna towards the others. He looked across the room and found Frido's eyes upon him, intelligent, speculative and kind.

Chapter 5

———————◆———————

ANTHONY LEFT OXFORD at the end of that summer term of 1938. He intended to live in London, to read for the Bar, to 'eat his dinners' – attend Hall at his chosen Inn of Court as an apprentice barrister with the aim of taking his final law examination in 1941. He had not read Law at University. No Law degree could shorten the obligatory and lengthy process he had now to begin, and concentration on undiluted Law for too long a period was regarded as narrowing and ultimately detrimental to a man's character. 'Quite right,' Anthony thought to himself, regarding with boredom the prescribed list of reading. He had taken a set of rooms in Mount Street, Mayfair, with his closest Oxford friend, Robert Anderson. Robert, also, was planning to read for the Bar.

At the end of August, Robert, like every other able-bodied and solvent inhabitant of London, was away. Anthony had been to Scotland for ten days, returning on 26th. He had some weekend invitations, but the first of these was not until late September. He was at a loose end. And on 29th, at Bargate for two days, he received a short letter.

> 'You may remember a little motorcar mishap at Langenbach. I am in London for a few weeks. It would be delightful to see you and your charming sister, so I write this line in case, perhaps, you are not away for your holidays.'

The letter, with some indecipherable flourishes, was signed 'Anna Langenbach'. How prim Anna, with her perfect command of English, could yet sound in writing and even sometimes in speech, Anthony thought delightedly.

He had felt a fool after that first, April, meeting with Anna – gauche, impulsive and blundering. Yet he had not been able to resist saying to her, when they parted at Arzfeld, 'I will write.'

71

She had said,

'No, no.' Then she had smiled and avoided his eye and said, 'Write? What about?'

'I have many things I feel I must say to you, can say to you!' They had had only a few short moments alone at Arzfeld before Anna returned to Langenbach.

'Many things!'

And he had written. It had been, Anthony recalled with embarrassed self-knowledge, an immature letter. He had told Anna that he had felt happier in her company than with anybody he had ever known. He had written as if she had no husband, as if making a lover's first, tentative moves. He had written that her face was before his eyes at all times, that he could not sponge it from his mind, that her voice was in his ears always.

'I know I shouldn't write these things to you. But I feel I must!'

It was a letter of appalling indiscretion, idiotic. He had written in May. There had been no reply. Perhaps a jealous Langenbach husband had seen an English stamp, suspected something, snatched the letter. Perhaps she was outraged. Or – far, far worse – perhaps she had simply laughed to herself –

'What a foolish schoolboy! I turned his head with one conversation! And our hands hardly touched!'

But there had been no reply. And now – as if nothing in the world had passed between them since April – there came this cool little note –

'It would be delightful to see you and your charming sister, so I write this line in case . . .'

She explained in it where she was staying.

'Anna – I'm s-s-sorry about my letter – I mean – you got it?'

Anthony's stutter was worse than it had been for some time. Anna smiled.

'Why are you sorry about it?'

They were lunching in a restaurant, two days after Anthony had received her note.

'Not sorry I wrote it. I meant it.' He held her eyes with his. He looked stern.

'That was wrong of you,' Anna said, near inaudibly. Conversation so far had been stilted, tension high. To eat was impossible. Anna tried to ease things.

'You've not told me about Marcia. How is she?'

'Marcia's in Vienna.'

'She's lovely. The Austrians will be mad about her.'

It was a hot summer. They made a pretence of playing with food, their eyes seldom leaving the other's face, serious, unsmiling. Anna spoke quietly, matters of no importance. She had explained that her grandmother, Mrs Briscoe, had married an Englishman after grandfather von Arzfeld's premature death. Born English and now again widowed, Mrs Briscoe lived in London. It appeared that she was particularly fond of Anna.

'My dear grandmother feels only the cold. She does not mind this. Her house is an oven.'

'London is no place for a heat wave, Anna.'

'No, but it is where I must be for these days.'

Anthony suggested they visit Kew Gardens.

'You know a lot about trees and shrubs, I can tell that. You'll love Kew, and there's space and air there.'

Later they walked slowly among the magnificent trees, forcing themselves to observe, exclaim, admire, hearts beating, aware of nothing but each other. At one comparatively deserted place of shade Anthony turned to face Anna and stood very close. She did not move away.

'Anna –'

Anna put both her hands on his upper arms and without a word rested her head on his shoulder. Quietly she began to sob. This could not end well. It was her doing. And it could not end well.

Anna's life had already been marked by sorrow. An infant in 1914, she remembered one or two visits from her father, a remote figure apparently always wrapped in an enormous greatcoat. She remembered smoke from a cigar, and a spluttering cough between rather overpowering kisses. That, she learned later, had been on his infrequent periods of leave from the Western Front, from fighting against his mother's relations. She had been five years old when he died in January 1919, in a field hospital still far from home, not from wounds but from influenza. Anna could recall no sense of bereavement. That period was what she came to know as the great hunger. Everybody in Germany was hungry – hungry all the time, hungry, sallow of face and evil-smelling: the hungry smell. Anna heard horrible stories of those days when she was older. The Allied blockade was maintained after the Armistice and it was said food was so scarce that children in the streets of big cities were in danger of kidnap. Anna never knew whether these whispered nightmares had substance. It was a time of humiliation, suffering and darkness.

Anna's mother, strict, loving, brought the girl up in her own image. Beautiful and gallant, Klara von Arzfeld was undaunted by loss, by famine or by penury. She started a dress-making business, specializing in the economical but elegant remodelling of clothes, using old material. Her taste was admirable, her industry tireless. She took on two, then three girl assistants. The business prospered sufficiently. She and Anna had been left poor and they remained poor. But they survived. They lived in Berlin.

From the beginning Anna had received inspiration from her mother's quiet, indomitable personality. She herself, anxious to help, was never allowed to sew. Her mother would say –

'Time enough for that later. Just now you must read! Work, study, read! Now is the time to develop the muscles of your mind!'

They went together every Sunday to the Evangelical church and Anna would pray with intensity –

'Make me brave, like Mother. Help me to love You, as Mother loves You.'

Arzfeld cousins were kind, and none more so than her father's first cousin, the lame, one-armed Kaspar von Arzfeld. Anna and her mother loved Arzfeld almost as much as did its owner. Kaspar, indeed, felt a glow whenever his cousin's widow appeared. A shy widower himself, he secretly asked himself sometimes the question –

'Perhaps we . . . might it not be a happy out-turn –?'

But Klara was scrupulous. Kaspar would say –

'Klara, you'll stay as long as you can, with little Anna? Certainly until Easter?'

'No, no. The business can't wait for that. You're too kind.'

And Anna heard her murmur once to herself –

'It wouldn't do, I'm afraid.'

To Anna, she would say –

'We must never stay long at Arzfeld. They're dear, kind people, and we love them. And they love us. But we're independent, you see. We manage our own lives.'

Once, with no apparent subject in mind, Klara said to Anna,

'In *some* things, Anna, not many, one must never settle for second best. In some things in life only the best is right.'

When she said, later that evening,

'How I wish you had known your father, Anna, little love,' Anna was sure she had been thinking of Cousin Kaspar von Arzfeld.

Then, at the age of nineteen, Anna had fallen in love.

She knew it without the smallest doubt. This was, she knew with absolute certainty, not an infatuation, not a surrender to flattery, not a passing, immature passion. This was immensely important. Astonishingly – for Klara was a strict and in many ways conventional parent – she blurted it out to her mother. She finished with the words,

'I've had a revelation, Mother. Nothing can be more important than this, than Clemens and me.'

To her amazement, her mother, who had listened silently, said quietly,

'Yes, I think so too.'

Then Anna understood, not only that her mother's love and understanding of her were even greater than she had already known, but that her mother had really loved her father.

His name was Clemens Starckheim. Anna was at university, Clemens on the first step of a journalistic career. They found every thought, every mood coincided.

'We're too much alike! Don't they say love needs opposites?'

'Not always. You see we're two halves of one soul, separated long ago and always looking for the other.'

75

Sometimes they could sit in silence, content simply to gaze at each other.

'How can one find simultaneously enormous excitement and perfect peace in another person?'

'Oh, one can, one can! Clemens, does everybody experience real love at some time?'

He held her tight.

'No. Not like this. Only a small, select brother and sister-hood, a privileged elect. The rest have something different. Nice, but different.'

'Clemens, how *can* you know?'

'Sh-sh-sh.'

Clemens was pale, dark-haired, fervent. She had been just twenty when she ran up the stairs to the Berlin flat one evening in 1933 having returned from the university, planned to go to supper with Clemens. Klara was waiting. Klara's eyes and expression needed the addition of no words. Anna said abruptly,

'When? How?'

'Anna -' Her mother, most unusually, was trembling.

'Yes. Of course. It's Clemens, isn't it?'

Tears now rolled down Klara's cheeks. She came to Anna, her arms outstretched. Anna pushed her away.

'He's dead!'

A nod.

'How?'

There had been quite a street battle that afternoon and Clemens, zealously covering for his paper, had been knocked down. Three young Nazis, it appeared later, had seen protruding from his coat pocket a copy of an illicit Communist news-sheet and had set about him. One kick, in particular, had done more damage than its deliverer intended and as they made off, alarmed, Clemens had writhed, suffered a haemorrhage and died before reaching hospital. There was irony, in that Clemens was as fanatically hostile to the Communists as to the Nazis. An old-fashioned liberal by conviction he had been slipped the news-sheet surreptitiously by a man in the crowd and intended to use it to show how the Communists were provoking the Nazis into excesses.

Anna immediately left university and found a job. She knew

she must drive herself forward with feverish energy or she would sink in a sea of misery. Klara had a business connection with a small textile firm. One day she said quietly,

'Dollmann's employ a lot of young girls. They want someone sensible, someone educated to handle them. They're having problems –'

'So?'

'Anna – could you do it?'

It was absurd. Few of Dollmann's girls turned out to be younger than her and she had no experience of giving counsel, exercising authority.

'I'll try it, Mama.'

She threw herself into it. After three months Klara's connection in Dollmann's said,

'That girl of yours, Anna – she ought to be Director of a firm herself one day! She's incredible! The girls respect her as if she were twice their age – yet they love her too! It's most unusual –'

And there was an admiring shake of the head. That girl is strong, people said to each other, that Arzfeld girl is really beautiful, with those eyes, that skin, that figure. But she's strong.

Anna applied herself, heart as well as mind, to her work. The von Arzfelds raised their eyebrows. The pain of Clemens began, a little, to pass, or at least to dull.

She had been busy at this for just eighteen months when she first met Kurt Langenbach.

'Anna!'

After a minute, with his arms now around her, Anthony said,

'There's never been much doubt, has there?'

'No. None. None at all.'

Anna knew, for the first time since the death of Clemens, that she had fallen deeply and genuinely in love. It was incredible, it was absurd, it was wicked, it was true. She had known it, like an electric shock, since driving from Langenbach to Arzfeld, with Anthony in tongue-tied silence. She had felt then, as she felt now, with half-terrified certainty, the enormous force of

Anthony's feeling. And she knew, insanely, that she responded to it. Completely.

Anthony quoted softly –

> *'If ever any beauty I did see,*
> *Which I desired and got,*
> *T'was but a dream of thee.'*

'Who wrote that?'

'John Donne.'

Anna sighed, her cheek resting against his. Her voice, most unusually, shook, and she tried, absurdly, to lighten the emotion.

'Anthony, darling, is one of us about to say that this is stronger than us, or some such nonsense? Is this all like a bad film?'

'No. A good film. With a star in the star part.' The tips of his fingers gently caressed the back of her neck.

One thing led to another with great rapidity. Robert Anderson was on holiday until the end of September and Anthony had the Mount Street rooms to himself: to themselves.

They were gentle, murmurous weeks. Weeks in Paradise. They learned about each other, absorbed the character, the past, the background of each other, at the same time as their bodies increasingly delighted in each other.

'You're younger than me, darling.'

'What the hell does that matter?'

'I thought this could happen. Perhaps I was wicked to write that note. People could say I pursued you. And I did.'

'You had to come to me. You must make – you must live – life with me –' he fumbled for words.

Anna smiled, 'Some of life, perhaps.'

Now that she had recognized the truth in herself, Anna was extraordinarily in command of the situation. Anthony sometimes felt, with a jealous twinge of inexperience, that his mistress was his superior in will-power, in love and, probably in intellect. Anna seemed to have to worked out so many things, to have calculated so many human situations so shrewdly. To talk to her, whether in bed or out of it, was joy: but was she feminine, yielding, vulnerable? At times Anthony felt inadequate. But when, if away from her, he recalled their love making, all else was blotted out. And with every day that passed Anthony also felt himself stronger, more assured.

Anna had found within weeks of marriage that she could never love the man she had wed so unwisely.

'Nobody made me do it,' she said. 'It was my own fault. He was handsome, clever, confident, rich. We were poor, you know. I wanted security, I was young, I was impressed. I was a wicked fool.'

Anthony hated to probe, or even contemplate Anna's marriage. He knew that it was Langenbach's whole character that repelled her.

'He has – Kurt has – nothing of his father,' she said. 'His father is a gentle, scholarly man. Kurt is ruthless, insensitive. I'm an object to him. If we both lived to be a thousand, he would never understand how I feel. That's the truth. He has no conception of what to love a woman – really love a woman – should be. Of course, I've accused myself, told myself it's my fault. But I think he'd be the same with anybody. He's – well, he's brutal. Indifferent.'

Anthony still found it incomprehensible that a woman of Anna's character could have married, apparently, against the instincts of her heart, but he preferred to steer conversation away from the subject. He did not think it wise yet to force the pace on that matter. Instead he implored her to return to England soon, 'To see her grandmother again.' She half promised –

'My grandmother is old now, and I love her, Kurt understands that. Now I would not like more than six months to go by –'

'Six months!' Anthony could hardly endure the prospect of six hours without his beloved. He met Mrs Briscoe. He had been surprised, at first, that Anna was prepared for the risk of such open acknowledgement of his existence.

'It's all right. I have told my grandmother that a friend of the von Arzfelds, who has stayed there, wishes to call on her. I would like you to meet her. She loved her first husband very much, and her only son, my father. She always likes to hear of Arzfeld.'

And Mrs Briscoe was, indeed, charming. She lived with

an agreeable and not noticeably downtrodden companion, introduced as Miss Platt. Her house in Wilton Place was pleasant. Her love for Anna was very plain. Anthony behaved to Anna, in her presence, with great formality. Human antennae, however, are sensitive where affection is involved, and Anthony thought Mrs Briscoe regarded him with a speculative if not unfriendly eye.

Then one September day Anna was gone, desirable and desirous, collected, wholly his when with him but ready, nonetheless, to return to a different world in which he could play no part.

'Of course it's a betrayal,' said John Marvell.

It was October 1938. John was trembling with anger, less articulate than usual. Stephen Paterson had never seen his brother-in-law so roused. He was astonished. John was always so extraordinarily peaceable, one who invariably saw an opponent's point of view. Yet here was John, who might have been expected to be heartily relieved that the Prime Minister had reached a sensible arrangement with Hitler about these bloody Czechs and had averted a war – here was old John, white with rage about the whole thing, weeks later. It was remarkable.

He, Stephen, had on many occasions taken an aggressively hard line about the German menace. John had been pacific, understanding. Then it had come to the crunch and John had become afroth with indignation while Stephen had accepted, as any man with experience of politics must, that although the Nazis might be a ghastly bunch you couldn't start a world war to stop them incorporating into Germany a lot of Germans unlucky enough to have been born the wrong side of an artificial line. John seemed to have no sense of proportion.

Furthermore, thought Stephen angrily, John was disloyal. The Government was doing its best. If defence of the realm was the point at issue HMG was taking air defence pretty seriously. What, in Christ's name, did old John want? An expeditionary force, to march to the support of Czechoslovakia?

'Abject!' said John Marvell. 'Abject surrender to a man who,

80

as is clear for all to see, will not now rest until he has enslaved most of Europe!'

'Steady, John,' said Stephen. 'The PM's pretty shrewd, you know. One of the sharpest we've had for a long time. He wasn't taken in. Hitler doesn't want a war. He's a nasty little squirt and he'll get away with anything he can. But he doesn't want a war. When the PM says he's done a deal with which all parties can live, I believe him. I reckon he's done us proud.'

'And I,' said John Marvell, 'reckon that he's shamed us. It may be inevitable to bow to superior force. But to pretend that it's honourable is an awful thing. We're all living a lie.'

'Nonsense, John!'

Stephen was upset. His allegiance to the Prime Minister was strong. He now half-regretted some fiery speeches about the threat of resurgent, Nazi-led Germany which he had permitted himself a year ago. One didn't want to be tarred with any particular brush. The thing was to have a sense of proportion.

'Living a lie,' said John. 'We know that we are weak, that we dare not outface this evil man. So we pretend he is less evil than he is, that we can deal with him on the basis of trust. We rationalize our cowardice.'

'Nonsense, John. And what's more, even if one looks at it from the simplistic, military point of view, we've given our-selves a valuable breathing space. We're getting stronger all the time. So even if the PM's got it wrong – and I don't believe it – we'll soon be in a better position to teach Hitler a lesson if it ever comes to that. Which it won't.'

'We will, will we?'

'Yes, we will. I happen to know a certain amount on that side and ministers have given the Party some pretty useful briefings recently. Our armament programme is really getting into top gear. And don't forget it's not only us who are getting stronger. It's the French. And the Czechs have only lost a strip of territory and a part of their population who are entirely German – both by blood and loyalty.'

'It's not that fact I mind,' said John Marvell quietly. 'It's the sense that we are running away from reality.'

'What reality?'

'The reality that Hitler is determined to take more. And more. He's on the march.'

'You're dramatizing.'

'And we are frightened and prefer not to see.'

They were standing in the inner hall at Bargate, too disturbed to sit, too angry to relax, too intransigent to change the subject, to smile, to agree to differ. Stephen supposed he'd better try to break from the confines of bitter disputation.

'Heard from Marcia lately? I suppose you and Hilda were pretty worried when things looked tricky that week in September.' For while Mr Chamberlain had travelled to Bad Godesberg, to Munich, Europe had, indeed, appeared close to war.

'Francis Carr is a sensible man. They'll look after Marcia all right, I have no doubt. From her infrequent letters she sounds happy.'

'How long do you plan to leave her there?'

John too, was striving to keep his voice steady, to allow his anger to cool.

'She is doing an eighteen-month diploma course. I believe it finishes at the end of 1939. Naturally, she may break it and come home if the situation worsens. So far, we have had no indication of anti-British sentiment making her life difficult, or anything of the sort. She sounds, as I say, perfectly happy. She will, of course, be home for Christmas.

'Did I hear the letter box, Robert?'

The afternoon post generally arrived in their rooms in Mount Street at four o'clock. The old-fashioned letter box flap in the door, brass and heavy, dropped with a satisfying smack when mail was pushed through it on to the mat inside.

Robert walked in.

'Two for you. Both from abroad I see. One an English hand. One –'

Anthony snatched his letters and pocketed them.

'I imagine you want privacy while you read them!'

'You imagine too much. I'm trying to work.' Anthony looked, unseeing, at a page of Commentary on Justinian for a further five minutes. They went very slowly. Then, after a fine display of note making, of leisurely preparation for the next day's work, he strolled to his bedroom. The first page of

82

Marcia's letter showed him that her troubles could wait. He tore the second letter open with trembling fingers.

Langenbach
15th October 1938

'My darling Anthony,
    Since those wonderful two weeks in London everything in life looks different. Colours are stronger, shapes more beautiful, music more melodious. Everything has become radiant. And it is all because I have found you . . .'

Anthony had written that life without Anna had no savour, was tedious, insupportable. He found himself, he said, bewitched, without appetite, energy or ambition. The only life he could envisage without agony was one shared with her.

'. . . you were already filling my heart when Kurt came on his leave from Spain in July. I was charming to him, very dutiful. He was, as usual, hard, rough, intelligent, cynical. I know, my own darling, that you do not like to think of my husband, that I have a husband – but we all have frames in which we exist, like pictures. We cannot easily step out of them. Langenbach is my frame. I did not have to choose it. I married a cold, clever, brave man. I do not love him – you know that. But he and his family are my way of life.
    Yet I must also live as Anna. When I came to England to see my grandmother in August I thought you might have almost forgotten me, or prefer to keep me at a distance. I had not answered your sweet letter. I had no claim upon you. But I could not stop myself from making the contact.'

Anthony's mind went back to 'the contact'. He could not erase the image of Anna from his mind and he wanted her all the time – absolutely, he decided with many a frustrated groan, all the bloody time. He saw her face everywhere.

'And what joy it brought us! With you I find warmth and ease and laughter. Of course to be your lover, your mistress (and I am proud of it) is to act a lie most of my life. With the most important part of me I am thinking of Anthony, wanting him, feeling I am part of him. The rest is mechanical – Langenbach, family, possessions. But these things are strong.'

'Damned, bloody strong,' Anthony muttered to himself, 'hellish strong. Of course they are.'

83

'You ask me in your last letter to leave these things. My dear, it would be absurd. It is true that I love you.'

Anthony was young enough to feel that those were the words which mattered –

'You beseech me to come to you for ever, to run away, ask to divorce Kurt. My love, believe me, I am not telling you our love was just an amusement, the passing fancy of a woman whose husband was away at the war. Nor am I saying that two weeks of love were not long enough for us to learn to know each other. I think I know you well, and you know me. But marriage and divorce and family and relations are real solid things. In Germany it is so. Also in England, I think. I cannot do what you ask. You will love others. It is perhaps better that you forget me. It is better that we say to each other – "It was beautiful. Now we say goodbye." I kiss you in my heart. I laugh and weep when I think of you.
　　　　　　　　　　　　　Anna.'

'Nonsense!' said Anthony out loud. '"Better forget me!" She doesn't mean a word of it.' There was a postscript on the back of the last sheet.

'It is best not to write here any more. If you write, send it to my grandmother's address in London.'

Anthony laughed delightedly. This was no breach, no severance. Reference to Mrs Briscoe's address surely knotted firmly once again the cord that bound them. Mrs Briscoe was discreet. 'I have told her,' Anna had said, 'that it is always possible letters are opened now in Germany. I have told her that if anybody wants to write to me with matters which – which might make trouble – the letter can be sent to me to her house, here in London. She will keep it. Then, when a reliable friend is in London I can make arrangements. It's not quick of course. But it is safe.'

'No,' Anthony thought, 'it certainly isn't quick!' He started to read Anna's letter again. Then he glanced quickly at Marcia's:

'Darling Ant (on)
You've got to help me. Will you please calm Mummy and Daddy down. I think they'll need it because I've written to them by this post to say I'm not coming home for Christmas.

I've got a wonderful chance to ski at St Anton with a blissful party of people and it's got to be Christmas week. I've written a *long* letter to them both but please try to stop them fussing or being hurt, or communicating with Cousin Francis to find out who the party consists of and all the Victorian stuff. Anyway, he and Cousin Angie wouldn't know, all my friends are Austrian, met through the art school, mostly –'

Before reading Marcia's letter carefully he started at once to compose a reply to Anna. His pen raced across paper. It would be, he reminded her, six months in February since she had seen her grandmother. It was already late October. His letters were likely to take time – he would write them regularly and send them, regardless of the absence of answers, to Mrs Briscoe's London address.

'I know,' he wrote, 'that you will be with me again in a very few months. And then I will be able to find better words, to keep you with me for ever. Let it be February, my darling – or March at the latest.'

He felt sick. March, 1939 seemed a lifetime away. Yet he also felt immensely more robust than ever before. Anna loved him. After separation, after ages, from afar, Anna loved him.

Chapter 6

BARGATE. MARCH, 1939.

'Anthony, my dear, we've heard from Marcia at last. She's coming home very soon, for Easter. Thank Heavens for it – it's about time.'

'I don't blame her for spending Christmas and skiing out there, Mother.'

'But *Christmas*!' Hilda Marvell had taken her daughter's long absence badly. 'I hope she's not getting involved with some undesirable Viennese. Marcia's so young – naïve, an innocent. I'm sure Cousin Angela is keeping her eyes open. Marcia needs guidance, protection.' Hilda sighed. They were walking in the garden at Bargate where a few bold shrub shoots were suggesting that winter was nearly past.

'Marcia's pretty well able to look after herself, Mother.'

'All you children think that. You're so mistaken.'

'Is Easter late or early? When exactly does she come?'

Marcia, it appeared, was planning to arrive on 14th March and to stay until the last week in April. Her letter had taken a surprisingly long time to arrive.

'14th March,' said Anthony. 'Good Lord, that's next Tuesday! I'd better meet the boat train in London and give her lunch and put her on a train down.'

Anthony had been considering how much to tell Marcia about Anna, but considering in a desultory way. Now the question was imminent. Brother and sister were close, and in one way he longed for the relief of confidences. There had been only one further letter from Anna – the courier service, via Wilton Place worked, albeit laboriously – but it had shown no diminution in love while still offering no explicit encouragement to any ambitious imaginings. As far as the immediate future was concerned, 'Plans are uncertain,' Anna had written.

But February – Anna's six-month point – had come and gone and all she had offered was the probability of a further visit to England 'some time in, or even before, the spring'. 'Whatever that means,' thought Anthony miserably. She had written, too, that Kurt had been given a further leave from Spain. Anthony had groaned. It might be some sort of relief to talk to Marcia. She was too young to understand, of course, but she was a sympathetic girl. There would be complications, irritation. He could imagine –

'What about her husband, Ant? I take it you're just her bit of fun, her fancy man? I suppose you know what you're doing – don't get into a mess, love!' He would find that sort of reaction hard to take.

On the other hand, Marcia had always been his confidante and the need to speak of Anna to somebody was almost insupportable. His closest intimate, Robert Anderson, was certainly not a suitable recipient of descriptions of Anna. He was too apt to snort impatiently at the weakness of humanity. One could talk about many things to Robert, but not easily about love. Anthony decided, as he paced the platform at Victoria Station, that he would talk to Marcia. He at once began to look forward to it, to the delicious moment when he could speak Anna's name aloud. Marcia would, inevitably, be agog to hear his news. She would be intensely curious about the state of his heart. He had arranged to take her to Mount Street, to give her lunch there before putting her on a train to Sussex. Over lunch he would talk to her of Anna.

The train seemed to be a few minutes late.

'Mr Marvell!'

Anthony turned. He did not at once recognize the middle-aged, plainly dressed lady who had apparently uttered his name and was smiling at him.

'Good morning, Mr Marvell.'

Anthony raised his hat. Something was familiar –

'I live with Mrs Briscoe. Margaret Platt.'

Of course! The companion!

'Good morning, Miss Platt. Are you meeting someone as I am?'

'Indeed I am. I'm meeting Anna Langenbach. Ah, this

seems to be the train now. Always rather an exciting moment, I think.'

Anthony felt his mind spinning like a top.

'I didn't know – I mean, is Anna – is Frau Langenbach –?'

Miss Platt was looking at him shrewdly.

'I had to send a telegram. She generally comes over in the Spring but Mrs Briscoe had a bad fall last week. The doctor is keeping her in bed and he's afraid of pneumonia. I knew it was important to get hold of Anna if she could possibly come.'

The train was now visible, moving slowly and remorselessly toward them down the platform.

'Luckily,' said Miss Platt, 'Anna *could* come. Her husband, Kurt, was at home for most of January and February but has now returned to wherever it is – Spain, I think. He's in the Air Force. So Anna was free and is due on this train.'

Anthony said quickly,

'And I'm meeting my sister who's arriving from Vienna!'

He felt unable to handle the situation of Anna arriving, seeing him, presuming he had somehow discovered her day of arrival, uncomprehending, angry even. Nor could he handle simultaneous explanations with Marcia, Anna, Miss Platt, as in some operatic quartet, full of repetitions and misunderstandings.

They were standing near the ticket barrier. The train stopped.

Anthony saw Anna before anybody else. She was walking, tracked by a porter, near the head of the throng of boat train passengers. She looked radiant. It was a cold, sharp morning and she glowed. Beside her, thought Anthony, his heart appearing to stop, her travelling companions seemed only half alive. Miss Platt swooped.

'Anna!'

They embraced. Anthony feasted his eyes. He was in for it now.

'See who I've picked up!' said Miss Platt with a chuckle, 'your friend, Mr Marvell. He's meeting his sister off this train. Such a coincidence!'

Anthony summoned up reserves of self-control. There must be no self-betrayal in the Platt presence.

'You will remember my sister, Marcia, Frau Langenbach. She is travelling from Vienna and must have been on the same boat as you.'

Anna, for once, looked less than entirely self-possessed. Passengers were streaming past them. The porter negotiated the barrier and turned, looking impatient. He called something.

'No!' cried Miss Platt, 'no taxi! I've got Andrews here with the car,' she said to Anna, 'I'll get hold of him!' She made a dart of surprising agility to catch up with the porter and bring him under control. For one moment Anthony and Anna were alone, alone amidst the crowd. Anthony muttered with shaking voice –

'It really was a coincidence, my darling. I'm sorry about your grandmother. I'll telephone – ask for news of her of course, talk to you. Oh, my love –'

'Is it the same?'

'Just the same! Oh, Anna!'

'My love! I had no time to get word to you.'

'Can I hold you and kiss you, here and now? I can't stand this!'

'No, my darling, no – oh, the wonder of seeing you again!'

Their faces were close. Miss Platt was invisible but must be hovering.

'ANT!'

'– *Wiedersehen*,' said Anna abruptly, looking and moving away.

'I walked past you once, you never saw me. Who was that you were with? How are you, anyway?'

Anthony kissed his sister. He had completely forgotten he was meeting her.

'Oh that! That was Anna Langenbach, do you remember? The von Arzfeld cousin who looked after us when Frido and I broke down and drove us to Arzfeld next day.'

He looked at Marcia. Even his brotherly eye could discern that she was looking remarkably pretty. Even prettier than before departure to Vienna.

'Lunch!' he said. 'If you can face it. Then I'll put you on an afternoon train. Were you seasick?'

'Not a bit. I'm ravenous. And it suits me well,' said Marcia,

'because you've got some listening to do. I've got rather a lot
to say.'

'Of course I'm sure,' said Marcia. Cheeks flushed and eyes
brilliant, she looked superb. 'Of course she must be irresistible,' thought her father.

It was the following day.

'Don't pour it out too quickly,' Anthony had advised. 'Get
acclimatized to Bargate first, make much of Mother and Father.
Father's not been too well. And you've been away over six
months. They've missed you like hell. Then talk about your
thing calmly, making it clear you're telling them good news.'

Anthony himself had been uncertain how good he thought
this news really was, that Marcia thought herself in love with
Werner von Arzfeld. He had been about to approach the
subject of Anna – delicately, confident of sympathy and interest, and suddenly Marcia had looked at him and said,

'I've got a bombshell for you all!' and proceeded to talk
about herself. It had not been the reunion he had planned. And
Marcia, Anthony said to himself, was only just approaching
twenty-one. She was painfully young. She had been – seduced;
he could find no substitute for the censorious, old-fashioned
word. And she seemed delighted with the fact!

'Let's get this clear. You're saying you want to marry Werner?'

'Indeed I am. And he's terrifically keen. But he thinks he
must do all sorts of proper things, approach the parents, all
that.'

'And what are you going to tell them?'

'I'm going to say that we're in love and he wants to marry
me, but that it's hard to make plans until he can come to
England and meet them. Werner, poor darling, must come
here on leave some time. But he never seems to get any. Just
the odd weekend.'

'And for those he goes to Vienna?'

'Once I went to Munich, stayed in an hotel. It was Heaven!'

Anthony said in a firmly older brother way, 'Marcia, are you
sure he is seriously in love with you and that he really wants to
marry you?'

90

'Of course I'm sure. He's potty about me. And I'm the same. It's all marvellous, Ant, but it needs a bit of finesse, you must see that.'

And when they had talked, at last, of Anna she had been perfectly sympathetic – but, somehow, disappointingly unsurprised. 'Of course I remember her, a heavenly person. Quite a bit older than you, isn't she?'

'Slightly. It makes not the smallest difference.'

'I like Werner being quite a lot older than me. It's bliss.'

'And you're really sure?' said Anthony for the fourth time. He felt a sense of doom, not unmixed with irritation.

'Of course I'm sure.'

'Of course I'm sure,' said Marcia. It was evening in the inner hall at Bargate. Nothing was making her task easy. They had listened to the nine o'clock news on the wireless. Earlier that day, German troops had crossed the Czechoslovak border. Now the field-grey uniforms were marching into Prague.

'So much for Hitler's absence of territorial ambitions in Europe,' said John Marvell. 'I wonder what the Germans themselves have to say about it!' He had tuned to a German station. The reports were confident and bland. There was something unctuous in the announcer's words, that a period of misunderstanding was being brought to an end by an invitation to the German Reich to bring Bohemia and Moravia under its protection. There was triumph in the air, reports of the troops' entry into the Czech capital, martial music. '*Preussens Gloria!*' said John. 'Yes, he's on the march all right. Now it will be the turn of the Poles. The German Army will lie along their southern border, as well as to their west.' He felt without hope.

Against this unpromising background Marcia had tried, with nervous excitement, to expound her feelings for Werner von Arzfeld, Lieutenant (shortly to be promoted Captain) of Panzer troops: now, for all Marcia knew, rumbling through Bohemia. 'Damn Hitler!' she thought. 'What rotten timing!'

The Marvells received her news, hesitantly presented, in total silence. After what felt like an hour, John said,

'I liked the brother. What was his name?'

91

'Frido. He's much younger.'

'That's it, Frido. What's he doing now?'

'He's doing his military service. He's at an officer school. Daddy, I'm trying to tell you about Werner, not Frido.'

Hilda snorted impatiently.

'Darling girl, you must see that there's likely to be a war.'

'I don't believe it. Werner doesn't believe it.'

'They've made no secret about their claims against Poland.'

'Oh, the Poles!' said Marcia impatiently. 'People over here don't understand about Poland. Over a third of the people in Poland aren't Poles – they're Germans, or Russians or something else. And the Poles have behaved really badly to them!'

'Nevertheless –'

'And that corridor of land, given to Poland and cutting off East Prussia from the rest. Ridiculous!'

'My dear girl, you're talking like Dr Goebbels. Anyway, the point is that after today, war can't be regarded as improbable, whatever the rights and wrongs. And you're saying you want to marry one of the enemy.'

'I'm saying I want to marry someone who loves me, whom I love, whom I know you'd both love. Ask Anthony – he's met him. He'll tell you how wonderful Werner is. Talk about "the enemy" is nonsense. Werner's family love England.'

'The fact remains,' said John from the depths of misery, 'that he's a German officer. And if you married him you'd have to share his life. Which is likely to involve fighting against this, your own country. You'd probably be pretty unwelcome in Germany too. Have you thought of all that? You might never see us again. For God's sake, darling, think what all this means at such a time.'

Hilda felt that they were losing the battle but that a small piece of territory might still be defended.

'Darling Marcia, we feel for you absolutely. All I ask is that you do nothing in a hurry. Don't go back to Vienna. Stay here. If Werner feels as you say he does he'll come over here, meet us –'

'I've promised to go back. Werner can't come here, not yet. He's in the Army. He wants to meet you, of course he does, but he's terribly busy, he never gets away. He's on some General's staff now, too.'

'Sooner or later he is bound to be able to take some leave and to come –'

'Provided we have peace,' muttered John.

'Then you can get some perspective on the situation. I'm sure he's all you say he is, and if so he'll find a way to visit us here. Quite soon. I'm certain of it. You've anyway planned to be here until the end of April – write and ask when he can come. And don't plan your return to Vienna until he's been here and we can talk things over.'

'No word from Marcia, Father, I suppose?'

John Marvell was paying one of his infrequent visits to London, and was giving Anthony lunch in his club. It was a hot, humid July day with thunder in the air. July, 1939.

'No recent word. As you know she wrote from Bargate to this von Arzfeld fellow, asked him when he could pay us a visit. He's too busy. I can well believe it. Then off she went.'

'Father, I don't think there was ever a chance of persuading Marcia not to go back to Vienna. She's head over heels, you know. When she's there she can see him.'

'So it seems. Anyway, she was determined and off she went. Seven weeks now. Your mother's almost out of her mind with worry. We've had three letters – full of affection, everything will turn out all right, still working hard at her art studies, that sort of thing. She's twenty-one, you know. She can do what she wants. And, of course, you've both got a little money of your own.'

'What do the Carrs think?'

'I wrote to Francis, your mother wrote to Angie. Believe it or not, they knew nothing of von Arzfeld! Complete surprise to them!'

Anthony did believe it.

'They wrote back and said she seemed very happy and they loved having her. But it seems she's got some alternative arrangement in mind and may be moving out.'

Father and son considered this in silence.

'What about you, old boy?' said John. 'We can't talk about Marcia all the time. How are you getting on? You've not been home for several weeks.'

'Well, as you know, I've joined the Territorial Army. I've been accepted for a commission if I undertake some training, do satisfactorily and so forth. I've been working at it most evenings.'

By now it had become unthinkable to Anthony, and most of his generation and kind to do otherwise.

'I'm glad,' said his father. 'It's best to have some definite duty if the worst occurs.' His voice was unsteady. He loathed the thought of his son in uniform. He added,

'I hope it won't come to it. I pray all the time.'

'There's been this big expansion of the Territorials,' said Anthony. 'That, together with the Government introducing conscription out of the blue, has put the Army in a pretty big muddle as far as I can see.'

'Time!' said John. 'That's what we need. Time, and yet again time. I'm not sure we're going to get it. I shall be surprised if we celebrate Christmas in peace.' He felt the weight of both public and private misery. He eyed his son.

It was a good thing that Anthony, in these recent months, had begun to look so much more assured, confident, even at times radiant. There was no girl, as far as his parents knew. Perhaps, perish the thought, he even felt some sort of excited anticipation of the crisis that must surely now come, anticipation like that of an earlier, doomed generation? Still, the boy's eyes were brighter than they had ever been; and he seldom stuttered now.

'If all goes well, I'll have my commission by December.' Anthony's mind was elsewhere. He patted his pocket. He could feel in it a folded letter, received three days earlier. There was also a telephone message he had scribbled down as it was relayed to him that morning.

The letter had taken two weeks to reach London.

When she had written it, Anna had sat long at her desk, looking at the sealed envelope. She had always despised people who pretended that emotions could be so strong as to master free-will. 'What I do,' she determined to say to herself, 'I do knowingly.' She often tried to decide why she loved Anthony as profoundly as she did – a young Englishman of a 'type' of which she knew a number and seldom found appealing. Within

94

minutes of first meeting she had felt that he had a quality unlike most of his kind. It was something in the way he moved, something in the intentness he devoted to his companion, something in the still-colt-like impulsiveness of the way he swung his body round to one when walking. Something, of course, in his physical beauty, something in his half-teasing voice, that now and then held tears in it. Something too in his deep and far from typical consideration in love, his instinctive ability, it seemed, to feel how she felt, whether in pleasure or in pain. Something, of course, like Clemens –

She sighed and took the envelope between finger and thumb, decisively.

'Well, whatever it is,' she said to herself, fearfully but exultantly, 'one loves.'

'There is no doubt about it at all, my darling. None whatsoever. I rejoice that it is so. Before writing to you I wished to reach clear decisions. Kurt, as you know, spent some weeks at Langenbach in January and February. I will say no more of that. Then there was that extraordinary, unexpected visit of mine to London in March. That visit where I was prepared for sadness with my grandmother's illness but which turned out so joyfully, with her recovery and with you, my Anthony. Even more wonderful than in October!

Be sure that the child within me is yours! By the middle of May I was sure. My child will be born in early December – that is what they think. For Kurt, and for his family, that can be believed. Kurt was here in February, I am saying to them it is likely to be November. It will be a little "late" that is all. It will be strange after several years, but the Langenbachs will be quiet and glad. Kurt – I am not sure. But his pride will help him believe.

I wish him to accept the child as his. You must, please, understand this. Not only will it be better for the baby, but today, in Germany, there could be serious difficulties if it were otherwise. I have written to Kurt that he will be a father, probably in late November.

If my health permits, and I am sure it will, I intend to come over to visit my grandmother in September. She is much better now but to leave it later will be difficult for me. It is now July but there are matters which keep me here.

Be happy for me, my darling, I have never felt better or calmer. Do not be angry or proud or resentful.

Anna'

95

Before Anthony had fully recovered his senses from Anna's letter he had been stunned by the telephone message. The telephone rang in Mount Street at nine o'clock that July morning.

'Mr Marvell? This is Margaret Platt. From Wilton Place. You remember –'

'Of course. Good morning, Miss Platt.'

'Mr Marvell, I'm afraid Mrs Briscoe has received some rather tragic news, and she thought it would be best to share it with you since you might not otherwise hear it and you are, she knows, a friend of the family.'

His heart had near stopped.

'Mrs Briscoe has just had a telegram. I'm sorry to say that Captain Langenbach, Anna's husband, has been killed in Spain. Having survived to the last day of that awful war. Some sort of accident, we don't know any details. He was about to return to Germany. Mrs Briscoe thought it right to tell you –'

'Yes – yes. Miss Platt. Thank you.'

'Poor Anna.'

'Yes. Oh dear. I – I'll write, of course. Please thank Mrs Briscoe. It was very thoughtful.'

'Goodbye, Mr Marvell.' She had rung off.

Anthony brought his attention back to his father with a radiant smile.

'Well, look after yourself, old boy. Going away for August?'

'I'm not sure.'

John Marvell paid the bill.

August, 1939.

'Mrs Briscoe, this is Anthony Marvell speaking. You may remember I called on you earlier this year, when Anna Langenbach was in London. And you were kind enough to get word to me last month about her husband. That awful tragedy.'

'I remember, Mr Marvell.'

'I wondered whether you had any news of Anna. I was so sorry to hear about her husband. I wrote to her – to Langenbach. I haven't heard anything, of course – there was no need to reply – but I had an idea she might be coming over.'

'I see.'

'And I – my family too, of course – would have loved to see her.'

'I can tell you that Anna hoped to come in September. Now I don't know. The whole situation in the world seems terrible, Mr Marvell. What's going to happen?'

'Terrible, worrying, I agree.'

'Anna has many reasons for worrying. She is in a delicate state just now.'

'Ah –'

'It doesn't look to me as if people will be able to come and go freely to Germany much longer. I'll get word to you if I hear anything. Would you like that?'

'Thank you, Mrs Briscoe. I would like that very much indeed.'

'Hilda just wired "Come home at once,"' said John Marvell to his brother-in-law. 'At the same time I sent a telegram to Francis Carr, "Urgently need your help to get Marcia home as soon as possible." You've spoken to the Foreign Office people, Stephen, and I thank you for it. Is there anything else we can do?'

It was 27th August.

'The Carrs will stay in Vienna until ordered to leave, of course. But it's still perfectly possible for Marcia to travel. Let's hope she sees sense. There's no question of closing frontiers yet or anything like that.'

'It's inevitable, isn't it, Stephen?'

'A few pacifists are still clinging to their illusions. But everyone on our side is pretty clear. Nazi Germany making a surprise pact with Soviet Russia! What can that mean but the go-ahead for Hitler? As you know, we've signed a formal defence agreement with Poland yesterday.'

Hilda came in from the outer hall. 'This has just arrived.'

She tore open the buff envelope and handed the telegram to John without looking at it and without a word. John knew that she sensed its contents as clearly as if she had seen the jarring capital-lettered sentences. He read aloud,

'WILL BE FINE HERE. WERNER AND I INTEND MARRY THIRD WEEK SEPTEMBER. INTEND STAY WITH AUSTRIAN FRIENDS. WILL SEND ADDRESS. ALL LOVE MARCIA'

It was dawn on 3rd September, a pale, clear dawn with superb visibility. Werner von Arzfeld looked out over the wide Galician landscape from the High Tatra hills. Before him lay southern Poland. The war was only two days old but already a large part of the Polish 'Cracow Army' seemed to have been destroyed within a few miles of that frontier over which General von Rundstedt's 'Army Group South' had advanced in the early hours of 1st September. The rest appeared to be in considerable disorder.

Since the beginning of August, Werner had spent most of his time in Slovakia, where 22nd Panzer Corps, to whose staff he was attached, had concentrated. He had been able to spend two perfect twenty-four hour periods in Vienna – a laborious train journey but no great distance. The second of those snatched absences from duty was now three weeks ago. He savoured it in his mind. Marcia had been as delicious as ever. Ah, when this Polish business was over!

Werner had only recently informed his family of his intentions. He had written a long letter to his father. Of course there were problems, but Kaspar von Arzfeld had so just a mind that his son was confident of his support. Meanwhile, by a stroke of good fortune, Werner had been able to arrange for Marcia to lodge with an Austrian family, distant relations of the Arzfelds, elderly, kindly, informal, understanding. Marcia had been perfectly happy with the idea.

'Casimir Rudberg and his wife have a nice flat. I have told them about us. I am writing to my father. It is all muddled, impossible to do things in the right sequence, because of the political situation. If your relations, the Carrs, leave –'

'But darling Werner, the Carrs can't leave. He's *en poste* here.'

98

'Yes – but if something happened, then the Rudbergs will be happy for you to live with them. For as long as necessary.'

Marcia had met them and been charmed. She had, for some time, been tiring of the Carr ménage and had made tentative enquiries about an independent flat. Of this, however, Werner strongly disapproved.

'At any time,' Werner had said, 'if the Carrs leave. Or before, if you like.'

Marcia had said softly,

'You mean, don't you, they'd have to leave if England were at war with Germany,' and had looked at him, for the first time, with a different look, a wounded, frightened look.

'I suppose in that case I'd be put in prison, or something!'

'No, no! It will be all right!' But he wondered. Ought not a man of honour, even now, to tell Marcia to pack her bags and go? He could not bear the thought. A little later he had said,

'I wish us to be formally betrothed.'

'What does that mean?'

'It means the world will be told. It means you will be recognized as my fiancée, my wife when circumstances permit the marriage. You will – you would – not be troubled if –'

'If?'

'If things get worse. And it will be proper, it will be expected then, that you stay with relatives of mine. Casimir and Amalie Rudberg will deal with some of the formalities for me. They were enchanted by you, of course. I wish we could do it more properly, my little Marcia, but times are difficult. Will your family be very angry?'

'Well, all in all I think it's best, too. So all right, Werner, my love. Let's be betrothed. It sounds great fun. But I do miss you terribly. I miss you all the time. In the night I want to reach out and touch you. When we're married can we be together always?'

'Soon, I'm sure.'

Then he had written to his father. He had spoken formally to his Corps Commander, General von Kleist. Although Werner was a very junior member of the Corps Staff, von Kleist had taken an interest in him and the Section Chief had said briskly,

'I think you had better see the Corps Commander.' Von Kleist had looked at him keenly.

'Your family approves, I imagine?'

'I am sure of it. My father knows the young lady, *Herr General.*'

'I hope you will not make complicated plans for family life. There is work to do here.' Von Kleist knew that 'Plan White', the operation order for the invasion of Poland had been approved as long ago as 15th June. Some people thought there would be a last-minute cancellation, a solution. Von Kleist was not one of them.

'Exactly so, *Herr General.* I should say one thing. My fiancée is English.'

'*Eine Engländerin!*'

'Yes. A good English family. She is studying in Vienna.'

The Corps Commander pursed his lips.

'This may be difficult, von Arzfeld. You realize this?'

'Of course, *Herr General.*'

'And it will, no doubt, be difficult,' thought Werner, as he looked through his binoculars towards a small Polish village in the middle distance. 'But I do not care.' The village had earlier been burning, apparently set on fire by the initial German artillery bombardment, but the blaze seemed under control, a little dark smoke drifting in the pale light. It was an exquisite morning, cool, tranquil. The sounds of battle were far away. Werner felt extraordinarily well. There was everywhere profound satisfaction in the sense that, militarily, things seemed to have gone very much according to plan. Now Fourteenth Army, of which General von Kleist's 22nd Panzer Corps formed part, was bound for the north-east on a great encircling movement – the southern pincer of a mighty trap to destroy utterly the Polish armed forces both west and east of the Vistula. The forward divisions were well under way. The campaign was already assuming the heady character of a pursuit.

There had been some fighting here and there for the Polish frontier positions. The enemy had struggled with considerable vigour in some sectors, and casualties throughout Fourteenth Army had been significant. It was clear from the first, however, that no authoritative hand was controlling Polish operations.

Fighting had been piecemeal, unco-ordinated. The Luftwaffe had cleared the way. Prisoners gave little evidence of knowing where they were or what their tasks had been. Polish deployment, indeed, had apparently been far from complete. One Polish company had been shot to pieces marching along the road from Cracow, apparently unaware that a war had started. And why on earth, thought Werner, had the Poles concentrated everything, as far as could be gathered, forward in the frontier area? It was simply asking for a breakthrough and an encirclement. They must have known they couldn't hope to defend a frontier stretching on a great arc from the Baltic to the Carpathians. 'He who defends everything defends nothing,' Werner quoted to himself complacently. Now, whether by design or desperate instinct, the Polish forces seemed to be streaming eastward to behind the Vistula. If they could get there.

'And then, with luck, it will all be over,' thought Werner. One had to trust the Führer's extraordinary flair for politics. It was unthinkable that Britain and France would launch a world war to interfere in a situation where everyone could see Germany had a strong case for rectification of frontiers and protection of minorities. There would, he supposed sadly, be huffing and puffing by them. This could be trying for Marcia. But it would blow over. The year before, a number of senior generals had been muttering that the Czech business must be stopped before it blew up into a world war. He suspected that his present general, von Kleist, had been one of them. They'd been wrong. Britain and France hadn't done a thing. The Führer's instinct had been right.

People like his father, of course, saw it all in a different light. They were appalled by the Nazis, by the bullying and swagger, by the way the Government seemed ready to ride roughshod over law, by the little jacks-in-office. Certainly some very unpleasant stories were current of what went on, of how opponents were treated and so forth. And there was the Jewish business. But as against all that – blemishes which time would doubtless cure or set in perspective – there was the fact that by diplomacy which was as shrewd as it was bold Hitler had put Germany on the path of self-respect once again. And now the Army was helping him to finish the job.

Werner's mind switched to Marcia, living now with the Rudbergs. He thought of her smile, her hair, her touch, her pale skin and dancing eyes. Onward to victory, and the quicker the better! And then, with luck, a long peace!

Werner walked from a small knoll, an excellent viewpoint, where he had been inspecting the morning, over to the two command vehicles, with tents attached, which served as the Corps Operations Centre.

'Arzfeld!'

It was his Section Chief.

Werner saluted. He was attached to the General Staff, and although not yet a formal member of it the attachment created that possibility. Werner was ambitious. He envisaged with pleasure the broad, red General Staff stripes which might one day adorn his breeches, the collar patches, the sense of membership of a great, historic fraternity.

'We want to move this group forward soon. Find the best place. Things are going fast. 17th Corps are pretty close on our left –' Werner nodded, his eyes on the Corps map. Roads were rudimentary in many places, and maps were inadequate. There had already been some confusion.

'Forward divisions are reporting no serious resistance anywhere this side of the river. A few snipers, nothing organized –'

The operational situation was perfectly clear.

'It looks as if they're trying to get away north, for the most part. All the better. The idea is to stop them withdrawing behind the Vistula as far as we can. We'll be making a broader sweep –'

The Chief of the operations branch had drawn a thick, ambitious line on Werner's map. To find a good place somewhere along it to which the Corps' tactical headquarters should move was Werner's task.

Soon he was being driven in a small staff car down a bumpy road toward the village he had seen from the hill top. Beyond, the road ran to Tarnow and the valley of the Vistula.

Werner noted with approval that his driver was Braun. He knew Gunther Braun rather well. A fellow Lower Saxon in a Corps drawn mainly from elsewhere, Braun liked, Werner knew, the chance of driving him. They raced through the little village into open country of wide, poor fields beyond. There were a few woods, in full leaf, well spaced, symmetrical. Road and farm tracks alike were crowded with military vehicles, interspersed with farm carts. Here and there was a blackened, burnt-out chassis. The weather was fine, fields and tracks were hard. There was little difficulty in driving past obstructions. Braun negotiated his way with erratic skill.

'They say we've won already, *Herr Hauptmann*! And the war only two days old.'

'Wars take longer to win than that, Braun, even in Poland.'

'Will others come in against us, *Herr Hauptmann*? France? England?'

'No. Now shut up and think about your driving. Take the small farm track to the right over there – up towards that wood. There's nothing else on it.'

They drew away from the main axis, from the flow of military traffic.

'Up to the crest and stop. In to the right here – stop! Good! I want to look –' He brought his binoculars up.

At that moment, some twenty yards inside the wood, one of the few skilled Polish snipers overrun by the tide of war settled his rifle firmly into the shoulder and brought the tip of the foresight on to the target. Two soldiers in a single German car. Nobody would miss them or find them for a little. Nothing else seemed to be coming up this track. Five minutes would see him safe back through the woods, able thereafter to melt into the mass of his countrymen, to evade this wave of field-grey scum. 'God avenge Poland,' he thought, 'and I'll send two on the way to meet Him.' He squeezed the trigger. Werner was standing and the bullet entered his stomach. Braun threw the driver's door open and the sniper's second round hit him in the head as he tried to throw himself from the car – a very pretty shot although, as the Pole acknowledged to himself complacently, a lucky one.

It was five hours later that same morning. At half past eleven the Marvells sat in the inner hall at Bargate. The voice of Neville Chamberlain was melancholy and dignified.

'It is the evil things,' he concluded, 'that we shall be fighting

103

against – brute force, bad faith, injustice, oppression and persecution – and against them I am certain that the right will prevail.'

'I feel sorry for him,' John Marvell spoke heavily. 'I haven't admired him these last two years or more, but I'm sorry for him. He's utterly wretched. And I doubt if he's the man for the hour.'

'We've got the King later.'

'I feel so useless,' said John, 'I'm under fifty, but they took me off the reserve – my leg –'

'Don't be absurd, dear. And there'll be plenty for everyone to do. Could we have prevented this do you think?'

'Perhaps. Early on, when too many people were vindictive and narrow-minded, capable only of seeing others' faults. That was the time for generosity and we were ungenerous. Then again later, when too many people – sometimes the same people – were frightened and self-deluding. But I'm afraid this man wants war. Not just the spoils of war. War. He wants to conquer.'

'Well,' said Hilda, 'all we can do is our best. Try to stay human and decent and generous and do our best. It won't be easy.' Her heart, like that of her husband, was near bursting with pain at the thought of her children, each differently menaced.

In admirable, broadcast words King George echoed her sentiment later in the day. The solemn, hesitant voice was heard in every British home.

'We can only do the right as we see the right, and reverently commit our cause to God.'

PART III
1940

Chapter 7

FRIDO DID NOT ANTICIPATE meeting many Generals, however long the war lasted, and he devoutly hoped it wouldn't last long. It had been, therefore, surprising and not a little alarming to hear his own name barked on a particular afternoon in March, 1940. A company from Frido's battalion had been detailed to provide security and ceremonial support for a distinguished conference in Western Germany. Generals, their red and gold collar patches as thick as falling rose petals in autumn, were congregated. Frido, duties appropriately performed, as he thought, was hovering diligently in the background. He had already, after a very short military career, learned that some people liked to be always in the way when Generals were around, heels clicking, salutes radiating homage, admiration. Frido's instincts were the exact reverse. To be inconspicuous was his dearest ambition.

He thus responded with sinking heart to the sharp call from his Captain. The great ones seemed to be dispersing in their cars. Guards were drawn up, drivers were standing at the salute by opened car doors. What now?

'*Leutnant von Arzfeld!*'

Frido moved rapidly. His Captain, steel-helmeted, boots gleaming, expression serious and devout, was standing beside what appeared to be a very senior general indeed. One of many.

Frido, heart beating, snapped to attention and saluted.

'*Leutnant von Arzfeld, Herr Generaloberst.*'

From his first moments in uniform Frido had felt, uneasily, that he was almost certainly unsuited to an officer's rank. It might have been more honourable, he several times reflected, to have remained, anonymous, in the ranks. He had so many doubts. He saw too many sides of a question. Could a man

107

lead others, who was himself so much a prey to uncertainties, unease? Then there was the oath.

> 'I swear by God this holy oath, that I will render to Adolf Hitler, Führer of the German Reich and People, Supreme Commander of the Armed Forces, unconditional obedience . . .'

and so forth. Everybody had to swear it, of course. It had been imposed immediately Hitler had assumed, together with the Chancellorship, the office of President when old Hindenburg died in 1934. But an officer must be sincere, responsible, single-minded, completely alive to what he was doing and saying: a believer. Frido, as in so many ways, was troubled.

It was Werner who had persuaded him. It always was. Werner had told him not to be absurd, had asked whether he thought he was the only German officer who was sceptical of some aspects of the National Socialist régime. 'You should hear my General when he thinks he's alone with his friends,' said Werner with a chuckle. Werner's position had always seemed privileged to some extent. As the respected Kaspar von Arzfeld's son, and a particularly promising young officer, he possessed and relished a status beyond that justified by age and rank.

'It's in the ranks you'll find the true believers, my boy!' Werner had said, putting an arm round his brother's shoulder. 'Now you work hard and distinguish yourself at Officer School, you earn your officer's tunic, you won't regret it. And you'll be among friends. That's what really counts if there's to be a war. Anybody will tell you that.'

To his father, a man of old-fashioned values, the matter was simple. If Germany was to find itself at war it was unthinkable that a von Arzfeld should not take his place in the officer Corps. Affairs of state were not for Frido. Military duty and military example must henceforth be his vocation.

Kaspar von Arzfeld, Colonel of the Reserve (retired), fifty-five years of age and lamed for life twenty years before, had managed somehow to insinuate himself into the local military district organization in charge of certain aspects of transportation and railway planning. 'One must do something,' he said, half-apologetically. His duty enabled him to live at home, to continue tending his beloved woods. But Frido knew, melancholy but comprehending, that his father liked, above all, the feel of his old uniform again.

So here was Frido, lieutenant in a Rifle Regiment of 7th Panzer Division, stationed in Western Germany, thoughtful, conscientious, concerned. There had been a whole week's leave at Arzfeld at Christmas. He had felt closer to his father than ever before, bound to him by their shared wretchedness at Werner's death. Werner, Frido thought with reason and without rancour, had always been the favoured, the first born, the satisfying son. From childhood, Werner had charmed all ages and both sexes, had exuded quiet strength, half-sceptical confidence, had never seemed to have a care in the world. 'I should have gone,' thought Frido. 'Father and Arzfeld needed Werner. It's different with me.' He thought it without morbidity for he had loved his brother dearly.

If such feelings existed in Kaspar von Arzfeld he never showed them. He looked for a long time into Frido's face and held his hand tight.

'Well,' he said. 'He went the way many of our family have gone. We shall not forget him.'

'Never, father.'

But there had been another shadow lying between them that Christmas, something referred to delicately in letters between father and son but difficult to get on terms with, resolve attitudes towards.

'Frido, you have seen the notice of betrothal sent out on behalf of Werner immediately before he fell – betrothal to Fraülein Marvell?'

'Yes indeed, Father.'

'You know that I was told nothing beforehand! Werner asked our cousins, the Rudbergs, to arrange this notification – it went only to our close family – in such a hurry that he wrote to inform me only after he had actually set matters in hand. And he asked these cousins of ours in Vienna to do it, instead of his own family, here at Arzfeld. He said there might be delays in the post – he was, of course, already in the field. The form of the thing, in consequence, was most peculiar, very irregular.'

'I expect he had some strong reason, Father.'

'Of course he did. He wrote it to me. He was determined to leave this English girl as his properly acknowledged fiancée. He did not wish to go to the war without arranging that. But it is still extraordinary. Heaven knows what her family think. Or what they know.'

'We haven't much opportunity to find out, Father.'

Von Arzfeld made an impatient gesture. 'So much hurry! Such neglect of how things are done!'

Frido said, embarrassedly, 'I suppose, father –'

'Naturally I thought of that. I asked myself if she may be going to have a child. I wrote at length and in confidence to Countess Rudberg. It was not easy. I do not know her well. She is, as you know, your mother's relation. But I wrote, and I was as direct as it was possible with decency to be. She replied it is certain this girl is not going to have a child.'

'But perhaps, Father, Werner couldn't know that for certain.' Frido's emotions were particularly confused.

'I see little difference,' said his father. 'If he had wished to ensure a child was born legitimate he should either have married or abstained. Or – taken other measures. If he merely wished to demonstrate to the world an intention to marry this girl –'

He sighed and shrugged his shoulders. Then he said –

'Whatever there has been between them, Frido, your brother died loving this girl, and wishing to make her his wife. That is the reality. And that indicates to us how we must behave.'

Frido was silent. His father looked at him hard.

'It makes it absolutely necessary that whatever our feelings, our reservations, we must treat Marcia Marvell as one of our family. We must regard her interests as our interests, her honour as ours. I have written to invite her to Arzfeld.'

'Has she answered?'

'Yes. She is at the moment, she says, trying to find work in Vienna. She has, of course, difficulties. She is an alien – an enemy alien. She has already been arrested once, and released. Countess Rudberg told me of it. The police have discussed her case with the Rudbergs, quite amicably. She is not to be interned because the betrothal, although not a marriage and having no legal effect upon nationality, apparently puts her in a particular category.'

'Where Marcia,' thought Frido, 'always belonged. And always will.'

'Because she was formally pledged to marry a citizen of the Reich, she is not to be interned. Apparently, she has to report regularly to the Police but her movements are not, at present, restricted. She could travel here provided, of course, that the authorities were informed. Her difficulty will be to find work.'

'It looks, Father, as if Werner has managed to protect her – posthumously. He's managed to get her into this special category.' Frido found difficulty in speaking. He loved his brother deeply, wept for him as only a brother can. At the same time he could not dismiss from his mind the image of Marcia, seen so seldom, desired so deeply. God forgive him, but was he glad that the Poles had rid him of the man who had won Marcia's body and heart?

'*Leutnant von Arzfeld, Herr Generaloberst.*'

'I'm glad to see you, von Arzfeld. I heard somebody call your name. Your brother was on my Staff in Poland. I wanted to tell you he was a brave and most efficient officer.'

'Thank you, *Herr Generaloberst.*'

General von Kleist looked at Frido.

'I knew your father well in the old days. In the cavalry. It pleases me to meet any son of his. In uniform.'

Frido knew that von Kleist had written to his father from Poland. Now he was on this front, in the west, although not, Frido thought, their own Army Commander. He was, Frido had heard, leader of some group of Panzer divisions, but not including their own 7th. 7th had just acquired a new divisional commander who had visited them, radiating energy, shooting out questions like a machine gun: but above that Frido's knowledge of generals did not extend.

'*Herr Generaloberst.*'

Von Kleist spoke softly.

'Your brother spoke to me, as his Commander, about his intended marriage, you know. I hope that matter has not caused distress to your father.'

'No, *Herr Generaloberst*, I do not think so.'

111

'I heard in Vienna that the young lady has formed another attachment. Well, good luck. And give my regards to your father.'

Frido saluted. Von Kleist smiled and walked to his car.

'Good news, von Arzfeld,' said Frido's captain that evening. 'We've got three days' leave the weekend after next. Then we've got a tough progamme, river crossing training, several big exercises, hard work right through to the summer. So make the most of three days off.'

Frido's short letter to Arzfeld announcing his imminent arrival crossed one from his father.

'My dear Frido,
    I have heard from Vienna that Fraülein Marvell would like to visit Arzfeld. I have said that she is welcome. There are, of course, formalities to complete but I am sure the authorities, when they understand the situation, will not trouble her or us. I am naturally confident that any intended bride of Werner's will be entirely reliable.'

'But less confident,' thought Frido, 'that this letter will not be examined by the censorship. Hence this unexceptionable sentiment.' He continued reading.

'Fraülein Marvell arrives here next Thursday. Lise remembers her with affection and it will be company for her. Lise is also going to enquire if there is any work in the hospital for which a novice could be trained. She thinks it is possible. So far this war has been merciful to most, but battles are not fought without cost. God be with you, my dear son.
                    Kaspar von Arzfeld'

So Marcia would be at Arzfeld! Frido's mind scratched at General von Kleist's words about 'another attachment'. Not that it was surprising, Frido thought, with a disagreeable sense in the stomach, only surprising that it had come to the ears of a general and not one, as far as Frido knew, resident in Vienna. But when he thought of Marcia at Arzfeld his blood raced in his veins. The week passed slowly.

Then he was again driving with Franz up the familiar dusty road.

'All well at Arzfeld, Franz? My father well? Any news?'

'All was perfectly well, Franz said. 'It's odd to see Herr von Arzfeld in uniform again – and he's as trim as ever, he doesn't put on a kilo. Is this war going on long, Herr Frido? We've settled the Poles now. What are we all fighting about?'

'The French and the English won't accept it, Franz. That's the trouble.'

'Ach, the French!' Franz grunted sourly. Then he said, 'English! We've got an *Engländerin* here, now, of all things!'

'You are speaking of Fraülein Marvell, Franz, who was to marry Herr Werner, had he not fallen in battle for Germany. You will speak with respect.'

Franz was unabashed. He had been long years at Arzfeld.

'Of course, Herr Frido. It just seems odd, that's all.' They drove on. Arzfeld came into sight round a bend in the road. 'Late March, and the trees starting into leaf,' thought Frido. 'A perfect time! A time to treasure in the mind!' War, even so placid a war as had so far been Frido's, gave peculiar sharpness and beauty to every beloved scene, gave a sense that it should be valued, savoured, stored, could not be taken for granted, might not last.

Kaspar greeted his son with quiet affection.

'The girls will be back later. Franz is grumbling at making two journeys but it is nothing. Their train arrives every evening at seven o'clock. Often Lise walks to the station in the morning.'

'How are – they?'

'Fraülein Marvell has been here a week as you know. She is charming and Lise is fond of her. It is, of course, not easy – for her. She must miss her own family. One has to say it. And – I suppose – her own country. I have had a talk with the authorities here. She must report her movements, but there is no reason why she should not work at the hospital – in a very subordinate capacity, naturally. It has already been arranged. She will make her home here.'

Kaspar was pleased when Frido gave him General von Kleist's regards. 'We were together as young cavalry officers, long ago!'

Frido made no mention of Kleist's reference to Marcia. And when she arrived in the trap, with Lise, his heart jumped as it always had on the infrequent occasions when he had seen her. His mind went back to his visit to England, to Marcia's laughing, teasing proximity at dinner at Bargate, to her flushed dishevelment when pursued by that elderly satyr, her uncle. And she looked, after a day at the hospital, a train journey, a drive, as lovely as ever.

'It is her colouring,' thought Frido, 'it is the texture of her skin, smooth like a rose petal. Above all, it is those eyes, so full of laughter and meaning.' He had prepared a few formal words about Werner – about *their* Werner. Werner had been, after all, her fiancé. But Frido's speech was pre-empted. Marcia jumped fom the trap, squeezed his arm and held up her face to be kissed.

'Darling Frido! Wonderful to see you again!' He blushed.

'You – you have started to work with Lise I hear?'

'That's it. Florence Nightingales, we!'

'Who is that?' said Frido puzzled.

But Marcia disappeared toward her room and Lise wanted to have him for a while to herself. She took his arm.

'It's light enough for a little walk.' She, too, squeezed his arm. It was, thought Frido, a sisterly gesture. As they strolled Lise spoke with enthusiasm of Marcia.

'I know she really loved Werner. I feel her to be my sister, even though they weren't married.'

Frido nodded. So far so good.

'You know there's someone else now. I don't blame her. She's young, Werner was killed seven months ago. She's lovely, every man must be after her.'

Frido said, 'It seems rather soon.'

'There's a war on. People can't stand back from life, mourning. Father doesn't guess anything of course.'

'Who is it?'

'It's a cousin – another Rudberg. Met her in Vienna, at Cousin Rudberg's house, where she was living. This one is Toni Rudberg. He's a Panzer officer, just like you.'

'In a Panzer Division?'

'Yes, 2nd. I know that because Marcia – well, to be honest, she finally decided to come here because Toni's Division's now in the west. She hopes he'll get leave some time, and be within reach. He seems to be mad about her.'

114

Frido digested this in painful silence. 2nd Panzer Division had been stationed in Vienna before the war: in fact it was known as the 'Vienna Division'. He'd seen nothing of them but he had an idea they were in von Kleist's command. Beneath his attention though such things might be, the old cavalryman might, Frido supposed, have heard gossip in Vienna or elsewhere about the condition of Count Rudberg's heart.

'He's older than Werner – he's a captain,' said Lise. 'I don't think he's actually a relation of ours although of course his Rudberg cousins were related to Mama. He sounds very attractive, I must say.'

With the part of his mind still capable of reflection Frido knew that the minutes spent in a small rubber boat crossing the river Meuse on 13th May 1940 were the longest he had ever experienced.

7th Panzer Division's march through the Ardennes had not been particularly eventful. There had been some fighting against French covering forces: mostly cavalry, from what Frido had heard. Then there had been a day or two in which they had all rumbled forward, checked now and then by, presumably, some minor action at the head of the Divisional column. But never for long. If a way could be found to bypass an action and keep up momentum it was taken. If a vehicle broke down it was pushed off the road without ceremony. Frido prayed that none in his company would suffer this fate. None did.

But then – only two days after crossing the frontier and starting this remarkable adventure – they had started to wind down the twisting, overhung roads to the valley of the Meuse. Much of the country hitherto had been high plateau, comparatively open and level, chequered by large woods. Here, by contrast, the trees and gradients prevented any movement of vehicles off roads. Traffic flow could be disrupted all too easily by accident or casualty. And here, for the first time, Frido tasted something recognizable as battle. Already his Regiment had advanced seventy miles. As their vehicles moved in the half-darkness of early morning toward the lip of ground below which ran the Meuse, French artillery shells began to fall near the river bank.

The *Panzer Grenadiers* of Frido's company jumped from their vehicles and moved down toward the assembly areas where assault boats were to be collected and carried to the water's edge. They knew that all bridges had been blown, in spite of earlier hopes that somehow a crossing might be rushed. The necessity for an assault across the water had been anticipated, and the operation rehearsed a good many times. Day was already breaking, although a thick mist hung along the river. 'When that lifts,' thought Frido, 'we'll be sitting ducks.'

Everybody moved fast. The company's organization was efficient. Practice had paid. Rubber boats were being inflated as fast as the men could manage and the first flight was being manhandled to the water. Heavier assault craft were being marshalled. No shell had fallen for five minutes.

Then Frido heard a sound with which he was to become sickeningly familiar – the rushing, whistling screech of an enemy shell about to explode in the near vicinity. Two men near him threw themselves flat. Frido did not know, afterwards, whether his own instinct to remain upright stemmed from inertia, inexperience, stupidity, some sixth sense that told him the shell would explode at a safe distance, or bravado. The soldiers picked themselves up, exchanging hasty glances, unsure whether they had disgraced the Wehrmacht. More reports sounded from the west bank of the river. Frido shouted an order and the next flight of assault boats were lifted forward. Each boat was meant to carry four men.

'The lieutenant's a cool one!' he heard one man mutter admiringly.

Then, without remembering exactly the sequence of events, Frido found himself on the water. For the first thirty metres, miraculously, there was no hostile sound or sign. The morning mist was still lying mercifully on the river but he could see the shape of the early sun through it, its light masked but its outline clear and menacing. At any moment the protective haze would be cruelly dispersed, thought Frido. He nodded to the soldier wielding the paddle and smiled. Conscious of little but fear and fatigue the man nevertheless registered gratitude. 'Some of them would shout at you,' the soldier

116

thought. 'As if anyone would be pouring out less than his guts to get to the other side!'

It was in mid-stream that Frido could first see clearly the dark line of the west bank. And it was in mid-stream that the French soldiers in bunkers and weapon pits along the line of the west bank could see him. The current was not fast but the boats seemed to be making agonizingly slow progress. The first noise was of French artillery once again. Some shells fell on the east bank.

'The following flights will catch it now,' a *Feldwebel* called out. 'They won't hit us on the water!'

There were some nervous laughs. Then Frido heard the sound they all dreaded: from the south, from their left, the insistent, clattering sound of French machine guns on the west bank. The men needed no exhortation to keep as low as possible in the boats but every soldier felt ten feet tall and wide in proportion.

'Ah-h-h!'

It was a long drawn-out scream from the boat next to them. Frido saw a soldier topple into the water, limbs still moving convulsively. The man wasn't dead. As he hit the water there appeared to be nothing but a scarlet mask where his face had been. There was another scream, as he threshed with arms and legs, blinded, in agony, about mercifully to drown. The west bank, their destination, looked very far away. There was still some mist. It thinned and thickened here and there, altering their chances minute by minute.

'Where are our own shells that ought to be silencing those damned Frenchmen?' thought Frido. He had seen artillery officers move into observation posts on the east bank but German shells were conspicuously failing to give the crossing the support it needed.

Suddenly the French machine guns started again. French artillery fire became heavier. They heard the shells screeching overhead. All seemed to be landing at the exact point on the east bank whence their little flotilla had been launched. Now there were, miraculously, only about forty metres to go, and as far as Frido could see there was no French position at the place on the west bank where they would make a landfall.

'Paddle, paddle!'

From the northward, from Frido's right, another machine gun clattered. It sounded disagreeably near. The next thing Frido felt was as if he were sprayed by a warm tap.

'*Herr Leutnant!*' yelled the man with the paddle pointlessly. Frido looked at his uniform and hands, crimson with blood. The soldier who had been crouching in the middle of the little boat looked extraordinary, grotesque. There was something missing. Frido recognized, with a sense which he later recognized as shock in its literal sense, that the man's head had been almost severed by machine gun fire. His blood had struck his companions like water from a burst pipe. The soldier with the paddle retched but by a remarkable effort, a triumph of fear over weakness, maintained his efforts. At that exact moment Frido heard the sound of the paddle striking the bottom. He shouted –

'Out! Out!'

The boat capsized as three men leapt from it and threw themselves into the water, wading frantically toward the bank. The headless *Panzer Grenadier* rolled into the Meuse.

Shouts could be heard along the bank. The mist was now clearing fast. Frido was able to see that a remarkable number of boats appeared to have made the crossing safely. A *Feldwebel* appeared from nowhere and saluted, reporting numbers. The company's next objective had been identified from an observation post on the east bank before they started – mist-shrouded, indistinct. Soldiers began running to the planned collecting points. There was much shouting and scurrying.

'The vital thing,' thought Frido, 'must be not just to reach some bit of ground, but to silence those damned machine guns.' For the sun was now up. The Meuse lay clear and silver beneath a glorious early summer sky. As he looked eastward, Frido could see no sign of the next company starting to embark. French shells were falling on the launch points with unceasing ferocity and machine guns were drumming away. One could see the strike of bullets as well as the grey spurts of shell bursts. 'I wonder if we're the first Rifle company across the Meuse,' thought Frido. 'I certainly hope we won't be the last.'

A few hours later he found a moment to thank God for sparing him and a large number of his company. Casualties

118

crossing the river had been surprisingly light. For several hours they had been isolated, as Frido feared, so devastating had been French fire at the east bank. This isolation had been unnerving, but otherwise they had not been much troubled. The French were manning their riverside bunkers, concentrating their fire on German attempts to reinforce, rather than spending blood and time in trying to deal with the enemy already across. And one German company was certainly inadequate, by itself, to attack the French positions firing on the river, widely separated as these were. Frido tried to organize a movement against two of the nearest of the bunkers, but they were difficult to get at. Instruction at officer school and previous practice had not prepared him for the launch of an attack from above against fortified emplacements lying beneath the overhang of a river bank, an attack supported either not at all or by artillery whose observers were all on the far side of the river.

'The French,' thought Frido, 'are winning this round.'

Then the situation changed – quickly and dramatically. There was a lull in the French fire. Suddenly everybody heard and recognized a new sound.

'*Panzers!*'

From where he was Frido could see back across the Meuse. He saw, shuffling their noses from small feeder side streets and then moving on to the road running along the river bank itself, the familiar sight of German tanks. There had been tank fire earlier, but from further back. Now the tanks were moving boldly on to the riverside road itself and starting to drive slowly north and south, turrets traversed westward.

First one tank, then another, then all started firing, at point blank range at French bunkers and machine gun nests across the Meuse.

'My God!' muttered Frido, 'they're dead if the French have got anti-tank guns down here! They look like moving targets on the range!'

But the Panzers were keeping up their fire and Frido could not see one get hit. After a little, a cheer went up from the few men round him who could also watch the scene. From the east bank of the Meuse boats were being launched again! No sound of French machine guns disturbed the sudden peace. The

119

Panzers had done their deadly work, pouring in shell after shell at a distance of only a few hundred metres.

From further to the west could be heard the sporadic sound of French artillery, and shells were still falling: but the mood had changed. Menace had dissolved.

'We'll soon sort those gunners out, once more of the Division and the general are across!' called Frido's Captain, suddenly appearing, voice and confidence greatly restored. 'Wait till we raft some Panzers over, wait till we get a pontoon bridge! We'll soon chase those guns away! We'll be in their gun positions in half an hour when General Rommel starts!'

Chapter 8

Eight days later.

Eight extraordinary days.

No reminiscences of his father, no instruction, no study of past campaigns had prepared Frido for anything like this. He found himself reflecting how unsurprising it was that man still turned to the evils and hazards of war if campaigning could be as exhilarating as this had been. There was nothing here of the carnage of old soldiers' tales described from twenty-two years before on the Western Front. No wire, no paralysing artillery bombardments, no muddy, churned-up ground, little physical destruction and, after breaking west from the Meuse Valley, extraordinarily little blood. French guns had at first given a lot of trouble and had hemmed in the German columns trying to debouch from the river valley: this had gone on for two days. But by 15th May, 7th Panzer Division's advance was meeting little opposition.

One of the biggest problems was how to dispose of huge numbers of prisoners without using an excessive number of men to guard them. As the Division rolled forward a French anti-tank gun sometimes picked off one of the leading tanks and had to be dealt with, but on the whole the enemy seemed keen to surrender and huge numbers of dispirited-looking French soldiers were marshalled in fields beside the road, dejected and bewildered rather than frightened, if their faces were anything to go by. Frido saw few civilians. They seemed to have abandoned their homes and driven or trudged westward. Some ran into the fields and gazed, little huddles of terrified and resentful humanity, at the driving columns. They made Frido feel uneasy. On the whole his *Panzer Grenadiers*, tired but exuberant, found these refugees objects of mockery rather than pity.

'Look at that old cow, wheeling an easy chair strapped to a perambulator!'

'Did you see the ones who tried to strap a bed on top of a donkey!'

'Hey – why've you left the piano behind?'

The mood was of laughter and gaiety.

War quickly drives out pity, Frido thought. But although he tried, fiercely, to keep part of his mind reflective and principled, he knew that he, like his men, was caught up by the winds of victory, the intoxication of rapid advance deep into the enemy's land.

Few chances, however, could be taken. It was as often as not judged prudent for farms or villages overlooking the Division's line of advance to receive one or two well-aimed rounds from a tank gun. Often they burst into flames. Sometimes a few enemy soldiers emerged in consequence – more often not. On one occasion the German advance was held up by a huge refugee column which had become mixed up with French military traffic, with a French force fleeing, making no attempt to deploy or fight; guns, carts, lorries, men, horses, all mingled in inextricable confusion. To make matters worse, the Luftwaffe had taken the column as a target and the road verges were littered with smashed equipment, household goods, and dead and wounded human beings both in and out of uniform, together with the mutilated carcasses of cattle and horses. Somehow the road was cleared, the stench was left behind and the Division raced on. The advance seemed to quicken as the spearheads reached further and further west.

'At this rate,' Frido said to his Captain, 'we'll soon reach the sea!'

The division's tanks were now well ahead of the *Panzer Grenadiers*. Deep into northern France they were skirting the town of Arras, said to contain an enemy garrison and thus to be bypassed and isolated. The country was open and ways around such obstacles were not difficult to find. Frido's own column was temporarily halted. There seemed some obstruction in a village. Some delay in front? He focused his binoculars north.

What he saw was startling.

Unmistakable, menacing, a line of wholly unfamiliar tanks

was moving southwards towards them, at a distance of under two kilometres from where Frido stood, on the outskirts of a small village. Between those tanks and his own vehicles and troops another minor road ran parallel to his own. This road was being used by a second company of the Regiment. They, too, were halted. Presumably they, too, had seen what he had seen. Thirty seconds later, two vehicles from the neighbouring company burst into flames simultaneously. Men were leaping from vehicles, diving into ditches and behind walls.

'Out! Out!' yelled Frido. He shouted a command or two, aimed at getting his soldiers into some sort of firing positions. He heard a *Feldwebel* take up the order. It was impossible to drive clear in vehicles – they were jammed in front and had closed up behind. To try to turn would be laborious and suicidal.

'Out! Out!'

The line of enemy tanks was closer. He could now hear machine gun fire, presumably from the tanks. A vehicle, two behind Frido's, exploded like a matchbox accidentally ignited. Most of the enemy's fire seemed to be going high. Men were cowering behind vehicles or in ditches. This was a new and disagreeable experience.

'Marvell, you speak German. You're urgently needed for a special job. You're going to be attached to another brigade headquarters, not ours, to help with on-the-spot interrogation of German prisoners.'

'German prisoners, sir? I didn't know we held them in unmanageable numbers!'

His Company Commander did not smile.

'We may soon. There's a big action due – a counter-attack. Now get cracking. Here's where you're to go. Jephson will drive you down. You've got to be there by nine o'clock in the morning at the latest. You'll be crossing the main refugee routes. Shouldn't be too bad.'

'Must I leave my platoon, sir? At this moment?'

'Stop arguing and get down there. It's nobody's fault but yours that you speak fluent German. You know perfectly well every linguist's name is listed.'

Anthony had spent six months as an officer. His commissioning had been advanced because of the imminence of war and he had been sent to a depot for four months with a large number of other junior officers, all more or less ignorant of military practicalities, duties or traditions, all more or less sceptical of the realism of such knowledge as was being imparted to them. Had war not intervened Anthony was scheduled to serve with his own Territorial soldiers, unskilled perhaps, but familiar certainly. As it was, the inscrutable ways of the Army whisked him away to a large training establishment where raw recruits and equally raw officers of the same Regiment were assembled together in huge numbers and somewhat mistrustful proximity. The winter had been frustrating.

'I wish to God I could have a platoon of my own! I'd learn much quicker with a little responsibility, rather than theorizing about how to command men and being treated like a delinquent schoolboy!'

'There's no demand for more officers at the moment, Marvell. There's no fighting, no casualties. It'll come.'

'Some of us will have rotted from boredom by then.'

'We've got to be patient. The Army's expanding, new battalions, new divisions. It'll come.'

And it had come. In March, 1940 Anthony, proud and refreshed, had found himself at last a junior commander in his own right, a warrior among his peers, in a Service battalion, and within weeks that battalion was in France. He had just about come to terms with the men in his platoon and the officers in his battalion when the alarm went on that May morning ten days ago. 10th May. The Germans had invaded Belgium and Holland! The long-awaited enemy offensive had started! The War had begun.

The ensuing days were chiefly noteworthy, in Anthony's mind, for lack of sleep. Fear, so far, was principally caused by air attacks which had been fierce, sudden and alarming. The battalion had twice been caught by the Luftwaffe on the move in vehicles – a most disagreeable experience, full of noise, explosions, shouts and acrid smells. Astonishingly, there had been no casualties. But all the time, after the first days, they were going back – back through Belgium, back towards the places whence they had started, back, back, back.

Of the German Army, Anthony had seen remarkably little. There were plenty of stories, of course, stories that lost nothing in the telling. It was said that German tanks had fallen in huge numbers on the brigade next door. German infantry appeared to have lapped like flood water round the flanks of a neighbouring division. Anthony had experienced none of these things. There was a good deal of artillery fire but it always seemed rather distant. The campaign had, for the most part, consisted of incessant marching, digging and waiting: accompanied by a great deal of explanation to his sceptical but, by and large, patient men about the destination of the march, the purpose of the digging ('I know we left the last trenches fifteen minutes after finishing them, O'Halloran. It'll be different one day. They'll save our lives') and the fact that some shrewd operational plan inspired the waiting. It was not always easy.

It would have been a great deal less easy without the aid of his platoon sergeant. In the few weeks of their service together, Anthony had come to the conclusion that Sergeant Chester was probably the best and certainly the nicest man he had ever known. A coal miner in civil life, a reservist who had originally served seven years from the age of sixteen, Chester was strong, very quiet and a mountain of loyal common sense.

'They'll dig fast enough, sir,' Chester said, 'when they've had a few mortar bombs among 'em. Like B Company.' For Chester's stories were gathered by the reliable word-of-mouth network of communication to which every senior non-commissioned officer in the battalion appeared connected, however widely they were dispersed. Chester passed on news only when it was true.

'Yes, I gather those bangs last night were on B Company. On the canal line.'

'That's it, sir. Jerry mortars. Very accurate they were. Two men and Corporal Jackson copped it.'

They had stood to arms throughout the previous night but although the darkness was full of distant firing nothing had happened on Anthony's Company front. He had been round the positions in the grey light of a drizzling dawn. Private Verity stood to attention in his slit trench. He wore his groundsheet, for the minuscule waterproof protection it afforded. He also wore an enormous, infectious grin. Verity

125

was very young. He looked about fifteen. Anthony had seldom seen him without a smile. Some NCOs would have been irritated by his unfailing, irrepressible good humour. 'What have you got to grin about, Verity?' they would have barked. Not so Sergeant Chester.

'Verity's a good lad, sir,' Sergeant Chester would say. Anthony thought so too. Something touched his heart as he looked into the sodden trench of this young man with his huge smile and his innocent good nature.

'All well, Verity?'

'Champion, sir. Will the Jerries attack us today?'

For Verity's zeal for battle was as unaffected as it was untypical. Mostly the men moved, grumbling but enduring, from one place, one task, one hazard to another. Verity was that curiosity, an enthusiast.

'I don't know if they will or not. Anyway, you'll deal with them, won't you Verity?'

'I will, sir!' More grinning as Verity tapped the butt of his rifle. He was a notably bad shot.

'Please, God, make me worthy of these people,' prayed Anthony. 'I know terribly little, like most of them.'

Withdrawal, thought Anthony, was a muddled, depressing business. There had been exhilaration in that first great bound forward into Belgium on 10th May. Since then, all had been puzzlement, rumour and retreat. And all the time the enemy – despised by the British at the outset as likely to be under-nourished, drugged by lying propaganda and lacking in initiative – was assuming in their minds magical proportions. From the first days euphoria and overconfidence began to be replaced by confusion, resentment and, inevitably, disquiet. The resentment fed on anecdote. Allies, both French and Belgian, were described in tale after tale as cowardly, ill-disciplined and, most certainly, disloyal. They didn't want to fight. They preferred the Germans to each other and to the British. Resentment fed, also, on stories about other arms of the British service, invariably unfavourable.

'Did you hear that, sir? RAF have refused to take on the Jerries until they get a day off?'

'When we came over, sir, there was a line of hundreds of tanks in the docks. Tank chaps, too. Black berets. Where are

126

they now? Why've we seen none of them? Jerry tanks going where they bloody like.'

'I expect there's a good plan,' said Anthony. 'We can only see a tiny bit of the front. As for the Air Force story, I don't believe a word of it.' The men grunted. They liked him. They liked his thoughtfulness, his way of giving them his whole attention, of never seeming patronizing or stuck up. They liked the way he laughed and somehow included them in the joke. They thought him bright, too: able to read a map, able to express himself – to find the way and to convince. They liked all that. It made them feel they were in sound hands. But they wanted to believe that others had betrayed them, let them down. Fear needs scapegoats. And beneath their patient humour the men were beginning to feel unease which was not far from fear, unease which stemmed from a sense that they were part of a machine under imperfect control. This unease could make them more vulnerable to stark physical fear when it came. The individual soldier's resilience and courage could be, and Anthony sensed it, undermined by mistrust of the powers in whose hands he was.

'Pity the lads don't know a bit more of what's going on,' said Sergeant Chester. 'It's hard for them, like.'

Now perhaps – even probably – there was going to be a fight, and Anthony would command these men in battle. It was 20th May. They had withdrawn to places not far from those whence they had moved forward ten long days ago. A lot of Belgium must have been given up, but it wasn't the end of the world. As for the rumours of a big break through south of them, south of the Franco–Belgian frontier, behind their right flank, Anthony was sceptical. An elderly officer had said to him at the Depot,

'Things are never as bad in war as the fellows in the rear areas tell each other. They panic first. I remember March '18.'

It had the ring of truth. But the Germans seemed to have dealt the French some nasty blows and certainly the Allied plan to hold from the Maginot Line northward, forward of Brussels, had gone up in smoke long ago. Now, however, it looked as if there was going to be a fight.

So that it was the last straw suddenly to be removed from

127

his platoon and sent miles into the blue simply because he could speak German! He made one last attempt to demur.

'When will I be released, sir? Am I to hand over –'

'God knows when you'll be released, Sergeant Chester is perfectly competent to command your platoon, now shut up and get off.' His Company Commander relented. 'The CO had a direct order to send you but he told me it will be for under forty-eight hours. Probably only twenty-four, if that. Off with you, and mind you wring the last drop of information out of the Huns!'

Heavy hearted, feeling a deserter, Anthony made his way southward. From his inadequate knowledge of the situation he tried to satisfy the driver's curiosity.

'Is it true what they're saying, sir –?'

'I don't know. Now step on it, I've got to be there as quick as possible.' Mercifully they were, as his Company Commander had forecast, crossing the main refugee flight paths.

On arrival at the brigade headquarters to which he was to be attached, more than an hour later than planned, Anthony's first impression was of a fatigue infinitely greater than his own. He reported himself and was curtly gestured to wait in a corner of the barn where most activity seemed to be. He waited. Waiting was a feature of Army life which even the inexperienced soon learned to accept. After about twenty minutes in the corner of the barn, while officers scurried this way and that, he was surprised to hear his Christian name uttered. Was it conceivable somebody meant him?

'Anthony!'

Anthony's face broke into what he felt must be the widest smile it had ever expressed.

'Robert! What the hell are you doing here?' It was indeed Robert Anderson. They had not seen each other since one weekend in London, in their early days in the Army. Robert had done his initial training in Scotland. Anthony had had no recent news of Robert's whereabouts or duties. Now he experienced, for the first time, the ineffable joy of unexpectedly finding a familiar and beloved face, feeling a warmth from sudden association with other, happier times, amongst the confusions, deprivations and anxieties of war.

'What the hell –?'

'I'm a Staff Officer! I know – you find that incredible! So do I! Well, I'm a sort of Staff Officer, anyway. Attached. Why are you –?'

Anthony explained his presence.

'Wonderful! I'll introduce you –' Robert took him in hand. 'They're very nice here,' he whispered to Anthony, 'but they're absolutely whacked. It's pretty good chaos, but never mind!'

Ten hours later Anthony was ordered to return to his battalion. Astonishingly, a small truck was travelling northward to Corps Headquarters, passing through the village where (according to the brigade location map which he regarded with misgiving) his own battalion was now deployed. He hitched a lift. As he huddled beside the driver he exhaustedly reviewed the day just over. The driver hummed a tune. He did not feel that the presence of an unbidden second lieutenant imposed silence.

'You want to go to Vencourt, sir, don't you?'

'Yes, it's where my battalion's meant to be.'

'We go through it. Came down that way this morning. Not bad most of the way.'

'It's a decent road is it?'

'Rotten road, like road, sir, if you get me. I mean not too many civvies on it. Refugees. What with them and the Frogs it took us an hour to go three miles yesterday.'

They drove on in the darkness. The road was packed but traffic was moving, albeit slowly.

'That right what they're saying, sir, that we're pulling out?'

'No, I'm sure it's not. We'll sort it all out, I'm sure of that.'

'Jerries pretty tough, ain't they, sir!'

'Yes. But we'll beat them. In the end.'

Traffic ahead seemed momentarily clearer. Suddenly the driver swore and braked.

'F– me!'

There was a small knot of people in some sort of uniform on the road ahead. They paid no attention to truck or horn. They appeared to be wearing overalls. One came silently to Anthony's window. His overalls looked more like pyjamas. They were all over the road, waving their arms. The driver lifted his window flap.

'Hey! F– off! You're blocking the f–ing road!'

Vehicles behind him sounded their horns. Several more of the pyjama'd group ran to Anthony's window. He was aware of grinning, slavering mouths, incomprehensible, whimpering sounds, and fingers scratching at the talc.

'F–ing loonies!' said the driver disgustedly. 'Gaols, loony bins, they're emptying 'em all!' He negotiated his way forward without too much scruple and Anthony heard a yelp.

'Steady! They can't help themselves, poor creatures.'

'We don't want the old Luftwaffe to find us halted here head to tail, neither, do we, sir?'

They drove on. Anthony's mind went back to the morning.

At first it had seemed as if he was, indeed, wanted for the interrogation of prisoners, that he had not been despatched on a fool's errand.

'Get down that lane,' the Brigade Major said to him suddenly, half an hour after his arrival at the barn. 'Just down there you'll find a Military Policeman with some SS prisoners. For God's sake try to find out what there is in front of us south of the main road. Then we'll send them back, but if they've got anything red hot we need it here and now, not when Division and Corps have digested it. We'll all be dead by then.'

'I'm not sure I know the questions to ask, sir. I speak German but I'm not –'

'Of course you're not. You know nothing, our Intelligence Officer's dead, you're not a soldier, you're useless, but you speak German and you just might be better than nothing. Look at this map.'

Anthony did.

'That's where we think the Germans have got to.'

Anthony had seen no map like this. He stood, appalled.

'This is what we're trying to do. Find out anything you can about the strength of Germans south and east of Arras and where they are. And who they are. Now get down that lane.' Anthony got.

It was about eleven o'clock in the morning – scorching hot, dusty. Anthony moved as fast as he could. He imagined from what the Brigade Major said that the guarded prisoners were only a few minutes' walk away. The lane was hedge-lined. It seemed empty. He looked at his watch. God, he'd been walking for eight minutes. Should he run? Was he on the wrong lane? Even if he got some useful information, a thing almost inconceivable, precious minutes would pass before he could bring it back. Should he go back and ask for a despatch rider? He'd probably be instantly shot for disobedience! The Brigade Major had seemed particularly ill-tempered. Then as he walked rapidly down the lane, Anthony saw to his left, in a field, an astonishing sight.

Tanks. British tanks. Lined up facing south. A low ridge to their front. A Corporal on a motorcycle came careering up the lane towards Anthony. As he approached his motorcycle engine stalled. The man jumped off, put the machine on its stand and started, with what looked like energetic expertise, to do something to the engine.

'F– thing, fourth time today!' he said to nobody in particular.

Anthony drew level, walking rapidly. 'Corporal, do you know if there's a Military Policeman with some prisoners further down this lane?'

'That's right, sir. By the first house.' He seemed to have done something satisfying to his motorcycle and threw his leg over to try another kickstart. Then his attention was caught by the line of tanks in the field beyond the hedge.

'Christ! First I've seen!'

'Good to see, aren't they!' said Anthony. 'I've just passed a lot of bloody infantry coming up this lane, two miles back,' said the Corporal. 'Bloody knackered! Been marching for three hours, they said. Meant to be joining up with this lot.' The engine started and he drove unsteadily off. Anthony hastened on down the lane. Next moment he heard a roar of engines. Instinctively he moved towards the shallow ditch. He had heard the Luftwaffe before.

This was not the Luftwaffe, however, and Anthony told himself he was a nervous fool. The noise came from the tank force starting up their engines. Anthony felt cheered. 'By the first house,' the Corporal had said. He started to run. His task could not now be far away. He could see as yet no house, but he was keen to start his interrogation, his extraction of vital information which might transform the battle for the gallant tank force, whose engines now sounded fainter.

Next, Anthony heard a hissing screech followed almost

131

immediately by a distant and sharp crack from a gun. Automatically and belatedly he dropped. About fifty yards away a small cloud of earth rose, fell and settled. There was a strong smell of explosive. The next shell and the next fell beyond. In each case the sound of the gun firing followed the scream of the shell. 'These are travelling fast!' Anthony reckoned. The firing appeared to be directed at the lane down which he was moving! He got up and marched on, somewhat more slowly. Then he heard, this time unmistakeably, a familiar roar and a frightful, deafening, screaming sound. Into the ditch again. Two German aircraft flew down the line of the lane. He saw the dust spurting from their machine gun bullets – or so he supposed. Or were they using bombs and was the dust being raised by the movement of the aircraft, so low had they dived? As if to answer him two shattering roars came from a point further down the lane. The aircraft tore westward. Immediately ahead Anthony heard shouting.

'Hang on here, Sergeant Ridgeway,' he heard a voice yell. He was approaching a blind corner. There was a clump of trees and the lane curved. Anthony moved on quickly and unsteadily. British soldiers! Laden, dust-covered, sweat-streaked British soldiers, lying against the hedges beside the lane. Presumably the Corporal's bloody infantry who'd been marching for three hours and were bloody knackered.

'Hang on, Sergeant Ridgeway! We're half a mile ahead of B Company.'

'Right, sir! As long as those Stukas don't come round again!' Sergeant Ridgeway yelled back. Anthony felt comforted. For the past three minutes the lane had seemed appallingly lonely. He found what appeared to be the Company Commander standing in mid-road, a lieutenant, who looked younger than Anthony and also looked hot and totally exhausted. He peered at Anthony.

'Where are you from?'

'Brigade Headquarters. I've got to do instant interrogation of some prisoners who are meant to be somewhere down here. Get the stuff out of them while they're still warm. Quicker to send me down here than march them all up and back. Or so somebody thought.'

The other laughed. 'You'll have to hurry. Not many still warm, I fancy.'

'How do you mean?'

'I mean there are a good many corpses in grey lying in the first farmyard you come to. There looked to be a few live ones too. With a Redcap standing over them. About two hundred yards, you're nearly there.'

Anthony looked at the other, who shrugged his shoulders.

'I expect somebody found it impossible to cart them back and thought it best to see they couldn't fight another day. Nothing to do with us. Anyway, they're SS – I saw the badge. The SS don't take prisoners, as I expect you know.'

'No, I didn't know,' said Anthony.

'You haven't passed some British tanks, have you? I know it sounds an absurd question.'

Anthony described their whereabouts. 'They were starting up.'

'We're doing an attack with them. We've been marching for three hours to get to the meeting place. I believe they've done one attack already.'

'Well, good luck,' said Anthony, 'I'd better get on. Good luck in your co-operation with the tanks.'

'I don't really think I've ever seen a tank before.'

There was a low humming sound in the sky, whose pitch suddenly expanded and sharpened.

'Stukas!' yelled Sergeant Ridgeway. They all three reached the same point in the ditch simultaneously. It seemed extraordinarily small.

'How long have you been in charge of these prisoners, Corporal?'

'About an hour, sir.'

'How did those ones – die?'

'Can't say, sir. Our Section Sergeant told me to get up here on my bike and relieve some infantry chaps who were guarding them. So I did. Then they sent up Corporal Evans and Corporal Hickens here.'

About twenty figures in field grey were sitting on the ground by a brick barn. The Military Police Corporal's rifle periodically pointed in their direction. Two other Redcaps covered the group. The squatting prisoners appeared extremely frightened. Along the fence which separated the farmyard from a field of standing corn were lying a number of bodies. They looked undramatic, untidy little heaps of jumble. Anthony did not count them.

'I want a few minutes with them, Corporal. Then they must be escorted back to Brigade Headquarters.'

So long had Anthony's march taken, so long was the way back, so imminent appeared the attack that he could not believe any information would be of the slightest value to Brigade Headquarters if deferred. He decided to see what he could discover in a very few minutes. He was, he thought, probably wrong to hurry it but it seemed best, and what seemed best was all he could do. He identified a *Feldwebel*.

'Bring him over.'

The Corporal shouted and pointed his rifle.

The German got to his feet and marched up to Anthony. Unlike the others he seemed uncowed. He stood to attention and looked levelly at Anthony. Obeying some instinct, Anthony said – 'In what part of the Reich is your home?' He felt absurd. Interrogation must be an expert's business.

The man looked at him, a flicker of surprise at the fluent German crossing his face. He shrugged his shoulders and gave his name and rank. SS rank.

'I asked you from which part of Germany you come. I imagine you're in the *Totenkopf* Division.' For in his short sojourn at Brigade Headquarters Anthony had absorbed as much as he could of the sketchy information about the enemy there was available. Division SS *Totenkopf* – 'Death's Head' – was certainly in the area of Arras.

The German eyed him boldly.

'*Herr Leutnant*, I wish to complain.'

'I'm not here to listen to your complaints. You can make them later. Where was your company moving to when you were captured?' Anthony spread his map before the man's eyes. Involuntarily the German looked at it.

'If I can engage his professional interest,' thought Anthony, 'I might – just – get somewhere.'

'We know you were retreating southward,' he continued to

the *Feldwebel*, 'towards –' he indicated the road to Bapaume. 'Isn't that so?'

It worked. 'No!' said the other. His soldierly dislike of inaccuracy overtook his discretion. 'No! We were driving westward. We were on the way to here and here –' he pointed on the map – 'We stopped only because of the enemy attack from the north.' He became aware of Anthony once again. 'My complaint, *Herr Leutnant*! Some of my comrades have been shot while prisoners. '

'If you have complaints, make them later,' said Anthony. 'Now is it true that the Division's leading Regiment has reached –'

It went on some time, longer than the few minutes Anthony had reckoned sensible if information was to be timely. Interrogation was punctuated by two other visits from the Luftwaffe. It yielded little, thought Anthony, but that little might conceivably be of use if he could get it back. Then another Military Policeman arrived on another motorcycle. More shouting.

'They've got to be got back, sir. Message from Division. As fast as possible.'

'I'm not surprised. Give me a lift back to Brigade, can you?'

'Hop on, sir.'

The infantry were now clear of the lane. They had been trudging past during Anthony's interrogation of the *Feldwebel* and two other junior NCOs. From the south came sounds of continuous machine gun fire and a number of particularly ear-splitting cracks from what could only be German guns. Anthony clung to the Military Policeman's waist and bumped along on the pillion. Shells were falling two hundred yards to their right. More sharp cracks.

'Those may be our tank guns in action.' Anthony did not believe it but liked saying it.

'Not them, sir,' shouted the Redcap over his shoulder. 'Ours are smaller guns than those. Those are Jerries.' Next moment Anthony found himself lying in the lane as the Corporal leapt from his motorcycle and reached the ditch. The same familiar, mind-shattering roar and screech. Two divebombers, followed by two more, came in low, firing over the fields to Anthony's

135

right. 'That must be where our tanks and infantry are advancing,' thought Anthony, picking himself up. He felt superior to the Police Corporal.

'Come on,' he said, 'they're well wide of us. We must get on, Corporal.' The roll of firing to the south was continuous now.

'I didn't get much out of them, sir. Death's Head Division.' Anthony conveyed his information rapidly. It related to a situation before the Germans had been taken prisoner. It was, he felt, hopelessly stale. But he had at least tried.

'You've taken long enough to get that little, God knows.'

'I'm sorry, sir. I took some time to reach them.'

'Well, it was just a long shot you might pick up something which could help this attack in its later stages. You haven't. And it's not having any later stages. We're calling it off. Now get back to your battalion, somehow.'

'Sir, I should report to you that a German *Feldwebel* I interrogated told me that some of the prisoners had been shot. By us.'

'Christ, we're in the middle of a bloody battle, we're up against a gang of murderers called the SS, and you come bleating to me about some Hun NCO's allegations. Go away!'

Robert Anderson blessedly retrieved him.

'Believe it or not there's a truck going your way in an hour. A taxi ride all the way! And unless there's a disaster I've booked your seat. *And* here's a cup of tea!'

'Robert, we've been attacking, is that right?'

'That's it. But the Germans lined up lots of guns, including a thing with the biggest barrel anyone's ever seen, meant for shooting at aircraft thousands of feet up, and now taking on our dear little tanks! Lined up that and other things. And that's the end of that. Meanwhile, these bloody Stukas have been over without stopping.'

'What happens now?'

'We're off.'

Anthony sipped his tea. Scalding hot, nothing had ever tasted better.

136

'Robert, I talked to one of the infantry chaps who was moving up to co-operate with the tanks. They'd never done it before. Hadn't the faintest idea what to do.'

'Well, who has? Not the sort of thing we've gone in for, is it? Christ, here they come again.' They both dropped as the familiar screech and roar burst upon them. The barn filled with dust. Anthony heard a man screaming beyond the open barn door.

'They've got the radio vehicle,' he heard a voice shout. 'Get over here quick some of you and give a hand with Sergeant Bragg.' To his absurdly self-satisfied relief Anthony found that he had lowered himself to the ground so circumspectly that he had avoided spilling his mug of tea. 'I'm getting rather good at being bombed,' he thought.

'Get anything useful from the interrogation, Anton?'

'Not much. Anyway, there was no way I could have told anybody quickly if I had. The prisoners were over a mile away. It was an idiotic idea to send me. I needed a bike or a radio or something –'

'We don't seem to go in for radios much.'

'Well, I was perfectly useless. And, Robert –'

'Yes?'

'Quite a lot had been shot. Of the prisoners, I mean.'

Robert frowned his familiar frown. 'Yes, it's being said that some of our chaps are pretty fed up, particularly with this SS lot, and aren't taking many prisoners. There's a story going round that the SS lined up some of our people and shot them. And of course our people feel they've got a lot of scores to wipe out. Not much fun being pushed back and bombed like hell and not given any chance to hit back.'

'Do you suppose it's true – about what the SS did to our people?'

'No idea.'

'Well, I've no idea, either,' said Anthony. 'But I rather think it's best – if one can – to be slow to believe atrocity stories about the other side in war. Not easy. But best.'

'Here's Vencourt, sir.'

Anthony had been asleep.

'God, I'm sorry, I've been no use to you. I dropped off.'

'That's all right, sir.'

Anthony climbed down into the darkness of a village street. He was in luck. Not only his own battalion but his very own company were in the quarter of the little town where he alighted. The truck drove off and Anthony found his way to Company Headquarters.

'Welcome back! The battalion's in reserve. We're moving off in three hours to take up a new position –' the map was spread on a kitchen table. 'They've had some food here, and about four hours' sleep. Not bad. Your platoon's in a ware-house a hundred yards down the road. Unfortunately the Jerry artillery's been rather active. They put down a lot of stuff an hour ago and actually hit battalion headquarters. Not badly, and everybody's been laughing. The Sergeant Major got a shell splinter in the arse.'

'Really?'

'No, not really I don't suppose, but the chaps have to tell each other things to keep their spirits up. Now get along, you'll get two hours with your head down, with luck.'

Anthony found the sentry outside the platoon billet.

'Is Sergeant Chester here?'

'In that corner, sir. Sergeant Chester?'

'No, don't wake him up.'

But Sergeant Chester was awake and present. They were in what appeared to be some sort of store room – large, dry, cavernous. One or two hurricane lamps cast shadows.

'Electricity's not working, sir,' said Sergeant Chester. There was a distant grumble of artillery fire. Anthony felt an extra-ordinary sense of comfort and homecoming.

'Have you had anything to eat, sir? There's plenty here. Plenty of local provisions so to speak.'

'Wonderful, Sergeant Chester!'

'Not bad, sir. They've eaten well, believe me. Lot of living off the land going on. Some of them's doing better than they've ever done. Needs a bit of controlling.'

'What else today?'

'Not much, sir. Long march. Digging. Some shelling this side of the canal line. The lads were pretty steady.'

A soldier appeared with what looked to be half a cold

chicken. He saluted with the right hand and extended the plate with the left. An enormous, trusting grin.

'Thank you, Verity. Thank you very much. I need that.'

But at that moment there was a sound like the approach of an express train. The whole dim interior was lit by a blinding light. At the same moment the mighty roar of an explosion was succeeded by the crash of falling timbers, plaster and masonry. Anthony found himself flat on his back seeing nothing, unable to breathe or to speak from the dust which filled throat and nostrils. He heard cries and shouts. He tried to move. Something was holding his right leg down. He felt warm dampness inside the right thigh. His own blood? 'Oh God, Oh God, I can't shout, I can't move, I can do nothing to help them – them or myself for that matter!' The dust seemed a little clearer. 'Am I alive and conscious, or dead or dreaming?' He tried his voice again. A croak came. There were cries, calls. He could distinguish voices. Some time passed.

'One over here!'

Another croak.

Anthony found himself on a stretcher. He remembered little, afterwards, of the next bit. Lights, the Medical Officer's face, other voices. Frightful pain in the leg. He yelled. Voice recovered.

'Take it easy, Anthony, you'll be all right. Splint will be fine now.'

'What – what?'

'Broken leg. Girder caught you when the roof came in. And you've cut your head.'

'What happened?'

'Direct hit. Bomb. You were right underneath it. Roof came in. You'll be all right. God knows how, it was only a few feet above you when it went off. We'll get you back to the dressing station as soon as we get hold of an ambulance.'

He presumed without interest that he was at the Regimental Medical Aid post in some other house in Vencourt.

'How many –?'

'Only two, we think. One or two scratches. Most of your chaps were lying down near the walls. Got away with it.' The Medical officer disappeared. An orderly moved in the background.

'Cup of tea, sir?

Anthony nodded. He muttered – 'Do you know who?'

'The Sergeant, sir.'

'Sergeant Chester?'

'That's him. A good bloke, as everyone knew. And another private. Don't know his name. Now you take it easy, sir.'

It was Verity, of course. It had to be. Sergeant Chester and Verity. Before the drug took its merciful effect in the ambulance Anthony found tears running down his cheeks. It had been a long day.

Chapter 9

———————◆———————

'ONE SHOULD, perhaps, be careful about believing atrocity stories about the other side,' said Frido softly.

Toni Rudberg looked at Frido with his sceptical half-smile. There were times – not many – when Rudberg reminded him of Werner, Frido decided, before lunch had progressed far. There was the same mocking confidence and – it had to be admitted – the same charm. But there were many differences. Werner, with all his easy manners, was a man of the north. He was at heart firm, serious. Could one say the same of this handsome, brown-faced, brown-eyed Austrian with his mobile features, his laughing manner to all, his apparent propensity to treat one as a confidential friend on first meeting? Was he not essentially frivolous, superficial? Rudberg had at once got on easy terms by reference to mutual acquaintances, relations even. About most he had something amusing, often something outrageous to say. He would accompany each remark with a delightful, satiric chuckle. He made his listener an accomplice. His gossip, his disloyalty were insidious. Frido found himself disapproving, wary, but he could not restrain his laughter. Rudberg's company was enjoyable.

The circumstances, too, were enjoyable. The last battles had found Frido's Division in Brittany. Thence they had advanced south, crossed the Loire, reached the great vineyards of the Gironde. And an armistice had been signed. There was peace. Most of France was to be left to French administration. It seemed reasonable to hope that the war would soon be over. Few people could understand why England refused to accept the verdict of arms in which the majority of sensible Frenchmen appeared happy to acquiesce. Why could the English not do the same? Then everybody could go home.

It was not to be. Instead there was talk of 'fresh operations'. A new training programme was initiated. Leave was confined

141

to an occasional day pass. The life of the troops was still comparatively austere. The focus of public interest shifted to the Luftwaffe. If the English couldn't understand that a page of history had finally turned they would have to be taught.

'You've been to England, you know them, von Arzfeld,' Frido's brother officers would say. 'What's the matter with them? Why the hell do they want to continue this war? It could be over. Nobody's threatening them if only they'll agree with the outcome here.'

Frido would shrug his shoulders. The English were certainly obstinate. They were, he thought privately, most unlikely to accept as final the result of *Sichelschnitt*, the German offensive in France and Flanders. He had, on his visits, found the English very agreeable; largely uncomprehending of the way history and events appeared to other nations including his own; firm in their prejudices, whether rational or no; but most agreeable. He suspected that one of these English prejudices, at the moment, was that the fight against Germany must go on – somehow, somewhere, for some reason; and felt pretty sure that after the air battles of the late summer this prejudice was likely to be ineradicable. He thought of Oxford, of his conversations with Anthony Marvell, of his visit to Bargate. He was disinclined to confide to his fellows the opinion that the English distrusted the Führer so deeply that they regarded negotiation with his Government as impossible. It was best to keep that sort of explanation to oneself.

Frido himself had, from its beginning, profound reservations about the War. He had always been upset by the strident mixture of populist heroics, peaceful protestations and sudden, brutal reversals of policy which had marked the Nazi era, had led to the invasion of Poland and had now made the Germans masters of Europe to the Channel ports. He often felt a sense of doom, of the whole German nation, family, friends, comrades, moving – chattering, laughing, singing – towards some unimaginable fate, deceived and self-deceiving: while even those who were not deceived had, it seemed, long given up hope of changing the course of events. Frido often thought of contemporaries of his father, old soldiers, rare visitors who sometimes appeared at Arzfeld, talking to Kaspar with long faces in low voices –

142

'Of course it's mad – quite mad.'

But at other times – and Frido was too honest not to admit it – there appeared to be not only exhilaration but justice in the way matters had gone. One did not have to be a National Socialist, Frido reflected, to feel some satisfaction in this hour. The French had triumphed for so long, boasted so loudly, behaved often so viciously, exacted from others with such lack of compassion when victorious. Deep in the collective memory of Frido's family and neighbours were two – perhaps only two – other historic occasions, other summers which could compare. Once, one hundred and twenty-five years before, Hanoverian regiments had helped Wellington smash Napoleon's Grand Army on the field of Waterloo, join hands with the Prussians at the end of the day and finish for ever, as it was thought, French domination over Europe. And Frido could remember vivid tales of the second occasion, could remember listening in his childhood to Grandfather, General von Arzfeld, a white-moustached veteran who would be ninety-one were he alive to see this day. Grandfather von Arzfeld had enthralled small grandsons with his recollections of a September day in 1870, of German regiments, hot, exhausted, dazed with victory as the evening came, as they realized, half-disbelieving, that these Frenchmen, disorganized, shattered, their Emperor's sword surrendered to the King of Prussia, were, indeed, the all-conquering French, brought to the dust at Sedan. Frido remembered every sentence of his grandfather's descriptions, could see in imagination the camp fires blazing, could picture the sweat-streaked faces and blue uniforms of the *landser* illumined by the flames, could hear the great hymn '*Nun danket alle Gott*' go up from every throat, from every part of the field as darkness fell. Such moments dent the painted surface of history like the forceful imprint of some triumphant, giant thumb. Frido could not suppress the feeling that he, too, had witnessed the making of a mark.

Life still held private moments. There had been exchanges with Marcia. Frido's first letter from her had taken three weeks to arrive – not abnormal for the field post office he was to learn. He guessed at once it was from Marcia – the handwriting could have been perpetrated by no German, and she had promised to write. He tore it open – simple, affectionate, short

143

– small bits of news about Lise and his father. Could he attempt greater intimacy, risk professions of warmer affection? He doubted it. It was impossible to put that sort of thing in a letter if one had made no move when with the girl! And Frido had made no move. He answered, miserably aware that it was a poor effort. But 'please keep on writing to me,' he ended, 'life without letters from you would be much colder and emptier than it is.' So Marcia wrote again. Now his heart gave its familiar jump whenever he saw her spidery writing on an envelope. And he hoped every day.

Then had come the unexpected moment when he was given a two-day pass and permission to visit Paris. It was the desire of every German soldier to do so: so far Frido had been unlucky, and had not pushed his application. His heart was at Arzfeld, and he hoped for Christmas leave. But the chance was too good to miss. As he signed the register at the hotel in the Avenue Foch a hand took his arm.

'It is! It must be the brother of Werner von Arzfeld. I am Rudberg! Toni Rudberg!' And of course Frido had to respond with friendship and correctness. They had mutual relations. Rudberg spoke as one who knew Werner.

And was he Marcia's lover?

They chatted. 'We're in the north,' said Rudberg. 'I've been to Paris quite often I'm delighted to say. I'm getting to know it pretty well!' He chuckled.

'Almost everything said about French girls is true. They're enchanting! Just imagine that some people are actually posted here!'

Frido nodded politely. He felt puritanical, unsophisticated.

'Let's lunch together tomorrow! I insist. I know we've got a lot to talk about. My cousins in Vienna are always talking about Arzfeld, about your family and your home.'

Of course Rudberg knew exactly the best place to lunch. They talked at length about the events of May and June. It was now the middle of September.

'Well, what about the next step? Are we going to cross the ditch? Or are we going to be able to shake hands with the English and all go home?'

'Neither, I think,' said Frido. 'It doesn't look as if the Luftwaffe have had things their own way. Unless the sky is clear of English planes I can't see the attempt being made. And it gets later every week.'

'Perhaps you're right. And won't they come to terms, then? Won't their honour be satisfied?'

'I don't think so. I don't think they'll agree to let us be – agree to the order of things we've imposed here –'

'A perfectly honourable armistice? Fair, generous terms for France?'

'The British won't see it like that. They'll demand restitution of everything before they abandon the war – Polish frontiers, everything –'

Rudberg shrugged his shoulders.'

'I expect you're right. Then it looks like a long, rather unprofitable business. We can't exactly get to grips with each other now they've all bolted from France! I can't see them coming back. And if we can't go there, what next?'

'I suppose it's up to the Luftwaffe. And I suppose the Italians will carry on attacking them in Africa, for what that's worth.'

'Ach – the Italians!' said Rudberg with one of his chuckles that wrinkled his entire face, most attractively. 'The Italians!'

Then he said, 'Let's go on talking about the English. There were some dirty things done at the end in France. There's been an inquiry over one incident, but it didn't really establish anything or lead to punishment. There's no doubt our dear *"Totenkopf"* Division, our SS friends, lined up a lot of Tommies, machine gunned them! Not quite in harmony with what we've been taught about the honour of the Wehrmacht!'

'Disgraceful!'

'Yes, but the *"Totenkopf"* say that the English shot some prisoners of their division first. At Arras.'

Frido made his remark about credence given to atrocity stories. He added,

'Anyway, it excuses nothing. Even if true.'

'Of course not, my dear Arzfeld! But military discipline doesn't entirely drive out human nature, does it! Even in the Wehrmacht!'

Frido, pacific, humane, self-questioning, felt the presence of Kaspar von Arzfeld and a long line of forbears behind his shoulder.

'If by "human nature" you mean acts of cowardly brutality, outside the rules of war and inspired by vengeance, then my answer is "Yes, military discipline should most certainly drive it out!"' He felt priggish, uncompromising and angry. Toni Rudberg was laughing.

'Well said! In the best "Prussian tradition"! I'm not sure, however, that it's going to be that sort of war. But I like talking about human nature – with all its frailties, it's more agreeable to contemplate than military correctitude if you don't mind me saying so! Of course you're right, my dear fellow, but I'm sure you understand me. And now let me ask you something.' His face, so quick to change expression, looked suddenly serious, almost for the first time, as he said –

'You know, I am acquainted with the lady to whom your brother was betrothed. I believe that she is now living at your home, is that not so?'

Frido knew that he knew it was so.

'I would very much like to see her again. And, of course, to meet your family.'

'There is only my father, Colonel von Arzfeld. And my young sister.'

'Yes, of course. Well, it looks – *if* we don't "jump the ditch" we were talking about – it looks as if I shall get a week's leave at the beginning of October. I had it in mind to ask your father if I could travel to Germany and visit Arzfeld. I would have written in July, after the armistice, but everything has looked so uncertain. Still as you've probably heard, there's likely to be demobilization of some classes. If you ask me, things quite soon are going to be nearly normal again.'

Frido said, 'My father, naturally, would be happy to hear from you. If you call at Arzfeld I am sure he will make you welcome.' He managed to make this sound as cold as possible.

'My lovely little Marcia,

Well, imagine! I have met your little Frido von Arzfeld, the one you're always rather tender about and describe like a small brother that needs protecting. He *is* rather like a small brother that needs protecting! He's incredibly immature, very stiff and pompous, very proper in all his reactions. He made me feel old

146

and wicked and cynical. I didn't find it particularly easy to talk to him.

Now listen! I told Frido v A that I "might be on leave" in early October: that I would like the chance to meet his family and "see you again". I had to say that, of course; even Frido isn't so dim-witted as to think I'd spend leave in Germany except to try to see you! I said I "might write" to your host, Colonel v A. He was very stiff about it. I thought, if I *didn't* mention it, that when he'd heard I'd been to Arzfeld (as I shall!) he'd reckon me a deceitful rogue for not indicating my intentions to him. I expect he reckons that anyway! I also wanted to see how he would react to mention of you (don't worry, my darling, my mention of you was very correct). I expect he's in love with you himself and hasn't dared say so. Or has he?

Anyway, if I get this leave in October (and it might even be by the end of September) I shall find a *"Gasthof"* to stay in, fairly near. I'll bring a friend with me who's got a sister working in Hameln: that's our ostensible reason for a visit "to take a few days off and explore a different and beautiful part of the Reich". Then I shall come and bow to your Colonel. And *you and I*, my sweetest girl, will make opportunities to meet. I wish you could come to Paris! But until things get a little easier I'm afraid it's out of the question for you . . .'

Marcia sighed. The letter had taken a fortnight to arrive. It was already the last week in September!

After Werner's death she had been sure that never, ever, would she love as she had loved him. She was oblivious of all but his loss. The appalling events which were engulfing Europe seemed remote, impersonal. War with the Poles had been quickly over: its sole significance was that it had taken Werner from her. War with Britain and France appeared totally unreal. So vivid had her life and experiences in Vienna been that they had largely blotted out her recollection of how people in England felt about the Germans and Austrians among whom the most passionate year of her life had been spent.

There was, of course, a large measure of self-deception in this. At heart Marcia recognized her situation as both false and miserable. She, an English girl, had refused to go home when war appeared almost inevitable. She had, without compulsion, remained in the enemy camp. At the crucial moment, desperately in love with Werner, she had evaded contact with her

147

cousins in the British Consulate General, she had told herself that the war scare would 'blow over', she had adopted a formula about it all being a misunderstanding, an episode which would soon be straightened out by history. The Polish business would be finished; Werner said so. Britain and France would find some framework in which new agreements could be made and peace return.

But Marcia knew very well in her heart that this was nonsense. Hard as she tried she could not shut out from memory the image of her father's grave face, and to her ears would come the sound of his voice, hating war, inexpressibly sad, saying, 'This man *wants* war. He is on the march,' with the quiet, unspoken conviction behind it that, at whatever cost, Britain should oppose such ambitions. To the death. This was no misunderstanding to be cleared by diplomacy, by compromise. This would, in all probability, be a fight to a finish. She sensed it without hope. It was an impossible sense with which to live at ease. It could only be made tolerable by the nurturing of illusions. An essential part of these was the pretence – and she sometimes managed to persuade herself, for a little – that the war was a charade which both sides had to present for domestic consumption until they could find some face-saving way of ending it. Meanwhile – and in consequence – they would try to do as little damage to each other as possible. Behind the bluster of Governments, the apparent inactivity on the Western front gave some colour to this view.

But then came the incredible, the overwhelming events of May and June, 1940. It was no longer possible to imagine that the war would soon draw to a negotiated end. Astonishingly, the Germans among whom she worked seemed to regard this as now much more likely.

'The thing's finished. The French have been taught a lesson, that's all. They never wanted to fight us, the ordinary Frenchman. The Jews, yes, perhaps – so now the French have seen sense there can be no possible reason for the British to want to fight us. What about?'

Marcia avoided all argument but she heard it swirling about her. Sometimes there had to be agonizing equivocation. The Party line would be voiced, even with courtesy, by some.

'Of course, Fraülein Marvell, we know ordinary English

people don't want this war. The Jews are very numerous there, that's the trouble isn't it? And the sort of circles who profit from war! We had them here last time, I can tell you!' Many people had been kind. Others had made savage remarks in a way which she was compelled to hear. Secretly, she wept often.

But it was not in Marcia's nature to brood. Ebullient and by temperament optimistic, her fits of natural depression, even despair and self-accusation, alternated with times of happiness. Mainly instrumental in producing those times were two people. One was Toni Rudberg.

Toni had first appeared at his cousins' home in Vienna at Christmas 1939. His name had been mentioned before that. Countess Rudberg had sighed and nodded in a knowing sort of way –

'Ah! Toni!'

He was her husband's nephew. She said to him,

'Your nephew Toni is a captain in this Panzer Division here, but he's not been to see us! He's not fighting in Poland any more. I expect he's busy.'

Count Rudberg nodded. 'Toni will come to see us if he's back here at Christmas time.'

His wife sighed again. She seemed to anticipate trouble. Marcia lived with them a life closely akin to widowhood. Many months must elapse in Rudberg eyes before it would be decent to bring her existence before a wider circle of acquaintances or family. And Countess Amalie sometimes looked at Marcia speculatively. There was no doubt, she was very, very pretty this little *Engländerin*.

But at Christmas Toni had appeared. Then he had re-appeared. Then he had contrived, Marcia was not sure how, to take her out to dinner without raising Countess Rudberg's eyebrows. He was by now again stationed in Vienna.

Then he had taken her out to dinner again: and started to show her aspects of Vienna which her previous study for an art diploma had entirely omitted.

And then she had found herself in love with him.

Marcia would not at first admit to herself that her feelings for Toni Rudberg were in the least serious. She had no confidante in Vienna and it is always hard to establish the truth of

149

an emotional condition purely by self-communing. She said to herself that Toni was good company. It was a relief after the kindly isolation of life in the Rudbergs' flat, endless discussions about her status, her 'difficulties', the attitudes of the authorities, the protracted interchange of correspondence with Arzfeld – it was profound relief after this wearisome, genteel imprisonment to find herself again escorted, entertained, finally wooed by an attractive man.

She did not in the least trust him. 'He is utterly unlike Werner,' she said to herself. Werner had had the same easy charm, the same dominant, assured masculinity. But Werner had, too, an inner seriousness, *three dimensions*, she told herself. He was a deep man. Toni, on the other hand, changed his moods, his opinions like quicksilver. She never knew if he meant a word of what he said. But when he told her he adored her she hoped that he did. She was not wholly unaware that she deceived herself. Even Marcia, on the whole innocent, English in upbringing, did not think that Toni was faithful to her while in Vienna. When away from her she simply could not imagine him except in pursuit of a woman, and probably of several simultaneously. Toni never spoke of such things as marriage. She could not connect him with any idea of a permanent or profound relationship. 'But oh!' she thought, 'how much I want him!'

And so, Marcia had fallen in love with Toni. They had become lovers. Her days were entirely spent in joyous anticipation of their next assignation. Toni had a flat in Vienna, and Marcia's acquaintance with the city and ostensible pursuit of art studies during the first months of 1940 made meetings comparatively easy. Sometimes he would call on his uncle and aunt and deliberately pretend he scarcely knew her.

'Ah! Fraülein Marcia! How good to see you again!'

His easy smile, his laughing brown eyes in a bronzed face disguised the fact that only twenty-four hours before they had been ecstatically in bed together on the other side of the Ringstrasse. It made it even more fun, and it provided huge emotional relief from the sombre reflections about her situation which otherwise crowded in on Marcia's mind.

Then Toni had told her he was leaving Vienna. It was March, 1940.

'Oh, beloved! Oh, darling! When?'

'Very soon. But listen. I mustn't tell you where I'm going –'

'To Germany, it must be.'

'To Germany, it must be, as you say. Now Cousin Amalie has said the Arzfelds want you to go and stay. Why not? You don't belong to dear old Werner now – and I was fond of him, believe me, but that's past – you belong to me. But it would be proper to visit your ex-fiancé's family. And you know them.'

'Would I be near you?'

'Well, if I got a short leave it might be easier than visiting Vienna. I could stay at some hotel nearby, make some excuse, call on the Arzfelds, and we'd make plans, spend some time together. Just at the moment it seems as if you wouldn't be stopped travelling.'

The other person who brought relief to Marcia's unhappy and anxious heart was Anna Langenbach.

She had not been many weeks at Arzfeld when Lise said one day,

'Of course you remember our cousin Anna Langenbach? She received us when we broke down in Anthony's car near the Langenbach house.'

'Of course. She was charming! She drove you here afterwards and I met her.'

'She's had a sad life. She had a baby, you know, a little boy, last winter. And months before that her husband was killed in a flying accident in Spain. Poor Anna!'

Marcia said nothing of Anthony's passion for Anna. It was their business, it might have been transient, unimportant, despite Anthony's seriousness about it. Probably Anna would only be embarrassed by his name. Poor, darling old Ant! Marcia's eyes filled with tears Lise did not comprehend. As naturally as she could she said,

'Does she still live with her parents-in-law? They were nice, I remember you saying, quiet, nice people.'

'Yes, it's her home of course. And there was no other son but Kurt – Anna's husband. So the little grandson is precious to them. Franzi. She looks after him wonderfully, she's a

151

perfect mother. But sad and lonely. She's very capable. She's going to come and stay here, with Franzi, for a few days in September. Perhaps even for two weeks.'

And Anna had arrived, complete with charming, serious Franzi. On the second day of her visit, a Sunday, the girls were at home. Sunday was no rest day at the hospital but on this occasion both had been given a holiday, as occurred every few weeks. Marcia felt Anna take her arm.

'Lise wants to have Franzi to herself, believe it or not! Let's go for a walk.'

They walked in woods which brought Werner vividly to Marcia's mind. The trees had been opening to the spring then, when she and Werner had ridden through the beechwoods. Now autumn was in the air. Marcia felt gripped by a great desolation. Yet she had work to do: somewhat to her surprise she found work at the hospital a profound relief. Its very squalor helped heal her mind, assuage her guilt. Lise was sweet, her father remote, a little embarrassed, always courteous and kind. But oh! The loneliness!

They sat down on a fallen log.

'It's a lovely place, isn't it?'

Suddenly Marcia found herself shaking with sobs. Anna put her arm around her.

'Poor little love! I know how you must feel. You lost a fine man.'

'It's not that. At least, it's not just that.'

'I can imagine the other things.'

And Marcia found herself pouring out her heart. She talked of her predicament, of her home, of the terrible sense that by some light, spontaneous, love-directed decisions a year ago she had burned her boats, had placed herself in a terrible no-man's land in this war, fair game for the hatred, the weapons of both sides, had become an interloper, a suspect in Germany and a traitress to England.

'Anna, you've got English blood, do you understand me a bit?'

'Of course. Your love crossed frontiers. It was inconvenient, highly indiscreet. But it was not wicked.'

'God knows what my family think of me now! And will I ever know? I think it would be better if I were killed. This

152

bombing – it will be heavy in Germany one day, I expect. It would be better if I were bombed. Then the problem would be over.'

'Yes it would, but these things are not always easy to arrange!' Anna's arm was firm and comforting around her. 'One day, perhaps, I will tell her certain things,' Anna thought, 'but not yet. Not quite yet.'

She said, 'Life is still ahead of you, Marcia. The world is a difficult place, in certain ways a terrible place today. But it will not always be so. Nor will you always be alone.'

Then Marcia told her about Toni.

Anna laughed – kindly but aloud.

'Toni Rudberg!'

'You know him?'

'Everybody knows him or about him. I've met him twice, I think, and I *quite* understand your feelings. He's very charming. But you should not hope too much. He is not a serious person.'

'But I have to hope too much,' said Marcia. 'Otherwise I couldn't face the days. I have to hope. And I'm not sure what to hope for, except Toni. Now fighting has started properly I can't hope for one side to smash the other in this war because it would mean the smashing of people I love. Toni, or – or Frido and the Arzfelds – or you: or Anthony and all the people I love at home.'

'A cause may go down,' said Anna neutrally, 'and individuals survive.' With what Marcia imagined was an attempt to lighten the atmosphere, Anna added –

'I suppose your brother is in the army?'

'Bound to be,' said Marcia. 'He was in the process of becoming an officer when I left England. But I don't know. I don't know whether he's alive, how can I? I know nothing! I'm in enemy territory.' She started crying again, despising herself for it. And Marcia remembered Anthony's voice, so tense, so utterly determined, so unlike the usual stuttering, teasing Ant – his voice saying – 'None of you will ever understand. I'll love her till the end of time.' He might be different now, he might be dead, or crippled, or married. But it might – it just might – still be the same. Suddenly she said,

'He loved you, Anna!'

To her surprised consternation she found that Anna's head was on her shoulder. And Anna was crying too.

'Some day,' she murmured obscurely, 'some day –'

They walked back to the house together. And at the house they found that the postman had called and Toni's third letter to Marcia had arrived – the letter which announced a possibly imminent visit to Arzfeld.

'Anna, there is a friend of yours who telephoned an hour ago. Herr Schwede. He says that he has to go to a conference in Kassel in two days time, 26th September. He will be passing Arzfeld tomorrow. He will call at about three in the afternoon. He announced, firmly, that he would present himself! No hesitation about it!'

'Ah! Herr Schwede.'

'He sounded anxious to see you.'

'Herr Schwede's always anxious to see me.'

'Anna, an admirer! And Marcia and I won't see him, we'll be back at the hospital tomorrow!'

'Herr Schwede is the Party *Kreisleiter* of Langenbach. He is very active. He travels a lot on Party business. It is not surprising that he is going to Kassel. Nothing about him is surprising.'

'Is he charming? After all,' said Lise softly, 'Nazis *can* be charming!'

Anna seemed to be considering her words carefully. When she spoke it did not seem to be with exasperation or distaste, but with a sort of scrupulous exactitude.

'Herr Schwede is certainly the most odious man I have ever met. And perhaps the worst. I don't intend to know him well enough to discover. I'm glad that neither you nor Marcia will be here. I'm glad Cousin Kaspar will be away at his office. Herr Schwede would disgust him.'

Lise looked troubled.

'Perhaps he's not as bad as you think, Anna. Some of them, even some of the very aggressive ones, resent us particularly – von Arzfelds, people like you, like us – because they think we despise them. But if we show friendliness I'm sure it's possible to disarm that feeling, bridge the gulf. It can't be right to make enemies of them.'

'My dear little Lise,' said Anna with more impatience than Marcia had yet heard in her voice, 'you don't know what you're talking about. I doubt if you've ever met anybody even of middle seniority in the Party.'

'I doubt if I have.'

Anna spoke now more softly.

'And I doubt also whether you – perhaps whether any of you here – have faced, inwardly, the things these people have done and are doing to Germany!'

Lise looked at her with consternation.

'Anna!'

'That is what I see when I see Herr Schwede.'

'Well, what does he want from you, Anna?'

Anna looked sternly at her. There was a silence.

'Herr Schwede comes, most weeks, to Langenbach on some pretext or other,' she said. 'Everything about the man makes me shudder. Everything.'

The afternoon seemed suddenly very cold.

Chapter 10

⸺⸺⸺◆⸺⸺⸺

EGON SCHWEDE ACCEPTED a cup of coffee with a bow of
exaggerated gratitude. He was a man of middle height, with a
brick-coloured complexion and brown hair with reddish tints
in it. His often bloodshot eyes were of pale blue.

Schwede was bull-necked, burly and broad-shouldered. His
habitual expression was one of suspicion, and his brow was
furrowed in what appeared a perpetual scowl. When he smiled,
which was surprisingly often, he succeeded only in looking
conspiratorial and ill-natured. It was impossible not to suppose
that the smile was caused by the discomfiture of another. The
same applied to his laugh, infrequent but exceptionally loud.
It seemed to express not gaiety or amusement but bitterness
and contempt.

But Schwede was formidable. He had personality. He dominated individuals and assemblies. He inspired alarm – but
it was alarm mixed with respect because Schwede was also
extremely efficient. He was pertinacious, thorough and, despite
the somewhat ponderous brutality of his appearance, he was
quick-witted. He had a nose for a situation. If there was
something amiss Schwede sensed it. If there was concealment
in a conversation, in the response to some question or comment
he detected it, he smelt it. He had, from the first, mastered
the Party apparatus in Kreis Langenbach. Every underling
feared him. So did most of the population.

Schwede was an early member of the National Socialist
Party. He could look back to the long years in the wilderness,
when to be a Nazi in Kreis Langenbach meant exposure to
taunts, incomprehension, ridicule; sometimes physical threats.
He had withstood all that. He had forced men to reckon with
him when precious few stood with him, had wrung from them
unwilling respect.

'You'll see! One day it'll turn out as I'm telling you! Germany

156

will rise again, have dignity again, get rid of the alien filth who've sucked her blood for so long, ruined all of us here, lied about us –'

He had never inwardly compromised. Sometimes instructions had come down which he found hard. Sometimes for tactical reasons the Party hierarchy passed the word that there had to be support for the Communists, the Social Democrats even! Headquarters were subtle, no question of it, and Schwede believed in absolute obedience. But he found these manoeuvres unpalatable. For Schwede was not only odious. He was sincere.

And his hour had come – that wonderful hour in 1933. A sufficient majority to win the crucial vote in the Reichstag and enabling laws, so that the Führer could get on with the job, supported by the Party, could dispense with all the wretched, so-called democratic humbug which had deceived and exploited the German people. It had all happened amazingly fast, so that Party dominance of the principal institutions of the State had been achieved in remarkably few years. Nobody was sure about the Army. You only had to look at some of the senior officers when they couldn't avoid some Party occasion! Resentful, looking down their beaky noses! Sneering! As for the rest – the Police, the Civil Service and so forth – they'd all toed the line, sufficiently at any rate.

In Kreis Langenbach there were few problems. One or two tiresome individuals had soon yielded to a little persuasion. A quiet word had, on the whole, sufficed to make them thoughtful. One journalist on a local paper had given trouble – refused to take a warning, been silly. He'd had to be taught a lesson and he was, as Schwede knew, now in the process of learning it somewhere else, somewhere a good deal less agreeable. The only three Jewish families in Langenbach had bolted in '38 like a lot of others all over Germany. They were all shopkeepers and their shops were now in decent hands. No, on the whole he, Schwede, had a straightforward, amenable bunch of people to look after, to provide with some political leadership and understanding, to help. They'd been slow to comprehend the Party and its ideals at the beginning but after 1934 there was soon no murmuring and he wasn't one to bear grudges. He also knew that even up to Gau level they had the sense to appreciate that this was not simply coincidence. On a recent

157

liaison visit one young sycophant had said to him, with an obsequious smile –

'The Gauleiter himself remarked the other day, when he was looking at some statistics – "of course Langenbach's all right. Schwede's there, what do you expect?"

With such achievements, such *harmony*, such sense of unity and purpose all about him, it could not fail to be a nagging pain to Egon Schwede that in one direction he was achieving nothing at all – or so it had appeared until recently. And this was in a matter which stirred him, body and soul, most deeply. The matter of Anna Langenbach.

Schwede's career had been successful well beyond his political activities, and had brought him from humble beginnings to the management of a local brewery. The brewery was a small, family affair – an excellent, small, German, family affair. Schwede got on well with his employers. He had always given loyal service. He liked brewing. He had made himself a master of the art and worked at all hours. As he rose in the hierarchy of the brewery, he tolerated not the slightest slackness or imprecision. Such leisure as he had, he devoted to the Party. He had never married. Quite early on during the Weimar days, the senior partner, head of the family, had drawn him to one side.

'Schwede, we deeply admire your patriotism. As you know, we share it. Of course we have to be discreet, in our position. But it's a great thing for the company to feel that the brewery is being served by one who has so committed himself to the cause of Germany!'

That was before 1932. He had nodded, satisfied. Later, all the members of the family who mattered joined the Party. They certainly didn't lose business by it either, he reflected contentedly. And after 1934 they offered him a seat on the Board of Management on generous terms. So Schwede was well established financially. He now had shares in the brewery. He was esteemed in Party and District. Everybody was anxious to shake his hand.

But Schwede, master of his surroundings, admired, courted – and, as he knew without displeasure, very generally feared – had found it impossible to penetrate the icy reserve of Frau Anna Langenbach.

158

He had naturally made it his business to call at Schloss Langenbach. The old people were unimportant, of course, past giving trouble, or being effective one way or another. He'd met the Major, Kurt Langenbach, twice only. He knew his reputation as a brave airman, one who was performing useful service for Germany: teaching the untrustworthy Spaniards how to conduct themselves in aerial warfare. Langenbach had been – Schwede grunted resentfully at the memory – remarkably off-hand.

'Ah, Schwede, isn't it?'

'*Kreisleiter Schwede, Herr Major.*'

The Major had been scarcely polite. Schwede fumed. He could picture the conversation, the contemptuous smiles after his departure from Schloss Langenbach.

'Curious world, when we have to entertain employees of the brewery, in case they do us harm!'

'As I could,' Schwede would mutter to himself after such bitter imaginings. 'As I could!'

But he had acted with prompt correctitude when they heard the news of Langenbach's death in that air crash. He had appeared, spruce in Party uniform, had saluted, bowed, his manner expressive of honourable grief at the passing of a German warrior. The young widow herself had received him. Perfunctory words were spoken. He knew he did it with dignity. He had seen her often before, of course, but this occasion was the first on which he had seen her alone.

She had thanked him, equally perfunctorily. Finally, awkwardly, he had murmured some further words and risen to leave. Then Anna (he thought of her always as Anna, licking his lips) rose from her chair. How beautiful she was! How elegant in her sadness!

'Herr Schwede, I wish to ask you something.'

'Frau Langenbach?'

'There is a family in the village who appear in some sort of trouble. They are deeply distressed and afraid. Will you please act in such a way as to put their minds at rest?'

She named the family. Schwede was appalled.

'Frau Langenbach, these are confidential matters but I know I can rely on your discretion.'

'You can.'

He told her that the family in question were suspected of having been party to an arrangement whereby one of the Jewish tradesmen who had fled from Germany the previous year had managed to expatriate some savings. There were technicalities. It was complicated – it appeared that the family had not, strictly speaking, acted illegally – but they had probably done a favour in a most indiscreet way. In what most decent Germans would regard as an unpatriotic way, no less.

'But if they have done nothing illegal, why have you threatened them? You have left them terrified that they may be – imprisoned somewhere – even without being formally charged.' She looked at him, opening wide her beautiful eyes in what appeared puzzled distress.

'They behaved most unwisely, if nothing else, Frau Langenbach. These were Jews.'

'Perhaps. But law is law is it not? And there are plenty of new ones. Yet you say these people have not broken the law. And you know, Herr Schwede,' Anna had continued, 'there is talk that people sometimes disappear in our country, just because somebody in the Party thinks it best.'

'Nonsense, Frau Langenbach.'

'I know and you know that it is nonsense – stupid, lying, talk. But surely it is best to stop foolish people thinking it by giving them no reason to think it? I am sure you agree.'

Schwede was far from agreeing. People had to feel there could be trouble if they misbehaved themselves. Society demanded it and the cumbrous processes of law were inadequate to satisfy that demand. He said nothing, however. He looked at her hungrily. What eyes! What skin! And in black – marvellous! She was manifestly pregnant but that altered her desirability not one bit. No more than did her widow's weeds.

'Anything you can do to set ignorant people's minds at rest would be most considerate – *Herr Kreisleiter*!' And then she smiled. It had been a cold smile and a cold extension of the hand, but as he took it he had felt blessed.

Thereafter, however, matters had not progressed. He had quickly sorted out the delinquent family.

'So! There are complaints of harassment, are there? What am I to think of that? Frau Langenbach tells me you've been bothering her with your troubles, telling her stories about your innocence! When you and I know that your behaviour has been very – very questionable, shall we say!'

'*Herr Kreisleiter*, let me assure you absolutely.' The man was terrified. Schwede eyed him.

'Here's what you'll do if you want to start convincing me you're a good German – and if you want to help me persuade people at Headquarters you're a good German –'

And Schwede prescribed a course of action. The man would approach Frau Langenbach and would assure her, 'In a way that convinces her, without double-talk,' that the *Kreisleiter* had been really helpful, had accepted assurances of good behaviour, that previous errors had arisen from misunderstanding.

'You were misled by the Jew, eh?'

'I was misled by the Jew, *Herr Kreisleiter*.'

'Swine!'

'Swine!'

Schwede put his face very close to the other's.

'And there'll be no mistake about this. You're perfectly happy and untroubled now, Kettner, aren't you?'

Kettner said he was. A diminutive man, he wished he could stop sweating and trembling. The Kettners kept a small provisions store.

'*Herr Kreisleiter*' I would consider it a great honour if you would give me your opinion on this bottle of cognac. It has been imported from France. One doesn't know, of course – I believe some of my customers –'

Schwede took the bottle, fixed the donor with a hard stare, nodded and left. But his next meeting with Anna had been infuriatingly disappointing. He had called at the Schloss after a decent interval to say that in the matter of the Kettner family he had 'put their minds at rest'.

'It was a misunderstanding. Herr Kettner was unwise, it preyed on his conscience, he got things out of proportion.'

Anna had nodded gravely. She did not refer to Kettner speaking to her. Schwede decided not to call on Kettner again. The man smiled at him ingratiatingly whenever they ran into each other but there was no means of knowing exactly what had passed between him and Anna. If Schwede ever found out that the little fool – but he turned his thoughts away from that.

161

The rest of his next visit to the Langenbachs had been filled with brief, trite sentences. Anna seemed resistant to being drawn into more intimate conversation, and Schwede almost wished for more Kettner-like misunderstandings in order to produce some connection between them, some ripple on the glacial surface of her composure and her indifference.

But Schwede called at Langenbach again, 'to check there are no problems with which he could help'. He made it into a habit.

Once he said,

'I wish you to know, Frau Langenbach, that anything which worries you, any assistance which you need, if you apply to the Party you will not be disappointed. It is one of our first duties to care for the families of fallen German heroes, in any way we can.'

'Thank you.'

He had tried to make it more personal, but she managed always to leave him feeling exasperatingly inept and boorish. She was never discourteous but he could get nowhere. Months went by and this great crusade of war began. The child was born. He called to offer congratulations, to hope 'all was well'. He seldom saw the old Langenbachs on these visits. He suspected them of ambivalent feelings about the Party in general and himself in particular, and he didn't care a damn that they were probably avoiding him. He came to see Anna.

Then, after that drab, first winter of the War, came the wonderful spring with its triumphs over the French and British. It had always been made clear to Schwede by the authorities that he was a man whose services were indispensable on the home front. Nevertheless he was, as he stressed to all and sundry, an old soldier at heart. He was forty-one.

'They've got softer than we were, these young lads, I can tell you, but they've done well, no question.'

He had been called up in 1917 but a bad attack of pleurisy had kept him at duty in training establishments. Still . . .

He had paid what had become a regular call at Schloss Langenbach.

'Wonderful news is it not, Frau Langenbach?'

Anna said – 'And let us hope it will bring peace nearer.'

162

'Of course. German victory and European peace. Frau Langenbach, it must often be lonely for you here.' For Anna the fact that this was true made it no less offensive.

'No, there is always much to do. My little boy still needs a lot of attention after all! And the affairs of Langenbach are a lot for my parents-in-law, who are not young.'

'Still, the company of a baby and two old people – greatly respected old people, of course – is not much for a lady like yourself, Frau Langenbach, a young, beautiful lady like yourself.' Schwede had rehearsed this speech to himself. It was, he knew, terrifyingly bold. Why did all his confidence, his courage, his power to dominate ebb swiftly away when confronted by this calm, exquisite young woman? It made him savage but he could not cure it.

'Like yourself!' he repeated. He smiled, with what he intended as respectful tenderness. But all Anna said was, as usual – 'Thank you, Herr Schwede. I assure you I am very well.' Her smile was as cold as ever. He had been told by her of her intended journey to Arzfeld. Anna knew better than to seem evasive with Schwede, or to take him by surprise in any way that could arouse suspicion. She told him that she intended to 'pay a visit to relations'.

'Good, good,' he had said, with jealous currents flowing through his mind. 'Are those Langenbach relations perhaps?'

'No, relations of my own. Colonel von Arzfeld. I intend to stay several weeks. Everything is in order here.'

He knew the name. He had found out all that he could about her family. Furthermore, he knew that her son was the sole heir to his grandparents and that Anna had a major life interest in Langenbach, as befitted the child's guardian. None of this made her less desirable. And at this parting he was certain he detected for the first time a warmer note, a melting. She looked directly at him as she took his hand. There was meaning in it, he was sure. The truth, he reflected, was that at least a year must elapse after Langenbach's death before so noble a woman could entertain thoughts of – of that kind. And now, in September, 1940, it was only just over a year. For the first time in that year Schwede felt hope.

It would, however, be essential to keep up the pursuit, the pressure. She must be aware of his feelings – his tender

163

confusion when with her, the frequency of his visits, the ardour of his expression, the generosity of his professions of desire to help her. All these must surely have conveyed their message to one so sophisticated and yet so feminine! It was not difficult to find business that would properly take him southward. An instructional conference at Kassel which he had been requested to attend 'if convenient, *Herr Kreisleiter* Schwede' (indication of privileged status) could be reached by a journey via the Wesertal. He would call at Arzfeld. He would call – at least in his own eyes – as something not altogether unlike an acknowledged suitor.

'Some more coffee, Herr Schwede?'

'Excellent.'

He sipped it, happy to be in Anna's presence, but, as always, ill at ease. Was it not extraordinary, he asked himself in rare moments of self-communion, that a man should be wracked *simultaneously* by embarrassment and by desire? He could not feel comfortable or relaxed with Anna. He admired her, and the cooler she was the more his admiration burned him and the more insignificant he felt. But at the same time he wanted her fiercely – so fiercely at times that it almost stopped his breath. And with what he was confident should properly be called love went, by now, great rushes of resentment. Rot any woman who could reduce Egon Schwede to this! Meanwhile, he sipped his coffee.

They spoke of the war.

'The British are paying a price for their obstinacy! The Luftwaffe are giving them a bad time, by all accounts.'

'Let's hope we don't suffer the same thing back, Herr Schwede. One day.'

'Not much fear of that! The *Reichsmarschall* has seen to that side pretty thoroughly!'

He looked at Anna. They were sitting outside the house, on a paved, sheltered terrace. The late September afternoon was warm. Arzfeld looked beautiful.

'This is a delightful place, Frau Langenbach! It is green, peaceful – one feels a truly German heart beating in such a place, as if it were alive. Don't you think so?'

'I am very fond of Arzfeld, yes.'

Anna was wearing a thin, flowered blue and white frock. Her slender arms, like her unstockinged legs, were bare and brown. Her hair was kept back from her wide forehead by a red velvet band. A bracelet with charms upon it was around one delicate wrist. His eyes drank in all this. He made his move.

'I have several times admired that bracelet, Frau Langenbach. It is charming, if I may say so. I hope you will permit me to offer a small gift, to be added to the symbols already on it.'

He drew from his pocket a small box and proffered it. The jeweller in Celle had guaranteed quality. Anna, taken aback, accepted the box and opened it before finding words or an appropriate reaction. Inside the box, lying on cotton wool, was a tiny gold swastika.

Schwede smiled fondly, nervously. He felt a certain relief. This moment, keenly anticipated, had also been dreaded. Suppose she found some reason to reject the gift? But would she – would she dare? To slight the Party emblem – when offered by a high Party official?

Yet he certainly did not wish acceptance to rest on such considerations, proper though they were. It was essential, indeed, that he should show how personal was the gesture, how devoted the tribute, a gesture from the heart. Schwede put his coffee cup down on the light garden table between them, a flimsy affair covered with a red and white check tablecloth. He rose.

'May I?'

He took the charm.

'The catches on these things are often awkward. It has a small ring to clip to a bracelet link. It is easier for another to fix. Allow me!'

He took her hand. Then he took her forearm – delicious! – and laid it on the table beside her while affecting to peer closely at the bracelet, to examine it for an appropriate link to which to attach his gift. He could smell her skin.

Anna found her voice.

'Herr Schwede, I am afraid I cannot accept your kind gift for my bracelet.'

'Not accept it? Ah, Frau Langenbach, it is nothing –' He stepped back, leaving the box on the table.

'You see, these – these charms on my bracelet – were all given to me at some time or another by my late husband. It is precious to me on that account. I feel that it has to be – preserved.'

Schwede was enchanted. This was exquisite sensitivity. It was truly German sensitivity. And how amply it spoke of the womanly tenderness he was sure existed beneath the cool self-possession Anna showed to the world.

'Frau Langenbach, I understand your feelings perfectly – perfectly!'

'Please do not think me ungrateful.'

'On the contrary, if it be possible you are higher than ever in my eyes! I only ask – in that case – that you keep this present – this little gold *Hakenkreuz*, our *Hakenkreuz*, keep it in its little box and one day, perhaps, find some other way to wear it. That is what I ask –' Schwede was trembling, 'Frau Langenbach! Anna!'

Anna seemed to be considering. She said 'Thank you' so softly that he could barely hear it. He extended his hand. Anna, looking at him in some surprise, took it. Schwede felt, with absolute assurance, a current pass between them. If he were bold now he could break through the barriers of reserve she had – reluctantly, unnaturally – erected. The swastika, as might be expected, had done the trick! He could tell from the touch of her hand, from the look in her eyes, that she was responding! Responding to the passion of a vigorous, warm-blooded man who, she must now fully realize, adored her! Schwede felt glorious, a conqueror. Saying again, 'Anna!' with immense fervour he took two rapid steps to her upright chair and threw his arms around her shoulders. His hands found the bare flesh of her upper arms. He sank to a position half-kneeling beside her. Anna appeared to be wriggling somewhat. The touch of her skin brought him to a frenzy. He pressed his mouth to the lovely place where her neck rose from her shoulders.

'Anna! Anna!'

'*No!*' said Anna, loudly, struggling ferociously. She managed to get halfway to her feet. The contortion involved

166

in freeing herself from Schwede's powerful, questing hands overturned the light table which crashed to the ground with two cups upon it. Table cloth, broken china and coffee dregs were strewn upon the flagstones, together with the small gift box. Schwede stood up with some difficulty. He tried to maintain the momentum of what had been, by any reckoning, a difficult assault to launch.

'Anna!' he said again. He extended his arms wide and took a step towards her. Anna had by now put several yards between them and was looking with what appeared nervousness towards the house. Schwede supposed she feared that the crash of broken china could have been heard within and might provoke the appearance of some third party, embarrassing to them both. His guess was right. Marthe, the old cook, was in the kitchen and Anna had no wish for an already deplorable situation to be complicated by the arrival of unbidden reinforcements, by subsequent explanations. In fact, Marthe was stone deaf and heard nothing. Franzi was sleeping soundly in his cot near an open window but appeared to have been undisturbed by the hub-bub.

'Anna!'

Anna said, 'Herr Schwede, please help me pick up this china.' Before he knew what he was doing he found himself on hands and knees, collecting pieces. When it was done he found it hard to recreate the excitement, the glory of that moment when he had, for however short and unsatisfying a moment, held her in his arms.

'Now, Herr Schwede, I think it best if you leave at once. I will try to forget your surprising behaviour.'

Schwede extended a hand. Anna ignored it.

'If you go round the corner of the house you will reach your car.' Her voice was icy.

He looked at her. One should never take 'no' for an answer. She was resisting but it surely only meant that he must push harder at the door. He bowed. It wasn't altogether unexpected. He had even rehearsed his closing speech.

'I am afraid my feelings got the better of me. Please believe that those feelings are of the strongest, the most sincere kind.'

Anna said nothing. Schwede smiled with melancholy fondness. He extended his hand again. What would happen, he

167

wondered, if he grabbed her again, really went for her this time? Was there much to lose? He eyed her and swallowed. Better not.

'One moment,' said Anna.

She darted to where she had been sitting and returned with the little box. Put it into his outstretched hand.

'Goodbye, Herr Schwede.'

'We shall meet shortly,' said Schwede, short of breath and confused in mind. 'I shall call again soon, when you return, at Langenbach. You have misunderstood me.'

Anna shrugged her shoulders.

'I see no point in your calling at Langenbach, Herr Schwede and I don't think I have misunderstood anything. It seems to be you who have suffered from misunderstanding of the position. Of your position.'

'I understand my position perfectly,' said Schwede, his voice shaking again but now made unsteady by a number of emotions of which lust was only one and by no means the predominant. 'I understand my position perfectly. I am *Kreisleiter* of Langenbach.'

'I did not mean that. I mean that you appear to think I might welcome – attention from you. That is far from being so. It is the exact reverse of the truth. I find your presence distasteful. And, as I have said, I see no point in your calling again.'

'I am *Kreisleiter* of Langenbach,' Schwede heard himself saying, as from a great distance. 'As such, many things are my concern. We shall be seeing each other, I promise you, Frau Langenbach. I promise you that!' He did not afterwards remember how he left the terrace.

Anna heard, with relief, the sound of Schwede's car driving away. She supposed she had been immensely foolish. It had been unnecessary to tell him so bluntly that his physical presence repelled her. She could have been more gracious while still keeping him at a distance. She could, she supposed, have brushed off his oafish attack without so ruthlessly wounding his pride. Instead she had acted as she felt. She found Schwede disgusting and the fact that he was in a position to do harm – or good – to her and hers had counted with her too little.

Anna sat for some time with her head on her hands. 'I was selfish,' she thought, 'self-indulgent. What does it matter that the beast paws me? By being so sensitive I might endanger other people whom I love.' For she had few illusions about what Schwede could – and would be prepared to – do. 'I wish I could talk – talk to anybody,' she thought. But to confide was itself somehow repellent. A child like Marcia, despite a year in the Reich at war, could not possibly understand the menace, the dangers of being branded as hostile to the Party. The sheer spite which could wreck lives.

Or take them.

Anna knew that she could not speak of Schwede to someone like Kaspar von Arzfeld, her cousin. He would be angry, but if he acted he would only make trouble for himself. He had no influential contacts in the Party. Besides, what had Schwede done? Tried to kiss an attractive woman whom he fancied – to whom he was, he apparently thought, paying honourable court! It might be socially distressing to a von Arzfeld or a Langenbach, but it was hardly a crime! And in the new Germany the lofty attitudes she and her kin represented were a great deal more reprehensible than any conduct of the *Kreisleiter*! Schwede had done nothing for which he would or could be taken to task. His only fault was to have failed. That would make of him an enemy.

Anna felt very isolated. Franzi was still asleep. Neither Kaspar nor the girls would return for another three hours. She found the companionship of Marcia half-solace, half-torment. She loved the reminders of Anthony that Marcia's presence provided, a few tricks of speech or movements of body where brother was brought to mind by sister. But she was also tortured by those reminders. Anna had never been able to find relief for her love and her pain by confidences. She had none near enough to her who could be trusted. She was, besides, a woman not given to sharing her emotions, to self-display. And how to find words, anyway, which were not utterly banal?

Anna knew by now that if she never saw Anthony again she would love him, unreasonably, unsatisfyingly, foolishly, but without the smallest doubt and for ever. She knew that he was far more to her than the young man who had moved her as no other, more than the father of her child, more than she could ever describe to somebody else. It made no sense, and she had no desire to make sense of it. It was simply there, a cancer, irremovable. 'Oh God!' she sometimes muttered. 'How I long for him!' Normally Anna loved solitude. Today the memory of Schwede oppressed her and she needed another human being, anyone, to remove the taste. She lifted her head. Surprisingly, she heard the sound of a distant car on the farm road to the house.

'My God!' she thought. 'He's coming back.' Her first instinct was to wake Marthe. Then she would pick up Franzi, go to her own room and lock herself in. She would tell Marthe that she was feeling unwell, and would keep Franzi with her. She would say,

'If a gentleman calls tell him you regret but I've asked not to be disturbed.'

She moved towards the house. Then she stopped, and stood frowning.

Damn Schwede! Damn the bullying brute! Why should she, Anna Langenbach, hide from the man in her own cousin's house? She would sit where he had left her! Let him try to attack her again, threaten her, try to ingratiate himself with her, do his damndest! She would see him in Hell before she fled from him. Anna heard the car stop and its door open and shut. He would probably assume she had moved from the garden. He would enter by the front door as he had when he first arrived. Let him do so. Let him find her! She would say – 'Have you forgotten something, Herr Schwede?'

She guessed correctly – through the open windows she heard footsteps in the house. Then – she deliberately did not turn her head – she heard him hesitantly approaching. A gentle, apologetic cough. What delicacy! Then a silence. He was standing in the french window. Anna spoke over her shoulder in as indifferent tones as she could muster.

'Have you forgotten something?'

'Almost but not quite forgotten, Frau Langenbach, how elegant you are!' said a laughing voice, not Schwede's. 'After all, we have only met twice! I apologize for this sudden intrusion. Toni Rudberg.'

170

Chapter 11

———————————◆———————————

FAITHFUL TO HIS LETTER to Marcia, Toni booked a room in an hotel not far from Arzfeld, and hired a car locally. His friend, he with the sister in Hameln, occupied himself separately, although Toni often brought him fluently into his conversation, helping to dispel the idea that he, Toni, was on a particular quest.

'He's a nice fellow, Berckheim. He promised me I'd admire this part of the country, wanted to show it to me. He was quite right.'

Toni's manner to Kaspar von Arzfeld was considerate and charming. With grave demeanour he murmured to him how much he appreciated the opportunity to pay his respects to the family of a comrade, 'Whom all deeply admired.' In fact, Toni had only met Werner twice, and since – with the excellent sense he had in such matters – he supposed that Marcia would have confided in the women of the family about their relationship, he was careful to say his reverend words about Werner in Kaspar's ear alone. It would not do for the others to think he was using their bereavement to mask his own pursuit of a girl. He could appear to them a heartless humbug. Instead, he wished to stand well in their eyes.

He had reasons for this which went beyond Marcia and which took shape as the week went on. Each afternoon Toni visited Arzfeld, greeting the girls as they returned from work, meeting them several times at the station. On the second occasion, with great show of respect, he asked Marcia if she would dine with him, 'to talk a little about Vienna'. His eyes were dancing. Kaspar von Arzfeld was, of course, the only member of the household unaware that Toni and Marcia would find, in all likelihood, plenty to do as well as talk about Vienna. Lise exchanged a quiet smile with Anna, whose complicity she had established after Marcia had confided in the latter.

171

That evening Kaspar said gently before they went to bed:

'I think young Count Rudberg has taken quite a strong fancy to Fraülein Marvell, to our little guest Marcia. It is perfectly understandable!'

So that it was occasion for no particular comment when Toni invited Marcia to two further evening exchanges.

'She has had a sad life for a young girl and she is anxious all the time,' said Kaspar. 'It is good for her to be admired, to see someone other than ourselves.' He felt benevolent and reflected on his own tolerance. Once, such behaviour –! But times were different. And Werner was dead.

Toni, meanwhile, had taken to arriving at Arzfeld ever earlier in the afternoon. By these means he invariably found Anna by herself. He managed, indeed, to have an hour's conversation with her on the first occasion and nearly two hours thereafter. And Anna enjoyed it. He was excellent company, and her life, most of the time, was both solitary and dull.

Toni, as always, had formed his ideas extremely fast. On the first evening at the *Gasthof* before going to bed he had had an evening drink with his friend, Berckheim.

'Are there a lot of them at Arzfeld beside your young lady? A large family?'

'No, nothing like that. It's quiet, lifeless. There's the young Arzfeld girl and Marcia Marvell – they go to work in a hospital every day, by train. And the old Colonel, Kaspar von Arzfeld, has a job at the District Headquarters. He's back in uniform. So he's away all day too.'

'Nobody else there?'

'Well, they've got a cousin staying at present, with a baby. A widow. Frau Langenbach. She was born Arzfeld. I found her there when I first called, unannounced.'

'A widow? Widow of Kurt Langenbach – Luftwaffe?'

'That's correct. She's travelled a lot. I met them once or twice in Berlin. He was killed in Spain.'

Captain Christoph Berckheim, Toni's companion, was a local man and well-informed.

'She's been left extremely well-off, you know. Her child – I suppose the one she's got here – will inherit everything from his old grandparents and people say that there are *very* generous provisions for the mother. It's a splendid property.'

172

Toni shrugged his shoulders with ostentatious lack of interest. He hadn't known. But the information accelerated within
him a sensation he had recognized within minutes of meeting
her again. He found Anna Langenbach enormously attractive.
Of course Marcia was irresistible, adorable: her youth was
delicious, her high spirits and her mischief, her *schelmerei* were
pure intoxication. She was like a figure from a rococo fresco,
an eighteenth-century nymph. Being in bed with Marcia was
not a thing to tire of easily. He chuckled lasciviously at every
recollection. The hotel was a pleasant place and he'd managed
to wangle enough petrol to drive her home at about midnight
each time. All rather rushed, but by God, it was worth it!

And yet, and yet –! Marcia was English, and in an impossible
position, no doubt of it. Sooner or later – he switched his mind
away from the possibilities but they refused to be banished.
At present, he gathered, she was adequately, if insecurely,
protected by her status as the late Captain Werner von Arzfeld's
fiancée; and, no doubt, by the good words put in by both the
Rudberg and von Arzfeld families – 'for what that's worth!'
Toni reflected gloomily. It couldn't last. Sooner or later, as an
enemy alien, she would try the patience of 'The Authorities'
too far. It only needed one false move, one sharp word in the
wrong direction by Marcia at the hospital, the malicious whim
of some jack-in-office. Marcia, poor girl, could find herself in
a nasty situation.

Which might, of course, involve anybody thought to be
particularly close to her. If these people, Toni said to himself
thoughtfully, once got suspicious they never let a matter drop.
They were as implacable as they were boorish. And Marcia
had the quality – endearing in many ways – of seeming wholly
indifferent to dangers once she had given her heart: and he
thought, with a mixture of complacency and uneasiness, that
she had certainly given her heart to him.

He knew she wept at the anomalies of her position. He
consoled her for that in the only way he knew. He enjoyed
using his somewhat limited stock of English with her.

'Darling, I am very, very loving of you.'

'No, Toni, that's not entirely right. But never mind.'

But Toni didn't think Marcia realized fully 'What *they're*
capable of!' Her naïveté, enchanting so often, had power also

to irritate. And, alas! there could be no question of any lasting relationship. Their communication with each other was as limited as it was delightful. He thought of it with strong emotion. But he thought also of Anna Langenbach.

What a charming woman! So intelligent, so cultivated, so amusing! Her figure, tall, slender, graceful was a delight. She had the skin of a young girl. Her eyes, her smile, her expression were enchanting. And he knew she liked him. He had been careful, very respectful. If there was really something to play for here it would need adroitness, patience. But he'd sensed it from the first moment.

And then – (Berckheim knew everything about people in this part of the world) –

'There are very generous provisions for the mother. It's a splendid property.'

Toni had little money and was conscious of the fact. He also felt – the feeling had, as far as he could tell for he was not introspective, come both suddenly and recently – that married life might bring certain compensations for the loss of liberty it officially entailed. He was, he thought, rootless. He had let his small flat in Vienna. His mother was dead. He had no brothers or sisters – a plethora of cousins but nowhere to call home, no place in which to feel an interest, an involvement. He was, he reflected, a nomad: something, too, of a parasite for all his officer's uniform and military responsibilities. Somewhere, some time, he could surely start to build foundations for a more settled life.

He told himself, of course, that for an officer it was absurd to have such notions in wartime. Nobody knew what would happen, who would survive or in what sort of society. On the whole Toni lived from one week to another. He was efficient, quick-witted, enterprising. He knew he was well regarded in the Army, although no doubt classed a light-weight by the more pedantic. His natural aptitude was for military service. He liked the challenges, he enjoyed danger. He took his pleasures when and where he could. He was happy-go-lucky. He was only thirty-one, still young, there'd come a time to settle down after the War. God knew how old he'd be after the War.

But now, out of the blue, came the idea of Anna Langenbach,

an irresistible creature, decorative, intelligent, of good family, available – and rich. From what he'd seen Lower Saxony wasn't too bad. There was the religious question of course, but he didn't expect her Protestantism was immovable. Anyway he felt indifferent on the subject. The Viennese were more tolerant in matters of religion than these northern relics of the Thirty Years' War!

There was, of course, Marcia. That sweet, sweet girl. Suddenly he saw the beloved curves of her body before the eyes of his imagination and sighed deeply. How complicated was life! Never mind, he had arranged to take Marcia back to dinner to the hotel that evening – and after that! He sighed again, breathed a little faster. He was sitting in the garden at Arzfeld in the late afternoon, the day before leaving for France. Anna was with him. This would be his last hour with her. This was going to be the last evening with Marcia. Another sigh.

'You sound sad, Toni.'

'This has all been so peaceful, so like Heaven,' he murmured. 'To leave it – ah, Anna!' He took her hand gently and pressed it to his lips.

'How long were you out of action after getting bombed, you careless oaf?'

'Only six weeks. It wasn't much of a war wound. Lots of blood from some head cuts and a broken leg. What they call superficial. What about you?'

'Untouched. I took as few risks as possible. The whole thing was rather a mess, wasn't it? But all one felt was relief at getting back.'

'Here we go again!'

The sirens began to wail. Anthony and Robert were in London, sitting in a night club off Regent Street. On the table was a bottle of whisky marked, 'Mr Robert Anderson'. They had consumed half of it. The place was crowded, noisy and companionable, a cellar decorated with a number of suggestive posters, a deafening band, a tiny space for dancing, virtual darkness and a clientèle largely known to each other, the men mostly in uniform.

'We're an odd nation, war or no war,' Robert shouted,

'when one really has to come to somewhere like this if all one wants is a drink with a friend after midnight. And then one has to pretend that one's ordered the bottle beforehand and that they're holding one's stock for one!' This elaborate subterfuge was indeed necessary, with supporting documentation, in order to circumvent the licensing laws. An overworked police force made periodic raids to enforce compliance.

'Well, if one has to go to a cellar this seems as good a one as any!' Anthony held his voice steady with an effort. The band had just been temporarily drowned by the mighty crash of an adjacent bomb exploding. Since the roof had come down on him at Vencourt he had found, to his shame, that the sound of sirens, the whistle and roar of bombs caused him to sweat.

'I'll get over it,' he said to himself. 'I'll get over it. I'm a little gun-shy, that's all.'

They talked of the times through which they were living. 'I wouldn't have missed this summer in England for anything,' said Robert. 'It's been a splendid sensation. Do you think we're going to be invaded?'

'Somehow I doubt it now. It's mid-October. Although I don't see what the Germans can do *except* invade us. We're not going to give in. And they're not going to persuade us to give in by bombing us.'

'I suppose the submarine thing may make life difficult.'

'Difficult, yes. But in the end the Navy will cope. They always do.'

'They always do.'

They poured more whisky into their glasses, a little drunk.

'How long a leave have you got, Robert?'

They had met, purely by chance, at three o'clock that afternoon, walking in opposite directions along Piccadilly.

'Week's leave,' said Robert. 'I'm going to Scotland on Tuesday night. See the family. If there's a train running. How about you?'

'I'm at home till next Thursday.' Anthony had, he said, been remarkably fortunate. Most of his battalion had got away from Dunkirk on the second but last day of the evacuation. Anthony had preceded them, moving by hospital ship before the main body of the British Expeditionary Force had begun their enforced departure from France. After a generous fortnight of sick leave he had rejoined his battalion in early July, limping but fit, to find that he had not, as he might have expected, been omitted from the first list of short leaves they had enjoyed since Dunkirk.

'We're lucky. Our rôle means we're to get some time off now. Then we relieve another division, and go without leave until God knows when. Until Hitler invades, I suppose, or rings us up to say he won't. But I've been idling in and out of hospital so long I really thought they'd keep me at duty. Jolly nice of them.'

So Anthony, for a week which had just begun, was again at home. Bargate was a wonderful oasis of peace. To return to it from hospital on sick leave had been sheer delight. It stood in particular contrast to the turmoil, the fear, the uncertainty of that extraordinary May in Belgium and France. Bargate had seemed like Heaven – but familiar, thought Anthony, as I suppose Heaven could hardly be. Or could it? And now he was profoundly grateful for the chance of another week there, after what had only turned out to be a short return to his battalion at the end of his sick leave.

The war had not left Bargate undisturbed and nobody wished that it should. There were evacuees – two families of London children, one co-operative and delightful, the other surly and suspicious. Hilda was coping with them skilfully and firmly. Preston, the butler, was beyond the age of conscription to any particular duty and was 'managing' with loyalty and a good deal of complaint, zealous for air raid precautions, waging unremitting war against the evacuees: and Hilda's cook, Mrs Riding, grumbling a good deal at the exigences of the rationing system (generous as yet), was producing edible meals. Otherwise there was no domestic staff and rooms were shut save dining room and inner hall. But it was quiet at Bargate. It was almost as it had always been. There was no sense of crisis, no alarm.

Most of John Marvell's county and charitable activities continued to demand his time. It was a relief to be busy, although the trivial character of some of the business irritated him, so far was it from the great drama through which they were all condemned to live. 'But somebody has to keep things going,' John thought, 'and these little concerns make up life, after all. They are worth attending to as well as fighting for.' He had joined the Home Guard. The evening news was invariably listened to on the radio and John tuned in again at breakfast time: but the war had assumed its inevitable place in the background rather than the forefront of life.

When they talked of Marcia it was with pain, but pain steadily endured. As much as could be had been done, by contacts with the American Embassy. There were, not unnaturally, a great many such problems put to the Americans. No direct word of Marcia had been received. At times the Marvells' fretting showed, though they took pains to be cheerful with Anthony.

The band in the cellar struck up a new and popular tune and people began to sing.

'At home,' said Anthony. 'At home at Bargate until next Thursday. I can always get up for a day or a night. The trains have been pretty good. I stay at the Club.' Anthony belonged to a large, many-bedroomed Club, a place of convenience rather than companionship, impersonal, useful, and so far undamaged.

'Could you come up and have dinner on Monday night?' asked Robert. 'There's a rather nice American who's just joined their Embassy here. He's been in touch with my mother. He's going to dine with me.' [Robert's mother was American].

Anthony nodded – 'I think so, yes –'

'Bill O'Reilly. William Standish O'Reilly, Junior. He was at Oxford – well before us. He's bound to be interesting. Before going back to the States last month, and now coming here, he was at their Embassy in Berlin! So he can tell us how people rate our chances – both in America and Germany.'

'Their Embassy in Berlin! How extraordinary that people still *have* Embassies in Berlin!'

Robert considered this. 'Well, I suppose the truth is that pretty well everyone does. Except us, of course!'

Anthony said that he'd be delighted. The 'all clear' was sounding and they made their way a little unsteadily up the steep cellar stairs to a Regent Street lit only by a harvest moon.

'Oh, there's not much doubt about it, we weren't good enough,' said Robert Anderson somewhat sharply. He and Anthony

178

exchanged glances. They had already discussed with each other their reactions to the fighting in France and Belgium with the sort of defensive self-mockery Englishmen adopt when confused or ashamed. Neither, however, relished the prospect of breast-beating before William Standish O'Reilly, Junior. His question had been courteous enough – what did they think primarily had gone wrong? He was, they had both decided, a nice man. But wounds were still raw.

'I reckon,' Bill O'Reilly said, 'that the French hadn't got their hearts in it, right from the word go.' They were dining in a restaurant immediately south of Leicester Square and so far the evening had been air raid free.

'You're talking to two pretty junior officers,' said Anthony lightly. 'I only saw things at worm's eye level. But I don't think it can all be blamed on the French. Neither they nor we were ready for the shock.' His mind went back to Arras. How did one convey to this agreeable American the paralysis of the will, the sheer numbness created by enemy air power and fast-moving ground forces, apparently irresistible, destroying any coherent pattern of defence, violating every preconceived notion? So that leaderless men, stunned, fearful, came to act only as if in a bad dream? There had been stories of French soldiers acting as unbidden traffic police, waving on German columns. To one such as O'Reilly this must betoken treachery or moral collapse. To Anthony – who had no idea whether or not the tales were true – such a thing was perfectly comprehensible.

'Never mind,' said Robert. 'There'll be a return match. Somehow. Some day. Now tell us about Berlin.'

O'Reilly told them.

'Their successes have stunned the victors themselves. The generals – you don't get any whispers these days of the sort of disenchantment in the Army which was certainly there before they went into Czechoslovakia. Hitler mocked their fears. He's been proved right. He's riding high.'

Did this mean, Robert and Anthony wanted to know, that the Germans were confident about an invasion of Britain? Bill O'Reilly shook his head emphatically.

'What's on Hitler's mind all the time is relations with Russia. They've got this pact. It's important to both sides. Germany's

179

getting her imports from the East, the Soviet Union's importing stuff from the rest of the world and exporting it straight to Germany. You'd be amazed. But the Soviets are fencing with the Germans all the time about their relative position in the Balkans – in Rumania, Bulgaria and so forth. Each wants to strengthen his hand vis-à-vis the other. Same in the Baltic States. The Soviets just marched in and occupied them when the Germans were busy elsewhere, and the Germans didn't like that one bit. They're having one hell of an argument about it.'

'Thieves falling out.'

'You can say that. But it's still covered by a lot of smooth talk.' The question every diplomat in Berlin asked himself, Bill O'Reilly said, was whether German–Russian relations could worsen to the point of war.

'They're watching each other like cats. But we don't think Russia's ready for it yet.'

'It must have been tedious enduring air raids in Berlin knowing that if you got knocked off it would be by friends!'

Bill grinned, 'I don't think any of us minded that. A British air raid was good news. But air raids aren't disturbing people much. Not yet, anyway.'

From the whole conversation, indeed, Anthony formed the picture of a Germany less concerned, at the moment, about the war than was embattled Britain. Bill conveyed the impression of a Reich unthreatened, triumphant, looking forward to the fruits of victory – very different from the sense of living, invigorated, through great peril which prevailed that summer in England. Bill acknowledged it.

'That's right. That's most people. But the top guys are discouraging complacency. The Party line is that the rough stuff still lies ahead. And of course there are, thank God, a number of thinking, decent folk who are appalled the Nazis have gotten such reflected glory, and who pray for a setback.'

'Although a setback for the Nazis would involve a military defeat! Not easy, I suppose, for a patriotic German to swallow!'

Bill agreed. 'That's the problem,' he said. 'That's sure their problem.'

Bill O'Reilly had been in Berlin four years, a long posting by any standards. His special subject at University had been nineteenth-century German history and he had been a fluent German speaker from his Oxford days. The assignment had been natural.

'We've a small Diplomatic Service,' he said, 'and less of them than you'd suppose know a lot about Europe.' He had thus been a witness of every step along the road which had led, so inevitably it seemed, to European war.

They spoke of Spain. The nationalist victory had brought satisfaction to Germany. Bill regarded it sceptically. He did not take the idealistic view of the Civil War which had brought stars to the eyes of so many of his compatriots.

'Franco's no German puppet. He'll get all he can out of them but the Spanish are about the most obstinate guys in the world.'

'Did German help to Franco amount to as much as the Republicans said?' asked Robert. Bill spoke expertly. This had been his department. He had also known personally a number of German officers who had served in Spain and he had, where opportunity offered, discussed the war with them.

'You had to measure what they said against what you knew, of course, but you got a feeling for it. There weren't huge numbers of Germans there, but they sent some good ones. One of the brightest of their airforce officers, for instance, was there – killed in an accident after the fighting was over as a matter of fact. Guy I knew quite well. I'd met him and his wife often in Berlin before he went to Spain. Guy called Langenbach. And there were some other pretty sharp fellows there, I know that.'

Anthony's attention had wandered for a little to other tables. Several acquaintances were dining at the restaurant, and contacts in wartime were fleeting and treasured. Then with the speaking of a familiar name, he felt as if a high-pressure hose of cold water had struck his left ear, leaving him shocked and breathless.

'Did you say Langenbach?'

'That's right, Kurt Langenbach. One of the Luftwaffe's ablest, they always said.'

'I've met some of his family. I was in Germany in 1938.'

'Well, Kurt was already in Spain by then –'

'Yes, I met his father and mother. And his wife. At their home near Hanover.'

'Is that so? Well, I used to see quite a bit of Kurt and Anna when they were in Berlin. She was a lovely girl – real lovely. She was half-English or something, you know.'

'Yes, I remember that.'

'When Kurt went off to Spain, some people said they'd not been getting along too well. Kurt was pretty close to the Nazis, in my opinion, even if he wasn't a Party member. I reckon he approved of a lot they were doing, even if he looked down his long aristocratic nose at them personally. There are plenty like that. That wasn't Anna's line at all. Still he came on leave now and then, must have, because she had a baby, a little boy, born after Kurt was killed. Born well after the start of this war in fact.'

Anthony said, 'I didn't know.'

PART IV

———•———

1942

Chapter 12

'IT IS EXTRAORDINARY what he writes to me, perfectly extraordinary,' said Kaspar von Arzfeld for the fourth time. 'Our friend Rudberg,' he added again, unnecessarily. 'Such an interesting letter. But perfectly extraordinary.'

It was the third winter of this peculiar war and he felt a good deal older. That golden summer of 1940, when France had been beaten, when England might have seen sense – that seemed, now, a long time ago. That was before the start of this strange, limitless adventure in the east, the adventure that had started on 22nd June, 1941, the invasion of Russia. Operation *Barbarossa*.

'An extraordinary, interesting letter.'

'Are you going to read it to us, Father?' Lise was daring.

'Some of it is not for girls, it is soldiers' talk,' said her father firmly. 'He knew I would be interested. One reads about it, of course, but there's nothing like hearing at first hand from a young fellow at the front. Makes all the difference.' He returned to the letter.

'Is Toni well?' asked Marcia gently. She had had no letters since Toni had 'gone east' in common with a large part of the Wehrmacht. Nor, although hoping a little, had she expected any. Now it was winter. January, 1942.

'He sounds well. It's hard for them just at the moment of course. The Bolsheviks were saved by that winter of theirs. I'll read you part of the letter.

> "Dear Colonel von Arzfeld,
>   I owe it to you –"

Well, all the first part is how happily he looks back to his visits here last year and the year before. Very polite of him, certainly. And he's just left his job, he's been with a Corps Headquarters until now and he's about to return to the staff of a Panzer division.'

'Like before?'

'A different one. And he's promoted! He's a major! He'll be pretty well in charge of the operations staff, I imagine. He's doing very well.'

'You said his letter is extraordinary, father.'

'Yes, his descriptions are vivid, amazing. He's given me a wonderful picture of the advance last summer. Of course he has to obey the censorship rules, no saying where events took place although he's writing of nearly six months ago. My guess is that he was with the Central Army Group. On the Moscow front with von Bock.'

'But we didn't get to Moscow.'

'No, of course not, the strategic line of pressure was shifted,' said Kaspar rapidly and a little uneasily. 'That's not the point. And of course, their damned winter slowed things down. All the same von Bock got within sight of the place, drove a mighty wedge into the Russian front. I'll read you some excerpts, you girls. Toni Rudberg was writing about the events of last August, you see –'

Corps Headquarters always moved in a number of groups. Each group consisted of a small column of vehicles, a few officers, a number of drivers, clerks, orderlies and signallers. Each group had a certain inner cohesion, played a particular and indispensable part in the corporate professional life of the Corps Headquarters. The Headquarters was only fully functioning, only its entire self, when all these groups were again brought together at the end of a day – or a series of days. On the line of march Corps Headquarters was largely useless, its role temporarily assumed by a small advance party, its commander ranging the battlefield as he generally did, far from the advice, the support, of his staff. Corps Headquarters lived only for the moment when its various parts could be re-assembled, arranged in harmony with each other, each playing its appointed part in the control, the management, the intellectual inspiration of the Corps – a Corps of three Panzer divisions, totalling no less than 450 tanks when at full strength.

Meanwhile, and on the move, the groups of Corps Headquarters were often widely separated from each other, sometimes by design to reduce the threat of Russian aircraft knocking out more than one group, sometimes – and now more often – because of the difficulties of movement upon the appalling roads which made near impossible any systematic march discipline. Each group drove toward the distant horizon, sometimes with inadequate knowledge of how its companion groups were faring. The Corps Commander was somewhere miles ahead with a small command group of three vehicles, and a tiny handful of privileged Staff officers, who gave the impression when they returned to base in the evening of running the Corps advance unaided, more than a touch of patronage in their attitude. The main staff, the brain of the body, was lumbering along far to the rear, able, it seemed, to contribute little. Yet all appeared to be going extraordinarily well, although the speed of the first days of the advance seemed to have slackened. The only operational decisions necessary tended to be how far to advance the following day – how much further, during the next twenty-four hours, to penetrate into this limitless country. And their commander's guideline for that was usually simple – 'as far as possible'. The groups of Corps Headquarters moved unevenly forward under the infinite skies.

The drivers of vehicles got tired. Everyone sickened of the eternal dust, and the heat was taxing. But there were compensations. The country, with its low, rolling hills, its great forests and enormous rivers was beautiful. It conveyed an incongruous serenity. The villages of wooden houses had a certain primitive charm. Great fields of sunflowers lit the landscape with a periodic blaze of gold. Everywhere the horizon seemed a hundred miles away. For much of the time there was a huge silence. It was mercifully different from everybody's idea of war. There had been, of course, some mighty bombardments in the first days, considerable expenditure of tank and artillery ammunition on both sides as the Soviet forces near the frontier had been encircled by a sequence of giant pincer movements. But thereafter the forward march, hectic, heat-ridden, had seemed for the most part extraordinarily free from

187

the sights and sounds of battle. When one of the groups of Corps Headquarters halted for a fuelling break, a stretch of the legs, one could often hear, far to the east, the grumble of guns. Somewhere out there Russian rearguards must be forcing the German spearheads to deploy, to bring artillery into action, even to manoeuvre. Then there would be quiet. A few shouted commands would get vehicles started, men mounted. Staff officers would climb stiffly into cars or the front of trucks. The group would resume the advance. And behind the Corps, as every soldier knew with some inner relief, was a mass of marching divisions, men and horses often covering thirty miles a day. It was August, 1941.

Toni Rudberg looked lazily at the country as his car bumped uncomfortably along. The road, the main Corps axis of advance, ran along a broad, shallow valley. Astride it woods crowned low hills, extending back as far as the eye could see, and connecting with each other to make a great forest on either side. If one had to go to war it was good to see new lands, savour fresh experiences. Toni had been pleased to be attached to this Panzer Corps Headquarters – and in the operations branch, too. If all went well he might next go in a more senior position to another headquarters, possibly again to one of the Panzer divisions, whether in this Corps or further south. Just at present, however, there wasn't much chance to show zeal and efficiency. The General was doing it all from the front, and Corps Headquarters was trundling along a dusty road all day, from one lice-ridden village to another. The driver braked and switched off the engine.

The operations group appeared to have halted. A military policeman was reporting to the vehicle in front, a car in which rode Toni's section chief. Along this stretch the road wasn't too bad. The forest, dark and seemingly infinite, started about a kilometre away on either side. Green meadows sloped gently upwards from road to treeline. A cluster of the usual wooden houses meant that this place probably had a name, but Russians didn't appear to go in for maps and those issued by the General Staff before the campaign had proved remarkably inaccurate. There was a shout.

'We're likely to be half-an-hour here.'

'It could be worse,' thought Toni. An orchard and cherry

trees stood behind the row of houses. He watched an old Russian woman feeding geese. She called out something which he didn't catch, although his Russian was improving – soldiers' Russian, perhaps, but serviceable. The old woman was joined by a fair, pale-skinned girl. Both wore peasant clothes and headscarves.

'Really she's rather sweet,' Toni said to himself. 'A delightful little thing. These people with their grave faces, their sad eyes, their wooden shacks, this extraordinary, limitless land – it transports one from 1941 to the middle ages. It's all so – so disorganized, so untidy, so primitive!' He went to the largest of the village houses. An old man stood humbly in a corner and bowed as Toni nodded to him. Toni noted with approval that somebody was brewing tea. He took off his cap and belt, yawned, and looked at his watch. Just four o'clock. Two other staff officers were in the room. They exchanged comments about the day's march so far. The August sun had made them sleepy.

The spring of 1941 had not been without complications for Toni. He reckoned that he had survived them with a good deal of adroitness. He had paid discreet but assiduous court to Anna Langenbach. This was to some extent by letter and he fancied himself as a skilled and sensitive letter writer. He had also, however, driven to Langenbach to see Anna while visiting Arzfeld on two further occasions early in 1941, while enjoying a delightful time with Marcia Marvell. This had demanded finesse. Toni knew that Marcia and Anna were fond of each other. His method had been to take, or appear to take Anna into his confidence. This, anyway, produced a certain delicious intimacy. He explained how Marcia and he had fallen light-heartedly in love, in Vienna.

'It was nothing. She was sad after your cousin was killed, she was lonely. I was available – she was living with cousins of mine and I was in the Vienna Division as we called it. She's charming, a sweet creature. But I know *you* can understand that a man's capable of deeper feelings, that it's unfair to himself *and to another* to pretend his feelings are more profound than they really are!'

189

'Haven't you pretended exactly that to her?'

'No! I don't think so. You know how it is. And I hate to give pain. I expect I'm a worthless creature –'

'I expect so, too.'

'Yet all I want, Anna, is your good opinion.' He took her hand with a fine show of nervous delicacy.

'You will not have that if you lead my dear young friend Marcia Marvell to think you love her when you don't.'

'Ah, I know, I know! And how I shrink from brutality! Of course I realize it's I who created this situation – but please, Anna!' and he looked with great and serious tenderness into her eyes. 'She's far from indifferent,' he thought.

'What a rascal he is,' Anna said to herself, 'and how terribly attractive a lot of women must find him with the wave in that dark hair, with those eyes which express so much emotion, a little of bit of it genuine now and then perhaps!' She smiled, but there was irony in the smile, a scepticism which Toni chose to ignore. Anna felt entirely detached. Toni was profoundly mistaken – a rare thing for him – in supposing her not indifferent to his charms. She saw him clinically. Her feelings were for Marcia.

Toni was not without principle. Indeed he thought of himself as an honourable man as well as practical – and kind. No man of sensibility could just drop a girl. There had to be gentleness, time. He had to admit to himself, too, that the temptations of Marcia's body were not such as to make him hurry to abandon her, seldom though he saw her. But Toni told himself firmly that he could not forever put off the matter of a breach with Marcia. If he was to appear honest in Anna's eyes, if she were ever to take him seriously – and how devoutly he wanted that – then the question must be tackled. If he tried to ride two horses simultaneously much longer his breeches would be bound to split.

On his last day at Arzfeld, therefore, he had gone as far as he decently could, painfully, seriously. It had been April, 1941. Toni's Division, one of the last, was secretly moving east. He had secured four days' leave. He had taken Marcia's hand and walked with her through Arzfeld woods: a glorious day.

190

'Marcia, I must tell you that I shall not be coming here again. Anyway, not for a long time.'

Marcia had wanted to know why not. Toni had no high reputation for discretion, but even he could say little. She asked – 'Is it this business in Greece?'

'I can't say what or where it is, and I don't know much, darling, but it is so. You may not see me again.'

Marcia looked at him, troubled.

'Why do you say it like that?'

'Well, war is like that for all of us, isn't it? We're like autumn leaves, blown in a gale, swirling around, not our own masters. And the gale is blowing over most of the world. But Marcia, I don't want you to feel tied.'

'I do feel tied.'

'No, I mean it. I haven't the right. I've not asked you to marry me, or anything like that. I've got no settled future, I'm a soldier, I'm not Werner von Arzfeld with woods and fields awaiting him one day – no, please let me finish. I think you and I should – should thank God for what we've had together and not expect anything from the future. I want you to feel free. Believe me, I hate saying that! It makes me feel horribly jealous! But I must. And oh! my little heart, how I shall miss you!' He held her tightly. There was a long, loaded silence.

Marcia said, almost inaudibly – 'There's someone else.'

'No, don't think like that, Marcia. This is more important than that sort of thing. I have to think what's right to do. I'm going away – much further than before,' he muttered recklessly.

Marcia appeared not to have heard him. She said again, as if to herself,

'Yes, there's someone else.'

Then – and he found the memory so painful that he could hardly face it without tears – she had simply taken his arm, smiled sadly into his face, and said softly, in English – 'I expect you're right. Anyway I do thank God for you, my love, and I always will, whether that's right to do or not. And may He keep you safe.' Then she had walked back to Arzfeld quickly and alone.

This scene, which Toni recollected with pain mingled with

191

a certain sentimental satisfaction, was the last time he had seen Marcia. 'And I suppose I may never see her again,' he thought, 'but I'm sure I behaved correctly, honourably.' He had written a quick letter to Anna Langenbach:

'I have done as you advised – I have been honest. Oh! how agonizing these things are. But how I bless you for your wisdom and inspiration.'

So far no answer.

Toni's sense of rectitude was strengthened by a most disagreeable incident which had occurred just after his taking up his new duties at Corps Headquarters – immediately before the campaign started on 22nd June. One afternoon he was summoned by the Chief of Staff.

'Rudberg, this is *Sturmbannführer* Schramm of the Security Service. There is a matter on which he wishes to speak to you personally. I have agreed.' The Chief of Staff left the room. He looked embarrassed.

Schramm was a heavily-built man with a dark pencil moustache, shaved above and below. Toni thought he looked repulsive. He wore the uniform of the *Sicherheitdienst*. Like the SS they had a rank structure different from the Army's. A Party man. Toni looked at him haughtily. What did this oaf want with a Rudberg, a gentleman? Schramm had sat himself down at the Chief of Staff's desk and was looking at some papers. He appeared entirely at home.

'Captain Rudberg, I've got to investigate a report I've got here. It concerns your personal affairs.'

'What personal affairs?'

'It has been reported that you have a close relationship with an Englishwoman. That you, a German officer, are – shall we say attached? – to a woman who is, at the moment, at liberty in Germany but who has members of her family fighting for the enemies of the Reich.'

So that was it. Even a year ago Toni would have simply knocked Schramm down. But things had changed a lot. 'Keep your temper,' he said to himself. His voice was less than steady.

'The lady to whom you refer was the fiancée of a distinguished German officer, who died fighting for Führer and Fatherland. She has chosen to live among us. I understand that

192

the State authorities – subject to understandable safeguards – are content that she should be, as you put it, at liberty.'

'I know all that.'

'Furthermore the lady is working as an auxiliary nurse, a work of humanity – and of service to Germany. As to her family – I know nothing of them, but since they are English I have no doubt, as you say, that some are fighting against us.'

'Quite so.'

'Then I cannot see why the matter is raised by you as a matter of security.'

'Captain Rudberg,' said Schramm, 'this lady,' he fingered a sheet of paper, 'this Fraülein Marvell may be harmless, as you say. But we have to consider whether she is a – shall we say, a suitable companion? – for an officer who might, I am told, be promoted to positions of even greater confidentiality.' Schramm smiled, displaying some gold in the teeth. It was not an appetizing sight. He continued, his voice soft and courteous –

'I'm sure you understand, Captain, that a man in your position, a man with your responsibilities – your possibilities – has an obligation to be free from, shall we say, complications or question marks. On the security side. They can so upset a man's life.'

'I assure you, *Herr Sturmbannführer*, that there are no complications. No question marks. And, as you know, the late Captain von Arzfeld was formally engaged to this lady. No questions were raised then.'

'There wasn't time,' Schramm said drily. He looked at Toni steadily, as if soliciting a further comment.

Toni heard himself saying –

'It is, anyway, unlikely that I shall be seeing Fraülein Marvell again.'

'Ah,' said Schramm contentedly. 'That seems to me to make matters simpler, Captain Rudberg. Much, much simpler.'

The atmosphere in the Russian kitchen was stuffy but the tea was particularly welcome.

'I expect there'll be night work as usual,' Toni yawned.

'There's rather a charming little lass feeding geese, did you see her? Like someone from the Brothers Grimms' tales.'

'Your eye's always the sharpest, Rudberg! But I doubt if time's going to allow –' Suddenly they all leapt to their feet. Outside the house there was a confusion of shouts, a babble of warnings and commands.

'What the Hell –'

Seizing belts and caps they rushed out to the road. One of the transport *feldwebels* was pointing excitedly.

'There, *Herr Hauptmann*, there!'

A number of soldiers with light machine guns had been pushed hurriedly into ditches and down behind the corners of houses on the village edge.

'There! There!'

Toni brought his binoculars up on to the forest fringe a kilometre away to the south of the road. He gasped.

'My God!'

Out from the trees were moving, in leisurely fashion, three separate columns of horsemen. They formed up in a near continuous line parallel to and facing the road. They appeared to be three or four ranks deep.

'God, there must be five hundred at least!'

Toni breathed deeply. The scene was being played out in complete silence. Every eye and every binocular was on the forest.

Suddenly there was an irregular but perceptible flash of sun on metal, rippling up and down the ranks.

'Look at that, they've drawn sabres,' yelled Friedmann, Toni's colleague in the Corps operations branch.

There was a distant roar of engines. Far to the south four ground attack aircraft of the Luftwaffe could be seen flying eastward. Somewhere near the horizon was a renewed rumble of artillery. Modern war appeared to be starting up again. The lines of horsemen seemed to shimmer. They were moving.

'Every man down, weapons ready, fire on command!' The little group were so concentrated that one shout could reach them all, or nearly all. And, astonishingly, no other German columns to east or west were, for the moment, in sight.

'Operations Group, Panzer Corps Headquarters,' thought

Toni, 'about to receive cavalry.' It was a pity tea had been interrupted. His mouth was dry.

Then twenty voices yelled the same words –

'Here they come!'

Toni's binoculars were still up. There was no doubt of it. They were indeed coming – at full gallop. Riding stirrup to stirrup, sabres held high. If Operations Group Panzer Corps Headquarters had decided not to receive cavalry but to mount vehicles and distance themselves the moment was certainly past.

'About seven hundred metres! Five – four –'

'*Feuer frei!*'

The Spandau light machine guns opened up, their short, high-pitched bursts sounding as if a giant were ripping huge sheets of paper. Two heavy machine guns, mounted on vehicles for anti-aircraft protection, had been levelled, Toni saw with approval, their platforms steered quickly into positions from which they could fire. Individual soldiers were now opening up with their carbines.

'*Feuer frei!*'

Toni watched, holding his breath. It was a fascinating, an appalling sight. At first, he was only conscious of the number of horsemen still galloping towards them. For some moments the charge appeared to have lost little impetus. Then he saw that he was looking at a mere handful of cavalrymen riding on – and at a larger number of riderless horses. The latter began to swing left and right, to gallop outwards and then back, neighing wildly, terrified by the frightful noise of the machine guns.

The Spandaus kept up their grim work. Toni could now hear shouts from the surviving horsemen. They, too, must be realizing how alone they were, how few, and were swinging outwards and making up the slope towards the treeline, every man for himself, crouching low over his horse's neck. Machine gun fire was going high but Toni saw half a dozen brought down, though whether bullets struck horse or rider or both it was too distant to say.

The main body of Russian cavalry had been cut down within two hundred metres of the point the line had reached when the Germans opened fire. Horses in the front rank had fallen in huge numbers, bringing down those behind them. Through their glasses Toni and his companions could see the frightful mass of writhing horseflesh, with, here and there, the prone or crawling figures of soldiers. The sounds of terror and confusion were clear. The nearest stricken men and beasts lay at no more than 150 metres distance.

'Stop firing, there! Stop!' whistles blew. There was the hiss of a bullet passing harmlessly over their heads, and then another. A few cracks could be heard from the mangled mass of carcasses.

'Watch out, now! The live ones have got their carbines, they're down behind horses, watch out!'

Certainly no chances could be taken.

'Poor brutes,' Toni muttered. He couldn't take his glasses off the ghastly sight.

'Schmidt's reporting it! Get them mounted, we're moving on,' somebody shouted. The air was full of excitement, of men telling each other of particular incidents or phenomena observed.

'Fantastic, Rudberg! The Luftwaffe and a tank fight in the morning, advance thirty kilometres, Battle of Borodino in the afternoon! What a sight!'

'There's not much that can be done for those poor devils, sight or no sight!'

'Schmidt's reported the incident and the approximate casualties –'

'Our horses are suffering enough from this campaign,' said Toni, 'but at least we don't go in for the "*arme blanche*". And I'm glad of it. Men make war. Let them pay for it.' He climbed into a staff car beside the driver. The man was in a state of something like ecstasy.

'That was quite a battle, wasn't it, *Herr Hauptmann*!'

'It was a massacre. Now shut up and watch where you're going. We don't want another cracked sump.'

'Well,' said Kaspar von Arzfeld, 'Rudberg is certainly having an interesting war.' He had read out excerpts from Toni's letter to the silent Marcia and Lise.

'It all sounds rather horrible.'

'War is a harsh business. Soon we shall have news of another campaign.' For a telegram had arrived two days earlier;

'Lieutenant von Arzfeld wounded but recovering well. Will be granted sick leave on discharge from hospital probably in March.'

The nature of the wound was not normally disclosed in such telegrams but Kaspar had got busy on the telephone from District Headquarters, and had returned the following evening with a grave face, touched with a certain relief. Frido was in hospital in Poland. He had been wounded in Southern Russia.

'Unfortunately Frido has lost his left foot – the lower left leg has been amputated. He was lucky to survive. The vehicle in which he was travelling drove over a Russian mine.'

Marcia and Lise were appalled. But by winter, 1941 the hospital at which they were working was beginning to fill with cases evacuated from the east, and they had no difficulty in imagining other and grimmer injuries. Frido without his left foot would still be Frido, gentle, enquiring Frido. Some of the men they tended would never be recognizable. Marcia, too, was able to give voice to a sentiment which Kaspar von Arzfeld could not entertain without offending his traditions –

'It ought to mean, at least, that he won't have to go back.'

'Frido will be distressed at any wound that prevents him serving his country,' said Kaspar sternly.

'Of course. Still, it would be awfully nice if he didn't have to go back, wouldn't it?'

And when Kaspar went to bed that night he reflected on Marcia's words.

'What a strange girl,' he thought. 'Her ways are not our ways, she only thinks of individuals' small happinesses, not of the destiny of nations! All women are to some extent like that, but this one –'

He told himself for the hundredth time, with understanding, that Marcia's position was intolerably difficult. How could one expect her to understand that to a German officer it was the darkest of fates to be prevented from serving in the hour of the Fatherland's peril? He ruminated on Marcia's words as he undressed and knelt to pray beside his cold bed. He was fond of her.

'It would be awfully nice if he didn't have to go back.' He

saw, as so often, in his mind's eye the face of his eldest son, who had loved this girl. He sighed, and thought again of Frido, committing him to Divine protection. He prayed to be saved from self-indulgence, from putting self and family before ideals. But –

'Yes,' he whispered to himself, 'yes, it would be – good – if he did not have to go back.'

Chapter 13

IT WAS NOT UNTIL April, 1942, that Frido eventually reached Arzfeld on his eagerly awaited sick leave. There had been 'complications' after the original amputation; a battle against gangrene, narrowly won. When he eventually arrived Lise wept for joy: but in the privacy of her room came other tears, of anxiety, of distress for her beloved brother.

For Frido was not only terribly thin. He was like a shell from which the inner creature had been anaesthetized and extracted. Outwardly, in spite of what he quietly assured them had been excellent treatment in hospital ('I haven't had such luxury for years!') he was pale, drawn, praeternaturally silent. Lise, who had always been close to Frido, found that she could establish no contact with him. He seemed without animation and so uninterested in life around him that Lise several times found herself wondering whether his brain had been affected.

His manner to Marcia was so 'correct' as to be chilling. She thought, on his first evening home, that she could discern a possible reason – a political, a general rather than a personal reason. By tacit agreement the international situation, the whys and wherefores of the war, were seldom discussed at Arzfeld, and Marcia was grateful for the delicacy with which they shielded her from this. It now appeared, disconcertingly, that Frido only showed life if talk turned to the war. He seemed unable to leave the war alone. On that first evening he stared straight at Marcia after supper. His habitual expression was now so grave that he almost looked accusatory. His father and sister, at least, would have been surprised to learn that as he looked at Marcia his blood was, once again and most painfully, on fire. His words were cold.

'Well, since I was last here, our war has become world war. Goodbye to any hopes of peace in our time!'

'You've been here since this Russian business started,

Frido,' said his father. 'You were here briefly last July before you went east, remember?'

'I didn't mean that. I meant that now we are also at war with America. We are at war, simultaneously, with the largest land power on earth and the two largest maritime powers. To say nothing of the greatest industrial power in the world. Rather a lot for Germany to take on, don't you think?'

Kaspar disliked the turn of the conversation. 'America is chiefly concerned with Japan,' he muttered. 'There's no question but that they forced war on Japan. I can't imagine why.'

'I have no doubt,' said Frido flatly, 'that there will, nevertheless, be some effort available for use against Germany. Anyway, England now has America and American production behind her. It is a different situation from that a year ago. Completely different.'

His father nodded judiciously. Frido's voice was unexpressive as he continued.

'It will be a long war. A very long war. Fought to the death.' Marcia looked at him.

'He does not hate us,' she thought. 'He can't hate anybody. But he is in despair.'

Frido had thought for a long time about how much he properly should say to his father about the war. His mind, always ambivalent about the whole business, had been entirely made up by what he had experienced on the Eastern Front. There was now so much that was loathsome, so much that made him shudder as his mind ranged over it, that he had at first decided only to produce a few soldierly reminiscences, perhaps to discuss the 'general military situation', insofar as an intelligent but very junior officer and an elderly colonel of the Reserve could do so. Kaspar von Arzfeld was, of course, avid to hear all he could. Second only to his joy at welcoming his younger son was his eager anticipation of hearing at first hand something of the Russian campaign. 'How I wish I could see it!' he had grumbled to the girls a hundred times: he had fought in Galicia in the First World War. Now Frido would enable him to see it. This far, Frido had anticipated and would oblige.

But Frido had other memories, dreadful, disturbing memories which it had been his instinct to keep from his father.

He felt that the simple patriotism, the traditional habits of mind of the old colonel could be so confused, so shaken by some of Frido's tales that there might be a collapse of confidence between them. Frido feared that Kaspar, outraged by some of the things Frido had seen and could recount, would tell himself, 'The boy's exaggerating!' It would be easier to avoid excessive frankness, simpler to put certain unspeakable things from his mind, to play a part – a straightforward, modest part – and to tell his father (accurately as far as it went) only the sort of things Kaspar wanted, eagerly, to learn.

Frido, lying in hospital, slowly getting accustomed to the idea of one day being fitted with a replacement leg, managing his crutch, exercizing himself conscientiously and laboriously in the small park beside the hospital – Frido had decided against this prudent course. His relationship with his father had always been a little stiff. He loved and revered Kaspar, but he had always feared him – feared, at least, his disapproval, his incomprehension. Frido had felt himself less satisfactory than Werner, as a von Arzfeld. Yet he wholly respected his father's standards of morality. And there had come a moment, in hospital, when Frido had said to himself – 'Of course I can – I must – speak to my father of *these things*. There can be little hope for mankind, and surely none for Germany if I cannot speak to such a man of *these things*. But it will be hard.' He had felt happier thereafter. He felt he had resolved upon a small, hesitant step down a long, dark passage.

'It looks to me,' said Kaspar, 'as if your old comrades are soon going to be pushed off on another big adventure. Southward.'

He was standing over one of the many maps which adorned his study table. Frido was sitting in a chair, pale, crutch beside him, sufficiently attentive. He had given to his enthralled father a full account of the fighting in Southern Russia at the tail end of 1941. After their triumphs in the Ukraine, after the capture of Kiev and the great encirclement of Soviet troops in the Kiev cauldron, after the crossing of the Dnieper river, the German 'Army Group South' had advanced south and east towards the Sea of Azov. Field Marshal von Rundstedt's command formed thus the northern arm of yet another giant pincer. The southern arm of that pincer was the Rumanian army, advancing eastward from Bessarabia, moving across a great, empty landscape where often for days on end no enemy troops were to be seen.

But as 1941 drew towards its close the Wehrmacht had to admit failure over a large part of the immense front, a front extending more than one thousand miles from north to south. Fresh Russian armies had been drummed up from the eastern regions of the Soviet Union. Field Marshal von Bock's Army Group Centre, inadequately equipped for winter warfare, freezing, famished, confronted huge counter-attacks, and barely hung on to their positions facing Moscow. The emphasis of the high command, after much acrimony and vacillation, was now on the south: on the Crimean peninsula, the great industrial areas of the Donets, Kharkhov, Rostov, the Don.

'The Russians counter-attacked, Father, as you know. Immense counter-attacks, huge masses of men advanced from the east against our forces who were battering their way southward into the Crimea.'

Kaspar nodded, 'Von Manstein,' he murmured.

'Exactly. And then the whole of our Panzer Group was sent south and we, in turn, attacked the northern flank of the Russians who were threatening Manstein. But there were enormous gaps throughout the southern front, Father. A lot of Russia is like the sea . . .' Frido talked on, the 'popular' map of the Eastern Front spread on the table beside him. His father nodded, following every move, digesting his son's impressions, asking a quiet question now and then.

'The weather broke in mid-October, of course,' Frido said. 'None of us could believe the high command expected decisive results from offensives started so late in the year. On the Central front it even started snowing in October! And the mud! My God, the mud! We've got no decent winter equipment, whether against the mud, water or ice. Men are suffering from frostbite in very large numbers – ears, noses, toes – and so forth. Frostbite kills, father.'

Kaspar sighed. An experienced soldier, all his instincts were against criticism. Organizing the supplies of a great Army

202

was inevitably more complex than even the most intelligent youngster generally supposed.

'At least our battle equipment, I imagine, was superior to anything the Russians could bring against us?' he said.

'Not at all. Their best tanks – their T34s – are better than ours.'

'*Better* than ours?'

'Certainly. And whether you're talking of machine, man or beast, the Russians are better prepared for the winter. They understand it.'

Some Soviet units, Frido said, hardly fought at all, their morale suddenly cracked, their only desire surrender. Others held out with extraordinary, chilling tenacity. Their endurance of hardship was something the German soldier, himself no weakling, found a perennial miracle.

'They live on grass if they're cut off from food. They survive in holes in the snow.'

Kaspar looked again at the map. He had, more recently, heard a good deal of which Frido, hospital patient or convalescent, could hardly be aware.

'Well,' he said, 'at least the winter's now past. As I say, I think your old comrades will soon be on the move again, south. That's what I believe.'

'You mean the Caucasus? It's been rumoured for some time,' said Frido quietly. 'It's mad, of course.'

'My son –' said Kaspar von Arzfeld sternly.

'Mad. I agree that it looks as if that's where we'll go next. And it's mad.' Frido stood up, took his crutch and started swinging his body about the room.

'Oh, we'll advance through the Caucasus all right. That's not the point. What comes after? When the Army is already so extended that a strong Russian thrust – a really strong Russian thrust – anywhere, could tear the whole front open.' In a low, unemotional voice, his eyes wide open, remembering, Frido started describing some of the Russian winter attacks.

'The more he talks the better for him,' his father thought.

'They attacked on one occasion across the frozen Don. We saw this great mass of men move down toward the far bank. Our artillery opened up and we heard a fearful wailing and screeching. Then they started coming towards us again, flowing towards us like the sea, and we could see that it was, in most cases, the second wave who had simply taken the places of the first. We saw them climbing over the men in front, yelling and laughing. Laughing! It was a horrible sound, amid all that blood and pain. I don't think there can have been a sober man there. They were drink-mad, insensible.

'They came down to the river, to the Don. Their arms were linked. They had neither the ability nor the thought of using their weapons. Something – drink, demons, – was driving them on, a human tide, screaming "Urra", swaying, thousands followed by other thousands, marching across the great frozen river towards us. Nearer and nearer.

'We were thin on the ground on the Don front. When they were about half-way across our machine guns opened up – the Don is over a kilometre wide there – and the whole lot came down. We could hear those yells of drunkenness and savagery change to screams of pain and terror as our fire found its mark, brought men down, and others staggered and fell, unable to free themselves from their comrades who'd been killed or wounded next to them in the ranks. The machine gun bullets, where they didn't strike flesh, threw up a fine white spray from the ice, rather beautiful. We could see men trying to claw at the solid ice as if they could burrow into it. It was like a great dark, obscene pool of blood spreading across a white carpet. The carpet was the icy Don, the pool of blood was a mass of suffering, writhing, bleeding creatures – more animal than human, or so I'm afraid we all felt –'

'It is shocking,' said Kaspar von Arzfeld austerely, finding his voice, 'shocking for any command, of any nation, to commit soldiers to battle in such a way.'

'Shocking, Father? Perhaps. But it was successful.'

'*Successful?*'

'Oh yes, successful. You see the second wave was immediately followed by a third. And they were protected by the bodies of their predecessors until they were much nearer our bank. And by then, you know, our people were getting low in ammunition. It's not as if we had huge numbers of machine gun posts; and the Russians were going to keep on advancing. "Urra, Urra!" Of course, the cost to them was immense –

horrible. But we pulled our people back. We had to. I know the Russians can't do that everywhere. Their losses have been unbelievable. But where they decide there is a real operational need to punch a hole they won't shrink from a terrible casualty bill – they'll punch that hole. Is that such bad strategy, Father? From their point of view it can surely be argued that an expensive success is still a success: that only failure is really expensive – when there is nothing to put on the credit side of the account.'

Frido was speaking with a sort of chilling irony, as if he could understand certain processes of thought, could even respect them intellectually while finding them entirely odious.

'They have always held human life lightly,' muttered his father.

Frido looked at him thoughtfully. Then he started talking of something different. He spoke of the extraordinary hatred, hatred beyond the ordinary stresses and violence of war, which the campaign in the east seemed to have generated. He told Kaspar of many things.

'The pain and sufferings of war are cruel,' said Kaspar. 'We soldiers understand that although we do not speak much of it. It has always been so.'

'Yes, Father, of course violent death, wounding, the shrieks of men with half their bodies burned away – of course these are terrible; but any soldier who does not expect to see and hear such things, if not to endure them, is a fool. I am not speaking of such things. I am talking of something else.'

Frido told his father of how his company had re-taken a village where a number of German prisoners had been held before being marched to the rear – prisoners taken in one of the first Russian counter-attacks in the summer of 1941. These prisoners, one and all, had been murdered immediately the German attack was in its turn renewed. There had been a chance, Frido acknowledged, that they might have been liberated – freed to fight against Mother Russia once again. No such risk could be taken by their captors. They had been cut down by machine guns and, in many cases, mutilated. Frido spoke quietly.

'Their private parts had been cut off and stuffed into their mouths. Their hands were bound. Those who had survived

205

the bullets had been bayoneted. It had all taken a little time. The lucky ones, of course, died when the guns spoke. None of us knew what they had suffered before that. Large numbers had had their eyes gouged out. I don't think that was done to corpses. There was too much blood. That's what our men found when they retook the village.'

'These are primitives, savages,' said his father grimly. 'It is like fighting against tribes from darkest Africa, not against a people which, until a few years ago, was a Christian people. This is what Bolshevism has done to them!' His voice shook.

Frido seemed to consider, dispassionately.

'I don't think one should say, Father, "*was* a Christian people". In many ways they are still. I have told you frightful things. They were true. But there's another side. When we first went in, last year, we were often given a warm welcome. We opened up the churches, restored them to worship – you've read of that. It was very popular. Religion had been viciously persecuted. We were the people's liberators from the Bolsheviks.'

Kaspar had indeed read of that. 'It made me very proud,' he said. 'I wish these Americans and English who have allied themselves to the Soviets, I wish they understood this. They think that was German propaganda I suppose.'

'It certainly wasn't that. It happened and I saw it. The terrible thing is that the effect is being entirely undone. We had the people as our friends.' Frido was hopping with his crutch up and down the study, up and down. He spoke in a low voice, pausing often.

'They could still be our friends. But now they never will be. Now there is the sort of hatred I've described, the sort of cruelty, savagery, barbarity.

'Do you know what is going on behind our front, Father? No, you cannot. And I will tell you. Or I will tell you a few things. A few little examples.

'A friend of mine was slightly wounded at Kiev – von Hamelstein, the one in our division, I've spoken of him, you know his uncle. He rejoined us after only three weeks. Hamelstein travelled up to us by road most of the way, as it happened, and he went through a number of places the division had passed during the advance. He talked to a lot of officers on the way forward. He told me, privately, what he had discovered.

'There are special units established for security in the rear areas. Enormous numbers of Russians have been murdered – quite simply, murdered. By our own people. In one village all members of the Communist Party – about fifty – had been herded into a barn and shot.

'In another place – a town – Hamelstein learned about the Jews. The Jews, of course, live – or lived – mostly in the towns. In this place there were over two thousand. They'd all been rounded up – men, women and children – and taken to a field outside the town. Then, covered by machine guns, they'd been made to dig a long ditch – about two hundred metres long. When it was done – and it seems they did it, perfectly docile, largely scrabbling earth out with their hands – then they were shot, the lot. And the *Einsatzgruppen* – that's the special security units, so called, the units who do this job – organized some tractors, from the local collective farm to push the bodies into the ditch and cover them. The tractors were driven by Russians, and as the final act they were shot as well and toppled into the ditch. Then the tractors were collected by other Russians. We're meant to be stimulating local agriculture, you see, it's going to help feed the Wehrmacht.

'Hamelstein was told about all this by an SD – *Sicherheit dienst* – officer who was drunk. And that was only one story.'

Kaspar von Arzfeld listened, his eyes never leaving his son's face, following that face, that figure as it swung on the crutch up and down, up and down. Kaspar sat as if turned to stone. Frido's voice remained expressionless.

'That is why, Father, I speak of the hatred which this campaign is generating. Don't misunderstand me. I'm not suggesting the Soviet Government or high command care a damn about their population, their civilians. In fact, there have even been incidents of civilians being herded forward in front of their attacks. Human shields. In an atmosphere so poisoned on both sides by cruelty and evil is it any wonder that men become beasts, and that mercy and decency die?'

Frido stood still for a little. Then he continued. He recalled for his father a phase during the winter fighting, on the Don front. He described how an experienced *Feldwebel* reported one evening. The front was static.

'We should send out a patrol again this evening, *Herr Leutnant.*'

'It's not necessary. We've had no orders to do so, we know all we can about the Russians, and it's twenty degrees below freezing.'

'It's not that, *Herr Leutnant.* There are three wounded men out there. And if we don't reach them the Russians will tomorrow. When we withdraw. We can't leave them alive to the Russians, *Herr Leutnant.* They were good soldiers. We must finish them off.'

It was often done. A patrol was risked on an errand of mercy, to make sure that wounded men did not fall alive into the Russian hands to meet a slow, horrible death as was only too likely.

'Let us sit for a little in the garden,' said Kaspar, who had heard all in a terrible silence. 'It is a fine evening,' he said mechanically. He heard himself saying –

'In spite of all you have told me, I hope the enemy's wounded are decently cared for by our own people.'

Frido considered, 'In the front line, certainly, by which I mean that our field hospitals, as far as I've seen them, do a wonderful job and according to the traditions of the service. They've saved many Russian lives. When I was operated on, for the second time – as you know, gangrene had set in, they were concerned – at that time there were Russian soldiers lying on either side of me. They were both charming boys, too, suffering badly and bravely. We were doing everything for them.'

'In spite of all,' said his father, 'I am greatly relieved to hear you say so.'

'On the other hand I've heard very bad things about prisoner of war camps, or some of them. I spoke to a *Gefreiter* who was operated on at the same time as me and recovering with me. He'd seen a lot of Soviet prisoners. He told me a favourite trick in one camp – where many of them were sick and half-starved anyway – was to make them draw lots, every fifth wretch was hauled out and made to stand against a wall with his hands tied above his head. Then a grenade with the pin drawn out would be put in each of his trouser pockets. Our people thought it was amusing. The *Gefreiter* who told me – of course his tongue was loose, he was in a state of post-operative shock, I suppose – said,

'"You see, *Herr Leutnant*, our men knew that that was nothing compared to what the Ivans did to our prisoners," which I expect is true.'

'I cannot believe it!' said Kaspar, finding his voice, 'I cannot believe it! You have not seen such things yourself!'

Frido looked at his father with sadness.

'No, Father,' he said, 'I've not seen that myself. But, unfortunately, I can believe it. You see, it's that sort of war. Not the sort you fought twenty-five years ago. Not the sort we fought in France. It's a different sort of war. The sort I've been describing.'

Kaspar made a gesture of demurral –

'Surely –'

He looked at his son's expression and held his tongue.

It was indeed a fine evening. Kaspar rose from the wooden bench on which both had been sitting and took his son's arm. Supported by father and crutch Frido swung the full length of the house in silence. There was in the air an exquisite smell of spring.

'It's that sort of war,' said Frido, almost inaudibly. He added, in a near whisper, 'and that sort of Germany.'

Kaspar could find nothing to say. The sort of sententiousness which, surely, was the appropriate response from a father immersed in a tradition of duty to a doubting son seemed wholly out of place. With a sense of charade he heard himself sigh and utter –

'Well, like many of our family you have drawn the sword for the Fatherland –'

'Yes,' said Frido tonelessly. 'Yes, Father. But doesn't it have to be a double-edged sword – with a back-stroke that can cut some standing behind one, some –'

This had gone far enough.

Girls' chatter and laughter sounded from round the corner of the old house. Frido's heart, as it always did and always would, lifted at the sound of Marcia's voice. He raised his hand in stiff salutation as Lise and Marcia walked towards them across the grass.

'Excellent news, Frido,' Lise called. 'Anna Langenbach is coming to stay for a few days. She's not been here for ages. She wants to see you very much. I've just had a letter.'

Anna had paid, with Franzi, one long visit to Arzfeld in the autumn of 1941. She had told a troubled Lise of how disagreeable the local *Kreisleiter* now was to her.

'He hates me, of course. I had to make clear I didn't want his attentions. It happened here, at Arzfeld.' Lise was concerned.

'Anna, you must be careful! You must be a little tactful, even if the man is horrible. There can be so much trouble made for you.'

'It's too late to think of that. I spoke as I had to, from the heart.'

Lise could imagine. Now, however, Anna wrote better news.

'You remember I spoke of a certain person here – he's departed! He's been enrolled to do "special work" for the Government-General in Poland. I'm sure it's very important.'

Nothing more. This must be a profound relief to Anna, thought Lise. The man might always return, and would periodically visit his home on leave, presumably; but the pressure of Schwede's mingled desire and hatred in the same small place had been removed and Anna must be feeling liberation. She could probably manage to avoid him if he only returned for short visits. Anna would be less anxious, more her previous, radiant self.

'She's coming on Tuesday!' Anna had also written –

'The more I think of Frido the more I long to see him and talk to him. He is so steadfast, his instincts are so good. I would trust him with my soul.'

Kaspar still held Frido's arm firmly. He spoke low. None but Frido could hear.

'Frido, my son, it is best, whatever you may think or feel, to say nothing of these things. These are difficult times. They are not – safe times. It is necessary to be very, very prudent.' His voice was unsteady and only just audible. His son looked at him with love and, for the first time in his life, with

210

compassion. Then Kaspar released his grip on Frido's arm and spoke to the girls with his usual agreeable courtesy.

'Excellent news, indeed, little Lise! Anna loves the summer here. I have told her that she should always plan to bring her little son to Arzfeld for every July. But it is good that she should come, too, in the spring. We cannot have her here too often.'

Chapter 14

———————◆———————

IT WAS December, 1942, and their fourth day on the hill. B Company had arrived in darkness, astonished and relieved to be told they had reached what they had understood was going to be a strongly defended objective – reached it without difficulty. Some shells had fallen among the rear companies as the battalion moved forward silently through the night, but these had, by good luck, done no harm. In front there had been nothing – no enemy machine gun fire, no mines, no reaction: nothing. The word had been muttered, 'Dig in,' and on stony and inhospitable ground they had done their best, scratching holes, enlarging them. Fear of the enemy's fire, so uncannily silent, struggled against exhaustion. 'Dig in.' In some places solid rock ordained that the erection of stone-piled breastworks had to replace the excavation of trenches.

'They look like grouse butts,' Anthony thought, as dawn began to reveal the battalion to itself.

Dawn did not come as a friend. Anthony was now a Captain, second-in-command of B Company. He and his brother officers, the day before their attack, had had the opportunity to look at the landscape from a neighbouring hill, to study the objective. They had seen, as if looking at a stage from far back in the dress circle of a theatre, the large, bare hill they were to assault that night. The hills of Tunisia were dark in colour. From a distance they looked grey and forbidding, with the rough, ridged texture of an elephant's hide. The lower ground was brown, with much scrub. Here and there were fields – patches of earth where there appeared to have been attempts at cultivation, to European eyes haphazard and unsystematic. Yet Arabs tilled this ground, and presumably owned it. As Anthony looked through his binoculars at the objective B Company was to attack in a few hours' time, two Arabs rode out on donkeys into the low, intervening plain: they

212

dismounted and began to work, scratching the resistant surface of the ground, pausing often in their labours, desultory, seemingly undeterred by the occasional sights and sounds of battle. Guns sounded in the distance. There was a sort of absurdity in the scene. Yet, for a little, these Arabs engaged in their primitive agriculture seemed more real in their struggle for survival than did the contenders for that dark, silent hill where a battalion of strongly entrenched German troops would try to kill the attacking British as they climbed up and along the elephant's hide, and must, therefore, themselves be efficiently killed. It was not the Arabs' quarrel.

And then, in darkness, there had been silence, anti-climax. No opposition. Arrival, by every calculation, at the correct point, unopposed. An hour later dawn had come, and as the early morning mist cleared every man could see that the crest they had reached was a false one. Ahead, and overlooking them, was a further crest. It was significantly higher. It had been invisible from their original observation point. And there was soon no doubt, no doubt whatsoever, that it was held by the Germans. Shells began to fall. Almost as bad was the fact that their supply route, the way they had taken forward, was, like most of their own positions, also overlooked by the enemy on the next crest.

It was the battalion's first battle. A few, like Anthony, had joined from another battalion after experience of that other battle, in France. To most men, of whatever rank, it was their baptism of fire. The first lessons learned were not new, but they were viciously taught. Anthony looked at the dark, menacing ridge in front of them, topped by black rain clouds, as dawn gave way to morning and shelling intensified.

'If I ever have anything to do with it, which is unlikely,' he thought, 'I'll never, *never* again sit down in front of an enemy who's occupying higher ground than me!'

The ridge beyond them was, in truth, only a little higher, but to the men of B Company it felt as if the Germans could peer into every British slit trench, could engage in observed target practice at their leisure. They felt naked and impotent.

Their spirits, nevertheless, were extraordinarily high. Every small fold in the ground was used to produce some sort of cover. Men worked with frantic energy to improve trenches, to find ground where digging was possible, to construct the bleak, sodden habitations of the battlefield and to carve some kind of protected way between them. In these circumstances the journey to or from a particular platoon's position was an adventure, the laughter and companionship found there something different from other laughter, other companionship. It had an edge to it, a nervous zest, profoundly experienced.

'I'm frightened most of the time,' said Anthony to himself. 'I'm soaking wet, I'm hellish uncomfortable, and I'm not even convinced that we're winning this little bit of the war. But there's nowhere – absolutely nowhere – that I want to be except here.'

On their second day he had to go back to attend for orders at Battalion Headquarters. When he returned to the scratches in the rock – half dug-out, half-cave fortified by piled earth and heaped stones – which constituted Company Headquarters, Anthony found an extraordinary sense of homecoming. Away from the little world of B Company he had felt a stranger. The Company Sergeant-Major, Phillips, held out a mug of tea to him when he returned.

'Tea, sir?'

Anthony looked at him and thought he had never known friendship until that hour.

It was hard to decide whether wind or rain was worse, although often, of course, they came together. The rain filled such trenches as could be dug. The wind struck with an icy, penetrative power which none of them had experienced before. German shelling was alarming but sporadic, rather than insistent: until the fourth day there had only been six casualties from shelling in B Company. Men were encouraged to leave the trenches and stretch their limbs, to show by this small act of defiance that their spirits were unaffected by the enemy's guns, to warm themselves in the occasional sun. Some might then be too slow or too unlucky to take cover again before a German salvo arrived: but it had not happened yet and the hazard, Anthony reckoned, was well worth it.

The worse aspect of their life was the sense that they could do nothing to hit back. They heard with enthusiasm the sound of British artillery, pounding positions the far side of that menacing crest line above and beyond them, answering the

German guns which harried themselves. But although it was at first hourly and then daily expected, there was no German attack. The men of B Company had no chance to use their own weapons. Their fate had been to advance in darkness, to halt, to dig, to find themselves overlooked, cut off, vulnerable: and then, simply, to endure. There was, they supposed, no thought of withdrawing them. It did not seem that the high command contemplated, just yet, a further attack. And the Germans appeared content to wait, to drop shells among B Company with intermittent ferocity, and to bide their time.

Supply had to be entirely by night. By day, German binoculars could focus on every route that led to them, from any direction. Their supply vehicles were well to the rear, in some woods near the foot of the hill. Movement of any kind was laborious. Getting wounded men back off the hill had been particularly hard, and in this, as in most things, Sergeant-Major Phillips had played an heroic part. An abrupt, high-principled Tynesider, with a rough tongue, he had shown himself careless of personal safety and tireless where the life or health of a single man in his Company might be at risk. By now every man in B Company, from the best to the worst, would have lain down with an appropriate oath and gladly have suffered Phillips to walk over him had the Sergeant-Major, improbably, so desired.

Now it was mid-morning on the fourth day. Anthony's Commander, Major Richard Wright, was at a conference at Battalion Headquarters, near the base of the hill, close to the track which wound through woods in the valley behind them, connected to something like the outside world. It was generally expected that he would return with news, plans, orders. Perhaps they would be relieved. The day had started well. Supplies had come forward in the hours of darkness. Anthony had been at Company Headquarters.

'Mail, Captain Marvell, sir.'

Everybody devoured letters, letters able to transport them in imagination to another, safer, drier world; a world filled with regular sleep, predictable activity, a world sweetened by the bodies of women, the gentle, the soft, the personal. Sometimes there was no time to read a letter: it had to be stuffed into a pocket, eagerly anticipated, treasured. But whatever the pressure, a man would instantly and hungrily tear open a letter if he possibly could. Men shielded the precious paper from the rain with the improvised cover afforded by their groundsheets, buried their faces in their letters, eyes moving up and down the lines, lips moving.

For Anthony it was a good moment for the arrival of letters. Things seemed extraordinarily quiet. A mug of tea and some tinned sausage and beans had made a delicious breakfast. He settled into a corner of B Company's headquarter cave. The letter was from his mother. Hilda was an excellent correspondent. She gave enough – but not too much – detail of their quiet doings at Bargate, enough to bring its gentle peace instantly before Anthony's eyes. Hilda knew how to do this without the appearance of design. She knew how casual reference to some paintwork in dilapidation, to some village eccentricity, would evoke home vividly, catch at Anthony's heart. She never overdid it. Then she wrote of serious things, of books, of thoughts. Whenever possible, she sent books to her son, and he delighted in writing to her his views on them, responding, arguing. Their minds were not unlike. They had always been able to talk to each other. As he read her letter Anthony could smell smoke from the fire in the inner hall of Bargate, hear birds outside the windows, see a print hanging slightly askew against the dark panelling.

'Of course,' Hilda Marvell's letter ran, towards its end, 'the Americans now being in the war does mean one feels a *total* gulf between us and Marcia. Before, when the USA had diplomatic relations with Germany, one always had the feeling, however far-fetched, that something, somehow, might be done. Now there's a great, grim wall across the whole world and reaching to the sky. We're on one side of it, and our darling Marcia is on the other. She must feel like that too. I'm afraid I hope so.'

Hilda was Anthony's chief correspondent. His father wrote briefly and prosaically. Other men grunted with pleasure at letters from wives, sweethearts. There were the domesticated types who read silently, thinking of home, firelight, peace. There were the lechers, the boasters, who used letters as evidence of amorous triumphs, to be savoured in recollection, sometimes quoted aloud. There were a few who never received

216

letters at all, for whom the cry 'Mail' generally induced a determined concentration on cleaning a rifle, attention to some small personal task, an averting of the eyes, shamed by neglect. 'And I,' thought Anthony, 'I have no lover to write letters to me.' His lover, too, was on the other side of what Hilda called that great grim wall across the whole world. And could she even think of him now? Was she alive? And where? But although he thought of Anna with a longing entirely undimmed by more than three years apart he thought of her with a certain inner contentment. This woman had loved him, borne his child (if Bob O'Reilly were to be believed – and why not?) and was a woman of such quality as few of his luckier, more satisfied comrades could ever dream of. And he, at least, could dream.

There was a whistle and a distant crump. Shells falling on C Company away to the north, on their left.

Letter stuffed into his pack and left at Company Headquarters, Anthony walked across to B Company's right-hand platoon, putting much effort into demonstrating a nonchalance he seldom felt. Shelling in the Company area, the right-hand forward company of the battalion, had been light since the previous evening.

The platoon – the right-hand forward platoon of the entire battalion front – was commanded by Sergeant Brinson, a lugubrious, reliable man. The Platoon Commander, Lieutenant Peter Worldham, a cheerful, impertinent, irrepressible youth had been one of B Company's casualties on the second day. They'd heard nothing about him since. As Sergeant-Major Phillips had briskly organized the stretcher party which took him down the hill Anthony had had a word –

'You'll be all right, Peter.'

Worldham had smiled. Anthony saw the pain behind the smile and feared that the shell splinter had found the stomach. Now Sergeant Brinson managed the platoon, in an austere sort of way. 'Everybody does things in his own fashion,' thought Anthony, 'and there's no doubt Brinson gives them confidence. They feel that even the Germans wouldn't take liberties with him.'

Sergeant Brinson, for once, seemed less than alert. He gave

no sign of registering Anthony's arrival. He was leaning against the end face of his slit trench, his head apparently in his right hand, very still. Private Wilcox, who shared the trench with him, grinned at Anthony and saluted. He turned half-apologetically to Sergeant Brinson. It was beginning to rain again.

'Captain Marvell, Sergeant.'

Brinson did not move.

'Sergeant –'

'Sh – sh – sh!'

Anthony stood on the edge of the slit trench and looked down into it. If they heard that dreaded, familiar, rushing sound, the fanfare of a German salvo, he would have to join them sharply. Wilcox was large. The trench was not.

''Morning, Sergeant Brinson.'

Brinson now turned his head thoughtfully, saluted Anthony with deliberation, turned his head back in the previous direction and said quietly,

'Listen to this, sir!'

Anthony listened. The wind was not as sharp and cruel as it had been but it produced background noise to all other sound. No guns were speaking. For Tunisia it was a quiet morning.

'What is it, Sergeant Brinson?'

'Listen, sir!'

Then Anthony heard it.

The wind dropped for a moment and he heard it. Without question. The sound of engines, rising to a roar, falling to nothing. The intermittent, clattering creak of steel tracks. To the right of Sergeant Brinson's platoon the ground fell steeply to a valley floor. There had never been anything to stop the Germans, were they so minded, from driving past that right flank, moving along the valley, threatening the right rear of the Battalion.

There was another lull in the force of the wind. The sound came to them now more strongly and more steadily. Three things were certain. These were tanks. They were German. And they were not very far away.

Although Anthony did not know it, Richard Wright, his Company Commander, was at that moment making his way back to B Company in an agony of concern. Meanwhile, Anthony was in command. The sound of tanks rose and fell. The slope to the valley was convex. The enemy seemed to be moving around their right, towards the rear company of the Battalion. D Company.

An artillery observation officer had a trench near the lip of the hill, whence the valley could be observed. Anthony decided to visit him. He was not sure that it was the right moment to pay a call, strictly speaking outside the perimeter of his own company area. On the other hand he could see little. He felt a mighty need to know more of what was happening.

Anthony reached the artilleryman's post without incident. The latter, a young man with a high forehead and the manner of a junior and ebullient university don, had already won friends among B Company with his manifest enthusiasm and competence. He now pointed downwards with quiet enjoyment.

'There they are!'

There were, as far as Anthony could count, fourteen German tanks. They were moving, as he had assumed, toward the right rear of the battalion. The nearest was about a thousand yards away. They looked like beetles.

'They've shown no signs of turning this way,' said the Gunner quietly, 'and there's a battery of the regiment' ('he means his regiment – twenty-five pounders –' thought Anthony) 'in a position down there, when they turn the corner.' He brought his binoculars up again.

'Look at that!'

'That' was a body of German infantry, following the tanks. Small parties were moving in a rapid, workmanlike way along the valley floor and traversing the lower slopes of the hill. *Their* hill! Men were hung with ammunition belts for the light machine guns which many toted. The prominent stick grenades, and their helmets, unique among the combatant armies, gave their silhouettes a sinister fascination. The Gunner officer was talking urgently into the microphone of his radio set. It was a promising target for artillery fire, although the German groups were well dispersed.

Anthony looked to his left. It was surely unlikely that the enemy would neglect their hill altogether. They would, at least, seek to mask it, to sweep it clean of the British sufficiently to make sure their own advance up the valley was not overlooked by hostile observers. That implied a simultaneous attack any time now. The convex shape of the hill made approaches to it from below difficult to detect. It would also, Anthony reckoned, make the movement of tanks laborious, although not impossible. The lower slopes were not only steep: they were extraordinarily rocky. Any attack would be an infantry attack.

Anthony's view from the artillery observation post was a good one. He scanned as much as he could of the ground below Sergeant Brinson's platoon.

Then he saw it.

He held his binoculars firmly, focused on a particular outcrop of rock. One rounded stone on the surface was darker than the rest.

It shifted.

It disappeared.

Anthony swung his binoculars to a point further along the hillside. A thornbush was prominent between two boulders. Beside the thornbush were two dark objects, small, dead branches lying on the ground perhaps.

One moved sharply, followed by the other.

Anthony grabbed the Gunner's arm.

'There are helmets and boots coming up this hill. I'm getting back to the Company.' He pointed.

'Got them!' said the Gunner softly, his binoculars up. 'Got them!' He started talking rapidly into his microphone.

'Good luck!' said Anthony. His mouth was dry. 'You may not have much longer here. Some of them are bound to come this way.'

The other grinned.

'If I have to go back I'll scramble over to your Company Headquarters. If it's still there.' He returned to scrutiny of the valley, binoculars in one hand, microphone in the other. British shells were beginning to explode in the valley.

Anthony ran back to Sergeant Brinson's platoon.

'They're climbing up the hill below you. The Gunners will

220

hit them as hard as they can. I should think they're about seven hundred yards away.'

Brinson nodded sternly. His platoon, now at a strength of twenty-eight men, was posted for just this contingency and he implied that the Germans, for once, were behaving properly and obliging by turning up where expected. Brinson's riflemen and light machine gunners could engage any enemy climbing over the right-hand crest at a range of 150 yards exactly. Brinson liked that. It was close quarter work at which his men's marksmanship should be deadly. To have moved forward, further over the convex slope in search of a longer field of fire as some inexperienced soldiers might have done, would have been to expose his platoon to German tank and mortar fire at ever longer ranges. Major Wright, his Company Commander, had posted the platoons – skilfully. Brinson had sited every trench, moving round with young Worldham before the little fellow had been hit, getting his eye down to ground level, weighing it up. He had several well concealed observation trenches forward of the crest, manned at night. He had a pair of men as observers there by day. They had a covered route back over the crest and he'd withdraw them in good time. Brinson's men were in the proper place all right. He said quietly –

'Well, they ought to walk into a Battalion mortar task very nicely, sir.' For one of the pre-arranged tasks for the Battalion mortars was immediately behind the crest line over which German infantry, vulnerable, laden, would have to scramble to reach Brinson's platoon.

'Yes, we've got Corporal Jacks up here.' Corporal Jacks was a mortar fire controller.

'Are there a lot of them, sir?'

'I couldn't tell. They're moving up pretty slowly, keeping low. We only picked them up by chance. And of course it's steep going. I expect they're covered by tanks and mortar observers in the valley or on the far hill. They won't see you till they top the crest.'

Brinson's mouth was set, as ever, in a disapproving line. His eyes were calculating and calm. He fixed them on the near crest line. His men were all in their slit trenches. He had called a few brief commands to them, unhurried, businesslike. He communicated strength and confidence.

221

'Right, sir,' Brinson said. 'And the Gunner OP can see this hill face opposite us can he, sir?'

'He can. But there'll come a moment when he'll have to pull out. He's pretty exposed.'

'I've got Corporal Vincent watching from the forward trench. He'll probably see something soon. They'd hardly put less than a company at us, would they, sir?' It was an assertion, sensible, unalarmed. A German company probably meant about one hundred men, infiltrating between platoon positions, rushing section trenches amid a flurry of hurled stick grenades and close quarter machine carbine fire, all supported by Spandau light machine gun teams working their way forward from rock to gully, cleft to fold in ground, taking the defenders in flank.

'Hardly less than a Company. You'd better get Corporal Vincent back. Good luck, Sergeant Brinson.'

Anthony ran off. They both knew that the hill where they stood was very prominent, very commanding: a desirable piece of tactical real estate. Yes, the Germans would hardly launch less than a company at it. They might easily commit a battalion – several companies – at the same time as pushing tanks and infantry up the valley floor. The Germans by now knew perfectly well that their enemies could only get stronger, and that they were running a losing race against time. The troops of General Anderson's First Army, operating eastward after their landing in November at Algiers, had already been joined by an American and a French Corps. Far away in the Western Desert the British Eighth Army, fresh from their great victory at El Alamein under General Montgomery, was moving towards Tripoli and would certainly advance into Tunisia and join hands with First Army. The Germans must be doomed – in the end. Meanwhile, they were showing every sign of a vigorous, and possibly successful assault on the hill on which Anthony's men were deployed.

Anthony reached Company Headquarters. At the same moment, with a whistle and a series of cracks, the first German mortar shells began to hit B Company.

Chapter 15

JUST AFTER MIDDAY the first German attacks struck two of Anthony's three platoons simultaneously: they coincided, too, with the arrival back of Richard Wright at his Company Headquarters. Thereafter, events were confused for a period which Anthony discovered later to have been only about forty minutes. This was astonishing. It seemed in retrospect as if a whole day had been spent in that opening battle.

The German infantry worked their way forward by a series of short rushes, interspersed with agile crawling, to two small folds in the ground, one between B Company's two forward platoons and one outside the left flank of the left-hand platoon – not Brinson's. The effect was to produce, very suddenly, German machine gun fire that drummed inwards in sharp, staccato bursts at the forward platoons of the Company.

Immediately thereafter the assault came in over the lip of the hill – more infantrymen, accompanied by much shouting, aiming at Brinson's platoon and the right-hand trenches of its neighbour. There was a great deal of noise. German mortar shells were falling in clusters among B Company. These always seemed to Anthony to be directed with superhuman accuracy, as if able to search and find individual trenches and men. It was astonishing, after enduring intense mortar fire, to find anybody left alive: but most people usually were. Anthony wondered, without much confidence, whether Allied shell and mortar fire appeared to the enemy comparably lethal. British shells and bombs could now be heard exploding, their dust visible, beyond the crest to the front whence the Germans had come, along the reverse slopes of the ridge.

The machine gun fire was now deafening. The Spandau bursts sounded like some demonic dentist's drill. Answering them came the rather slower, friendly sound of the British Bren guns, firing from every section position. And every British rifleman was pumping bullets into whatever he could see of an enemy *landser* creeping or rushing toward or past him, now crawling among the rocks, now suddenly upright to loose toward a British slit trench a murderous burst of fire from a machine pistol, or arching the body, like a participant in some bizarre athletic event, to hurl a stick grenade. From every quarter of the Company area came the sombre cry 'stretcher bearers'. Sergeant-Major Phillips, quiet, indefatigable, organized them and a hundred other things. And Anthony, too, found himself doing what seemed a hundred things at once, most of them requiring him to shout at the top of his voice. Now Anthony could see the Company area speckled with grey bodies, bodies that did not move, did not seek to evade the bullets criss-crossing the hillside. There were dead and dying British soldiers in the slit trenches: by now there was no doubt of that. But all could see they had taken their toll. The direct assault from the front seemed to have been discontinued. B Company still held its ground.

The worst threat appeared to be from a party of Germans who had infiltrated into a hollow between B Company and their neighbours to the left, C Company. This hollow – ground into which neither company could easily see – was marked at the rim by a line of scrub. From that rim – at a distance of about two hundred yards from the left-hand platoon of B Company – what sounded like four German machine guns were firing. A burst followed every movement in B Company area.

There had been no firing for a little time when Wright jumped into the Headquarters trench with Anthony. Several slits had been connected to provide, as it were, a battle station and observation post for Company Headquarters. These were in turn ingeniously linked by a short excavated way down to the rocks, half cave, half dugout, which provided Company Headquarters with some working space. In this latter nest was their radio set, their link to Battalion Headquarters. Anthony had alternated between cave and trench during the flurry and confusion of the German attack. The trench had twelve inches of slimy mud at its base. It was a wretched place but it felt extraordinarily safe compared to the ground above it. Anthony had, for much of the last forty minutes, manned the radio set, kept Battalion Headquarters informed as well as he could, received in turn laconic accounts of what was supposed to be happening in other parts of the Battalion area. Then he had returned to the forward trench whence Wright had been doing his best to stay master of B Company. Now there was something of a lull.

Wright had been tireless – and fearless. He had encouraged every platoon in turn, exposing his body in what appeared suicidal fashion. He had, the Company would remember afterwards, seemed present everywhere, steadying men, helping them with a laugh or a curse at exactly the moment when doubt or terror was in danger of striking. Anthony knew that no small part of his own fears was that Richard Wright might fall; and Anthony still felt inadequate to taking his place. Yet Wright seemed positively to be courting a German bullet, inviting a fragment from a mortar bomb or a stick grenade.

And Anthony knew that he, Anthony Marvell, had, in some way, found himself upon that inhospitable hill. He knew that in the nervous minutes before Richard Wright returned he had acted and spoken decisively, had not been half-looking for the confirmation of others that he was right, had been in fact as well as by rank Captain of the Company. Later he had enjoyed being ahead of events, anticipating what the Company Commander would need –

'We'll have to get some more to 6 platoon.'

'I've done that. They're well stocked now.'

'Thanks, Anthony. Well done.'

Ever since 1940 Anthony had found himself growing in confidence and strength. He seldom stuttered now. He still had something coltish in his movements, still retained a recognizable amount of the undergraduate who brought to each new relationship, to every fresh companion, a certain impulsive intensity, generally mixed with laughter. But Anthony had grown up. Indeed, he sometimes felt almost middle-aged in his maturity. When he allowed himself to think of it he recognized the chief reason for this. Nobody who had been Anna Langenbach's lover – who was still, he sometimes thought painfully to himself, her faithful lover – could feel less than a man. And now, outfacing the Germans somehow on a bleak Tunisian hillside, he knew that he was, too, a soldier.

225

The rear platoon of the Company, No. 6 platoon, had been relatively unscathed. Posted on a sharp reverse slope where the hill behind them fell more steeply, these thirty men constituted a backstop. They were also largely protected by the pitch of the ground from any but high trajectory German shells or bombs. No. 6 platoon was commanded by the third surviving officer of B Company, Second Lieutenant Thomas Vane. He was a quiet, rather dreamy youth. Wright had, from Vane's first days in B Company, found him an irritation.

'Not an adult, yet,' he snorted. 'That's his trouble. Babyface.'

Anthony was less sure. He had observed Vane closely on their second day on the hill, when shelling for the first time was really heavy, and some of it appeared to be searching the slope where 6 platoon were entrenched. Vane showed not the slightest concern. Anthony had walked down to 6 platoon area and found the Platoon Commander sitting in the bottom of his slit trench reading. A vicious ten minutes of German attention had just concluded. Vane looked up, and struggled to his feet with a gentle smile. The Company Second in Command might find fault, although he didn't see why.

'Enjoying your book, Tommy?'

'Yes, thanks.' He held it up to Anthony's enquiring look. Homer! In paperback.

'I doubt if there's another Homer being read on any battle-front in the world in December, 1942, Tommy! How's it going?'

'Homer! Oh I enjoy it, it's a splendid antidote to – to rain, or things like that.'

'What about the last stonk? All well?'

'Yes, we've been lucky. It's a good place this. They pass over and explode a good fifty feet below us! The platoon are getting well used to it now, aren't they, Sergeant Cubbon?'

'They're all right, sir,' said Sergeant Cubbon.

Wright had first thought that Cubbon, a notably outspoken Battalion boxer, would despise Vane. Now, Anthony thought as he listened to the note in Cubbon's voice and watched his face, Cubbon was rather proud of him. That had been on the second day. Vane had said seriously as Anthony left,

'Is there anything I ought to be doing?'

Anthony had laughed.

'Nothing as far as I can see. Get back to the Iliad.'

Nothing in the intervening period had shaken Anthony's view that Vane was all right – perhaps even very good. Now it mattered. Wright squelched along the Company Headquarters trench and gripped Anthony by the upper arm.

'We've got to turn out those sods in the hollow. They've done quite a bit of damage, they're getting 4 platoon down.'

No. 4 platoon had lost seven men, several of them cut down by those vicious Spandaus in the hollow to their left.

'I'm going to pick up 6 platoon and go for them. Work round the contour, and pump in everything we can from 4 platoon. At the same time get all the gunner support we can, concentrated on the hollow.'

Artillery had the hollow registered, and an artillery observer was with B Company Headquarters and listening. He nodded. 'I've already been on and told them what you want to do, sir. All they need are your timings. But we won't get more than two batteries on it, I don't think. You see –'

Anthony cut in quickly –

'You say you're going to "pick-up" 6 platoon, Richard? Lead them yourself, you mean?'

'Of course. Can't send Tommy Vane on this one on his own.'

'I think he'd do it very well.'

'Well, we'll never know –' Wright gave out some quick orders, timings. Sergeant-Major Phillips listened quietly, his face impassive. A series of explosions sounded from nearer the crest of the hill, followed by a familiar cry –

'Stretcher bearers!'

The cry came from the direction of Sergeant Brinson's platoon. It was possible to reach this, moving along a contour of the hill with circumspection, avoiding the machine guns in the hollow.

'Bugger!' Wright stood up, careless of his prominence, head and chest above the slit trench lip. He yelled –

'Who is it?'

'Sergeant Brinson, sir! Mortar!'

'I know it was a mortar, you bloody fool!' Wright cursed meaninglessly below his breath.

Brinson and his brave platoon had not been dislodged by all the German assaults from front and flank. Beneath a hail of bullets and grenades Brinson had been steady, disapproving, unshaken. Now a mortar bomb had found him: poor, sour-faced, gallant Brinson. He had lost, although they were not yet sure of it at Company Headquarters, nine men out of his twenty-eight. The platoon would now be commanded by Corporal Fletcher, a Battalion weight-putter, phlegmatic, slow of movement and, some thought, of wit.

At this moment there came a confusion of shouting and some bursts of Bren gun fire from the left-hand platoon, No. 4. A handful of Germans could be seen to jump from the hollow and start to run towards 4 platoon. As quickly they jumped back again.

'Stretcher bearers!'

Sergeant-Major Phillips, organizer of stretcher bearers, marshalling, encouraging, never raising his voice, was active again.

'We've lost a large part of our right forward platoon, including the commander,' Anthony thought. 'The left forward platoon are shaken, and within close range of a bunch of Germans who are trying to get at them any minute. The only platoon of the three who haven't had it too bad is No. 6. Now Richard's going to lead No. 6 in a charge into the hollow. And if that settles *their* hash there won't be much of B Company left to face the next serious German attack.' He knew that he had a weakness, or he supposed it was such: he could see the gloomy possibilities of situations with too much ease. As if responding to his thoughts, Wright said,

'We've got to clear them out of that hollow, come what may!'

Anthony saw for the first time blood running down his Company Commander's wrist and Wright saw Anthony's eyes. His own voice was impatient.

'It's nothing. Now look –'

Anthony held up his hand. He heard a call from the cave.

'Captain Marvell!'

The signaller didn't know that Wright was with him. Anthony dived down and snatched the headset. The radio was carefully placed to gain maximum protection but in such a way that its aerial could perform its function. He listened to an

228

urgent voice from Battalion Headquarters. He acknowledged the message. Richard Wright appeared at the entrance to the cave.

'Richard, it sounds as if D Company were hit pretty hard by that tank attack up the valley, past us. What's left of D have been moved back to the woods. Couldn't hang on. Quite a lot knocked out.'

'Christ!' said Wright. 'That means –'

They stared at each other, thoughts of an imminent counter-attack by 6 platoon into the hollow temporarily obliterated.

'It means,' Wright said softly, 'that the bastards are between us and Battalion Headquarters. They're pretty well all round us. And all round C Company.' He gazed at Anthony, hardly seeing him, his mind working, his eyes bright. There was still blood running down his hand, through his fingers.

'He really is at his best,' Anthony thought, with a twinge – not for the first time – of rather jealous astonishment. 'He's enjoying this. I'll swear he is!'

'Right! I'm going to move 5 platoon back –'

'Sh – sh!' Anthony listened again and acknowledged again. It was a long message. It contained clear orders. He might have brought Wright to the set but Wright, surprisingly, was somewhat inept talking on radio. His blunt assurance, his decisiveness left him. He was apt to be hesitant and verbose. Anthony looked up.

'We're to withdraw tonight.'

'*Give up this bloody hill!*'

'Give up this bloody hill. C Company first, to the Pimple. Then us, through them.'

The Pimple was a round, convex bump over which the tracks ran to the forward companies. It was six hundred yards to their rear. Anthony told him the orders about timing. Wright's eyes blazed.

'We've beaten them! We've not been driven off this hill!'

'I imagine,' said Anthony, 'that if we were left here the Battalion would be sliced in two. And as we're not going back till the small hours of tomorrow morning, we've got plenty of time to show we've not been driven off this hill. We've got to hold it for hours still!' It was just before three o'clock in the afternoon.

'Is the whole Battalion going back, sir?' asked Sergeant-Major Phillips.

Anthony guessed so.

'We're to withdraw through C Company on the Pimple. We're to go into reserve in the area of that clearing in the woods where Battalion Headquarters were before we advanced four days ago. Behind those shacks we passed in the darkness, coming up.'

'Bloody place!' said Wright automatically. 'Right! It's not going to be easy. Unless we want to go back arm-in-arm with these bloody krauts.' He was muttering, thinking aloud –

'We'll have to put up quite a show, give the impression we're going for them, make them sit tight, give ourselves time to get away.' His head turned suddenly. Like a dog sensitive before others to an alien sound Wright could sniff danger or battle a moment or two ahead of the rest. He was never mistaken.

'Here they come again, sir!' called Sergeant-Major Phillips. The Spandaus had opened up from the hollow as Wright and Anthony raced up from cave to slit trench. At the same time a new wave of Germans came over the crest in front of what had been Sergeant Brinson's platoon. As before they came in short rushes, whistles blowing, words of command shouted, stick grenades hurled from now here, now there. Anthony could count about twenty. But the rush seemed to spend its force more quickly than before. Was it wishful thinking, or had the enemy lost heart?

'That's my lot, sir.'

Corporal Fletcher grunted the words in the darkness. Last platoon past the checkpoint. Wright had thinned the Company out from rear to front, keeping a bold face to the enemy, dressing B Company's shop window, up to the last moment. He had posted a patrol forward when darkness fell, in some trenches dug earlier and later abandoned when company losses mounted, but occupied by neither side. Wright re-occupied them, and later ordered a timely demonstration of fire and grenade throwing in the general direction of the German infil-

230

trators in the hollow, in the heart of B Company's forward area. Let those Germans be alerted – but defensive! Let them reconsider any attack plans of their own in the face of this aggressiveness! Under cover of this demonstration, noise ripping the air, the patrol slipped back and, on cue, the forward platoons stole away. Rear sections first: forward trench men last: each past a platoon checkpoint: each platoon past Anthony. And then on, in single file, down a steep stony track in the wet dark night.

'That's my lot, sir.' Corporal Fletcher, so far, was handling his responsibilities with aplomb. His breathing in the darkness was so stertorous that it seemed impossible the Germans did not share the information he imparted, just as his boots struck rock with a sound which, in Anthony's nervous perception, must be audible in Tunis itself. But from beyond the now abandoned trenches no sound came.

The line of soaked, tired, filthy and hungry men began filing off the hill: it had been decided to try to feed them after, not before, withdrawal. Next they should pass the Pimple, with C Company in position upon it. C Company sentries would be expecting them. Everybody's nerves were taut, the strain telling on men whose resistance was already lowered by exposure and fatigue. Men who had been gallant when the Germans had been advancing upon them, who had held their ground steadfastly, now stumbled through the night fearfully, without assurance. An accidental collision in the darkness evoked a savage curse, hissed with venom albeit between trench-mates, beloved friends. The rain came down without mercy. It would be light in about three hours, the grey, cold light of a Tunisian dawn.

The leading platoons of B Company must, Anthony reckoned, be approaching the Pimple by now. He was moving with the rear of the column, ears pricked for any menacing sound behind them. The men in front seemed to be halted, immediately sinking to the ground with what was, in small part, the soldier's instinct to get down, and in much larger part was sheer exhaustion. A whisper ran through the files in front. Anthony began to pass men, brushing his way forward down the sodden, silent column. A figure was standing in the middle of the track.

'Who's that!' It was a low, suspicious grunt, the only permissible mode of speech.

'Captain Marvell. Which platoon's this?'

'5 Platoon, sir. C Company's sentries just ahead. On your feet, lads.'

The column in front seemed to be moving again.

Men lurched to their feet, breathing their swear words, shifting the weight of their damp packs on their aching shoulders. At that moment a familiar sound sent them flat again.

'Get down, get down!'

Nobody needed the order. The first German shells hit the Pimple at exactly the moment when B Company was beginning to file through the covering position established there. Whistle, crump, crack, whistle, crump, crack – this was no casual, harassing fire. Concentrated, intensive, it could mean only one thing. A German attack! A German night attack against a company in hastily adopted, temporary, positions, with another company passing through them, on the march to the rear. To emphasize that this was, indeed, the situation, the unmistakable sound of several Spandau machine guns cut the night air. The Spandaus were firing from the flank of the line of B Company's withdrawal – from the direction of the valley down which German tanks and infantry had advanced that morning towards the Battalion's rear, overrunning the hapless D Company.

With a good deal of relief Anthony heard Wright's voice in the darkness, near at hand down the track. Wright was shouting. There was no longer the slightest need for quiet.

'Anyone seen Captain Marvell?'

'It's Major Wright! Anthony heard a man mutter, wholly unnecessarily, to his neighbour. Anthony, without surprise, recognized the touch of relief, of confidence in the soldier's voice.

'Captain *Marvell*?' Wright was bellowing.

'I'm here!' Anthony moved as fast as he could in the darkness towards Wright's voice. On either side of the track men were crouching, lying, wriggling into fire positions, facing the general direction of the Spandau fire. The German bullets were for the moment passing harmlessly high. Their hum could be heard by all and men burrowed as deep as they could into the ground, fatigue suddenly driven out by fear. Where C Company's positions were, only God knew. But perhaps Wright, also, knew? He was extraordinary, the instinctive warrior, whether in darkness or in daylight, whether wounded or whole. He seemed to know, like an ancient warhorse, an animal trained for war, where his and other troops were and should be, where an enemy was, what would happen – a minute before it did.

'I'm here!'

He could tell Wright's shape from other shapes. The Company Commander was standing beside the track, oblivious to Spandaus. He must have just cracked a joke. From the crouching men beside him Anthony heard a round of grateful, nervous laughter. He heard Wright call –

'And there's still three bloody weeks to go before Christmas!'

'I'm here. It's Anthony.'

Wright grabbed his arm and immediately swore. His outline looked somewhat distorted. In the darkness Anthony saw some lighter-toned surface hung on Wright. Wright's arm was in a sling.

'Are you all right?'

'*Shut up!* Corporal Thomson's patched up my arm, I'm perfectly all right.' Corporal Thomson was the Company Medical Orderly, thought to have ambitions toward surgical practice and keen on demonstrating his skills. He was known, unkindly, to the men of B Company as 'Crippen'.

'Are you sure Crippen's done the right –'

'Shut up, Anthony. And get down here.'

With his uninjured arm, Wright dragged Anthony down beside him, in the lee of a small cluster of rocks. Bursts of Spandau fire continued, sporadically.

'Anthony, I want you to get back to Battalion Headquarters as fast as you can. I'm going to keep the Company here as they come back – dig them in on the reverse side of the Pimple.'

Already, as he spoke, men were moving on down the track and apparently branching off it under some sort of control. Anthony heard Sergeant-Major Phillips's voice.

'It's obvious there's going to be a Jerry attack bloody soon. I'm not going to have it hit B Company strung along this

233

track. I've seen Freddie, agreed where we'll go.' Freddie Lang commanded C Company.

'We've got guides on the track, to lead the platoons to their ground. I can't raise Battalion Headquarters. Wireless packed in, and two signallers hit an hour ago, bugger it! Freddie's telling them what's happening as well as he can.'

Richard Wright was known to have a poor opinion of Freddie Lang. Relations between the two companies had, consequently, never been close. But they needed each other now. There was a hiss and a crump, several times repeated along the way they had just come. More German shelling.

With unwonted frankness Anthony said,

'You'll have nobody to take over if you stop one, Richard!'

'Freddie and I will be together. Run both companies together while we're here, makes sense. If anything gets me he'll command both.'

'Or if Lang is disabled,' thought Anthony, 'you'll command both. That would be good.'

Wright said,

'We must get the picture to Battalion Headquarters or there's no hope for anyone. At present the Battalion's sliced into small pieces.'

Anthony said, 'Right!' still feeling it was wrong to send him. He said, 'I'll tell Colonel Adam . . .'

Lieutenant-Colonel Adam Jenkinson commanded the Battalion. Another shell exploded, about fifty yards down the track below them on the route to Battalion Headquarters.

'Colonel Adam's been hit. Shell, this evening. I don't know who's at Battalion Headquarters. I suppose Freddie will be taking command but the Adjutant hasn't been through. Anyway, Freddie can't get away from here at the moment. Obviously.

'Get DOWN!'

More shells fell, and the German machine guns suddenly opened up again with sustained bursts.

'Here they come, I expect,' said Wright in a matter-of-fact voice. B Company had been filing rapidly down and off the track during their conversation. Wright's system was working. Somehow, somewhere, in whatever confusion of darkness, he would get his Company in some sort of defensible perimeter within supporting distance of C Company and would handle the Germans when they came. This sounded as if it would be very soon indeed.

'Off you go, Anthony,' Wright said, still in his matter-of-fact tone. 'Tell them what's going on. We and C Companies can't get back at the moment. We'd be caught on the run and the Jerries could drive wherever they like. If we can hang on till morning, here at the Pimple, somebody can make some sense of it all. We'll get word to them, somehow, that you're on the way back, but put it across, for God's sake, to whoever thinks he's running the Battalion tonight.'

Anthony knew that he spoke truth. The Pimple commanded all routes into what had been the Battalion area.

'Off you go! Take Billings here with you. He's no good here, now we've got no bloody wireless. And look after yourself!' For the moment Wright sounded dubious. Private Billings, a spare signaller at Company Headquarters, loomed out of the darkness.

Feeling a deserter, Anthony moved down the track. Soon he and Billings were alone. He sensed rather than saw survivors of B Company filing off to the right, toward what Wright called the reverse side of the Pimple. There, he knew, the energy and the soldierly competence of Wright, supported by the intelligent anticipation of Sergeant-Major Phillips, would again make B Company a hard nut for the Germans to crack. And while those Germans dashed themselves like waves against the breakwaters of B and C combined companies on the Pimple somebody else – the Brigadier? the General? – presumably could and no doubt would find a way to restore the position in the Battalion's right rear, on the ground occupied until this morning by D Company. For as far as Anthony could imagine from his recollection of the map, from what he had originally seen of the ground, there could not be much – indeed was there anything? – between the Germans and Battalion Headquarters. Or, for that matter, between the Germans and the Battalion supply echelon in the woods far beyond: between the Germans and the heart of the brigade position.

Anthony had been once to Battalion Headquarters. It was in some caves, holes in a vertical rockface in the middle of woods. These woods stretched along the foot of the hill they had been defending, from which they had now climbed painfully down. They stretched, too, along the slopes running down from the Pimple, that bump to be passed in the night but now turned into an improvised fortress for B and C Companies. The caves were, Anthony thought, about one thousand yards from where he had left Wright. It was a long way in the dark. He moved as quickly as he could, stumbling now and then, pausing on occasion to ensure contact with Billings, hoping his sense of direction was not betraying him.

They had been moving for about ten minutes when there broke out behind them renewed and sustained Spandau fire and the sound of sharper explosions than the crump of shell or mortar bomb. Anthony looked back. The flashes were unmistakeable.

Grenades.

So the attack was going in! The Germans, masters of infiltration and assault by day, were not particularly enthusiastic fighters by night. They must want the Pimple badly. They must have more ambitious plans for the morning. From the Pimple came a mighty clatter of machine gun and rifle fire. Anthony disliked himself for not being there. He felt extraordinarily lonely. After they had received the withdrawal orders in the afternoon Richard Wright had suddenly said to him,

'You did very well, Anthony, it was a great help to know you were always being sensible in the right place. Thanks.' Then he had hastily spoken of other things. Anthony had been much moved. B Company was his family and they were at this moment, fighting it out on the Pimple. Without him.

'Come on, Billings!'

Billings was making slow progress, although the inferno of noise from the Pimple might have provided strong incentive to move away from it as rapidly as possible. Billings was a clumsy, maladroit man, his fingers astonishingly competent with a wireless set, his other limbs ungainly and shambling. Wright found him irritating and had small patience with him.

They moved slowly on. The track fell steeply at this point. Anthony thought he remembered it.

'Get down!'

The crack of the first shell's explosion was particularly sharp. 'A high velocity gun,' a tiny part of Anthony's mind reflected. Seven shells exploded. Each felt as if it were about three yards away, but five out of the seven hit the track, or ground near it, higher up the hillside, hit the route they had already traversed. Anthony had burrowed into the stony earth, tried to make his bulk as minuscule as possible. The hot smell of cordite was everywhere, and dust thickened the night air. He thought he had probably been unduly precipitate in his reactions and was glad they had been unwatched except by Billings.

'I'm getting windy,' he told himself with honesty. 'Getting windy after that bloody hill.'

'Are you all right, Billings?'

There was no reply.

'Billings!'

Billings was not all right. Lagging a little way behind Anthony he had dived into some bushes beside the track. The third shell had killed him instantly. Billings' legs extended from the bushes and Anthony tripped over them as he retraced his steps. He picked himself up and shone his torch on the rest of Billings. There was a small wound in his throat: very small, almost surgical. There was little of the blood, grime, sickening ugliness of much of war: little of what the cry 'stretcher bearers', the word 'casualties' now evoked in Anthony's mind's eye after the long days on B Company's hill. Billings, by contrast, had gone with great neatness and consideration. The awkward, untidy man had been treated by death with curious courtesy, with marked exactitude.

Anthony stood up. On the hill he had lost men he had come greatly to care about. He had seen them die, watched them squirm and moan from wounds which must lead to death before they reached the Medical Aid Post after a jolting, agonizing, journey. He had thought, 'I shall mind all this very much one day. But I can't feel anything yet. I haven't time. I've no feelings to spare.'

Anthony had not known Billings particularly well. He had found him dull and unsympathetic. Yet now the death of Billings hit him hard. He found himself hating the German gunners who fired the shell which found Billings. The man was so extraordinarily inoffensive! So clumsy, so unmilitary, so patently allergic to soldierly duty except where it kept him with his beloved wireless set. Billings was a man of peace. There was nothing to be done for him now. Anthony left him, with his small, tidy hole in the throat and hurried on in the darkness, alone.

Anthony reckoned that another three hundred yards should take him to the area of Battalion Headquarters. He had already entered the woods, small, twisted trees for the most part, yet making darkness more impenetrable. There was no moon. He forced his eyes to do their best but he tripped and stumbled a good deal. Perhaps it was more than three hundred yards? One generally over-estimated how much distance one had covered in the dark. It would be getting light soon now. Already shapes were more distinguishable.

He started to count his steps. He reached 140, and then, to his profound relief, saw something move beside the track. Battalion Headquarters sentries! There was often disloyal ribaldry among the rifle companies at what was alleged to be the slackness of routine at Battalion Headquarters.

'A few Jerry attacks would sharpen that lot up,' Sergeant-Major Phillips had observed with relish, after some doubtless apocryphal story of Battalion Headquarters' unsoldierly remoteness from real fighting.

'It will be different now,' thought Anthony grimly. After the morning's fighting Battalion Headquarters sentries were likely to be not slack but jittery. He moved cautiously. There were plenty of precedents for being shot by one's own sentries. The password was on his tongue. It would be better to walk with a certain amount of noise. He was sure the movement he had seen was no more than thirty yards away. They should be expecting him, although it was such a confused night that one could not count on this vital information having reached the sentries.

He crouched down and saw, without question, two shapes that were not rocks or bushes, saw them against the ever paler background of the night sky. It was the sentries all right

238

– about twenty-five yards away. Anthony noted with wry amusement that they were close together and could not possibly be covering each other in the approved manner. Battalion Headquarters! This would make an acceptable story in B Company! He strode forward.

There followed several sharp cracks, followed by a number of blinding flashes. Anthony found himself lying on his back without knowing how he got there.

'Grenades!' he thought, perfectly clearly. 'My God, they must think I'm a whole bloody company withdrawing.' He was conscious of no pain. But when he attempted to turn on his stomach, to crawl, he found that he could not move and the attempt brought anguish which he thought he identified as running down his left side. There seemed to be a great weight pinning his left thigh. Then he found that he was, for no reason that made sense, calling out –

'It's Captain Marvell!'

He remembered afterwards, when these things began to come back to him, a great deal of shouting. Words were distinguishable as from a great distance –

'*Nur ein! Nur ein!*' and '*Verwundet!*' and a little later – '*Offizier!*'

He saw a boot near his head. Then a voice spoke, very near. Fear, pain, were overtaken by irritation as Anthony heard the sound of a German, clearly fancying his fluency in English, showing off his skill with unconvincing idiom. And there was nobody to laugh with about it! The voice was patronizing and affected, the accent artificial.

'Well, old boy, I'm afraid you must be spending Christmas behind barbed wire!'

Anthony summoned up a flicker of resistance – '*Unsinn!*' he found he could do no more than whisper, '*Dummkopf!*' he added for good measure. He could not tell whether the croak was audible but the defiance was necessary even if childish.

Then he lost consciousness.

Chapter 16

———————————•———————————

TEN DAYS TO CHRISTMAS! Christmas, 1942! Toni Rudberg shivered. He stamped his feet ceaselessly on the earth floor of the peasant cottage to try to maintain some sort of circulation. The temperature was twenty degrees below zero and still falling.

Against the wooden walls of the cottage two command vehicles were parked and Toni, now a Major, had set up the Divisional operations staff cell in the cottage itself. With casualties and illness having taken their toll he now found himself virtually running the Operations Staff of the Division. They'd moved south some weeks before to join what most people regarded as a doomed attempt to relieve Sixth Army from the south-west, to fight their way from the Don to the Volga and somehow link hands with the poor wretches in Stalingrad. It had been the first such attempt. In Stalingrad more than 200,000 German soldiers of Sixth Army were surrounded by what appeared to be most of the Red Army, pinning them in a great pocket west of the Volga.

Toni had been delighted to be assigned again to a Panzer Division, after nearly a year spent on a Corps Staff. One was nearer the troops, the action. A Divisional staff was small, intimate, congenial. But when he gazed at the sullen grey of the eastern sky, listened to the incessant grumble of the Russian guns and rockets pounding the defenders of Stalingrad, he found himself thinking with nostalgia of his last appointment, of a different part of the front. Above all, his mind went back to those extraordinary days in the Summer of 1941. The advance had been exhilarating, no question of it. They had been going forward – going forward huge distances over an empty landscape much of the time. Until the beginning of November the weather had been agreeable. Thereafter – the winter of 1941 was not a pleasant recollection. There had been no decent winter clothing, no effective winter equipment. Vehicles had been unusable, oil had frozen, automatic weapons jammed, supply had been laborious or non-existent. Instead of sweeping advances into this vast and melancholy land they'd had to sit tight, to hold positions where they happened to be – which were seldom positions any sane man would have chosen to defend.

Then had come the huge Russian attacks on the Central Front. Immense packs of men, advancing wolflike across the frozen ground in close order, inviting massacre, yelling, mad with drink, making no attempt to manoeuvre, to skirmish.

It was like a film he'd seen in Berlin long ago about the English being attacked by Zulus, although from his recollection the Zulus had appeared more methodical.

Most of the Russian troops who had carried out the great counter-attacks of the winter around Moscow had been oriental divisions from the Soviet east. Again and again the defenders had given ground because there simply wasn't enough ammunition for the machine guns and mortars to stem the flood. Toni had been shaken on one occasion by seeing at first hand the sense of self-preservation which even the hardened German *landser* could display. He had been sent to visit a forward regiment and was lying behind a bank of snow beside a light machine gun team, one of half a dozen on the front edge of a wood. The Russian attack was the third in two days. Toni watched the leading ranks through his binoculars as they stumbled forward in the snow. Maybe one thousand metres, he thought, and glanced at the nearest machine gunners. The *gefreiter* in charge was an old soldier, grizzled, hardbitten. A minute later the Spandau opened up. The Russian shrieks were audible in the crisp, icy air.

'Urra! Urra!'

There were German shouts from left and right of Toni and a yelled order from the team next to him.

'Back, right away!'

'What the hell –' roared Toni. He was a Staff officer, visiting in order to report first-hand impressions, but he knew that no withdrawal had been authorized in this sector.

'We're going back, *Herr Hauptmann*. You'd better come. Quick.'

'Why –'

'You don't think we've got the ammunition to stop that lot!' the man said contemptuously as he shouldered cartridge belts and bent to lift a box. Toni looked at him. Should he shoot the *Gefreiter* instantly, take command, restore the situation? He looked at the other machine gun teams. They were already climbing out of the snow-filled ditch into the cover of the wood and through it. Toni looked at the Russians. Six hundred metres.

'Better come along, *Herr Hauptmann*,' said the *Gefreiter*. 'There's plenty of Russia behind us. If we stick to this bit of it for another three minutes we'll never leave it.' Toni moved back without a word.

It was the same everywhere, this second winter. There was the conversation he had had with an old friend only two weeks ago, here in the south. They'd met during what passed for a rest period – a few days' lull before this last desperate attempt to relieve Stalingrad. Von Wrede was with an infantry regiment, a battalion commander, several years younger than Toni. Most infantry battalions were commanded by lieutenants by now. Wrede was a friend from carefree, peacetime days. They'd once been in the same ski-ing party at St Anton, raced each other, drank together until all hours, chased the same girl. Toni had won the chase but they'd always got on well. Wrede appeared a different man now. He not only looked older than Toni, Toni thought without pleasure: he, a youngster, actually looked like an old man.

'Rudberg, these men have got to have some rest, some relief. They're fine men but they've been pushed too hard. They're losing confidence.' And von Wrede told him that during the great Soviet advances of mid-November, 1942, those attacks which had smashed the Rumanian army, torn a great hole in the Don front and encircled Stalingrad, his Sergeant-Major had come to him one evening and saluted.

'Are we to retire tonight?'

'No, we're staying here.'

'*Herr Oberleutnant*, the soldiers –' the man was embarrassed. More, he was wretched. He told von Wrede that unless orders were given to withdraw he had information – reliable information – that there was a plot to kill the officers and withdraw willy-nilly. There were no loyal, dissentient voices: none, at least, that could be relied upon to stay firm.

'They know they may be detected, shot. But they count on the confusion to get away with it. And they're saying – what's the odds? If we stay here, it's a Russian bullet or bayonet. For the lucky ones,' the Sergeant-Major muttered. For the less fortunate, as every man knew, torture and mutilation were the hazards of wounding or capture by the Red Army.

Toni heard his friend, aghast. Von Wrede held the Knight's Cross of the Iron Cross.

'What happened?'

'I talked to them. We went back. I pretended I'd decided myself. They knew, of course. And they were ashamed. But the trouble was that they were right. It was a hopeless position and every *landser* realized it. I made out a report which squared it all up, of course, not particularly relishing the prospect of being court-marshalled and shot myself. It wasn't too difficult. You know how chaotic things were just then –'

Remarkably, letters from home continued to arrive. They took a long time, but even in the most unpromising conditions the field post office worked. There might be no more mail before Christmas but Toni had one letter in the pocket which could bring before his eyes, smarting as they were from the bitter cold, scenes of peace, beauty and tranquillity. Unfortunately, Toni reflected, even war could not eliminate the emotional complications which beset man's life. Of course all one's energies, here on the Don, were concentrated upon survival and the performance of rigorous, unpromising duty. But one could still find a few minutes now and then to dream, and dreams were confused.

Since the Russian campaign started, Toni had had no leave in Germany, no leave for eighteen months. On every occasion when there had been a chance, an operational crisis had intervened. There had been the appalling winter in front of Moscow, and then he'd been promoted, given this new job, greater responsibilities; and now it was winter 1942! Toni had, therefore, had to pursue Anna Langenbach by letter. The more he thought of her, the more he told himself that this was an extremely sensible thing to do. He was able to recall Anna's face and figure with huge approval – she really was a lovely woman, one in a million, he decided. And the more this damnable business of war depressed him (although he had to admit to enjoying a good deal of it. Despite his frivolity Toni was a soldier through and through) the more he thought with longing of the possibilities of a home, a wife, calm, prosperity! Small references by her to domestic concerns had long persuaded Toni that his information was accurate and that Anna was rich. He was sure Anna cared for him, was attracted to him. He made her laugh. They talked the same language. It was too bad that circumstances had not enabled him to get her into bed. That would have persuaded her! But she was a mature woman, she understood life. Anna Langenbach, née von Arzfeld, was, Toni had convinced himself, the ideal mate for Count Toni Rudberg.

But Anna's letters were so – so *cool*. When he asked her something directly – and the passage of time was leading him, against his instinct for tactics in these matters, to be more direct, more pressing – she either disregarded the request or question, or treated it as if it were a trifling matter which she would 'think about'. He asked for a photograph of herself –

'Believe me it will make an immense difference, out here, if I can be reminded daily of the face dearer to me than any other.'

She had replied that she had no decent photograph. She had even written –

'You must content yourself with one of your little Viennese beauties. Surely you haven't thrown them all away?'

This might be coquettish, teasing. But Anna was not coquettish. Her letters were invariably thoughtful, intelligent, strong. They had the effect of making him desire her company ever more violently and at the same time gave her an aura of remoteness. She was so extraordinarily self-contained. Had he touched her inner self not at all?

And in September, 1942, after being disappointed of yet another leave, Toni had (with what he reckoned was particular skill) laid bare his heart, his hopes. He had written that – comparatively short though their acquaintance was – he sincerely loved her. He had described himself as unworthy of so much beauty, courage, intelligence –

244

'The sheer quality you possess, Anna, unlike that of any other woman I have known or dreamed of –'

but as a man, nevertheless, who had perceived in Anna *for the first time in life* a woman with whom he felt capable 'of better things'. He had ended, unequivocally, by saying that he was asking for hope that 'If I survive this extraordinary campaign' she would become his wife. He had concluded –

> 'I cannot believe that any man could be with you and not wish to love you. And no doubt many would deserve that more than I. But nobody – absolutely nobody – could outdo me in the fervour and energy with which I would love you if allowed to do so. Your face is before me every waking hour. Yours until the end of time.'

'That makes it all pretty clear,' he thought, as he committed the letter to the field post office. Then there had been a long period of waiting, a period filled by the murderous activities of the Red Army and the ceaseless demands on the scanty Panzer reserves of the Wehrmacht. But ultimately a letter had arrived.

And Anna's answering letter, the one in his pocket, had been harsh. Toni thought, easily, that women often went through the motions of rejection while strongly hoping that the rejection would itself be disregarded, that the lover would persist, ardour strong enough to warm the coolest heart. But in Anna's case it was hard to believe that she was playing. She had a sort of terrible sincerity.

She wrote that she regretted giving him pain, but –

> 'I somehow doubt whether I shall really do so, in spite of your protestations. You are not fundamentally serious, and I am. I know very well, for instance, that when you first decided to – shall we say show an interest? – in me, you were still protesting undying love for Marcia Marvell: a sweet girl whom I love and whom you have injured.
>
> You have injured her because you have treated her as a toy, from which to extract pleasure . . .'

'And give it!' muttered Tony irritably.

> 'She was young and vulnerable, and you set out to make her love you. You succeeded. Does that make you proud? I fear it probably does, that it simply represents a little conquest, some

pleasant memories of love-making before passing on to something else. It is not, my dear Toni, that I criticize your amours
or their number. It is simply that I could not myself take
seriously one whose approach to life and love is so essentially
uncommitted. It is not that I should fear your infidelity. It is,
I am afraid, that such an attitude betokens, for me, a personality
that is, fundamentally, uninteresting.'

'*Letzlich uninteressant!*' This was almost the most painful
part of the letter to accept and Toni read it three times, put it
away in his pocket and periodically took it out and read it
again.

'Uninteresting!' Yes, it hurt. And it brought to mind other
expressions, sentences Anna had let fall from time to time
when they used to talk lightly, happily, at Arzfeld, sentences
spoken so casually as to imply complete sincerity. She had
referred to a man they both knew, shrugged him off as of little
consequence. Toni had demurred, smiling –

'Surely he's admitted to be highly attractive – to women?'

'Oh yes,' Anna had said. 'But you know how some attractive
men can also be great bores!'

Once he had spoken of someone as being proud. Anna had
said,

'Not proud, I think – not at heart. Vain, certainly.'

'What's the essential difference?'

Anna had considered, laughing.

'Well, I think pride can be an intelligent sin – a sin, of
course, but consistent with a good mind. Vanity, I think, is
almost inseparable from silliness.'

Had he imagined it, that her eyes, her lovely, laugh-filled
eyes, had looked at him, in saying it, with particular meaning?

And she was surely being unfair. She cited the case of Marcia
Marvell. She was fond of Marcia. Yet he had explained things
frankly to Anna at the time. It was hardly a crime to enjoy
a delightful little affair with a lovely girl and then, after a little,
aspire to a stable – an entirely honourable – relationship with
a mature woman of beauty – and, the world being what it is,
of property.

'Or if that's a crime,' Toni thought sulkily, 'it's a pretty
criminal world.' Yet as he formed these sensible, worldly
opinions he could not rid himself – and sometimes he felt,

246

uneasily, he would never rid himself – of the image of Marcia, the recollection not only of beauty but of a personality as fresh, as clear – and as effervescent – as a mountain spring.

All this was complex and depressing. Toni's taste was for simple, carefree and uncluttered human relationships, physical enjoyment, melody, laughter, a few tears perhaps. But, as he had always recognized, there was in the case of Anna Langenbach a great deal at stake. If it was to be won there was, he supposed, justice in the fate which made him sweat for it. Meanwhile, he thought ruefully, it was by no means certain that he would see Anna, Marcia, or for that matter, home, ever again. Toni's spirit, however, was resilient. Although he could look forward to no leave in Austria or Germany in the immediate future there had been a wonderful break in the clouds the previous afternoon, 14th December. The Division was shortly going into reserve for a while after continuous fighting since arrival on the Don front. Toni's Divisional commander, a man of particular kindness and charm as well as ability, had taken his arm –

'Rudberg, you should have a few days off. I insist. I know your record. You've been wonderfully fit, and no Russian bullet or shell has hit you. The result is, in this job like in your last, you've done everybody's work. Seven days off and no argument. Starting next Monday.'

It was true that even Toni had been feeling near the end of his tether. The troops in the foxholes, or trudging through the snow were harder tried, physically, but they got at least some periods of rest. For the staff, Toni thought, the war goes on all the time. Fight one battle, plan the next, the pressure never eases. Furthermore, Toni – and he was admired for it – was always going forward, visiting the troops, getting impressions of the fighting. It was only recently, as temporary chief of the operations section, that he had been largely confined to Headquarters and Headquarters, in this Division, was pretty far forward. Toni knew that he had the name of a cheerful, efficient officer – and a name by now pretty widely known. He also knew, however, that he was stale and tired: and now he hadn't much hope of Anna to keep him buoyant. Seven days off, his duties safely entrusted to another, could be a wonderful restorative.

247

Toni wanted to get as far away as he could, but the claims on aircraft were such that any attempt to travel to Germany or Austria was out of the question. Providentially, he had earlier befriended a Rumanian Colonel: and by a supreme stroke of luck a telephone call to ask for his good offices had disclosed that the Colonel was himself flying to Bucharest – on Sunday. It was easy to advance his own leave by a day. There was a seat obtainable and the distances weren't too bad. Toni and the Colonel had discussed the possibility weeks ago, as something unlikely ever to happen. Now it was within his grasp.

'You'll like Bucharest, Rudberg,' the Colonel had winked, 'I'll show you round!'

Bucharest after the Don front! It had sounded like Paradise. There was nothing he could do about Anna, and he'd see things more clearly – and no doubt, write more eloquently – after a break from this appalling scene of desolation. The icy wind sighed and moaned round the corners of the cottage. 'Here's to next week!' Toni thought, spirits high again. It was Friday. He'd heard delightful things of Bucharest.

An orderly entered and saluted. He handed Toni a piece of paper. It was marked for him, personally. Toni saw that it was a hurried note from the Divisional Commander who was, as usual, with the forward troops.

'The Army Group Command urgently wishes an experienced officer to fly into Stalingrad to report to Sixth Army and to compile a report on certain questions after personal observation. The Army Group Commander has just been with me. Captain Eicholz from Headquarters was due to fly yesterday and has been taken ill. There are difficulties in sparing another from the Army Group staff. In view of our impending move to reserve the Field Marshal has requested, and I have agreed, that you shall fly into Sixth Army area this afternoon. Instructions will reach you direct from the Army staff later this morning.'

Below his initials the General had scribbled –

'I regret this but it is necessary.'

The likely fate of General Paulus and Sixth Army in Stalingrad overshadowed the Don front. Sixth Army had been the spearhead of the Army Group in the victorious advances of the late summer. One great expedition, General von Kleist's Army Group A, had advanced into the Caucasus while behind it General von Weichs pushed Army Group B toward the Volga. Sixth Army eventually found itself in a huge salient whose tip was the city of Stalingrad. And in Stalingrad the Red Army was hanging on desperately to the Volga banks and to various pockets which the Germans, in savage fighting, failed wholly to eliminate.

Toni, like every other staff officer on the Don front, remembered vividly what happened next. In November the greatest Russian offensive of the war crashed into the Rumanian Army on the Chir and the Don. The Russians developed a huge pincer movement against the flanks of the salient that led to Stalingrad. By 22nd November Sixth Army was encircled. Thereafter, Paulus could only be supplied by air: or not at all.

It was generally supposed that this situation would not be allowed to last long. It was, all thought, inconceivable that a whole German Army – and there were said to be 230,000 men in Stalingrad – would permit itself to be throttled. But those, like Toni, with some knowledge of the workings of the High Command, knew that the Führer had forbidden any attempt by Paulus to break out of the encirclement. Sixth Army was to stand its ground. It would, Hitler promised, be supplied. The Luftwaffe would never let the Army down. And in the spring, when mobile operations became practicable again, Sixth Army would find itself once more in the van. Meanwhile it would do its duty. There had been a relief march from the south-west, but German tank strength in the Panzer divisions was so low that the attempt seemed already to be failing in its object; and one of the three Panzer divisions engaged had had to be withdrawn to deal with yet another crisis on the northern flank of the salient. Without permission to fight their way out, and without further hope of German troops in sufficient numbers being able to fight their way in, Sixth Army settled, shivering, to meet its fate in the ruins of Stalingrad.

As he flew toward Gumrak airfield, by now the only serviceable strip, Toni glanced again at the paper he had been given. Background statistics: Sixth Army needed 600 tons flown into the pocket daily to make operations possible, and 300 tons for mere survival. Further background statistic: Luftwaffe average delivery during December 140 tons. Commander-in-Chief's decision: an offensive west from the pocket was an absolute necessity in order to open a land line of communication.

'And how is that likely to be possible?' Toni respectfully enquired of the Army Group Chief of Staff, who had briefed him personally before departure. 'How can that occur, *Herr General*, if Sixth Army has, at the same time, to hold its positions by the Führer's order? And if its supply position is so bad that, as far as I can see, it must be almost out of both fuel and ammunition?'

The other looked at him without expression.

'There's to be a conference to discuss it with Paulus. What I want from you are some clear impressions of the real state of Sixth Army. Statistics are one thing. We all know that where the spirit is right one can achieve great things with every material odd against one. It's possible Sixth Army are exaggerating. They originally said they could only hold out until today!'

Toni saluted. His smile was as disrespectful as it was possible for a General Staff Officer to be.

'Exaggerating!' From what he'd heard the plight of Sixth Army had been, if anything, understated. He'd managed to visit a severely wounded friend who'd been flown out ten days earlier: one of the lucky ones. Brenndorf had held his hand tightly:

'The *landsers* are permanently frozen – already. Fingers, toes, dropping off. No food – and it's getting worse. We're down to a hundred grammes of bread per man. Do you know we're killing most of our horses to eat them? And we're digging the corpses of horses out of the snow –'

'Take it easy, Brenndorf, old friend, you're out of it now.' – 'I'm out of it. What about them?' Brenndorf was lying, feverish, in the field hospital near the airstrip. 'What about them? They're living among the rubble like animals, freezing, famished. You remember winter '41 – believe me it was nothing to this. We can't move – no fuel and now no horses. The Russians infiltrate between us, they scuttle around like sewer rats. There are Ivan snipers everywhere and our fellows have to exist on a few rounds each – if they're lucky. And as often as not they've no finger to shoot with. What the hell do they think they're doing, leaving a whole Army like that?'

'Sh, sh!' Toni said automatically. He glanced around. Nobody was taking an interest in Captain Brenndorf's delirium.

'The men are lousy – they're rotten with disease, they stink to heaven. Some of my battalion have had dysentery for the whole time, they're so weak they can't stand. I've seen men fall into the snow and they've had to be left there to die. Pray God they did so before the Russians got them! But Rudberg,' Brenndorf held his hand tightly, 'Rudberg, they're still magnificent, our fellows. They're suffering, God, how they're suffering! But give them one bowl of filthy stew, get some together with enough limbs to shoot and run and you wouldn't believe some of the things we've done! We've still mastered them! We –'

'Hush, old fellow. I believe you!' Toni left him.

That was ten days ago. It must be worse now. If it could be.

Toni's light aircraft was delayed in take off. He talked to the pilot.

'It's pretty good chaos at Gumrak airfield, *Herr Major*, I can tell you.' Toni nodded.

'It's a big job to get these tonnages in to one airfield, turning aircraft round in time, clearing the airfield of stores and so forth. I can imagine. And the snow can't make it easier.'

The pilot laughed. 'That's true. Often there's been no flying at all. But that's not the worst of it. At the far end they have a job to fight off our fellows trying to help themselves. They've a real security problem I'm told.'

Toni looked at him. 'You imply that some of the troops are out of control?'

The pilot looked uneasy and shrugged his shoulders.

'These stories always get exaggerated, *Herr Major*. I expect it's a small, criminal minority, who've lost their self-respect.'

'It always is,' Toni said half to the pilot, half to himself. 'It always is a small minority,' and he wondered what he would find.

They took off at last. The light was fading rapidly. Out of the window Toni saw great fires blazing as they approached the pocket.

'They've fired a lot of our own dumps,' the pilot said through the intercom. 'Couldn't defend the perimeter, couldn't cart the stuff back. No transport, no fuel, no horses. Burnt it to stop the Ivans getting it. Pity.'

A lieutenant approached Toni as he walked from the aircraft. The sky was darkening. Grey, ruined buildings stood out like tombstones from the dirty snow of airfield and surrounding landscape. From what Toni knew was the perimeter of the pocket a steady pounding of artillery could be heard. Russian artillery. The flashes lit the horizon. An icy wind swept the tarmac.

The lieutenant saluted and reported his name. In the half-light Toni saw his pallor and the sunken eyes of exhaustion.

'And although he probably works hard he's certainly better off as regards shelter and food than the wretched *landser* in the infantry companies,' thought Toni grimly.

He saluted in turn and held out his hand – with a smile. Even in Stalingrad, Toni Rudberg had a smile which could arouse response. He drove away every thought that he might be on the way to Bucharest and a few days of warmth, peace, colour, normality. He smiled as if, in all the world, he wished to be nowhere but here, on the Volga, in December, 1942. The other gave something like a smile in return.

'Welcome to Sixth Army!'

Chapter 17

THE HEADQUARTERS of Sixth Army were housed in a number of interconnected underground bunkers, near Gumrak airfield and railway station, deep excavated and well protected. The staff officers, clerks, orderlies and telephonists Toni observed as he was ushered into these sombre depths, moved slowly, ponderously, as if somehow expressing in their apathetic limbs the expectation of calamity. There was a nightmare quality in Sixth Army Headquarters. Toni reported to the Chief of Staff in person. Visitors, particularly visitors of junior rank with a mission to 'report independently', were not naturally popular with any command. There had, Toni knew, been plenty of such visitors to Stalingrad. All had brought back the same message. Whether in handling visitors or in describing their problems to the outside world by teleprinter Sixth Army must, Toni thought, by now feel that they were conducting a dialogue of the deaf.

The Chief of Staff looked at him cynically.

'I'm surprised it's thought necessary to ask for another "independent report"! The facts of the situation here must be clear to everyone by now.'

Toni inwardly sympathized with him.

'*Herr General*, I hope that anything I report will have the effect of being useful to Sixth Army, not the reverse.'

'What do you want to see? I'm proposing to send you to the 51st Corps.' He pointed to a map on the wall. 'They tell me you're to fly back by 20th December at the latest. That gives you four days.'

'*Herr General*, I would like, above all, to attach myself to an infantry regiment, preferably one in the city itself, in contact with the enemy. Perhaps on the Volga front.'

'That can be arranged, of course.' The Chief of Staff

shrugged his shoulders. He glanced at a larger map of the whole front.

'From this morning's report it looks as if another big Russian attack is starting on the Don, in the north. I expect your Division will be involved. The Soviet Voronezh Front are throwing in everything from the north-east.' He nodded dismissal.

That, at least, was not Sixth Army's responsibility, although it made even less probable the success of any attempt to break through to them from the west. Toni digested the information. It was no doubt true that his own Division – with all of the thirty tanks they had left after the recent fighting! – would be involved if there were another big attack on the Don. He expected they'd already been breaking it to the troops that there was to be no brief period in reserve as promised. He felt like a deserter to be away from his own Divisional family, his own Staff comrades, his own commander at such a time. But no deserter would have chosen to escape into Stalingrad! He saluted and left the bunker.

Toni peered over the edge of a chipped stone window sill. The air was icy but now and then it was absolutely necessary to breathe a change from the evil stench inside. It wasn't the fault of the troops – their way of life condemned them – but the result was nauseous.

About Toni was the shell of what had once been a block of workers' flats. The peeling paint of a title in cyrillic script was still decipherable on one outer wall and Toni could translate it – 'Workers Block Red Dawn'. The upper storeys of the tall building had been gutted by fire but the street level and extensive cellars were usable. Fragments of collapsed ceiling and fallen masonry littered the floors. Broken glass was everywhere. Dust invaded nostrils and lungs and never seemed to clear. It was always possible that a salvo of Soviet shells would bring down on their heads some more of the precariously lodged brick and stonework of the upper building but this possibility – like all the others, all of them worse – was dully accepted by the remaining men of the detachment of Combat Group Schroder, a unit of 305th Infantry Division. Toni crouched by his window, binoculars in hand.

254

In the day and night Toni had spent with this Combat Group, moving from detachment to detachment, from one pile of rubble to another, he had often recalled, and with agreement, the words of the wounded Brenndorf.

'They're still magnificent, our fellows, but God! How they're suffering!'

These men were indeed suffering. By any rational use of language they were starving. The tiny bread ration, the limited quantities of decayed horseflesh, carefully husbanded and stirred into a soup, were insufficient to sustain the human body in any sort of physical activity. Toni noted their lassitude, their slowness of reaction, the dumb resignation more terrible even than mutiny. These men had given up hope. They would have been unsurprised to learn that that very day – it was 18th December – their Army Commander had received a direct order from Field Marshal von Manstein to assemble his forces and break out to the westward. They would have been equally unsurprised to be told that General Paulus, placed as he was under the direct supervision of the Army High Command, the Führer himself, had declined to obey the order, which conflicted with his instructions from the highest level that in all circumstances Stalingrad was to be held, that no thought of breakout was to be countenanced if it involved giving up ground.

They would have grunted, only half comprehending. They had ceased to believe or trust. Every human being's energies, whatever his rank or intelligence, were concentrated on the difficult business of survival from one hour to the next. Outside the pocket the last relief attempt, made by units at pitifully low strength, was already stumbling to its unsuccessful end. For weeks to come there would be further rumours, expectations of other similar attempts. The men of Combat Group Schroder felt little but scepticism at such tales when they heard them. Indeed, they felt little of anything save cold, hunger, pain and fear.

Yet, Toni recognized with an unusual surge of emotion, they were still fighting. While he had been with these men there had already been two Russian attacks. Small-scale, savage attacks – now here, now there and apparently unco-ordinated, wearing down the defenders by their incessant ferocity – formed the pattern of the fighting in Stalingrad. Toni's blood had

255

been fired by seeing with what courage, skill and discipline those attacks had been beaten off. The Russians had come without warning, leaping over rubble in the streets, aiming bursts of fire with machine pistols at every glassless window or door as they rushed forward, uttering their weird cries, covered by sustained machine gun fire from upper windows of the blocks they held. Schroder's men had been at first held well back from the windows, seeking cover within the buildings themselves. Then, as the Russians came closer and started to appear at windows and doorways the Germans opened up with everything they had at point blank range. At the same time they struck the attackers in flank with machine gun fire and grenades from the upper floors of an adjacent block: a group was specially placed there for the purpose. Then, the *landsers* started to move forward, firing, hurling grenades from within the huge building itself. The Russians stopped, dropped – and fled. Two attacks followed each other with exactly the same sequence.

'They'll get wise to our system,' said Toni, to the non-commissioned officer next to him. He felt an enormous exhilaration. 'They'll find a way round.'

'No, *Herr Major*, the Ivans always do the same thing.'

From those attacks, eleven 'Ivans' could be counted in the snow. As Toni watched, the blood running from the head of a wounded Russian began to freeze. The man himself was propped upright and stationary against a wall, so hung with weapons and ammunition, so dark and misshapen in his quilted felt clothing, that he looked like a Christmas tree leaned against a woodman's shed awaiting purchase. Toni could not see whether he was dead or not but he did not fall. The frozen blood had the appearance of some sort of obscene decoration.

The *Feldwebel* in charge of the detachment grunted. He'd found it strange that a General Staff Major should come and live in their cellar, even for an hour, but he'd given up looking for any proper order of things in Stalingrad. It was hard to snap to attention all the time, *Herr Major* this, *Herr Major* that. But he had to admit that this one seemed a decent fellow. He not only talked to you, asked sensible questions and listened carefully to the answers: he also gave the impression of enjoying himself, God help him!

'Of course,' the *Feldwebel* said to himself sourly, 'the Major's only here as a tourist. Short visit. And you can tell from his face he's well fed.'

It was indeed true that outside the Stalingrad pocket there was no great shortage of food on the Don front. But Toni's ebullience and laughter did something for these men. Nobody had heard laughter for a long time.

'Have we taken many prisoners?' Toni was looking at the human Christmas tree. He kept his voice casual.

'There were a lot early on, *Herr Major*. The General ordered that they were to be sent back to the Russian lines. We couldn't feed them. It seemed – still, that was the order.'

'What happened?'

'They wouldn't go! Preferred to chance their luck with us, I suppose. There are lots of Ivan wounded, of course, but a great many more German wounded. In the cellars mostly, where they haven't managed to collect them in the dressing stations.'

'Thirty thousand wounded men have been flown out already,' said Toni casually. It was one of the statistics in his briefing. The *Feldwebel* said nothing. Privately he guessed it should be a hundred thousand at least. They'd lost half their strength from wounds or sickness even by the beginning of December.

Two hundred metres down the street was a barricade of rubble and concrete blocks. It was at this Toni had been peering from the window ledge.

'Did we put that barricade up?'

'Yes, and we held it for ten days. The Ivans tried to drive us off it. They failed. Then, when we got short of men, the Lieutenant pulled us back here. You need fewer men to hold this end of the street.'

'I can see that. Do the Ivans man that barricade from the other side?'

'I don't think so, *Herr Major*. I think it's between the two sides, in no-man's land you could say.'

Toni's task was to observe and report upon the general condition of the fighting troops. Neither his sense of military propriety nor his instructions gave him latitude to involve

257

himself in tactical details. He was a visiting General Staff Major, not a Corporal: although, during the last attack, he'd found a light machine gun whose Number One was wounded and settled down to use it in a most effective fashion. The men had been amazed but they'd liked it. One had even chuckled –

'We've only got ten belts of ammunition for that gun till they get supplies to us, *Herr Major!*'

Toni had smiled back grimly. For the truth was that, despite his instructions, despite the disgusting conditions, Toni was enjoying himself, as he always did at moments of challenge. He could not stand aside from action. Now he looked at the barricade, considering.

'It might be best to demolish it. It's giving them too good a covered approach. If we knock it down we'll be able to sweep the whole length of the street. Break them up earlier.'

'We'd need an assault gun or a Panzer,' said the *Feldwebel* dubiously. 'We've seen none of those in this sector, *Herr Major*. We're on our own. And the barricade does block assault by an Ivan tank!'

'That cuts both ways.'

Toni's binoculars were up again. He ached for even a small detachment of armour, something with which to attack, surprise, shake these Russians, knock them off balance. The *Feldwebel* nodded. No doubt the Major would convey his ideas on the tactical situation to Captain Schroder in due course. Whether the latter would relish them was questionable. Toni was still looking thoughtfully down the street.

'I want to have a look beyond the barricade. I'm going along that broken wall between us and the next detachment. Then I'll scramble to somewhere from where I can see over. I shan't be long.'

'*Herr Major*,' said the *Feldwebel* respectfully, 'I have been made responsible for your safety. One can never tell when an Ivan sniper will appear. You will be in the open.'

There were already many thousands of wounded German soldiers lying uncared for in the Stalingrad cellars. The medical teams did their best but ambulances were as short as was fuel. The *Feldwebel* already had five men in various stages of suffering. He didn't want to add a damaged Major to his responsibilities.

Toni looked at him coldly.

'Nonsense. One can't climb to the upper stories here because they're falling down, you said so yourself. So in order to see I must get out and up. And you know that no possible sniper position overlooks that wall.'

The *Feldwebel* shuffled to attention with an inward sigh. Toni slipped his spurs into his greatcoat pocket, jumped lightly from the window sill and scrambled with agility up a pile of rubble to the top of a broken wall that ran parallel to the street and toward the enemy.

The men from Combat Group Schroder watched without emotion. He seemed a good sort, but if he wanted to get himself killed quickly that was his business. Toni moved nimbly along the wall, reached the far end where it joined the jagged corner of another ruined building, climbed a few feet and brought up his binoculars. He was, as far as the watching *Feldwebel* could judge, in full view of any Russians hidden behind the street barricade.

Nothing happened. No shot rang out. Toni's body was silhouetted against the leaden sky beyond the barricade, although the *Feldwebel* acknowledged grudgingly that it was probably more difficult to observe from the opposite direction.

'The bloody fool's got away with it,' he thought with relief. 'Now, he'll come back.' And that same bloody fool, who might be one of those said to bear a charmed life, would presumably then go away and leave them alone.

Toni, however, was not yet disposed to return. He looked to his left. The bodies of Russian soldiers still lay in the snow. None moved. He supposed they were all dead: from every point of view he hoped so. But to his right his attention had been attracted by something unexpected.

On the right-hand side of the wall along which Toni had clambered – hidden from the men of Combat Group Schroder in the building from which he had started and also hidden, as far as he could judge, from any other German detachment in adjoining blocks was a small, enclosed yard. No upper windows gave on to it. It appeared to have no direct access to any street. Toni supposed that in other times, when these buildings were standing, various doors gave on to the yard. It probably housed rubbish bins and an incinerator. There was a manhole cover

259

in the middle of its rough concrete floor. The surrounding buildings on three sides had suffered varying degrees of destruction. Toni's wall formed the fourth side. It was a squalid little area which overlooked nothing, led to nowhere and appeared to have, in present circumstances, no tactical significance. Toni surveyed it from his perch without particular interest.

As he looked the manhole cover appeared to move. Toni stared, fascinated. Had he imagined it? Everything seemed still and desolate.

Toni instantly decided to inspect further. But if he climbed down to the yard would he be able to haul himself up again? He didn't want to be caged in this depressing little rectangle which neither Army appeared to think worth occupying or even watching. He saw, however, that the corner of the building on one side of the yard – the corner nearest Combat Group Schroder's detachment – was damaged in a way which would certainly afford footholds, so that he could easily climb out of the yard at that end, regain the wall along which he had scrambled and thence descend to Workers Block Red Dawn. Below him there was an intervening, sloping cornice and if he steadied himself for a second on that it wasn't much of a drop into the yard. He started to lower himself from the ledge on which he stood. The cornice was almost his whole height below the top of the wall, however, and as his boots found it he realized that there was no question of hauling himself up again. Field boots and a greatcoat weren't ideal climbing gear, Toni grinned to himself, panting, as he balanced on the cornice, ready to loose his hold on the wall, twist his body and jump. The important thing was not to do something inept like spraining an ankle:

'Among the casualties in the heroic Sixth Army it is necessary to report one gallant Major of the General Staff with a sprained ankle!'

He retained his grip on the top of the wall for a moment, spreadeagled against its surface before committing his whole weight to the cornice, turning and leaping. He glanced down. He had already decided that what he was doing was unnecessary and perhaps unwise and wished very much to be at the top of the wall again.

At that exact moment the manhole cover moved again.

This time there could be no mistake about it. The manhole cover was pushed up strongly by a pair of arms wrapped in thick quilting. These arms were immediately followed by a fur cap and then a body swathed in shapeless garments and hung with a machine carbine. With astonishing rapidity the body was followed by others. They appeared to have run a ladder against the inner wall, and were now swarming into the yard.

Toni was spreadeagled, hanging and uneasily balanced. He was above and about fifteen metres from the manhole. It took a fraction of one second for his mind to recall, too late, what he had been told. The Russians holding the Volga front had tunnelled inwards from the steep banks of the river, into the city sewers, brought them into use as underground communications and approaches. Then Toni's hold on the top of the wall slipped and without further calculation he dropped into the yard. He heard rather than felt a bone give in his knee. Fur caps, yells, quilted bodies! Greatcoat flapping, cap knocked off, boots slithering as he tried to regain his feet, hand moving uselessly to his revolver holster, Major Count Rudberg found himself involuntarily joining a patrol of twelve Red Army soldiers of the Soviet 62nd Army.

'This one's got to go back to Headquarters. Over the river.'

It would be best – perhaps essential – Toni had decided, not to let it be discovered that he could speak and understand Russian – not, at least, until a later stage if at all. He was still dazed from the extraordinary moments which had followed his capture several hours ago. There had been a hubbub of voices from the soldiers around him, clearly dumbfounded at this booted apparition that had suddenly dropped into their midst. One seized his revolver and binoculars. Another gave him a savage blow in the crutch which doubled him up. Toni remembered seeing a carbine muzzle lowered towards him, and a shout which might have checked an immediate bullet. He could distinguish no sense in their discordant cries. He felt physically sick.

Later he deduced that there had been argument as to whether the taking of so unexpected – and, perhaps, important – a prisoner justified abandoning the task for which, presumably, the patrol had been ordered out. The latter, probably, was the deployment of a number of snipers. Toni now recalled being told that snipers used the sewer tunnels to great effect. It was unlikely that the patrol's orders covered the taking of a Major of the General Staff! The decision must have been a difficult one, Toni thought later when he had leisure to ponder. Somebody took it, however, and Toni found himself unceremoniously booted down the manhole, into what was, clearly, one of the main sewers of Stalingrad. Had the decision gone the other way, and the patrol continued with whatever was its original mission, it was likely, he guessed, that he would have ended his days in the little yard.

There had followed a nightmare procession along the sewer for what felt like and doubtless was several miles. For the first part of their journey it was necessary to move doubled up, in a position of almost unbearable discomfort. After what seemed at least an hour but was probably ten minutes they reached, mercifully, a larger, higher sewer tunnel and could move upright. Most of the march was conducted in silence, although occasionally the leading Red Army soldier turned to call some words, indistinguishable by Toni, to the rear of his little column. The only light was provided by a torch held by the leader. There was, at intervals, a paling of the darkness, perhaps coming from manhole covers removed in areas under Soviet control. Rats scurried between their moving feet. The men were trudging along apathetically, Toni in the centre of the file. Periodically the muzzle of a machine carbine was shoved into the small of his back with brutal force. The pain in his knee was excruciating. He found it difficult to keep up but the carbine in his back propelled him, stumbling, onwards. At one point he fell over a heap of sacking. The smell told him it was a body. He soon found that, wherever a little light came through, indicating the nearness of a manhole, there would be bodies. He guessed they were in various stages of decomposition. The stench was indescribable. The Stalingrad sewers were communication routes, tombs – and, of course, sewers. Toni retched, and received a sickening blow at the base of the spine by way of reward.

He supposed he was as likely as not to find death at the end of the tunnel. The Russians were known to have a short way with prisoners, and had announced their view that the German General Staff was a criminal organization. Toni told himself that, if he survived the first stage, the moment when front line soldiers might say, 'He's too much trouble. Shoot him!' he might last longer. Perhaps he already had survived that first stage. At a higher level they would certainly wish to interrogate him – if they ever heard about him. That would mean survival for a little. He limped painfully on.

Toni realized, as yet in a blurred sort of way, that if he were to keep any sort of mental balance he must discipline his thoughts, try to control what images should or should not be allowed to invade the mind. Already, as he groped his way along through the darkness and the fetid air, he felt strong temptation to self-accusation. It had been idiotic – and improper – for him, a visiting Staff officer, to carry out a private reconnaissance and get himself into this sort of mess. It was impossible to justify it as 'getting to know at first hand the conditions under which the troops had to live and fight'.

On the contrary, he had behaved like an adventurous adolescent. He was a danger to the Wehrmacht through what he might ultimately disclose (he switched his mind from this aspect as well as he could). He would certainly have got the brave, patient detachment of Combat Group Schroder into trouble for not looking after him. He was leaving his own Divisional Headquarters, quite unnecessarily, without one of their principal staff officers when they were already short-handed and likely to be facing the prospect of a new battle on the Don front. Perhaps most reprehensibly of all, he had failed to produce the report which he had been sent to Stalingrad to compile. He had failed to do even his limited best to make others understand the ordeal of the gallant men of Sixth Army. He should be brought before a Court Martial. Perhaps one day he would be. If he survived.

Suicide would be a perfectly honourable, perhaps the only honourable course for a failure of duty so complete. Deprived of a weapon, Toni nevertheless saw little difficulty in losing his life if he so decided. In fact it ought to be particularly easy. An attack on one of his guards, for instance, would surely bring instant death from a Russian bullet or bayonet. But that seemed an inappropriate gesture – the sense of it would be lost, nobody would ever know. Suicide in such circumstances, after all, ought to be an act of semi-public atonement. No, to court death as secret self-punishment for failure as an officer wouldn't do. Anyway, things might turn out a little better than the worst. There would be other officer prisoners. There might (although he felt dubious on this score) even be the possibility of liberation by the Wehrmacht. There might, one day, be freedom again. When Germany had won the war! He found the latter consummation as difficult to envisage as any, but one never knew, something might turn up. The important thing was to survive, clearly no better than an even chance; and to remain sane, which might be at least as difficult.

'But you never know,' said Toni to himself. 'I was born lucky!'

He hobbled along down the sewer, in a good deal of agony, towards, as he rightly supposed, the banks of the Volga. Somewhere above his head, no doubt, little detachments of men like those from Combat Group Schroder were shivering hungrily among the rubble, bloodshot eyes blinking from grey, unshaven faces, frozen fingers curled round triggers, Sixth Army fighting off unremitting Soviet assaults among the ruins of the city of Stalingrad.

The little column halted. Ahead the darkness was dissolving. They had, it seemed, reached the end of their journey. When Toni emerged, half blinded at first, into the grey, cold light soldiers closed in on either side. A sack was thrown over his head. It was a nerve-racking moment, perhaps to be one of his last. Then he was pushed, slipping and slithering, down what felt like a muddy chute, although his heel caught the edge of a step, showing him that it was some sort of stair. The atmosphere was even colder than before. He tripped and fell, in darkness. He cursed in German and received a numbing blow in the small of his back. Next moment he was yanked to his feet and the sacking was pulled from his head.

The dug-out in which Toni was standing appeared to have been cut into a cliff face. Through a large round hole in one wall he could see sky and hear sounds, including the sound of water, which seemed to come from far below. This dug-out, he thought, must be in one of the cliffs overhanging the Volga.

It was from these cliffs, from the west bank where they held a shallow bridgehead into the city, that the Russians had tunnelled with such extraordinary effect. The dug-out walls were dripping, the air damp and chilling to the bone. The place was about three metres square. A kerosene lamp stood on a table.

At the table sat two men. One wore the shoulder straps of an officer on his greatcoat. On the other, who was in shadow, Toni could discern no mark of rank. The latter spoke first, in a lilting, broken German. His voice was high-pitched. Both he and his companion wore fur hats and smoked pungent, Russian cigarettes. The reek was strong.

'Your name?'

'Major Rudberg.'

'Your unit?'

Toni described himself as attached to Sixth Army Headquarters. It was strictly true at the time of capture, and it could do no harm.

'What is your position at Sixth Army Headquarters?'

'I was attached to the Army Staff for a particular task. Temporarily.'

'What particular task?'

The conventions dictated that interrogation must be limited to the eliciting of certain specific facts. The conventions, Toni decided, were hardly likely to apply. He would do the least possible damage to his comrades and to Germany, and be judge, while he still had strength, of how and what to answer. And he would, somehow, survive. The immediate problem was how to comport himself so that these particular Ivans would think it desirable to keep him alive: and to send him to the rear. What sort of command post was this, he wondered. Battalion? Regiment? He looked neutrally at his interrogator.

'I was to report on the state of the German troops in Stalingrad.'

'Report to whom?'

'The Staff of Army Group Don.'

'So you are on the Staff of Army Group Don?'

This was getting more difficult. Toni was anxious to avoid, as long as possible, questions touching his real area of knowledge, the strength, composition and capabilities of the divisions of Army Group Don, the troops outside the pocket, the German Army on the Don front. At that moment, however, the man at the table with the officer's epaulettes started to mutter in Russian to the interrogator. Toni kept his face blank. He distinguished a word or two. They seemed to be reminding each other of something. Toni heard Epaulettes say, 'Yesterday', and, 'Orders from Division'. The other nodded. He looked at Toni and then spoke in Russian to the soldier standing behind him. With sacking again pulled over his head but with a faint whisper of hope in his heart Toni found himself hauled up the slippery steps of the dug-out to cleaner and drier air above. He had no picture of his surroundings to help compose the mind. He could envisage nothing.

He heard the words, 'This one's got to go back to Headquarters. Over the river.'

Toni reckoned he had been walking for nearly two hours. His watch had been dexterously snatched from his wrist when the sacking was first put over his head. After emerging from the dug-out he had been prodded along steep, slimy paths, falling often. At last he had found himself treading on boards, resonant, slippery. The sacking had been taken away. Jammed between Russian soldiers they were crossing the great river on a creaking, paddle-driven ferry. Then he had been pushed and harried up the east bank and along a track of beaten snow. He seemed to be escorted by only one soldier. After walking a short way they appeared to be alone, trudging through the snow beneath a leaden sky. Toni reckoned that it must be about three o'clock in the afternoon.

The pain in Toni's knee was sharp and showed no signs of diminishing. Every step was torment. Nausea had been replaced by hunger. He felt incapable of a long march: a long march, however, looked to be his fate. He limped on as well as he could. His escort shuffled along behind him. Toni glanced at him periodically. In his mind he christened him Vassili. If they were going to spend some time together he had better have a name, if only in imagination.

Vassili's face was barely visible. His fur cap had ear-pieces, and a mouth and nostril cover – Toni could see eyes which looked at him incuriously. He wore felt boots, huge, shapeless articles which were undoubtedly warmer and more serviceable than anything in German use – and greatly preferable to Toni's field boots, in which his legs were so frozen at the start of the march as to raise doubts in his mind as to whether they were still attached to his body. Vassili had a rifle with fixed bayonet slung over the shoulder. Marching along behind Toni he periodically uttered a strange cry which somehow penetrated the mouth cover and was interpreted by Toni as an instruction to move faster. There was nothing to be done about this.

Toni, twisted with pain, felt the temptation strong, now and then, to sink into the snow, to let the man shoot or bayonet him – or simply leave him to die, here on the icy Volga steppe. Every pace brought a fresh twinge to his knee. His face, unprotected from the wind, was frozen. He supposed he would get, probably already had, frostbite. His nose would drop off. His gloves, although fleece lined and, miraculously, still in his possession were of little use. He kept his hands in his pockets. He supposed he still had ears because he could hear the crunch of snow beneath his feet. He trudged on, looking at the ground five paces ahead. The biting wind sighed and sang. The will to live is strong but it was ebbing in Rudberg.

Toni heard, once again, a meaningless call from his escort. He plodded forward and then felt, dully, the new pain of a blow between the shoulder blades. It was the butt of Vassili's rifle. Toni turned. Vassili was stationary and shouting something. He appeared to be commanding a halt. Toni turned again, apathetically. Then he saw the reason.

Trudging towards them through the snow in the opposite direction was another Russian soldier. He and Vassili called greetings to each other. Soon they all formed a bizarre threesome beside the track. The two Russians evidently knew each other. They took no notice of Toni. Toni could now distinguish their words. The chance of a social occasion was too great to miss, and each soldier lowered his mouth cover and fumbled in his pocket producing tobacco and paper. Soon they were rolling, lighting and puffing cigarettes. They chatted, oblivious of Toni. Eventually the soldier who had met them said,

'What have you got here?'

Toni listened with interest. He could follow them pretty clearly although he took care to show nothing.

'A Fritz. An officer, I've got to take him to Headquarters.'

The other looked at Vassili pityingly.

'You know it's another hour's march?'

'Yes, I know,' Vassili drew on his cigarette.

'Well, why don't you shoot him?'

'No, Comrade,' said Vassili seriously. 'That won't do. I've been ordered to take him.'

'You could say he collapsed on the way. The snow will soon cover him. They'll never know. Here, I'll shoot him if you like, my rifle's dirty already. Otherwise you've got three hours in front of you by the time you get home again.'

'I know,' said Vassili regretfully, 'but Headquarters know he's coming. I'll end in the snow myself if he doesn't arrive.'

The other digested this. He seemed to find the conclusion depressing. He turned to Toni and looked at him, considering. Then he spoke to Vassili again.

'Well, if you won't shoot him and you won't let me shoot him, you might at least look after him better.'

'How – better?'

'Well, the poor fellow's absolutely done in, anybody can see that. Here, Comrade,' he said to Toni, without any reasonable expectation of being understood. 'Here, you'd better have a cigarette.'

He rolled one, shoved it with a grin between Toni's frozen lips, and produced a light. Watching with satisfaction as Toni puffed, he felt in his pocket and produced a bottle. He took a swig, roared with laughter and held it out to Vassili, who drank greedily. Then its owner recovered the bottle and pushed it at Toni.

'Go on, Comrade, it will do you good. You never know when a drink will be your last. It's a terrible world, Comrade – a terrible, terrible world!'

PART V

1944

Chapter 18

———————◆———————

JOHN AND HILDA MARVELL led a separate existence from the American officers who had largely taken over Bargate in the autumn of 1943. Relations were cordial, contacts few. The Americans belonged to the communications unit of a large Headquarters in Flintdown. They were invariably courteous. Colonel Schultz, the Commanding Officer, a large, sallow-faced man from Illinois with rimless glasses, was particularly friendly. Hilda loathed having them in the house, and despised herself for loathing it.

'They're a long way from home,' she told herself. 'And they certainly didn't ask to come. And what am I doing to win the war?'

Nevertheless, she could not help herself – the military presence sprawling over Bargate was a defilement. Grey vehicles with huge white stars painted on them crowded every yard, driveway and paddock. Noise was incessant.

'It would be no better if they were British,' thought Hilda. 'In fact in many ways it would be worse.' The Americans were generous and good-mannered. Individually, Hilda found them endearing. The fact remained that the heart of the house no longer beat for her and hers. She and John inhabited three rooms on the first floor, where a small washroom had been converted to a kitchen for them. Apart from the few Marvell rooms, Bargate – inner hall, drawing room, dining room, billiard room and all the rest – was part of General Eisenhower's command. It was 31st May, 1944.

'They've been up at all hours these last few days,' said John. 'They've hardly had their clothes off as far as I can see.'

It was six o'clock in the evening and he had made the same remark three times. They were sitting in their small upstairs sitting room.

'Do you think the invasion's about to begin, John? I've

271

always thought it would happen on the anniversary of Dunkirk. The end of May, the beginning of June.' It was a futile speculation, something to say. John shrugged –

'I don't think that the American Command, which must largely decide the matter, is likely to be sentimentally influenced by memories of Dunkirk!'

Everybody in England was waiting, of course. It had to be this summer.

John felt he had been snubbing to his beloved wife.

'No, I've no idea, my love. These American fellows jump about such a lot, seem to be rushing to and fro all the time, one can't tell if anything unusual is up. Nor should one, of course. Security, you know, walls have ears, all that. And these chaps are the signals outfit of a Corps Headquarters, pretty important –'

There was a knock at the door. John opened it and uttered friendly greetings.

'Do come in. Darling, it's Colonel Schultz.'

Schultz came into the room carrying a parcel, glasses flashing, an enthusiastic smile on his face.

'Mrs Marvell, Mr Marvell, I wanted to call on you this evening because these days we never know when we might be called away suddenly.'

'We understand.'

'There could be no time for proper goodbyes. That would make me sad. Mrs Marvell, I'd like you to know how much I and my boys have appreciated being in your lovely home. Maybe I'll get the opportunity to say this many more times and if so I'll do just that. But just in case, I wanted to say it now. Ma'am, it's been a wonderful experience.'

Hilda felt particularly guilty.

'And you've been wonderful too, Mrs Marvell.'

More guilt. This, Hilda thought, was especially untrue. John said, 'It's been a great privilege for us, Colonel, to be able to do anything to help you. Personally we've done little, I'm afraid. But I hope you've found the house convenient.'

'It's a wonderful old place, sir. I'll always have some great memories. And believe me, I can imagine it's no fun having strangers tramping all over your home.'

The garden had suffered most, Hilda thought. They were

assured that compensation for damage to the house would be scrupulously assessed and they had little doubt of it. The Americans appeared so lavish and to command such immense resources that the Marvells were unworried. And what does it all matter, Hilda said to herself irritably, garden, furniture, inanimate things, what do they matter? These men are going to war, going to fight our battles as well as their own, going to risk their lives, may never see their families again! And how extraordinarily, terribly nice they are! She felt confused and close to tears.

Schultz was addressing John Marvell.

'Mr Marvell, I have here a small present. It's rather a special whisky. I know you like Bourbon and I believe you'll appreciate this.'

John thanked him profusely. In providing periodic benefits of this nature, the Americans had been kind well beyond the call of manners, and probably beyond the limit of regulations. They did not seem greatly concerned about the latter. Schultz looked pleased. Hilda laughed.

'Don't you think we ought to open it, and have a drink together? As Colonel Schultz said, he never knows when he'll see us again. There may not be many more opportunities.'

The bottle was opened. Schultz smiled, gratified. Then he looked serious and cleared his throat.

'Mrs Marvell, may I ask, have you had any word recently of your son?'

John shook his head. Hilda said brightly,

'We had a letter a month ago. They can't say much, you know, but he was alive and not, as far as one could tell, sick. Of course, we haven't the faintest idea where he is.'

'It's been a long time, ma'am. A long time of anxiety for you. I can just imagine how this last year and a half has been. Well – let's hope we'll soon be getting on, finishing it.'

When Schultz left them Hilda said, 'Do you think any of the ones with German names – like Colonel Schultz – feel any reservations about this war? I expect lots of them are only second generation Americans. They must have close relations in Germany. They can't find it easy to regard them as automatically vile.'

John looked at her. 'And do we? Do we regard them as

273

automatically vile? What about that charming young man, Frido von Arzfeld, whom Anthony brought here? I know the name upsets us because of little Marcia, but he wasn't vile. He was decent and delightful. Darling, we've got to fight against the temptation to lump everybody in the same pot of iniquity because we're at war with their beastly government, we really have.'

Hilda pursed her lips. 'I don't think women find it easy to feel like that. That delightful young man, as you call him, may have been spending the winter of 1942 trying to kill Anthony. I think you're too forgiving, my dear.'

They generally tried to avoid subjects of contention between them and long practice made them good at it, but the habit sometimes failed.

'I doubt if one can be,' said John, suddenly feeling exhausted. 'But I know it's all too easy to forgive injuries done to other people. Still, if Frido von Arzfeld spent the winter of 1942 trying to kill Anthony, at least he failed. I wonder if he's alive. Arzfeld, I mean.'

'When there's no air raid, when the sun is shining, the *Grunewald* can almost persuade one there are other things than war.' Klaus Becker, like his companion, Frido von Arzfeld, had been wounded in Russia. Disabled, one empty sleeve pinned to his jacket, he had recovered sufficiently to be posted to the staff of the Army High Command, in Berlin, *Oberkommando des Heeres* – OKH. He had arrived at the end of June, 1944. Frido, who had for two years been attached to the Headquarters of 'Home Army', was delighted. They were old friends.

'You manage damned well with that wooden foot of yours, Arzfeld! I can hardly keep up with you.' They were walking together on a Sunday afternoon in July, both freed for a few hours from duty.

Frido walked surprisingly fast. He was silent that afternoon. The heart had been pounded out of Berlin by Allied bombers and there were few people minded to stroll light-heartedly in the summer sunshine. When Frido at last started to speak he talked in a low voice and Becker had simultaneously to gallop to keep up and to bend his head, for he was particularly tall.

Frido said, 'I wanted to have this talk here, outside. Outside one can speak freely if one's careful. Indoors one never knows.

'I've been told to make certain things clear to you. General von Tresckow vouched for you. We know you're reliable.' Von Tresckow had once been Chief of Staff to 'Army Group Centre' on the Eastern Front. Klaus Becker had been a promising adjutant at that Headquarters before returning to his regiment, a tall young man who radiated calm, principle and purpose. He had attracted confidence. Now he looked at Frido, listening, expressionless. He knew that von Arzfeld was, as he put it to himself, 'All right': but a man could not stop his heart beginning to race when conversation took this turn. What was coming? What would be required?

Frido was continuing in the same low voice –

'You've heard about yesterday?'

'You mean the false alarm? Orders sent out from your people, troops started to move and then everything cancelled? Yes, of course – and there were all sorts of rumours, I can tell you! But then we heard it was an exercise, a sudden unannounced alert to test the readiness of the troops for Operation "Valkyrie", isn't that so?'

'Valkyrie' was the codename for mobilizing home forces in case of emergency – an emergency which, during Frido's time in Berlin, had been imagined as possibly being caused by a revolt of the huge numbers of wretched, conscripted foreign workers within the Reich: by some other internal disturbance: or even by an Allied landing on the north German coast, though few people had ever thought that likely. 'Valkyrie' involved in the first instance the Berlin Guard battalion and all troops who could be raised from the staffs of training schools and depots near the capital. It was decreed by 'Home Army' that every installation must find men for operations in such an emergency, and guards were to be rushed into Berlin to secure Government offices, telephone and radio centres and other key points. While the emergency lasted, 'Valkyrie' placed legitimate authority firmly in military hands.

'Valkyrie' had been ordered, suddenly, the previous day, a Saturday, 15th July. Then, a few hours later, it had been cancelled and the troops ordered back to barracks.

'It wasn't an exercise,' said Frido.

'An alarm? I don't believe it! Even at my humble level we in OKH would have – besides nobody could imagine England and America starting another invasion here, when they're doing pretty well in France.'

For there were no illusions within the Army High Command. Field Marshal von Kluge's front in Normandy might crack at any time. His signals grew more desperate daily. The Allies had landed on 6th June, 1944. The long anticipated Anglo-American invasion of the Continent had been under way for nearly six weeks. German attempts to push the invaders into the sea had utterly failed. Every soldier knew that when the British and Americans finally broke out from the expanding beachhead in which they were precariously hemmed, there would be little organized defence feasible between the Channel and the Rhine.

Frido began talking, quietly, flatly. He had been ordered to brief Becker. Becker listened with a heart half-troubled, half-exalted.

On the previous day, Frido said, the Commander-in-Chief of Home Army, General Fromm, and his Chief of Staff, Colonel von Stauffenberg, had flown to Hitler's Supreme Headquarters at Rastenburg in East Prussia. They had been ordered to attend a conference with the Führer himself, to describe the progress made with weeding out men within the home and training establishments in order to man new divisions. This operation had been largely entrusted to Fromm.

'We don't think it's going to work miracles,' interrupted Becker conversationally. 'They're pretty sceptical in OKH. The barrel's been well scraped.'

Frido ignored him, and went on in his matter-of-fact voice. Becker listened with a curious feeling in his stomach.

In Colonel von Stauffenberg's briefcase had been a bomb. The bomb was to be set off by a time fuse. The fuse depended on the breaking of a capsule which would spill acid on, and snap, a tiny wire. This, in turn, would release a striker on to a detonator cap and the fuse would be ignited. A ten minute fuse.

'It's an English fuse. The *Abwehr* have plenty of them and it was easy to get them until Canaris went.' Admiral Canaris, head of the German counter-espionage service, *Abwehr*, had been dismissed five months earlier. He was, Frido said, 're-liable'. The function of the bomb was to kill Hitler.

Thereafter 'Valkyrie' was immediately to be ordered. But instead of securing Government offices and communications against some internal threat or some revolution, the purpose of 'Valkyrie', Frido explained, was to get control of the machinery of government for a new, anti-Nazi administration, dedicated to making peace.

'All of which is organized. General Beck will be Head of State. Dr Goerdeler, Lord Mayor of Leipzig, is to be Chancellor. Field Marshal von Witzleben, Commander-in-Chief of the Armed Forces. And so on.'

'What happened?'

'We heard Stauffenberg had landed at Rastenburg, with Fromm. We ordered "Valkyrie" straight away. We knew he'd not fail – he's been the life and soul of the whole business and it all turns on him. The General – Fromm – sits on the fence. He'll emerge as his Chief of Staff's benevolent patron if all goes right – assuming he survives. If it doesn't –'

'But it didn't!'

'No, it didn't. At the last moment Hitler left the conference room. So, of course, no bomb.'

'And meanwhile "Valkyrie" had been ordered!"

'Yes. Fromm, of course, was with Stauffenberg in East Prussia. When they got back and we learned what had happened – or not happened – at Rastenburg we had to cook up a story about a practice alert, an exercise. I don't think Fromm believed a word of it but it suits him to pretend. He's been trying to have it both ways for over a year.'

They walked on, more slowly now. Becker said,

'One heard rumours – earlier attempts –'

'There were indeed earlier attempts. Something always went wrong. It never came to the point – although, to be accurate, a bomb was actually put on *his* aircraft once, flying back from Russia. It didn't go off. But now everybody's absolutely determined – it's *got* to happen. There can be no more waiting. It's got to happen – by one means or another.'

Becker was silent. Frido was not sure whether his companion's lack of response implied dissent.

'You agree, I hope?'

'Yes – but the urgency –'

'My God,' said Frido, his voice for the first time a little louder, 'we can't go on like this! It's obvious the war is lost. Within months the Red Army will be in East Prussia. We're certainly not going to push the English and Americans into the sea. We're just about holding on in Italy. Germany is being systematically destroyed by these air raids. Of course we can't wait.' He stopped, wheeled and stared at Becker.

'And it's far worse than that – far, far worse. There are worse things even than defeat if it's defeat in a decent cause. But look at the things that have been done by these swine – in our name! That are being done all the time! One can't breathe until –'

He stumped on.

'Until the principal swine is dead?' said Becker, near inaudibly.

'Of course. That's the key to everything. Without that nobody will be moved. They'll be stifled, hesitant, mutter about the oath –'

'I think many soldiers feel strongly about the oath. Germans are serious about such things.'

'Then they had better,' said Frido, 'enquire in their hearts whether they can reconcile it with the creed many of them recite conscientiously on Sundays. Germans have the name of being serious about such things too.'

The moral issue was not new to Klaus Becker, and the strength of feeling he shared. His temperament was to provoke antithesis in an argument. There was one practical point he had secretly felt for a long time from his own observation, that these people (and he felt both proud and nervous to be of their number) disregarded. He put it to Frido.

'Whatever orders are given by generals, I don't believe the ordinary German soldier is ready to go against – him. That's the problem, in my view.'

'When he's disappeared they'll change, start opening their minds to the truth. They're fine fellows, after all, they've simply been mesmerized.'

'I'm not so sure,' said Becker. 'The ordinary soldiers, the young ones anyway, *believe* in Hitler. They think he rescued Germany from the old gang with their disaster-laden policies

278

– that's how they see it. We must face the fact that to most young Germans, not all, this – Goerdeler, Beck, von Witzleben – will simply look like a step into a gloomy conservative past from which Hitler rescued them.'

'There are also young idealists in Germany, young people who have discovered enough of what National Socialism is doing and are revolted by it.'

'Some, perhaps. But the young people I'm chiefly concerned with are in the ranks of the Wehrmacht. And I think most of them are – loyal to the Führer.' Becker said the last words with an ironic inflexion, wryly. He shrugged his shoulders. What of it, he seemed to say. If we have consciences we must obey them, however lonely the road.

'We can't think too much of that,' said Frido abruptly, who shared the same anxiety, 'we mustn't worry about that. We've got to have faith. We've got to light a torch. Then men will rub their eyes and feel they've emerged from darkness, as Stauffenberg says.'

'And your part in all this?'

'A humble transmitter of commands and information, knowing nothing and obeying orders. A captain at a desk in an office in the Bendlerstrasse. But placed where another might question certain orders, be dismayed at certain information. And in the light of yesterday's events, it's been decided an extra link is desirable between the Bendlerstrasse and OKH. We knew your name, of course, and I was able to speak about you personally. Now here's what you've got to do . . .'

'Becker? Arzfeld here. Supper this evening? Seven o'clock?'

'Thank you.'

It was three days later. 19th July. That evening they sat in a cellar-restaurant that had survived air raids, not far from the Tiergartenstrasse. They sipped wine and Frido said quietly, conversationally,

'Thursday. Tomorrow.'

'Same plan?'

'Precisely. Same conference, reconvened. Same object, same method. He'll send word when it's done. We won't act till then.'

'You mean he'll wait to telephone –?'

'No. The Chief Wehrmacht communications man is a friend. He'll do it while – my master – is on his way back to Berlin.' Frido lifted his glass. His smile was exultant.

'To Thursday!'

They walked away from the restaurant an hour later. It was a warm night. There was no air raid. Their footsteps echoed. They had the narrow, moonlit side street to themselves.

'I shall speak to you, tell you what's happening all the time. You're my only authorized link with OKH. And you know whom to tell what in OKH.'

'I do.'

'We shall send signals to the Military Districts direct from Home Army. You've heard Rommel's been wounded?' It was a statement. All Germany knew that the wiry, tough Field Marshal Erwin Rommel had been hit by an enemy air attack in France two days before.

'Was he –?'

'Ready to serve, yes. A late sympathizer, but helpful. He doesn't know our plans, but he would have reacted after the event as we wish. It's a pity he was hit. And we know that they've moved to arrest Goerdeler, but he's gone into hiding. Of course others – Leber and others – were arrested earlier this month.'

They were only names to Becker. Whether names like this would command the confidence of the hard-bitten, suffering *landser* at the fronts he was unsure. Frido took his arm, eyes shining in the moonlight.

'Until tomorrow!'

They parted with a handshake, Becker extending his left, his only arm and holding the other tightly. Frido sat all night by the window of the room he had rented in the southern suburbs of Berlin. No Allied bombers disturbed the German capital that night. It was hot and sultry. At five o'clock he washed, shaved, put on a clean uniform and set out on a bicycle towards the Government quarter. His artificial limb impeded his bicycling now as little as it slowed his walking, and he covered the distance in excellent time.

The headquarters of Home Army was in the Armed Forces

Building in the Bendlerstrasse. Frido shared his office with two colleagues on the Staff, a captain and a lieutenant. Neither had become intimate friends of his, with neither had he ever discussed anything more serious than their shared professional concerns, and neither was privy to the great enterprise which had kept him sitting awake and restless all night. But neither, he was sure, was a zealous National Socialist. They were intelligent, painstaking officers with good records at the Front in both cases. One, Koller, had been wounded in the Caucasus and the other, Hoffmann, was suffering still from stomach disorders acquired in North Africa. He did not think, when the moment came, they would be particularly inquisitive or obstructive. But he could not trust them.

The room itself was at the top of the building, reached by a large, old-fashioned staircase with heavy mahogany banisters. It was a wide, high-ceilinged room, excessively cold in winter. In the heat of July it was pleasant. Frido reached it early that Thursday morning. This would arouse no comment. He was known as a hard worker, had a great deal of paper to sift, proposals to analyse on the organization and equipment of the planned new divisions of Home Army. He had frequently needed to be at his desk half the night, unless driven to the shelters by the fearful sounds and sights of Allied bombardment. Frido had already arranged that this day would be dominated by discussions in other parts of the building about one of his particular responsibilities: discussions, for the most part with his section chief, one of the conspirators. His frequent absences from his own desk would be regarded as normal when he sped off.

'To the Major – again! It's these charts, we'll never get them finally approved!'

If he were summoned more often than usual it would be unsurprising.

'Arzfeld! The Major wants to see you urgently!' and he would be able, minute by minute and hour by hour, to maintain contact, to know what was going on during this, the day of German liberation.

'*Dann bricht der Tag,*' he hummed from the *Horst Wessel Lied* '*Der Deutschen Freiheit an!*' 'But a very different *Freiheit,*' he prayed. 'God be with us!'

Surprised to hear the austere and conservative von Arzfeld hum so much as a stave of the Party song, one of his companions, Hoffmann, looked at him and was struck, as he said afterwards, 'by the air of nervous excitement Captain von Arzfeld had that morning'.

Frido arrived at the Bendlerstrasse and climbed to the top floor at half past six. At five past seven he received his first summons. The Major, his direct superior in both the army and the conspiracy, looked at him levelly.

'He's taken off. From Rangsdorf. The General's not going. He's taken off! He's airborne!'

Later, Frido was able to recall every moment of that extraordinary day, to sort it into tabular form in his mind, to settle the sequence of events over which his mind travelled restlessly again and again. And from others he gradually came to piece together the story of what befell 350 miles away in East Prussia, as well as elsewhere in Berlin.

Rastenburg

At a quarter past ten in the morning of Thursday, 20th July, Colonel Freiherr Schenk von Stauffenberg arrived by light aircraft at the airstrip at Rastenburg, accompanied by one adjutant. He ordered the pilot to be ready to take off on the return journey at any time after midday. He was due to attend a conference at one o'clock with the Führer and a number of other dignitaries including Field Marshal Keitel, Chief of the Armed Forces High Command, *Oberkommando der Wehrmacht* – OKW. The conference might always be advanced in time, and in fact he soon learned that it had been brought forward to half past twelve.

Stauffenberg drove through two heavily guarded barriers. Rastenburg was protected by a double cordon of perimeter fences and sentries. The headquarters itself, the 'Wolf's Lair', was still being strengthened and further fortified. It consisted of a large number of separate compounds of huts and concrete bunkers. Wooden huts were being reinforced by concrete facing. Stauffenberg was familiar with the place. He sought the Chief of OKW Communications, General Fellgiebel.

Berlin. Midday.

'He's seen Fellgiebel. Fellgiebel will get word to us when it's done. Then he'll block communications into and out of Rastenburg.'

'The conference has been brought forward from one o'clock to twelve-thirty. Mussolini arrives at two-thirty at Rastenburg.'

'But there's no question, *Herr Major*, that *he* –?'

'None at all, I understand. He'll be there. Not in his own conference bunker but in a temporary room he's using while the Todt people work on the protection and the defences. He'll be there in half an hour from now. You'd better find some pretext to report to me, Arzfeld, at about a quarter to one.'

Rastenburg. 12.35.

The temporary conference room was thirty-five feet long, wooden walls inside a concrete casing, ten windows and a massive central table. It was a hot day and the windows were all open. The participants began to file in.

Set back from the passage running from the visitors' assembly hut to the conference room was a telephone exchange; several telephones on which conference participants could take or make urgent calls, and a *Feldwebel* in charge. Stauffenberg, dark-haired, of striking good looks, was walking immediately behind the tall, burly figure of Field Marshal Keitel. He paused for a moment at the telephone exchange.

'Colonel von Stauffenberg,' he said loudly to the *Feldwebel*, 'I'm expecting an urgent call from Berlin – information I need for my presentation to the Führer.'

The man clicked to attention in acknowledgement. Keitel turned his head and nodded a salutation. Stauffenberg looked at his watch. It was 12.36. The conference was starting a few minutes late: they had only just received the summons that the Führer was ready. One minute earlier Stauffenberg had put his hand inside a bulky briefcase he was carrying. He had lost one hand in the fighting in Tunisia but was agile at manipulating his artificial limb. He had held the briefcase in the crook of one arm and inserted the other hand. With it he had broken a small capsule.

At 12.37 Stauffenberg took his place at the conference table. Four places to his left was Hitler. He placed his briefcase against the left side of the table leg beside him. The opening presentation of the conference began.

'I've got to take an urgent telephone call,' Stauffenberg whispered to Colonel Brandt, his neighbour at the table and an acquaintance of long standing. Brandt nodded. Stauffenberg looked again at his watch. 12.40. He slipped from his place and unobtrusively left the room. Brandt shifted uncomfortably on his feet. In doing so he knocked over Stauffenberg's briefcase, and bent to pick it up again. He glanced round. No sign of Stauffenberg returning. Still on the telephone.

One minute later, at 12.41, Stauffenberg was standing by his car.

Two minutes later again, at 12.43, with a crash like the explosion of a heavy artillery shell, the conference room burst into flame and smoke amid the sound of smashing glass and collapsing girders.

At 12.44 Stauffenberg, with his adjutant, drove up to the first barrier.

'Colonel von Stauffenberg. Going to the airfield.'

'I shall need to check with the duty officer, *Herr Oberst*. There's been some sort of accident, some emergency.'

Stauffenberg waited. In the duty officer's room, one to whom Stauffenberg's name was sympathetically known took the call from the guardroom.

'Yes, all in order,' he said crisply. Then he rose and stood looking out of the window. 12.46. Both barrier gates opened, sentries saluting. The airfield was twenty-five minutes' drive away.

Berlin. 13.15.

'Becker?'

Frido tried for seven minutes to make his connection. Switchboards were having a difficult day it seemed.

'Becker, we've had word –'

Becker kept his voice non-committal. They had agreed that guarded speech would suffice for security in the urgency of the moment. No telephone could be regarded as safe although

284

some – and some very senior – officers were remarkably slow to take the point. Becker said,

'Word? Ah – all right, I hope?'

'Not entirely,' Frido was less successful at controlling his voice, try as he might. 'The event took place but not – it appears – with exactly the full consequence planned.'

Fellgiebel's telephone call to Berlin had come through at one o'clock. He had been cautious and somewhat ambiguous but the conspirators had received the impression that, while the bomb had certainly gone off and Hitler had been injured, his injuries were not known to be fatal. Stauffenberg, Fellgiebel presumed, was flying back. He was certainly nowhere to be seen.

And there were now divisions of opinion in Berlin. Some thought it madness to launch 'Valkyrie', to set things afoot in the capital, until they knew for certain that Hitler was dead. But what if he wasn't? It was unlikely that the explosion of a bomb and the sudden disappearance of Stauffenberg would long remain unconnected.

Dangerous as it might be, another call was put through to Rastenburg. But General Fellgiebel was obeying his instructions to the letter. No communications were possible with the Führer's headquarters. There seemed to be an inexplicable breakdown. Efforts were being made to deal with it.

Berlin. 15.00.

'*Herr General,* there has been remarkable news. The Führer has been killed. There has been a bomb, an assassination at Rastenburg!'

General Fromm looked up at his visitor. Head of the *Wehrmachtamt*, in the same building in the Bendlerstrasse. General Friedrich Olbricht. They stared at each other, holding each other's eyes levelly for ten long seconds. It was three o'clock that afternoon.

'When did you receive this extraordinary report?'

'A little time ago. We've been trying to corroborate but can make no contact with Rastenburg. You've heard nothing?'

'Nothing.'

'There will be, undoubtedly, special orders, special measures necessary –'

Fromm nodded, still looking at him.

'We must contact Rastenburg. Somehow.'

'At present it appears impossible,' said Olbricht. He sounded, thought Fromm, unsurprised at so protracted and unusual a collapse of communications. Entirely unsurprised.

Berlin. 15.15.

'*Herr General*, it's Rastenburg, the *Generalfeldmarschall*.'

Fromm held the telephone tight.

'Fromm here!'

Keitel's voice was agitated. He sounded shaken. His news, however, was given without equivocation. He asked Fromm whether he had heard any rumours.

'Rumours, yes. Is the Führer safe?'

'The Führer, thank God, is entirely safe. There was an attempt to kill us all. Several dead, many injured. It's been terrible! But by some miracle the Führer, although injured, survived.'

'He's not – incapacitated?'

'On the contrary, it happened just before one o'clock and at one-fifteen he appeared among us all having been patched up, changed his clothes, looking cheerful and composed. He's truly wonderful, Fromm. We've had the Duce here – he's still here. The Führer's entirely in control of the situation.'

'Wonderful!'

'Now we've got to get to the bottom of it – quickly. I raised no objection when Himmler said the Gestapo must have a free hand to question whom they like – Army officers, everybody. One can create no possible obstacle in these circumstances. It's the least we can do.'

'Of course.'

'Has Stauffenberg returned?'

'No,' said Fromm carefully. Keitel told him that Stauffenberg was known to have left the conference room before the bomb exploded, 'So he must arrive with you soon.' There was a further interruption on the line. Fromm snapped into the telephone that he would undoubtedly wish to speak to Rastenburg again later. He sat back in his chair and considered the tips of his fingers thoughtfully. There was a knock on the door. An adjutant. Four o'clock.

'Herr General, I thought you would wish to be informed that retired General Beck has just entered the Bendlerstrasse. In civilian clothes.'

'Has he?' said Fromm. 'Has he indeed?'

Rastenburg. 16.05.

'This is an odd one!' exclaimed the lieutenant in charge of the monitoring department of the OKW communications division.

A telephone call had been intercepted and recorded from the *Wehrmachtamt* in Berlin. It was to the effect that Field Marshal von Witzleben had been appointed Commander-in-Chief of the Armed Forces. The lieutenent looked at the typed record in astonishment.

'They're calling each military district with the same message!'

His Captain seized his cap and moved like a sliver of mercury. Within minutes the transcript lay on Keitel's desk.

'In the name of God,' snarled the Field Marshal to his Adjutant, 'what is happening in Berlin?' He started to dictate a signal to be telephoned or sent by the fastest possible means to the commander of every military district in the Reich.

Berlin. 16.40.

Stauffenberg burst into the Bendlerstrasse building and went up the stairs, taking them two at a time. The office of General Olbricht was the scene of what looked like a funeral wake. The ageing General Beck, Olbricht himself and several others sat in armchairs in silence. Everybody heaved himself to his feet as Stauffenberg strode through the door. There was a gasp of interrogation and relief.

'Stauffenberg!'

Berlin. 16.50.

'Becker?'
'Becker here, Arzfeld.'

'Our friend's back. The signal is going out to all military districts. You know its terms. The first message – about the top man – went out half an hour ago. Please start taking action as agreed. Tell all those on the list at OKH.'

'It's going out in spite of the uncertainties, the –'

'Certainly,' Frido spoke fast and emphatically. 'S. – you understand?'

'Of course.'

'S. made everything electrically clear as he always does. By now we've gone too far to stop. Of course there will be counter-instructions from – from the other place. But if everybody now plays his part here in Berlin the operation can be completed satisfactorily. People will fall into line. We've given the local people word to go.'

'In your General's name?'

'In our Field Marshal's name!' said Frido. He sounded buoyant once again. Becker thought that this particular conversation would hang them both if the dice rolled wrong. He said – 'You've heard, I take it, that there has already been a message to everybody from – from the other place, saying that no orders are to be obeyed unless they emanate from there?'

'That may be so. But if things go as they should in the next two hours there will be – moral authority – here in Berlin. It will be compulsive. The clock has already struck.'

'Right,' said Becker. He put down the telephone and moved towards the door of his office. He felt afraid.

Berlin. 17.00.

Fromm looked at his Chief of Staff.

'What's happening, Stauffenberg? When did you get back here? I want a full report –'

'*Herr General*, it's my duty to tell you that you must consider yourself under arrest. A room has been prepared.'

There was a long silence.

'You are placing your own commander under arrest, Colonel von Stauffenberg?' said Fromm calmly. 'Why?'

'Explanations must wait. I regret it. There is danger to the Reich. Operation "Valkyrie" has just been ordered.'

'By whom? And against what threat?'

Stauffenberg ignored these questions and left Fromm under guard. Soon the first troops would be moving into the Government quarter of Berlin. They had lost hours, he thought to himself angrily, but he mastered the anger and summoned up those reserves of faith and serenity which had invariably inspired all around him. The important thing now was to secure Berlin and to get the Head of State, General Beck, to speak urgently to the various Commanders-in-Chief in the field. Of course their enemies would try and overturn matters with the SS – they'd always been ready for that. 'Valkyrie' provided for army reinforcements from Potsdam. If real energy was shown the ring could be held. General von Hase, Commander of the Berlin District, had, Stauffenberg knew, been waiting hours for word from the Bendlerstrasse. Now at last he'd received it, and set the Berlin Guard Battalion moving towards the centre of the city.

Rastenburg. 18.00.

'Here's another signal from Berlin, on a wide distribution, telling commanders to secure their communications and respond only to – wait! There's something else coming through!'

The lieutenant felt immense excitement. What a day! A man in SS uniform stood by the door of the monitoring office, alert and interested.

'A very illuminating run of signals,' the latter said contentedly, 'very illuminating indeed!' He took a copy of the tape as the signal ended and pinned it to several others of the same kind.

Berlin. 19.30.

'Arzfeld, you heard the broadcast?'
'I did.'

There was silence between them and after a little Frido said, 'Well, goodbye.'

At half past six that evening all radio programmes had been interrupted for a special announcement. It stated that, in spite of rumours, the Führer was alive and well, and that later he would speak to the German people. At seven o'clock the Propaganda Minister, Dr Goebbels, had broadcast that a das-

289

tardly attempt had been made to kill the Führer and overturn the Government. The attempt had been made in order to strengthen Germany's enemies. It had failed.

Nobody was allowed to leave the Bendlerstrasse that night. At half past nine Frido walked slowly down to the main entrance. Soldiers of the Berlin Guard Battalion stood at the door both inside and outside the building.

'All movement is forbidden, *Herr Hauptmann.*'

'By whose orders?'

'General Fromm.'

So Fromm had been released from arrest! Frido did not at the time know that all troops were acting under the directions of the Commander of the Berlin Guard Battalion, Major Remer, who had received orders from Hitler himself. Fromm was exercising a little authority but it was to be shortlived. Frido retraced his steps. There were tanks at the end of the street, clearly visible from the windows. Tanks had been part of the 'Valkyrie' plan. But whose orders were they now obeying? And what were those orders? Nobody seemed to know.

And Frido did not dare ask too much. Colonel von Stauffenberg was certainly not in his office. Casually, Frido said to one of the colleagues in his room,

'Has anybody seen the Chief of Staff since he returned? He must know what's going on.'

'Must he?' Frido met a hard stare. Men were talking in whispers in every office.

It grew dark – a hot July night. Frido, for the hundredth time was walking down the stairs, making an excuse to visit another office, range the corridors. Many doors were locked.

Suddenly he became aware of an extraordinary phenomenon. The main staircase window, which opened on to the Bendlerstrasse car park, was admitting, from blacked-out Berlin, a blaze of light. Astonished, he climbed higher, shifted the corner of a blind and peered out.

The car park, in defiance of all regulations, was illumined by what appeared to be searchlights – probably, thought Frido, the headlights of military trucks lined up for the purpose. He became aware of figures moving in the shadows and some shuffling on the edges of the brilliant pool of light. He could only imagine one explanation. He turned away from the window and closed his eyes. A few minutes later he heard the shots.

They were walking, Becker and he, in the Grunewald once again. It was an evening ten days later, the first occasion when both had found it possible to keep a rendezvous.

Frido was beginning to piece things together. He had been interrogated twice: Becker so far not at all. Frido had, he thought convincingly, expressed ignorance of anything except what had been apparent. Yes, of course everybody knew that Colonel von Stauffenberg had flown to the Führer's Head-quarters. Yes, he had heard rumours of an accident at Rasten-burg during the afternoon. Certainly he was aware that Colonel von Stauffenberg had returned – not as a matter of dramatic import but expectedly: somebody had said, quite casually, 'the Chief of Staff's back'. Certainly he was aware 'Valkyrie' had been ordered, although his own responsibilities were not con-cerned with operations but with future organizational planning which had fully occupied his day. No, he'd not found the ordering of 'Valkyrie' 'suspicious'. It seemed a natural pre-caution if there really had been some sort of disturbance at Supreme Headquarters, it was what one would expect. Yes, he had been aware of an order informing all Districts and Field Commanders that Field Marshal von Witzleben was appointed Commander-in-Chief of the Armed Forces. The order had originated from the *Wehrmachtamt*, as one would expect, and had reached Home Army – in another part of the same building – as a matter of course. Naturally, everybody had been sur-prised, because it was generally thought that the Field Marshal suffered ill health, which had earlier led to his resignation from the position of Commander-in-Chief West. It was, he had to admit, curious but it was certainly no part of a captain's duties to question the matter. If the Führer were incapacitated, which was the presumption, it was not for junior officers to have opinions about his choice of who should be entrusted with the command of the Armed Forces of the Reich.

As to 'later events' that evening, he had been stunned and, naturally, deeply upset. Everybody had admired Colonel von Stauffenberg as a brave and highly efficient soldier. Frido had, he explained patiently, only once met General Olbricht. No, he had never had the slightest suspicion that either of these – or others whose names were repeatedly put to him – were not devoted patriots.

'And that,' said Frido grimly as they walked dejectedly along the same path they had trod in a very different mood a week earlier, 'was the exact truth.'

Becker knew pretty accurately what had occurred in Berlin.

'The Commander of the Guard Battalion, Remer, thought something was odd when he heard "Valkyrie" was ordered. On his own initiative he went to the Propaganda Ministry. He saw Goebbels, and told him that he had to take his orders from General von Hase, his immediate superior, and that these were to deploy his battalion around the Government quarter and await further orders from von Hase. Goebbels handed him the telephone. It was Hitler himelf – from Rastenburg. Goebbels had explained to Hitler that Remer would shortly be with him, and our Führer was able not only to show he was alive – Remer recognized that voice – but gave him direct orders and power over everybody in order to carry them out. Then it was simply "*Jawohl, mein Führer!*" Our people were prisoners.'

'And of course,' said Frido with despair in his voice, 'within minutes of German commanders everywhere being told that Hitler was dead and Witzleben was Commander-in-Chief, they were hearing from Keitel that this was false, treasonable nonsense. We lost about three hours. They might – they just might – have made the difference.'

Becker said, 'I doubt it.' He knew the doubt would be unpopular with his companion. 'I doubt it. Too many things were wrong. Nobody secured the radio transmission centres. In spite of what was done at Rastenburg the other side were able to communicate. I still think Commanders of Districts, Army Groups and so forth were unlikely to obey anyone else's orders once they knew Hitler was alive. And, as I told you last week, I'm sure the soldiers wouldn't have done so, whatever their superiors did.'

Frido disputed nothing. He looked as if he would never smile again. He said, 'It's all over now. It failed. I'm not ashamed to have been a small part of it. I'm proud.'

Becker looked at him shrewdly. He was fond of von Arzfeld but thought him rash. Frido's sombre defiance made Becker uneasy. He hoped his friend would not court martyrdom.

'Have you heard much about the – er – enquiries?'

'Oh,' said Frido indifferently, 'they'll be pursued in the usual way. Nobody dares speak of it, there are whispers, murmurings in corners – General so-and-so, Colonel such-and-such. You know Fromm was arrested after all? The Gestapo have got him. I've no pity for him. It was he that had Stauffenberg, Olbricht and the others shot that night. He called it an "instant Court Martial". It was murder – he thought they'd implicate him in the end, although they'd arrested him. He'd been nodding and winking for a long time. Then he told Beck to shoot himself. The old gentleman made a mess of it and Fromm had him finished off. They shot Stauffenberg and the rest in the car park. I heard it.'

They walked on in silence. After a little, Frido said softly,

'I'm sorry we involved you in this. They'll pursue every scent – even after us little ones. They'll not give up. For myself, I've cared about nothing else for a long time. I'm proud. But you were new to it. I sincerely hope –' He halted and said rather stiffly,

'I hope no harm will come to you, my dear Becker.'

Becker said gently, 'I'm proud too.'

'At present nobody would understand that. We're hated. Not only by *him* and *them*. I think most ordinary, decent Germans also hate us, think we've tried to betray them. As for *him*, he'll have an orgy of revenge. Did you see the article last Sunday in the Party paper?'

'"We must exterminate the entire breed!"'

'That's it. The entire breed. What our Führer in his broadcast that night called "a very small, aristocratic clique . . . ambitious, unprincipled, criminally stupid officers". Well, I'm happy to be of their number.'

'Ach, well,' said Becker evenly. He took his friend's arm,

'Maybe one day it will all be understood.' Becker was Swabian, with a Swabian's stolidity. He spoke without emotion, 'Maybe one day they'll all understand.'

Chapter 19

———————◆———————

IT WAS THREE MONTHS LATER, in October, 1944, that Robert Anderson walked into Oflag XXXIII.

'I couldn't believe it, that day in 1940,' said Anthony, 'that day when I got hit. And you of all people turned up!'

'No, it was you who turned up. I was where I was meant to be.'

'And then I simply ran into you in London, out of the blue. And now you're here! What would war be without coincidence!'

He felt better than he had since captivity began, twenty-two long months ago. For several weeks he and Robert were engrossed in exchanging experiences. As far as Anthony could make out, officer prisoners were moved at intervals of not more than twelve months from one camp to another. When first captured he had been shipped to Italy and handed over to the Italians.

'A bit of grenade got me on the left hip. At first I felt as if half my leg was blown off, but in fact there was little more than bruising, although it hurt like hell, and I passed out.'

'You're even more accident prone than me,' said Robert. 'Any bomb or grenade that goes off near you seems to hit you.'

'But never seriously. Anyway I soon found myself in Italy. And you can imagine the relief when we were taken over by the Germans, after the Italian surrender a year ago.'

Robert couldn't. 'Relief?' Captured himself in Italy by the Germans, in the Rapido valley at the start of General Alexander's offensive in May, 1944, he raised his eyebrows.

'Relief! The Italians were hell. One never knew what would happen next. No system. No discipline. I reckon that in military as in political life anarchy is crueller than oppression.'

'You haven't changed!' Nor had Robert. He still frowned

295

at the same time as he smiled. He still appeared furiously indignant with everything or nothing. He had acquired from battle or captivity no trace of tolerance. It was, Anthony thought, pure joy to see him. For a little, an old friend's companionship, the warming experience of being able to talk of shared memories, could dissolve the parched boredom of Oflag XXXIII.

Robert's regiment had sailed from England to Sicily in July, 1943 to take part in the invasion of the island. They had been committed to the Italian campaign in November and had taken part in the slow, bitter push through the mountains from Naples to Cassino. Then, at the beginning of the attack that would take the Allies to Rome and north to the Gothic Line in the Appenines, a German mine had smashed Robert's lower leg. A German patrol had found him. The leg was treated efficiently and was mending fast. Six weeks in hospital had been followed by a month in transit of one kind or another. Robert still limped but declared he was as active as ever. Oflag XXXIII was his first regular camp.

They talked of the Italian campaign, of the North African campaign. They speculated on how things were going in north-west Europe. They talked endlessly of Oxford, and discussed the possibility of taking their law studies further in prison.

'I've done a certain amount,' said Anthony, 'but not as much as I should. Perhaps with two of us – one might . . .'

Robert was frowning. He changed the subject. They talked of the possible course of the war. For the first heady days of September every British bulletin, eagerly and surreptitiously devoured, spoke of the great breakthrough that had taken the Allied Armies almost to the Rhine. Robert still felt something of that euphoria.

'We may be overrun in a matter of weeks if they go on like this!' Anthony felt sceptical.

'The winter's coming on. And the Germans must fight for the Ruhr even if they pull troops out of Italy and Russia. Mind you, before our people get here they'll probably move us again. East.'

Anthony had been in Oflag XXXIII for three months, a camp set in wooded country between Brunswick and Magdeburg. This was his third camp, smaller than some. About one thousand officers shared the twenty identical wooden huts. Anthony and Robert were, inevitably, in different huts. The most recent batch of inmates included Robert and were housed together, while Anthony was settled in another part of the camp with a number of old-timers who had arrived with him. The two spent, however, much of every day together. Anthony explained everything to Robert – the '*Appels*' – roll calls where the prisoners were interminably counted off by fives to check total numbers, courses of instruction, camp entertainments.

'The older prisoners will tell you that food was terrible at first. Now we're getting one Red Cross parcel a week. Not bad at all.'

Anthony described too, the 'parole walks' – outings by individual prisoners strictly on parole.

'And parole strictly honoured, I suppose.'

'Of course. What sort of a criminal lunatic would throw everybody's privileges on to the rubbish heap, as would certainly and rightly happen?'

At first Robert showed impatience with the petty *mores* of the camp. 'Surely I could swap places with somebody in your hut, if we explained it?' The huts were divided into rooms in each of which eight prisoners occupied four double-decker bunks.

'Then we could mess together. Because I was in hospital I'm not with anybody from our division, there's nobody I ever knew before. It would make a big difference – after all the Germans leave the running of the place to us, we can order it as we want, it seems to me.'

Anthony told him the proposal was out of the question.

'It would cause great offence to suggest such a thing and it certainly wouldn't be agreed. This is a very special sort of community you know. People – especially people who've been prisoners a long time – are sensitive. Very touchy.'

'But still,' said Robert softly, 'I suppose we could pair up for an – adventure – couldn't we? Or would that, too, run counter to protocol?'

Anthony considered him. 'Yes,' he said, 'I think perhaps we could.' Quietly, tentatively, they began to discuss that difficult, controversial question among prisoners: the possibilities of escape.

In earlier life Anthony had often deferred to Robert. Robert, with strong opinions and impatient, had liked to have his own way and Anthony had often smiled and let him have it. They had always been complementary and their temperaments seldom jarred. Robert always said exactly what he thought with a candour which could be brutal. Anthony, despite his charm, could sulk and be moody but he was seldom other than courteous. In prison he had not been bored by solitude, but had often been irked by enforced companionship. He disguised this, and had the name of a 'first class man'. Robert, a much franker personality, was from the start regarded as awkward and argumentative.

'Talks as if he knows the bloody encyclopedia by heart,' they muttered. 'Lays down the law.' But a few who got to know him better warmed to his openness and honesty.

And now it was Robert who had all to learn, Anthony who knew about prison life.

'There's an escape committee in the camp, of course. Anybody who has an idea puts it to the committee. It has to be approved. Then those who thought up the idea have established a sort of copyright. If they're sensible they do *not* talk about it, except to people who need to know. Of course any escape attempt generally involves a lot of people in preparation and back-up, besides those actually making the break.'

It was characteristic of Robert's restless nature that their first serious conversation about escape took place only a few days after his arrival, in the middle of October. Anthony explained the fundamentals of the challenge. An escape could be conceived as four different problems. The first of these was how to get out of the camp itself.

Oflag XXXIII consisted of two separate compounds. On one side of a partition wire were the prisoners' huts, on the other a camp for the German guards and staff. Surrounding the whole complex was a double wire perimeter fence about ten feet high, the inner and outer fences separated by a catwalk about five feet wide. The fences were strong, supported on poles bedded in concrete. Rolls of concertina wire were extended in the catwalk. It was a formidable obstacle.

At each corner of the camp rectangle there were watch towers, manned at all times by sentries equipped with machine guns, searchlights, and in telephone communication with camp headquarters, the guardroom and each other. By night, the perimeter wire was illumined by lights set in high stanchions at thirty yard intervals. By night, too, intermediate watch towers were manned (the longest sides of the perimeter fence measured about nine hundred yards) and additional sentries on foot were posted outside the fence at hundred yard intervals. And by night, mobile patrols operated outside the wire.

'There are dogs, too,' said Anthony. 'They enjoy showing them off to us – savage brutes, I'd not like to be brought down by one. I imagine they track pretty effectively as well. I've never come on dogs before – they're a rarity at Oflags. You could say we're unlucky.'

Two gates served the camp, each guarded at all times. Both gates were locked at the same time in the evening and never thereafter opened, as far as the prisoners could see, except for the occasional passing of the Commandant's car. It was clear that anybody, whether or not in uniform, had to present some sort of authorization to the gate sentry. One of these gates – known as 'The Forest Gate' because of its nearness to woods bordering the lane which ran most of the way round the outside of the camp – seemed principally to be used by administrative traffic, builders' carts and the like, or vehicles bringing supplies. The other, through which Robert and his party like all their predecessors had marched into captivity from the railway station three miles away, was known as 'The Main Gate'. Through it visitors, camp staff and the large number of civilian employees moved. There was plenty of coming and going at the main gate. There was a small amount of military traffic but most movement was on foot. Civilian workers seemed to arrive either by bus – a bus at morning and evening stopped in the lane outside the gate – or by bicycle. Bicycles were left in a park outside the gate: presumably by order.

Anthony described the character, the routine of the camp to Robert as they walked ceaselessly round it. The weather was cold for October, but after one circuit of the wire – a distance of nearly two miles – both were warm, and with warmth came optimism.

'Of course, getting out is the first – in many ways the hardest – nut to crack. Really, there are three main options. First, tunnelling. That means a mass effort. It takes a great deal of time, and conditions have to be right. We were working on one at my last camp. Here, for various reasons which I think are sensible, there's been no suggestion to start a tunnel. At least I don't think so, and I believe I'd know.

'Then there's the possibility of going through or over the wire. There've been ideas about scaling ladders. Unless we could find out how to fuse the perimeter lights and search-lights simultaneously it would have to be done in thick fog. And even if we could put out the lights, we think there's some sort of standby generator, which would anyway power the searchlights. The trouble with fog – and sometimes we've had some really thick ones – is that it's unpredictable. And escapes need meticulous planning, preparation and timing. One can't just decide to go when one sees it's a foggy morning! The scaling ladders, for instance, could probably only be put together immediately before the attempt – there are periodic searches, as you know, and our friends are pretty thorough.

'The third option is disguise. Plenty of people – soldiers and civilians – go out through the gates by day. One pretends to be one of them.'

Robert stared at him. 'That must be the hardest option of the three, isn't it? The clothes, the identity cards, passes or whatever they have, the language –'

Anthony shook his head. 'One can manage all that.'

He explained that in Oflag XXXIII knowledge was detailed and exact of the sort of documents every German – or foreign – traveller in the Reich needed to be able to produce on demand.

'We've built up the knowledge over a long time,' said Anthony. 'People bring more information from other camps and it's centrally collated, we've not had an awful lot of other things to do.'

Similarly precise was knowledge of the papers needed to gain access to Oflag XXXIII itself: or leave it.

'What's your chief means of getting information?'

'Bribery. We can get pretty well anything.'

The generous supplies of cigarettes and chocolate in the Red Cross parcels which every prisoner received were strong currency when negotiating with the German guards, with whom the prisoners established, on the whole, a comfortable relationship.

'They'll do anything for some decent cigarettes,' said Anthony. 'They never see them otherwise. And they'll swap Reichsmarks for prisoners' money, because the British Government has undertaken to honour it after the war, so they reckon it's a stronger currency than their own! We've got masses of money. It doesn't say much for their faith in the thousand year Reich, does it! But then not many of these chaps are likely to have had that faith for a long time – if ever. They're mostly old fellows, well beyond normal military age, and all they want is a quiet life. Or they're disabled in some way. They're a decent, good-mannered lot on the whole.'

But the guards should not be underestimated, Anthony warned. Old they might be, and without heart in their job, but they functioned still under the iron discipline of the Wehrmacht. They were, with good reason, afraid of being detected in their small acts of corruption and exchange with the prisoners, and this set limits. In an actual escape, whether manning a machine gun from a watchtower, handling a dog or conducting an armed patrol, they would undoubtedly do their duty.

Robert asked about the help a man might expect from within before launching an attempt. He learned that there were highly expert forgers in the camp, self-taught over the years, models of discretion. Given time they would produce all the papers an escaper needed for his particular plan. There were tailors who would create a fair semblance of anything, from a worker's civilian clothes to a German uniform. There was an excellent make-up department. There was an information bureau which could brief on the regulations and customs with which anybody

301

travelling through Germany must be presumed to be familiar. And there was a comprehensive map library – including detailed plans of the area within about two miles of Oflag XXXIII itself.

'That's the first matter, getting out,' said Anthony. 'I said there were four main problems. The next is how to get clear of the area. Any escape, once it's detected, sets off the alarm throughout the immediate area, obviously. One's got to have a well-thought-out idea how to cover, say, the first five miles. During that time there'll be patrols and, presumably, dogs active near the camp, and every authority, railway station, policeman and so forth for miles around will be alerted. So one wants a clear cut plan for the immediate action once one's through the wire.'

The third problem, Anthony said, was connected to the second and influenced it – and was fundamental to the whole matter. Where did the escaper want to go and how did he propose to travel?

'One can go north, try to get to a port, stowaway on a neutral ship – try to get to Sweden or somewhere like that. It's been done. From this place, that probably means Lubeck or Hamburg. Or Rostock, perhaps.

'Or one can go south, aim at Switzerland. It's a long way, but it's been tried. The third alternative is to go west – get into France, Belgium or Holland. We've heard of men getting home from there, helped by the resistance people. Naturally, that's the direction one's drawn to at the moment. If the Allies keep the pressure up one would hope somehow, by going west, to get into British or American lines.'

There was a good deal of optimism in the camp in early October, 1944. Robert's hopes were more fashionable than Anthony's doubts. News in Oflag XXXIII was as good as the Allies' broadcast communiqués, no more, no less. There were plenty of clandestine wireless sets among the prisoners. There was, at the moment, less talk of escape than of imminent liberation as the Allies seemed set to surge forward into Germany over a beaten Wehrmacht. But in the last fortnight of the month, it seemed to Anthony, a certain change of mood set in. Men were now talking of the winter. Robert was considering.

'One thing, Anthony. You explain it all very logically – the escape planning, the choices. But has much of this actually been tried – here? Or is it just talk? As far as I can see, as a new arrival, people seem pretty apathetic. They accept that they'll be here until the war ends. And what about you?'

It was a typically tactless and direct approach, but it was just.

Anthony said, 'It goes in waves. At my last camp I was, actually, part of the tunnel party but we were moved. Here there've been two pretty well-staged attempts. The first was "blown" – a search upset it the evening before it was due to start. In the second, five chaps got out, all were recaptured. I wasn't in either party.'

'And do you feel, now that we seem to be winning here in Europe, that it's not worth while?'

'Sometimes I feel like that,' said Anthony slowly, 'to be truthful. But talking to you has made me restless.'

Anthony resumed the subject of the escaper's third and great problem – where to go and how to get there.

'Wherever one decides to go there's a fundamental choice – is one going to try to get by with a bogus identity, be prepared to talk to Germans, face routine police checks, that sort of thing? If one is, then obviously one can move fast. One can go by train. Or is one going to avoid contact with any sort of people – avoid it like hell? That probably means lying up by day, travelling on foot by night, keeping out of towns, villages. Safer. Some people here would tell you it's the only way. Too many fellows have been hauled back and found themselves in the punishment cells because they gave themselves away on a train or in a shop. But it's much, much slower. And, obviously, it can be more of a strain on health and strength.'

'I suppose,' said Robert, 'that some chaps only speak English and feel ill at ease in any atmosphere in which English isn't being talked. They'd stand out. Their nerves wouldn't take it. Isn't that so?'

'Yes, some people couldn't possibly pass muster, as you say. But you've got to remember that there are plenty of foreign workers in Germany. Imperfect German or a blank stare doesn't necessarily give you away. But you're right, movement by night and avoidance of contacts is simpler, safer and probably better for the nerves.' Anthony added, 'Of course, the autumn's the best time for all this – weather's not yet too foul, longer nights in which to walk, some fruit and potatoes to pick or grub up without too much difficulty. I think a mid-winter break would be hell, and in the summer the odds are on the pursuer. He's got light on his side and there's too little time to move in every twenty-four hours. If one's going overtly, using trains and so forth, obviously the season matters less.'

They strolled on.

'And the fourth problem?'

'The fourth problem,' said Anthony, 'is how one actually crosses the frontiers of the Reich. Or, of course, the German front line.'

'Your German's pretty good, isn't it, Anthony?'

'Yes, I think you could say that. What about you?'

'Not bad,' said Robert, 'but I'm out of practice.'

'You can get practice here,' said Anthony softly. 'There are facilities for that, and you should start right away. If that's the way it's going to be.'

The two overalled electricians moved their wooden ladder to another of the light posts between the German compound and the prisoners.

'It's Whiskers and his mate,' said Oliphant languidly. He was, as usual, observing the labours of others with the air of one relieved that he did not have to share them. It was the last day of October. Oliphant was always immaculately turned out and Anthony, who had got to know him as well as any (for Oliphant was intimate with none), admired a man who seemed so entirely suited to imprisonment. Oliphant appeared so congenitally idle that the enforced inactivity of Oflag XXXIII plagued him little. He did the work apportioned to him by the Mess with goodwill and a charming smile. He pursued no hobby, studied none of the subjects organized by the prisoners within the camp to keep their minds from vegetating, played no games. He read a good deal and occasionally wrote a letter. Within days of his own arrival, Robert expressed irritation with Oliphant.

'It's unnatural for a man to show such inertia as Charles Oliphant. He's rotting. He'll end up good for nothing, physically or mentally.'

'I'm not so sure,' said Anthony. Oliphant often showed an even-tempered normality which surprised and a little shamed them all. Now he was sitting by the hut window, watching with good-humoured amusement the German electricians at their work.

'It's remarkable how often they have to climb up their little ladders and do something to those lights. I thought the Goons were meant to be mechanically efficient.' Germans were Goons to the prisoners. 'Do people have to change light bulbs or whatever it is as often as that at home?' Oliphant sighed, concerned at so much effort, even though made by others.

It was generally the same electrician, christened 'Whiskers' by the prisoners. He and his colleague seemed to be about sixty years old. They moved at all times from one electrical fixture to another like priests at the altar, solemn, dedicated, expert. Whiskers derived his name from a luxuriant grey moustache. The other, who limped, was clean-shaven and taller. Nobody had ever seen them speak to each other.

'I thought they only appeared on Tuesdays and Fridays. A routine contract. I'm sure I've got that right.' It was a Wednesday, and Oliphant frowned, as over a matter of high importance. Anthony responded.

'I expect if there's an actual defect they get Whiskers up any day of the week. Tuesdays and Fridays he makes routine checks.' And this desultory speculation was confirmed by the guard, known to all as Hermann. Hermann was a local man. Hermann was also heavily compromised. He had always been a cynic about National Socialism and the prisoners had enough on Hermann to hang him in his own indiscretions many times over. And Hermann was a tobacco baron. He had grown sleek from his dealings.

Hermann, in spite of his nation's admiration for hard, methodical work, dutifully performed, much admired Oliphant. The latter's appearance, Hermann acknowledged to himself, was what an officer's should be. This could be said about few of the prisoners. Gaoler though he was, Hermann

305

felt warmed by Oliphant's condescension. Oliphant hailed him on his next visit in his usual half-bantering way.

'Hermann, you know Whiskers –'

'Whiskers?'

'The electrician who potters about changing the same light bulbs over and over again.'

'Ah, that is Johann Meister. The one with the big moustache. The other is his brother, Fritz Meister. They have worked in the village many, many years. They have a small repair business.'

'I thought they came here two days a week, Tuesday and Friday. That's what I've always observed.'

'That is correct.'

'Now he's here on a Wednesday. Captain Marvell thinks he must have a duty to come whenever he's needed. Surely that makes his life most difficult?' Oliphant spoke with great seriousness. Hermann replied in the same tone,

'The Meisters have an agreement. If there is a failure they must come. It is true. But they do not like it, you are right. They are sometimes taken away from other work to do something small, maybe something on a Sunday which could wait until the Tuesday. Naturally, if there is an emergency they come. But often, they are called when there is no emergency. That they do not like.'

'You know them well?'

Hermann laughed. 'Ever since I was a little boy. Everybody knows the Meisters. They are like part of the staff here. And everyone in the village knows them. They resemble their father.' Hermann laughed again and made an expressive gesture, implying that the brother electricians had a weakness for the bottle.

'That must be awkward in their profession,' said Oliphant sternly. 'It needs great precision, good eyes, a steady hand.'

'Better when there's no emergency on Saturday nights!' said Hermann, chuckling. 'Only twice I remember them out here on a Saturday, and they broke three fuses on the lavatory wall light box trying to replace one! It could have waited, too, but the Commandant noticed a defective light on his morning inspection and there was hell to pay.'

'Do we always get electricians to replace light bulbs?' enquired Anthony. It sounded more like some British Trades Union practice than the National Socialist State. But Hermann became serious and said that the electrical system needed professional attention, even in small things. Some fool had fused all the lights once and it had taken the Meisters two hours to get out from the village and put it right.

'Meanwhile Oflag XXXIII was in darkness, eh?' said Oliphant.

Hermann looked at him thoughtfully. 'No, *Herr Hauptmann*,' he said. 'There is an emergency generator, although it does not come into action automatically. It was dark for only about four minutes. Perhaps five.' He seemed to feel he had gossiped enough, and shuffled away.

It was Saturday evening, 8th November, and already it was almost dark. The Main and Forest Gates of Oflag XXXIII were to be closed punctually at six o'clock. Thereafter, there would be no ingress or exit except by specific arrangement or on the authority of the Commandant.

The Meister brothers appeared at the Main Gate at seven minutes to six in their working overalls, their familiar small boxes of tools slung over the shoulder of each, their faces as expressionless as usual beneath their caps. The sentry on duty had seen them on previous occasions about the camp. He did not know them personally, but he was familiar with their reputation. Johann Meister was 'Whiskers' to the prisoners: to the more informed soldiery he was '*Rotnase*'. Fritz Meister, a more shadowy (although, if Hermann were to be believed, an equally self-indulgent) figure was always, simply, '*Der Bruder*'. As the Meisters approached the guardhouse, fumbling for their passes, the sentry chuckled inwardly. He caught a powerful aroma of schnapps.

The sentry, Krebs by name, looked perfunctorily at their gate passes.

'Evening, Herr Meister, I didn't know we'd had an emergency. I suppose you came in by the Forest Gate?'

'Naturally,' said Johann gruffly. 'And it wasn't much of an emergency. It could have waited. Now we'll be walking back by the lane to collect our bicycles from the other gate. You

307

shut both damn gates at six and we've not time to reach the other through the camp before it's closed!' It was true. Bicycles had to be left outside, and no sentry was allowed to waive the strict orders on keeping gates closed in order to convenience such as Meister. The Forest Gate was at the opposite corner of the camp, and a man needed a good ten minutes to reach it on foot.

'Ah, well, it's only ten minutes further by the lane, Herr Meister!' said Krebs pacifically as he entered the pass number and time on his log sheet.

'Only ten minutes! Wait till you're over sixty!' The Meisters strode off, a trifle unsteadily. Krebs, a kind-hearted man, thought of offering to telephone to the Forest Gate to request a stay in closing time but he knew there was no hope. Gate time was rigid. All he'd get would be a balling out from the *Obergefreiter* at the Forest Guardroom for making such a grotesque suggestion. What the hell did it matter that the elderly Meisters had a longer walk in the twilight – unnecessarily? What did that matter to Krebs, the *Obergefreiter* would yell. Anyway, why couldn't the two boozy old buggers have left their bicycles at the Main Gate?'

So it would go on. Krebs looked at his watch. In three minutes the guard would fall in, the gate would be locked, evening sentries would be posted, evening routine would begin. Krebs thought again of *Rotnase* with an inward chuckle tinged with envy. A walk in the night air would probably do them a lot of good! And it was perfectly true that they could have moved their bicycles to the Main Gate once they knew what and where the trouble was – and it was presumably on this side of camp. Come to think of it, why hadn't they?

Krebs picked up the telephone and asked to be connected to the Forest Gate. His mind never worked particularly fast, but something told him he would be happier if he could with complete certainty report to the *Gefreiter* of the guard that the Meister brothers, whose names were on his log sheet, were walking round by the lane to collect their bicycles at the Forest Gate. He could do so already, of course, but nevertheless –

He did not recognize the voice that answered the telephone. Not one of his mates.

'Krebs here, Main Gate. Just to check that two bicycles, property of the electrician brothers Meister, are outside the Forest Gate. The brothers are walking round by the lane to collect.'

'Wait.' After ten seconds the voice returned.

'No, no bicycles.'

'Poor old devils,' said Krebs. 'They must have had their machines stolen! Thanks.' He felt sad.

'It's not my responsibility to guard their damned bicycles. Anyway, why leave them here? They must have been drunk as usual. They've not been in this way. They've not booked in.'

'Not booked in?' said Krebs feebly. He felt the beginning of nausea. It was in the stomach now and moving northward with each second. The voice from the Forest Gate was still snapping.

'Not booked in! They must have entered by the Main Gate. So why leave bicycles here? Stupid old boozers.'

'Thanks,' said Krebs again. He rang off. The *Gefreiter* in charge of the guard moved out of the guardroom in a purposeful way. The light shone on the top of his steel helmet. In sixty seconds the guard would parade and the gate would be locked. Krebs marched up to him and stood stiffly to attention, right palm pressing against trousers, heels together, left hand holding sling of carbine over shoulder in regulation manner, logsheet held between fingers of right hand. He spoke to a point in the middle of the *Gefreiter*'s helmet.

'Permission to check the gate list from earlier hours of duty.'

'What the hell do you want to know, Krebs?' said the *Gefreiter* irritably.

'I wish to check at what hour the brothers Meister, the electricians, entered by the Main Gate.'

'I can tell you that. They've not been in at all. They were in yesterday and left in the afternoon but they've not been through the Main Gate today. Now get out of the way, Krebs, it's time for parade.' He shouted over his shoulder. Men turned briskly out of the guardroom, the day's duty over. Krebs stood as if turned to stone. The *Gefreiter* walked over to him menacingly. A fist in the stomach would stir him up, he thought. He began to roar.

'Krebs –'

'I have checked with the Forest Gate. The brothers Meister have not entered by that way either. Their bicycles are not there.'

'Krebs, what in God's name –'

'Well,' said Krebs, still rigid and hearing his voice as from a very great distance, 'they've just gone out, you see.'

Chapter 20

THE GLOAMING outside Oflag XXXIII swallowed them. They moved deliberately, unhurried, simulating at first a little tipsiness, listening with hearts beating for the shouts behind them, for the alarms to go. They walked for three minutes down the lane, lengthening the stride but not running. 350 yards. Then, at a point recognized from their planning, they dived into the forest to the right of the lane, found a path running north-west they knew existed and started running as they had not run in life before. Ten minutes later they stopped.

'Five past six,' panted Robert. They felt as if they had run half across Germany. It had been clear enough to see the ground and neither had stumbled, but all around them great beech trees reached towards the darkening sky and the light was thickening fast. They knew that a road ran north and south across their planned line of escape, two miles from Oflag XXXIII. They walked now, fast, listening, ready to sprint at any hint of close pursuit.

They walked for another fifteen minutes. There was still around them a great silence.

'The road must be pretty close.'

They had agreed to cross it with circumspection. It looked from the map to run straight through the forest. Patrols could reach it with speed, headlights probably illuminate it for a considerable distance. Beyond the road and roughly parallel to it after a further quarter mile was the river. They pinned hopes on the river.

'There!' Robert paused and pointed. The road appeared, slightly raised above the forest floor, about fifty yards ahead.

At that moment they heard the unmistakeable sounds of the camp alarm.

They had hoped for an hour. They had been given twenty-five minutes. It might well have been less, but time

311

had been wasted after Krebs blurted out his report, wasted on a fruitless attempt to locate the brothers Meister at home, wasted on an unnecessary and noisy emergency visit to the prisoners' lines.

Twenty-five minutes gave at least some hope.

'They'll have the dogs out,' muttered Anthony. 'We've got to risk the road. Race straight over it.' They began running again, broke cover and dashed towards the grey, cobbled way. There was no sound of vehicles, of man. There was no light but the fading November day.

'Over!'

They sprinted across and into friendly woods beyond. After another hundred yards of running through open beechwoods the ground began to fall away steeply. They paused, Anthony holding up his hand and bending double.

'Stitch.'

'You must keep going.' Then Robert grabbed his arm.

'Listen.'

Anthony had straightened up.

'I can't hear dogs.'

'I thought I did, but there's a good deal of wind.' It was a cold, dry evening with a slight breeze from the north. They both hoped that the fact they couldn't hear the sound of dogs meant the hounds were still leashed. They both knew it might not be so.

'Come on!' They strode on.

They knew the river could be forded. Only heavy rain, they calculated, would upset their hopes of wading, of getting across without a detour, and the weather had been good. Once a safe distance the other side they planned to remove and bury their workmen's overalls, clean make-up from faces, and continue in dry civilian clothes cobbled together by the camp tailors and carried in their rucksacks – rucksacks which were also the product of the tailor's shop.

And water would kill scent. It was, of course, possible that dogs would be taken to a point opposite the ford and start hunting, scenting from there. But there were, according to the map, several fords. They built some hope, too, on the fact that the river itself might be too far from Oflag XXXIII to be within the area of immediate search. And there might not, at first, be

312

an immediate presumption that they had gone west. Meanwhile –

'What's that?' It was Anthony, sharp-eared. There was no doubt of it now.

The deep, excited calling of the tracker dogs! Distance was impossible to assess.

They began running again. The slope grew steeper, the light became worse. Robert lost his footing and slithered down three yards of sheer bank. Then he exclaimed.

'Tracks! In fact a lot of tracks.'

They were at what appeared a junction of several tracks. Two great piles of timber showed the activities of foresters. There were, clearly visible, the ruts of cart wheels and the hoofmarks of horses, going in several directions.

'Let's hope they're recent,' gasped Anthony, 'and strongly scented.' He had never had a good wind and he wished he were in better condition. This must be a track intersection marked on their maps, studied assiduously. Unbelievably, they were on course.

'By my reckoning this track, half-right, will take us down to the ford. If it were light we'd see Bensdorf on the far bank.' Bensdorf, according to Hermann during his interminable gossiping about the locality, was a small, farming community, with neither military presence nor light industry to attract security precautions.

They found the ford and waded across. From time to time they heard the sound of dogs, but not perceptibly nearer. They skirted Bensdorf, found a straight farm road going north-westward as their little compass told them (another standard product of the evasion section of Oflag XXXIII) and marched on as fast as they could. After an hour they found a copse, changed and scrabbled away the earth to get rid of their overalls.

'Food?'

'No, we must get on. It's still only about five miles –'

By the beneficence of whatever providence cares for escapers the night remained dry. They stepped out, limbs aching but walking on air. Afterwards they swore to each other, probably with exaggeration, that they had covered twenty miles that first night. And then, before dawn, came the bliss of finding

313

that there was indeed another noble forest, a *Stadtforst*, where the map had promised it. They found a camping place, had their first meal of biscuit and chocolate and lit a fire to brew some tea. Then, in most friendly fashion, a November sun came out and they slept, each in turn keeping watch with drooping eyelids.

'If our escape is going to be like this the whole way to the Rhine, or wherever the British Army's got to,' said Robert, 'it's going to be all right. I've seldom felt so happy.' His joy was remarkable, and sincere – and not the least remarkable fact, thought Anthony, was that Robert Anderson had confessed so simply to happiness, without a frown. He laughed.

'It won't all be like this. It can't be. There'll be nightmares ahead. It's all gone much too well.' But they did not believe it.

It was their sixth day. They had walked by night, carried forward for the first forty-eight hours on a mood of exaltation after the miracle of the escape, the smooth outpacing of pursuit. Now, five days and nights later, they lay some thirty yards inside a young fir plantation, a typical daylight lair.

'One's invisible like this,' Robert always said confidently. It was essential to reach the safety of woods at least an hour before dawn. Then, as light thinned in the grey, eastern sky they would choose the haven for the day. A careful fire was generally lit if dry wood could be found, reducing tell-tale smoke to a minimum. On one glorious occasion they had washed thoroughly by a stream. There had been one day when they had felt vulnerable and lit no fire, the forest's silence broken by periodic, distant calls of woodmen. Once there had been a terrible moment. Moving freely after dawn in the depths of a wood searching for an ideal camping site Anthony suddenly froze. Ahead was one of the raised platforms which pepper the broad tracks in every German forest; but this platform was manned. The guardian or sportsman was looking the other way and they backed, silent and afraid, into the cover of the friendly trees.

Now it was the sixth day. As they lay in the dark of the trees, chilly and aching, they took stock of their problems.

314

The first of these was food.

They had brought in their rucksacks as much biscuit, chocolate and tea as they could carry: and on two days they had managed to scavenge some vegetables and some late apples. But it was later in the year than they had originally intended. Every day was a little colder, or so it seemed. There had been several cruel downpours, without the chance of drying clothes in sun the following day. Food was necessary to maintain health, strength, warmth and morale. And food was running low. Anthony and Robert knew that they were near the end of both supplies and tether. They knew they would soon be forced to go shopping, with all that entailed in terms of risk. They had broken camp openly, disguised. Thereafter, however, their plan had been to move by night only, to lie low, to avoid contact. It had worked. But now resources were all but spent; and there was a long way to go.

For the next and greatest problem was speed and distance.

'The fact is,' said Robert, 'that we're just not making enough ground.' They had been over-optimistic. Now, with five night marches behind them, they were, they knew, a few miles south-east of the outer suburbs of the city of Hanover. At this rate it was going to take a mighty long time to reach the Rhineland, where their hopes lay.

Anthony said, 'We've agreed the first thing is to get some more food, some reserves so that we can walk when we need to. When we've done that I think we ought to think again.' Robert nodded impatiently. They had been over this ground a day and a night before. Anthony continued, knowing it was contentious –

'Then – after shopping – I favour taking a train.'

They had discussed it. Anthony knew that slow, stopping trains were seldom searched. It should be possible to find one going in a westerly direction, to make some distance, to leave the train and walk for a while – and then repeat the process. Obviously the last phase – the reaching of Allied lines – was a different operation which could only be planned when nearer in time and space. Neither of them disputed the likelihood that it would be the most difficult feat to accomplish.

Robert, less confident than Anthony with the German langu-

315

age, German atmosphere, feared contact with the world. Walking through the dark, friendly nights, resting in the enfolding woods, had suited him admirably. But he recognized that there must be a change of method, at least for a while: new system: new risk. He said,

'Where shall we shop?' It was an acquiescence.

Anthony was studying their map.

'There's a small town about five miles from here. Villingen. We ought to move into it fairly late in the afternoon, try to buy what we want. Then it won't be too long before dark and if something nasty happens we've got a hope of getting to cover, even if we have to change direction.' They pored over the map, discussed details, agreed to move through the woods nearer to Villingen and to walk into it at about four o'clock in the afternoon. They refreshed memories of their identities, studied again their papers. They were two Dutch volunteer workmen, Jan Vogt and Pieter Joost, natives of Tilburg.

'We're on our way to catch a train to a factory in Dortmund, a new job. By the way, how's your leg?'

'It's all right,' said Robert shortly. Anthony knew that he had been in some pain, ever since Fritz Meister had limped out of Oflag XXXIII six days before.

'There are shortages everywhere, it's natural,' said Anthony sympathetically. The woman sighed cautiously. It didn't do to grumble.

'You're not going back to Holland? The English have begun to destroy it, brought the war to it, you know that –'

'No, we're on our way to the Ruhr, Dortmund. A new job. We're engineers. We were in Silesia.'

'It's a funny way to travel from Silesia to Dortmund by Villingen!'

'Certainly! You see we were turned off the train at Hanover, where we had to change. We had to give way to some priority movement people. We're hoping for a place on tomorrow's train. We thought we'd get out of town and see a bit of the country as we've got a day to spare. We've not had a day off for a long time, I can tell you.'

The woman looked at him without sympathy.

'I've got a man in Russia. They don't get many days off there.'

'No, I suppose not,' agreed Anthony respectfully.

'Best stay out of Hanover, anyway,' said the woman, more agreeably. 'Those swine have bombed it horribly.'

'So we saw.'

The woman lowered her voice. Discussion of air raids could be dangerous defeatism and was carried out with circumspection.

'We've been hit here, twice!'

'A little place like this! Fancy!'

'Not so little. There's the factory at the end of town.'

They paid, put the austere provisions in their rucksacks and walked away fast. Villingen was bigger than the map had suggested. The factory – it would have been undesirably inquisitive to ask what it produced – was on the edge of the town by which they had approached. It seemed to have been matched by a large estate of workers' houses, on the other side of the road, white, steep-roofed houses in neat rows. Rain began to fall heavily. Robert grunted.

'Do you think we could find an outhouse, some roof or other? It's rather tempting not to step out for the woods in this downpour.' The shop, the unaccustomed shelter had given them an appetite for cover. Their previous night's refuge was an hour's march away, in the wrong direction. Robert developed the theme.

'If we're going to take a train we could do it here. The first one we see. Get clear of the place. Then we could change trains at some big place and catch something going west.'

'That means going north, to Hanover.'

'Or south to somewhere else. Trains through any big station are bound to be unpredictable because of air raids.'

'I agree. Let's take the first train to anywhere that gets us clear of Villingen. Which will probably now mean first thing in the morning.' The woman in the shop had looked at them curiously. She had seemed puzzled at their explanations, despite the frequency with which foreign workers could be found travelling throughout the Reich. Anthony's imagination was always vivid. Was she at that exact moment talking to the local policeman (a friend, Anthony explained to himself morbidly, a frequent visitor) –

'I had two young fellows in here this afternoon. Two Dutch-men – on their way to a new job in the Ruhr. Engineers or something. Said they'd been turned off a train in Hanover and couldn't get another till tomorrow, so were looking round the neighbourhood. Sounds odd, doesn't it? In the middle of a war! And why come to Villingen? It's not a beauty spot!'

And the policeman would be responding, importantly,

'You are right to tell me all this!' And he would step off sharply to alert the police station and 'the usual authorities'. Perhaps it would be best, after all, to make haste to the woods. They walked on as the rain came down harder. Villingen straggled. They had thought to be leaving it but instead seemed to be approaching its oldest quarter. It was close on six o'clock.

'Look at that!'

To their left in the failing light was Villingen railway station. They were surprised by its size. It seemed to have an extensive goods yard. They remembered the warm response of the woman in the shop to any implication that Villingen was an insignificant place. Villingen had industry, a busy population. The railway station matched it.

It also, they soon discovered, had a small waiting room. Dimmed bulbs lit a number of benches. An ancient, uniformed figure was moving between them. There seemed to be no passengers. Perhaps the last train had left Villingen.

But the waiting room looked tempting. There was no slackening in the rain. Anthony marched up to the aged official and addressed him with confident respect.

'We are two Dutch workmen, *Herr Stationsvorsteher*, we have to catch a train early in the morning –'

Anthony doubted whether the old man deserved the dignity of stationmaster which he had ascribed to him but it did not seem to go amiss.

'We are engineers. Can we rest on the benches here until morning? We have nowhere in Villingen to go.'

'A train early in the morning?' said the old man. He looked shrunken and slow but his uniform of blue and gold was impeccable, his pride in Villingen station clear from his bearing. He looked at Anthony and Robert frowning, but Anthony thought that the frown was more of concern at his own difficulty with unpredictable events than suspicion of his visitors. 'Early

318

in the morning? That must be the Kassel train, the southbound train. It stops here at 5 o'clock. It stops at every station.'

'Exactly! It is that train we have to catch.'

'You can sleep on the benches here,' said the old man graciously. 'There will be nobody here until shortly before the arrival of the train from Hanover. Your train. But the room will be locked. You will be locked in. And the lights, of course, will be out, except for one bulb over there in the corner.'

They thanked him warmly. 'It does stop at every stop, that is right?' said Anthony.

'Every stop. For an express you would have to go north to Hanover. Your train stops all along the line –' he reeled the stations off. They bowed their gratitude and the old man moved away, raising his hand in salutation and farewell.

The first bomb fell at twenty minutes past four in the morning. Robert and Anthony simultaneously heard the screech of bombs and the thunder of gunfire, rolled off their benches and threw themselves violently to the floor, hitting it as the explosion deafened them. Dog-tired, neither had heard the alarm.

There followed a sequence of crashes, and the rumble of falling masonry. The station was lit by the flames of fires. As they lay on the waiting room floor Anthony found himself trembling. He was ashamed of his reaction to an air raid, deriving from 1940, but he could not help it. He had grown almost accustomed to shelling, but the familiar rush and scream of a descending bomb brought sweat. Robert seemed unmoved. They were, it appeared, still alone in the waiting room.

'I suppose they're going for the factory. Let's hope they're accurate.' Anthony risked a muttered sentence in English.

'Perhaps it's a railway junction or vital goods yard!' Robert grinned in the darkness. He had got to his feet and was standing at the door which opened towards the road they had walked along. The door was glass-panelled and barred.

'I'd say they must be hitting those houses we saw opposite the factory. Burning like hell. It's hard to tell but –'

'DOWN!'

Anthony saw Robert's figure framed against the night sky,

319

upright, unmoved. Next moment there was a crack like a thunderclap and the sound of glass smashing and splintering. A great rush of air swept the waiting room. The one dimmed bulb was extinguished and the place was lit by flames alone. All windows had been simultaneously blown in.

'Are you all right?' Anthony heard Robert shout. It was, he thought with a fleeting twinge of resentment, typical that Robert, who had been standing and by all the rules more vulnerable, should have been the first with a solicitous enquiry.

'*Schweig du, Dummkopf!*' he yelled. The station staff would soon be on the scene and they had best not find two British officers discussing in English the exploits of the Royal Air Force.

'Damn! Damn, Damn, Damn!'

Robert moved swiftly to him.

'Anthony, your leg!'

'It must have been a bit of flying glass. Nothing much.' Blood was soaking fast into his left-hand trouser, high up. He felt little. Robert put an arm round him. They were whispering, although the roar of fires and the high-pitched drumming of anti-aircraft gunfire made it unnecessary.

'Sit down. I've got my torch.' He knelt by Anthony.

'They seem to be going back to England, thank God!' It was true that no bombs sounded to have fallen in the minute that had elapsed since the windows splintered and flew.

'Let's have a look.'

Anthony could still feel little. He spoke softly and urgently.

'Robert, listen. Nobody must see this. They'd haul me off to a dressing station, first aid post, whatever they have here. They'd find my tally –'

An escaping prisoner always carried his tally, his prisoner of war identity disc. In the last resort it was supposed to be his salvation. Escaping prisoners of war could hope to be treated as such. Unidentified strangers masquerading as foreign workmen could expect to be dealt with as spies. Jan Vogt's papers would not stand expert inspection. Gestapo inspection.

'We'd both be done for. We must catch that train. It doesn't matter where it goes. We'll take tickets to Kassel. We must get clear of this place.'

'Can you walk?'

'I think so.' But he knew that he was bleeding freely. He felt giddy. He made a brave attempt to stand. Not bad. They each had a small medical pack in the rucksack and Robert produced it.

Anthony said – 'I'll keep a look out. They must *not* find I'm hit. They're too damned conscientious.' He lowered his trousers. He tried to say something about the idiocy of being hit three times in the legs in one war, but a wave of nausea hit him and he couldn't attempt the feeble joke.

There was a great deal of blood. Robert worked efficiently, applying a field dressing to the outside of the upper thigh where the wound was apparent. Anthony gasped at the pain. He could feel it now all right.

'Morphia?'

'No, I can cope.' He didn't dare dull the senses further. Thank God Robert was exceptionally deft.

'You'll have to try putting weight on it, old boy. We've got to find out what we can do.'

At that moment, there was a rattling at the door and a loud call. They recognized the deep tones of their friend of the previous evening.

'My windows! My windows! Are you safe, you two Dutchmen, both of you?'

Anthony was pulling up his trousers. The pain was now excruciating. The old man was picking his way across the waiting room through broken glass. There was dust everywhere. He was unlikely to move fast, but he had a torch and he would see blood.

'Ah, the swine! Most of the bombs hit the factory, and Rosendorf next to it! The swine!'

'Will the Kassel train come?' said Anthony in as level a voice as he could manage. The old man peered at him irritably.

'One cannot know for certain. If they attacked Hanover –'
His eyes and torch went to the floor.

'What's that? You were hit?'

'A bit of glass scratched me. It's nothing.'

'Are you sure?'

'Quite sure, *Herr Stationsvorsteher*.'

The old man nodded, relieved. He shuffled off and they heard him unlock the door to the platform. After a little he

321

brought a lamp and hung it in a corner. They sat down again on the bench in the near-total darkness. Five minutes later two other travellers appeared, exclaiming loudly at the broken glass, the absence of windows.

'I think,' murmured Robert, 'we'd better make ourselves scarce till the train comes.' Anthony nodded. The pain in his thigh was throbbing and he dreaded movement but they needed to distance themselves from fellow passengers. It had, he thought, looked a clean wound and clearly it hadn't broken a bone or, he supposed, cut any nerve. And as the bleeding seemed to have stopped, he presumed it had missed a principal artery. But he felt as if he could only walk a few yards. With Robert's unobtrusive help in the darkness he stumbled on to the platform and they found a merciful bench at the far end. And there Anthony sat in silence as a long, cold hour passed and as he made up his mind what he had to do. But the time for telling Robert was not yet.

The Kassel train was only seventy-five minutes late at Villingen. Robert had bought tickets for Kassel, leaving it open for them to decide how far actually to travel.

'We must get clear of this place,' Anthony had urged.

It might be best to go a short distance and then change trains and travel north again, go to Hanover where surely there would be a direct westbound train.

Robert helped Anthony aboard. He looked, Anthony could see in the cold half-light of a November dawn, more anxious than at any time since escaping. Before they mounted the train he whispered –

'Old boy, I really think – you've got to survive, we know the risks and all that, but I really think you ought to get to a doctor.'

'Quiet!' They found wooden seats beside each other as the train puffed slowly southward.

'We'll be unlucky to get a search. Small, workmen's train, early, stops everywhere.' Anthony was muttering to keep his own spirits up. His head was aching and he supposed that soon fever would set in. It grew lighter.

The train stopped at a station every few miles. They sat in

silence. One or two old men got in, with a gruff '*Tag*,' and settled in various corners. It was still possible to talk – to murmur softly. Anthony's watch showed that they had travelled for two hours from Villingen. He touched Robert's sleeve.

'How far do you think we've come?'

'We're moving very slowly. Forty miles? Not more.' Neither wished to evoke conversation by looking at maps or appearing uncertain.

'Yes, forty miles perhaps. I don't think we aroused enough suspicion in Villingen to –' He gasped suddenly. Pain shot through his thigh like a white-hot rapier.

'Listen Robert. Very carefully.'

Muttering, still holding Robert's sleeve tightly, Anthony told him the bitter truth. He, Anthony, could not go on. He knew his wound must have proper medical attention, and soon. There was no hope of getting that and evading detection.

'I'll try, of course. Dutch workman bombed and all that. But we both know it won't work. Pretty soon I'll be rumbled.'

Robert was silent. He knew that it was so. Anthony was whispering still, urgently.

'The important thing is to separate. There's no reason why you can't make it on your own. Your German's all right. Your leg's holding up well. Make for the Ruhr in small trains, changing as often as you can. Take most of my money as well as yours. Get out before you get into the Ruhr itself and start walking towards Holland. Then hope for the best. The war seems to have settled down on the Dutch–German border.'

'I'm not going to leave you.'

'Yes, you are. You've got a sporting chance. I've got none. The essential thing now is to separate. I'll try to lie low long enough to keep them off your scent. If I can.'

'I'd really rather –'

'Oh, for God's sake,' said Anthony, hitting him where he knew he could hurt, 'don't act as if you're windy of being on your own! I'm going to get out at the next station. Keep travelling. And good luck.' He did not look at Robert again, and was unsure exactly how he himself got off the train and limped away from the platform of a little station, five minutes later. It was a small place and at ten minutes to eight on a wintry morning there was, by some miracle, no attempt to cross-examine him on why a ticket to Kassel had been so wastefully misused. Every step a torment, he moved slowly away from the station. He had forgotten, in his pain and preoccupation, to notice the station sign and had no idea where he was. A café would soon be open: *ersatz* coffee, but hot. Then – he could not think far ahead. Suspicion might destroy him at any minute now. But every minute carried Robert a little further down the line.

One hour and fifteen minutes later, with some warmth inside him but with a leg he knew could support him little longer, with a sickening headache and a wretched heart, Anthony decided he must move from the café. He had stopped at the first one he had seen. Now he paid and walked into the town's small square. To have lingered longer would have aroused closer scrutiny. He could not kill time by walking. It was raining again and to settle on a bench in the square would be, and would appear, absurd. Robert needed every hour, every minute: but there was nowhere to go. It would be so damnably easy to link the two of them. Descriptions of two escaping officers would have been circulated.

'We've got one!'

'What about the other?' Then they would try every station up and down the line, catch the old man at Villingen.

'The two Dutchmen caught the Kassel train.'

'Two Dutchmen, you damned old fool! They were English!' It was all vivid to Anthony's fevered imagination. It couldn't be long now.

He thought about the forthcoming moment of surrender. A policeman? Perfect German, courteous propriety.

'Excuse me, *Herr Polizeioffizier*, I am a British officer, escaped from Oflag XXXIII.' Was that it? When in doubt ask a Bobby? The hot rapier stabbed his thigh again. His head throbbed.

The door of a fine old church stood open. In their endless conversations about escape in Oflag XXXIII the prisoners had discussed refuges, if one had to brave a town or village. A church was good, they said, wisely, drawing on the experiences of others, recaptured, ruminating. You weren't often bothered in a church. In a church it would be rare that a policeman would fix an escaper with a hard stare, would shoot out like a bullet that grim request – 'Papers?' In a church one could, with luck, sit, be dry, think about the next move. A church could be a sanctuary. Perhaps a few also admitted, if only to themselves, that sometimes a church had brought, unexpected and probably uncomprehended, not only rest but a certain, obscure comfort.

Anthony walked into the church, every pace bringing agony now. He sank into a pew near, but not too near, the door. The moment of truth was approaching fast. The pain in his thigh was devilish. It was an angry, hot pain, and he felt a sick certainty that infection was at work. He knew that he had a high fever. He was unsure whether he would even be able to summon strength to leave the church. He looked at his watch. Half past nine. Robert must be approaching Kassel soon now. He might even be there. He couldn't remember distances and he gave up trying.

He looked at his surroundings apathetically. It was, he supposed, a Lutheran church. There was no sign of a reserved sacrament, no sanctuary lamp, no lingering whiff of incense. The stalls in the chancel and the reredos were elaborately carved. There was a surprising amount of marble and gilding in the nave. The place was lit by high, plain windows but the day was grey and the interior dark. It seemed a mediaeval building with something of a baroque interior.

Anthony was conscious that he had the church to himself. So far, so good. He sighed. The end was bound to come soon. Then he would blurt out his identity, confess to some person in authority that he was an escaped prisoner, and the torture would be over. There was a movement in the back of the church and he turned his head. He felt extraordinarily sick.

It was the pastor. A small, neat man with a little goatee beard, wearing a shabby dark suit had emerged from some side door and was now moving up the aisle to where Anthony sat slumped. The pastor took a seat beside him and for a little said nothing. Anthony sat very still. It was nine forty-five.

'You are a stranger here? I have not seen you in our church before.'

'I'm travelling. I came on the train from Hanover.' No point in saying he didn't even know where he was, and didn't care.

325

Anthony was ready to add, 'A Dutch engineer, *Herr Pfarrer*, on his way to a new job in a factory in the Ruhr,' but he held it in. It might be that the moment of confession was anyway imminent, so why complicate it by a futile lie? And anyway why not waste, for Robert, a few more minutes by making this pastor, or anybody else, work for their information, take time to formulate their suspicions?

The pastor did not comment. He did not seem disposed to ask questions. Instead he said gently,

'The carvings in Kranenberg church are famous.'

The name reached Anthony as from a great distance. He listened to himself saying,

'I have heard of them. Did not the same carver work in an old schloss near here?'

'Yes. In Schloss Langenbach. You obviously know the area.'

Anthony heard his own voice as if it were another's. He had a sense of having no control over the words uttered.

'Once, as a tourist before the war. Is the Schloss still occupied by the Langenbach family?'

The pastor did not seem to find this enquiry peculiar. He answered in soft but resonant tones.

'Frau Langenbach, the old lady, is confined to the house, we never see her now. Her husband left this world in 1942. The son was killed, flying, in Spain. There is a little boy – a grandson. And a widow.'

'They live at the Schloss?'

'Naturally only in a small part of it,' said the pastor reprovingly. 'The young Frau Langenbach has a high sense of duty. She underwent some medical training – there was first a convalescent home at Langenbach, but that was moved to the Harz mountains, to more suitable accommodation. Now the village school is there.'

Anthony said nothing. The pastor went on, still with a hint of admonition in his voice –

'There is no question of visitors seeing the Schloss these days.'

Anthony nodded. He felt so feeble that he could make no sensible response.

'You do not seem well,' said the pastor softly. 'Are you sick in any way, my friend? You are not German, I think.'

326

Anthony spoke haltingly. 'I was slightly injured. An air raid, yesterday. Only a minor cut, it's been dressed. It gave me a bit of a shock, I feel weak. I'll be all right. I've got to continue my journey. I'm a Dutchman, an engineer. I'm moving from Silesia to a new job. In the Ruhr. Dortmund.'

'Sit here as long as you wish, my friend.'

The pastor moved towards the east end of the church where a woman with a broom, bucket and dusters had appeared and seemed to be busy.

Anthony closed his eyes

Anna Langenbach generally visited Herr Proser, the Pastor of Kranenberg, on Fridays. Proser was an excellent man. She had always appreciated his quiet, sceptical discretion. Sometimes he would say, 'These are difficult times, Frau Anna,' words in themselves innocuous, banal. He would hold her hand for a moment as they exchanged greetings, his eyes kind as they looked into hers, his mouth drawn with sympathetic feeling above his absurd little goatee beard. They understood each other. He would say,

'Is all well at the school?'

'I think so.'

'The enthusiastic Fraülein Wendel is well, I hope? A woman of strong convictions!'

They would smile at each other. Anna had never known him other than practical, sensible and self-effacing in any human dilemma. She attended divine service at Kranenberg on alternate Sundays, and on intermediate Fridays would generally try to call at the Pastor's house, to exchange a few words, to leave a package of garden produce in the right season. They would talk briefly, comprehendingly. The contact was comforting. So it was on Friday, 24th November.

'Is Frau Klarsen all right, cleaning the church as she should, Herr Proser? I know she's lost her husband in Russia, poor woman, doesn't know if he's alive or dead. Is she managing to do her work, in spite of it? You know her sister works at Langenbach – a great talker.'

'They are both great talkers, Frau Anna! Frau Klarsen is working as hard as ever. A conscientious woman, despite her

327

tongue. She's in the church now. I was talking to her ten minutes ago.'

'I'd better have a word.' Proser nodded.

'She will appreciate that. It's hard to find helpful things to say – and one has had to try to do it so often in these years. You have the gift, Frau Anna. You can quieten the heart's pain with a word. Your presence would help anyone.'

Anna was touched. 'I wish that were true.'

Proser stood up. 'The church is open. You may also find a young Dutchman sitting there – he's resting! The poor fellow was slightly wounded in an air raid yesterday, and arrived here by train feeling rather the worse for wear. He says he's all right. He's an engineer – on the way to the Ruhr. I told him I didn't mind how long he sits – he's been over an hour already, if he's still there! I told Frau Klarsen to let him be.'

'A Dutchman?'

'Yes, he's travelling to a new job. And, do you know, he went to Schloss Langenbach once – as a tourist. Before the war. At least I think he visited the Schloss, from the way he seemed to know something about it.'

'We used to have many tourists asking to see the house, on Sundays in the summer.' Anna sighed. Those days seemed far away, the coincidence uninteresting.

Anna found Frau Klarsen polishing brass work on the staircase up to the pulpit. She was working with ferocious energy. Anna spoke understanding, consolatory words.

'Ah, well, Frau Anna, there are plenty like me. As long as it's doing some good, that's the important thing.' Frau Klarsen cried a little, quietly and then took up her cloth again with an angry growl of contempt for her own weakness. Anna patted her shoulder, shook her hand strongly and moved down the dark aisle of the church toward the west door. There was Herr Proser's Dutchman, very still. She could not see his face in the shadows. She paused as she passed him sitting several places in from the aisle. Was the pastor right that his wound was superficial, nothing to prevent a long journey? She hoped so, poor fellow. She glanced in his direction. He turned his head and spoke. A whisper.

'Anna.'

It was Anna's turn to feel the faintness of astonishment and terror. He whispered again, without moving –

'Anna!'

Anna, hardly knowing what she was doing, turned and sat in a pew behind him and a few feet away. She looked at the altar.

'God. Beloved and all-comprehending God,' she said soundlessly. 'Be with me now. Be with me now.'

Chapter 21

———————◆———————

IT HAD BEEN in the spring of 1944 that Frido, on leave at Arzfeld, had last seen Marcia. Marcia and Lise had been about to start their grim adventure, to move east, to a hospital in Silesia.

Frido had put his arm round Marcia on a walk during his last afternoon. He started, nervously, to talk as Marcia had never heard him talk before.

'Marcia – all the time, in Berlin, I can see you if I close my eyes. I watch your face, a little flushed, eyes so bright, that little bit of hair running down your forehead, teasing your right eye –' He was pretending to laugh, but his voice shook.

'Darling Frido. Perhaps you'll be able to visit us.'

How unlike Werner he is, Marcia thought, while feeling enormous affection for him. Frido talked little these days, and never before about his own thoughts or emotions.

In April, the girls moved east.

Berlin   10th December, 1944.

'Dearest Marcia,

In January, in the New Year, I will have a few days leave. I wish, instead of going to Arzfeld, to pay a short visit to Silesia, to visit you and Lise. I can get a permit to travel. I know the area where you work, I have even been to the village where your hospital is! And I think of January all the time, because one hope I take with me to bed every night, and when I wake in the mornings I shake this pet hope and wake it up and keep it with me all day – bicycling to work, at my office in the Bendlerstrasse, in the evenings. It is the hope that one day, before too long, I will see you again.

This is my favourite small hope – to see you again not with the eyes of imagination, but alive, warm, real. But this hope

330

has a big sister, a grander hope which I also take with me wherever I go, and keep by me day and night.

This grander, more important hope is that one day, Marcia, I may be allowed to love you, and succeed in making you love me. Ever since I first saw you at your own home, at Bargate, do you remember? Ever since I saw you then, so young, so mischievous, so lovely, I have wanted you for myself. Of course, when Werner loved you, became your fiancé, it was impossible for me to think like that. I loved my brother. After he was killed I dared to think like that again, in spite of Rudberg, whom perhaps you thought you loved, in spite of others maybe – I dared to think like that again. I have to tell you this, Marcia, before I see you in January. I have to write it down. I have thought about it and I can do no other.

One day this nightmare we are living through will pass and it will be morning. I may not see that day – there are reasons why I say that. I have lost recently some dear friends. It is a difficult, dangerous time. But the morning *will come*, and just in case I am here when it comes I am not going to turn my big hope away. I shall find a way of getting word to you when I know for certain about my leave. Tell Lise everything. It gives me joy that you two are together. And do not be angry with me for what I write.

Now, Marcia, I am going to entrust a secret to you. It is not my secret, but I am allowed to tell you if I think it right. There is a piece of knowledge which should not be lost. If something were to happen to Anna Langenbach and to me as well, it would be lost unless somebody else knows. You are the right person to know.

You are very fond of Anna, rightly so. She is also fond of you. But what you do not know is that her son, little Franzi, is not the son of her late husband, Kurt Langenbach. He is the son of your own brother, Anthony Marvell.

They were lovers, he and Anna, when she was in England before the war. Franzi is his son, born after Kurt Langenbach was killed. Franzi may inherit the property of his so-called grandfather, but he is not a Langenbach. He is your nephew.

Kurt Langenbach was a brave, clever man, but he was a bad husband to Anna. He treated her without feeling. He had no gentleness in his character. I know that she came not to love him. It was the mistake of her life to marry him. She wanted security, she wanted to be able to help her mother, a wonderful woman, now dead. And Langenbach was an interesting man. She was entertained – dazzled, maybe. But I also know that Anna is a woman of very high character. If she were unfaithful

331

to her husband it could only be because she felt that he, himself, had broken their contract by his behaviour: and because she loved another with her whole heart. That other was your brother, Anthony.

Anna told me all this long ago – only me. She wished me to know because, if something happened to her, she wanted another person to know the truth. She paid me a great compliment. She said she knew, whatever the circumstances, I would act rightly in the matter.

She said to me, "If at any time you think it right you can *tell Marcia* Franzi is her nephew." And I think now I should do so, because my own future is so uncertain, just at present. I shall, naturally, not entrust this letter to the post – with all that means – but will take advantage of the fact that an officer of this branch, a trusted colleague, Captain Hoffmann, is visiting the exact area of Silesia where your hospital is in the next few days and has undertaken to deliver the letter to the hospital personally!

I kiss my little sister and I must now end by writing the three simple words which this long letter has tried to convey to you – I love you!

Frido.'

'"Not entrusted to the post – with all that means!" "My own future uncertain! Lost recently some dear friends!" He certainly has – still, there's not a great deal to help us here, *Herr Sturmbannführer.'*

Egon Schwede looked at his subordinate grimly.

'I don't agree!'

'"This nightmare we're living through" – it's defeatist stuff, certainly, disgusting for an officer of course, but . . .'

'That's only part of it, you idiot. The letter stinks of disaffection. But we already know all about von Arzfeld – he's only where he is in case he can still give us a few heads. No, look at this so-called secret he tells this girl! And don't forget she's English, sister of an English soldier!'

'But that was gone into, wasn't it? She was going to marry this one's brother. She's nursing now, not far from here.'

Schwede brushed this aside. 'Times have changed. We've been betrayed by too many of these so-called gentlemen, this scum. We're more vigilant now. But it doesn't matter whether she's English or not. Look at the "secret" as he calls it!'

His companion, *Sturmführer* Molde, looked.

'He's been concealing a serious criminal offence. This woman, this cousin of his, Langenbach, has been breaking the law in the most shocking way. She's been pretending that an illegitimate child – by a foreigner, mind, who may be a Jew or have Jewish blood for all anyone knows – pretending that this child is the son of a dead officer of the Wehrmacht. It's incredible! And Arzfeld, *a German officer* has been concealing this. He's guilty of connivance.'

Molde nodded subserviently. He remained unconvinced. He said, 'All the same, *Herr Sturmbannführer*, I wish we had a clearer reference to his relations with some of the others. After all, we reckon Arzfeld's own guilt can be established already. The argument for not finishing with him was that he might still give something away. There are a lot of gaps to fill in and we're dealing with a conspiracy against the Reich. This letter is all about their miserable private lives.'

'It all hangs together,' said Schwede. 'It's evidence of a criminal conspiracy. It shows these people up for what they really are – immoral, devoid of any principle, false to every German idea –'

He choked. Molde was looking again at his own copy of Frido's letter.

'Do we allow the letter to reach its destination?'

'Of course we do, you fool! What would Hoffmann say if it didn't arrive? Hoffmann's doing his duty and we want to keep Arzfeld trusting him. It was Hoffmann who tipped us off he was up to something in July, remember? We owe something to Hoffmann.'

'When will Arzfeld be pulled in?'

'When the Gestapo judge it right. They have great experience,' said Schwede sententiously, 'in the difficult matter of exactly when and how to bring criminals to justice. But I suspect that this so-called secret he has been keeping will help, when they decide to pull him and crack him. He won't be expecting it. It will give them something to ring the changes with – swing from that to his relations with Stauffenberg and the rest of the swine, and back again. You need variety in interrogation, and surprise. Oh, we'll have his head all right! And screw a good deal out of him before, I wouldn't wonder!'

Schwede tried to sound dispassionate, but as he reflected

on the contents of Frido's letter he felt jealous and uncontrollable fury. And to think that he had been offered the chance of returning to his own Gau in Lower Saxony after Christmas, probably in a more senior position! If it would serve the Reich he should accept the offer. He should indeed!

Molde reached for a folder. A thought struck him.

'*Herr Sturmbannführer*, you spoke of the woman – the one with the child – as a cousin of his – of Arzfeld's. The letter doesn't refer to her as a cousin.'

A nerve twitched in Schwede's forehead. 'I thought he wrote of her as a cousin,' he said gruffly. 'Why does she confide in him if he's not a relation? Anyway, it's not important.'

'It's near your own home and former place of duty, of course, isn't it? I imagine you know of these people.'

Schwede's mind went back to his one encounter with Major Kurt Langenbach, to the latter's arrogant smile, his unconcealed contempt for the pretensions of the little Nazi brewery manager, the dismissive tone in which he said, 'Schwede, isn't it?' Schwede adjusted his memory.

'Major Langenbach,' he said to Molde softly, 'was a close friend of mine. A true hero. One should never allow personal feelings to affect duty, but I can tell you my shame on behalf of my dead friend is hard to set aside. Now get on with your work!'

Anthony was lying on a mattress on the floor in an attic at Schloss Langenbach. He had only blurred recollections of how he got there. He remembered moving from a church, every step a painful, uncertain adventure, beside Anna into a wet street beneath a grey sky. Somehow he had then found himself stretched in the back of a small farm cart. Then there had been pain again, clip-clop-clip-clop, that had surely gone on for hours. Anna's voice was whispering, 'stand – not for long'. Then her arm had been round him – a steep, winding stair. He thought he'd said, 'I can't do it,' and she had said fiercely, 'You must, I can't carry you.' He remembered saying at one point, 'I'll sit down for a little,' and Anna, he was certain, had hissed 'NO!' and made him drag his torment and his fever on and on, up and up. He didn't know how long ago that was.

Nor how much had happened, how much was dream. But today, whenever today was, he felt clear-headed and able to think lucidly.

Anna had saved him and hidden him. She had also nursed him. He reached down to his thigh. It was efficiently bandaged. He felt weak but he knew he was recovering. He also felt extremely hungry. He didn't suppose it would be sensible to try to get up but he wished there were less of a draught. He looked at his surroundings.

The attic was huge and dusty. It had obviously long been used as a storeroom for unwanted furniture, boxes, antique luggage and broken harness. There were several skylights, and it seemed a bright day, for pools of sunshine lay at intervals on the wooden floor. The exposed roof beams and rafters were immense. Anthony coughed. He saw the dust swirling in the sunbeams that struck the nearest skylight.

At that moment there was the sound of a door opening. He knew that step already, as it approached where he lay.

'Anna!' He found that he could speak, though weakly. 'Oh Anna! It wasn't a dream! It's you!' He felt too feeble to worry about what terms they met on – enemy, lover, captor, saviour. His eyes moved over her face like fingertips.

She knelt by the mattress. In the forthcoming weeks they always murmured – the size of the place and the solidity of walls and floors meant that to whisper was unnecessary, but it was unwise, too, to raise the voice. He took her hand.

Anna had a handkerchief bound round the head. She looked, as she always did, both supremely efficient and very beautiful. She left her hand in Anthony's and smiled at him.

'You are better. You are different today. The fever has gone completely.'

'Anna, where exactly am I?'

'You are in one of the attics at Langenbach. The east attic to be precise. It is a storeroom, as you can see, and nobody visits it but me.' She explained to him in a matter-of-fact way, that every visit to dress his wound, to care for him, to bring water or supplies had had to be made at night – or, at the earliest, in the evening.

'The village school occupies part of the floor below, the first floor. My mother-in-law never moves from her own room off

335

the hall. She can no longer walk. I have a girl who does most of what's needed in the kitchen and two women who work here by day, cleaning. They live in the village. They would at once know if you were in a bedroom. I couldn't conceal it. But they never come up here.'

'How long have I been here?'

'Exactly nine days. It's 5th December. You had a bad wound in the thigh.'

'It was a splinter of glass. From a bomb. An air raid. We were at the railway station.'

'"We"?'

Anthony nodded and then sighed. He supposed in some extraordinary way they were still on different sides and he'd best say the minimum about Robert. Or were they?'

'My leg doesn't feel too bad now.'

'The splinter missed every main nerve and artery. It went through muscle and flesh. You were very lucky. But it started to become infected quickly, and you had a high temperature. Now it's just a question of getting your strength back, and the tissue's mending.'

Anthony lifted her hand to his lips and started kissing it gently, lingeringly. She smiled, still a practical smile but, he noted with joy, with the love that he remembered in it and in her eyes. Was it really possible that after years of separation, amidst the chaos of a world war, committed as she was to an opposing side in that war, she could – did – still love him? As he knew, and had never doubted, that he loved her? Or was this a delirious dream?

Anna patted his cheek with her other hand.

'You're not going to be fit for – very much – for a little time, you know!' She bent and kissed him on the lips.

'Anna, you must be running a terrible risk having me here. I was going to give myself up, you know. I'm an escaped prisoner of war, the worst that would happen to me would be the punishment cells.'

'I know you're an escaped prisoner of war.'

He looked at her and he knew with humble and astonished joy that to this woman her human duty had been instantly clear.

'I knew it at once. That wasn't difficult to guess, although

336

first seeing you gave me a fearful shock! But now you can't move – as you are. And if you gave yourself up they'd start asking how you had your wound dressed and so forth. No, my love, you must stay for a little, until you are strong enough to walk properly.'

'Can I really stay here without being found?'

'Yes, but you must do exactly what I say. You must never leave this attic – I've got a wash basin, I'll bring water every day, empty it for you. I've got an old – what do you call in England, those old-fashioned lavatories one empties by hand?'

'Commodes.'

'I've found one, and lifted it up here – very heavy! Later, when you are really better, it should be possible for you sometimes to come down, maybe at night.'

'If there's nobody but your mother-in-law, bedridden, a girl cook and two cleaning women by day, then there's no human being to set eyes on me after the end of school, is there? Perhaps I can explore a little more quite soon.'

His hand, still without strength, moved, caressing, from wrist to forearm.

'It is not so that there is no other human being, not at all,' said Anna. 'There is also Franzi. Your son.'

Several weeks went by and the winter grew harder. As Anthony grew stronger so did his restlessness increase, but so also did all his old passion for Anna well up again. She was strict in the régime which she imposed and he obeyed her absolutely. He could imagine what she was risking. She brought him books from the library at Langenbach. Sometimes she brought a newspaper and he tried to deduce from the manifest lies and distortions what was actually happening in the war.

They talked of Marcia. Anna spoke of her with affection.

'Frido loves her, you know. There was another, a man called Toni Rudberg. Attractive, promiscuous – I think she lost her heart to him. He disappeared, like so many, somewhere in Russia. But Frido has always loved her.'

'It's caused us all – my parents – awful pain, her being here. I can't get used to the idea of Marcia, spending the war – well –'

337

'On the other side? And courted by German officers? Your little sister? Is that what you mean?'

'I suppose that it is.' But it was both wonderful and poignant to hear that Marcia was well.

On the subject of Franzi, Anna was adamant.

'He must not see you. Children cannot understand secrets. It is essential that he knows nothing – is in a position to say nothing. He is five years old, very bright. He would ask questions, say something unintentionally to Hans, the garden man, or to one of the cleaning women. Or to Fraülein Wendel, she is always keen to talk to him.'

'Fraülein Wendel?'

'She directs the school. A Nazi. She distrusts me.' It was astonishing how easily they slipped into a sort of normality in conversation, despite their bizarre circumstances, Anthony thought. Franzi, however, complicated life greatly. Anna looked after him entirely herself as well as taking the major part in over-seeing the farm at Langenbach and caring for her mother-in-law. There were a thousand things to be done or to arrange in the old house, trying to maintain its existence under the shadows of war. Anna seemed to do the work of five women. And accompanying her much of the time, it appeared, was Franzi. Sometimes she would appear in the attic by day. Anthony would say.

'Stay for a little!'

She would explain, Franzi had been promised a story, or a ride in the donkey cart or a game in the snow. She brought Anthony's food for the day early, with a thermos of ersatz coffee he drank with gratitude and distaste. Then she came in the evening, with something cooked. They ate together then, perched incongruously on collapsed chairs long declared redundant in the Schloss.

'Couldn't we go down?'

Anna would shake her head. Franzi was a light sleeper. It would, Anna said firmly, be utterly disastrous if he saw Anthony.

'So I am not to meet my son!' Anthony was resigned.

But once, when the school was not in session, on a Sunday, he persuaded a somewhat nervous Anna to take him to one of the first-floor rooms with a window opening on the garden.

'I'll be very quiet. I'll lock the door. I'll not show myself at the window, I promise. Take him into the garden, let me watch him through the window. I'll sit on the bed, well back from it.'

'Franzi's going to the house of the farm manager – a social call, there's a four-year-old granddaughter! I'm taking him there and collecting him after an hour or so.'

'Take him past the window, across the grass there.'

She had done so and Anthony feasted his eyes on his son. Later he heard three taps, their special signal, on the door of the bedroom and unlocked it. Anna was smiling, her eyes shining.

'You saw him?'

He nodded. Anna came in. Anthony asked himself, 'What exactly am I feeling?' But he knew the answer now.

'So that was Franzi. That was our son.'

Anthony had looked at the little boy at first with disbelief, with a sense of detachment. He could not easily think of Franzi as flesh of his flesh, a son, a Marvell. Suddenly, as he had watched, Franzi had turned and raised his left hand high above his head, small fist clenched in a gesture of triumph or emphasis to something he was shouting to Anna, something Anthony could not hear. And Anthony immediately remembered that his own mother had always reminded them of his, Anthony's, childhood gesture of the raised fist. It was the same! Great God of bequeathed characteristics, of mysterious and inexplicable inheritances, it was the same!

Hilda had often bored them, affectionately –

'Anthony was a proper little Communist! Clenched fist salute, only it was always his left fist and he raised the arm high so it wasn't quite correct, I suppose!'

'Oh, Mother, we've all heard about Anthony's salute!'

Franzi had raised his arm again, shouting, inaudible through the heavy, closed window. Anthony felt weak. He could not now take his eyes from Franzi. He followed every move the child made with fascination. He longed for this moment to last. All too soon, Franzi was away, running, calling, radiant, untroubled.

'So that was Franzi, that was our son!'

It was, he told himself, his dreadfully weakened condition

that made his eyes swim with such easy tears. Anna understood. She kissed him gently, held his hand firmly in silence. Anna understood well and the understanding brought her contentment.

'Only Frido knows,' she whispered. She had explained that she had, some time previously, thought it right to confide in Frido. 'I hope that does not make you angry?'

'It makes me proud.'

A little later Anthony said,

'Who is in the house?'

'It's empty except for my mother-in-law. On the other side, off the hall.'

Anthony drew her down beside him on the huge four-poster bed, his arm firm around her.

'You've got much stronger this last week, my darling!'

'Yes,' said Anthony, his hands busy, his mouth buried, his heart beating. 'I think so too. Much stronger.'

After that he used to say, 'When's Franzi going to see his little friend again? Next Sunday?' And she would chuckle and say that something, perhaps, might be arranged.

Sometimes Anna would spend some hours with him in the attic at night, but she was nervous of this, always afraid that Franzi might look for her, find her nowhere and start hunting or even disturb old Frau Langenbach, leading to subsequent questions and complications. Yet in spite of the discomforts, the concealments, the absurdities of their situation, their love-making gained from the dangers with which it was surrounded. Anthony's physical hunger for Anna grew with what it fed upon. She was like a gazelle, he thought, large-eyed, slender-limbed, desirable, elusive: elusive – yet always and quickly caught if within reach! He could never have enough of the smoothness of her skin, of the way she came to him with such smiling, frank enthusiasm of the body, of the immense pleasure she took in giving pleasure.

One day Anthony whispered,

'My darling, I've never really understood how you came to marry Langenbach. You didn't love him, and you're the last woman in the world to marry for money, or position.'

Anna looked solemn.

340

'It was a crime. I told you it was wicked of me, long ago, in London. But –'

She told him, caressing him, stroking his hair, that although Kurt Langenbach quickly showed her that she could never love him he was an interesting man, 'It was impossible to be bored with him! He was quick and original. Interesting!'

And Anthony said, as evenly as he could, 'He must have touched *something* in you, darling!' It was as easy, he found, to be jealous of the dead as of the living. Anna told him, very seriously, that her marriage had been able to help her beloved mother. She had seldom talked of her mother, who had died suddenly only a year after the marriage to Kurt Langenbach.

'I tried not to let her know I was unhappy. But after she went, it was very lonely.'

He learned more and more of Anna's early life, loves and recollections.

They made love with ever-increasing urgency and energy. Anthony listened to Anna's soft tones as she talked, and realized he was seeking to record them on the phonograph of his mind, to be able to play that beloved music over and over, when lovers were separated, all afar.

One evening, Anna said, 'Listen, it's Christmas next week. I must spend all my time with Franzi. The school children start their holidays tomorrow.'

Anthony suffered, as he had several times in the last few days, a twinge of bad conscience.

'When am I going to go?'

'My darling, your leg can't be strong enough. You've recovered a lot of energy remarkably quickly,' she squeezed his arm, 'but the truth is I cannot, I simply cannot allow you to do what you need to do, which is to walk, to strengthen your leg muscles. They will get stronger, and you should walk up and down at night, all you can. But you're not yet fit to travel in the way you tell me an escaper has to travel.' For Anthony had talked often of his plans, and although he supposed it was just possible that Jan Vogt could make another train journey without instant discovery, he knew how arduous it was going to be to walk and run, to burrow and hide and somehow make his way through German positions to British or American lines. In mid-winter.

341

In weaker moments, Anthony thought that perhaps the best plan would be to wait until the Allies crossed the Rhine and entered Germany. It couldn't be long. Then many of the problems would, surely, solve themselves. But on 19th December, the day after this conversation, Anna brought a newspaper to the attic in the evening. Anthony was feeling particularly restless. There was snow on the ground and a good deal of snow covered the skylights. The atmosphere was close and depressing.

He glanced at the headlines.

'This must be nonsense!'

He read that the British and Americans 'Were in full retreat' in Belgium, and that the victorious Panzer Armies of Generals Dietrich and von Manteuffel were marching through the Ardennes and about to cross the Meuse. The Meuse! Anthony refused to believe it. Nevertheless, something must have happened, and whatever it was didn't sound as if it had brought nearer the day of a triumphant Allied march into Germany. Or the day when an advancing British Army might find, whatever they made of it, Captain Anthony Marvell in the arms of his mistress: or, perhaps, playing in the garden of Schloss Langenbach with his five-year-old son.

Christmas passed. Anna brought further newspapers to the attic. They told Anthony that the Führer had ordered the troops in the west to pass, temporarily, to the defensive. But one day, during the first week of January, 1945, Anna came to the attic as usual, but looking drawn and wretched. At first she said nothing, gave him a glass of wine, poured one herself and sat down on one of their ancient, battered chairs.

Anthony saw her looking at him with a frown of concentration. 'I don't know what exactly to do. You see, your existence depends on me. You're not yet strong enough to leave. And God! I dread your leaving! But I've got to go away for a little, some time soon.'

'For how long?'

'Two days perhaps. One night. I shall arrange for one of my cleaning women to sleep in the Schloss to be with my mother-in-law. On the ground floor.'

'Of course I'll be all right, don't be absurd! Will you take Franzi with you?'

'Yes. I must pay this visit before the school holiday ends. It would be much too dangerous to be away and leave you here with the Wendel woman poking about on her own.'

'Anna, I'll be perfectly all right. Give me some apples to eat, whatever you like. I'll be able to go at night to the first floor for water and so forth. I'll be careful. Anna will you tell me, what is this visit you must pay?'

'It's to Arzfeld, which you know from long ago. I must see my cousin Kaspar von Arzfeld.' She went on, almost inaudibly. 'Frido has been arrested. He is to be brought before the court, it seems, in about three weeks' time. Kaspar is to be allowed to visit him.'

'Why – arrested?'

Anna looked at him steadily. 'My love, you can't hope to understand a lot of things that are happening here and we daren't ask much ourselves. Just be glad that you have the quite simple task of finding your way, with a wounded leg, through the backdoor of one Army and in at the front door of another! I shall go to Arzfeld for the night, next Tuesday.'

She started crying gently. Anthony had read of the July plot in Oflag XXXIII but knew little of its spread or significance. He supposed Anna was referring to it. These, he reflected, were waters in which it was difficult for an Englishman to swim. He kept his arm round Anna's shoulders and they sat for a long time in the dark. After a time she said,

'There's another thing. There's an odious man, a Nazi official, quite senior in Himmler's SS, that sort of thing. He used to be the Party boss here. He's been for several years with the SS in Poland. He's a horrible man, called Schwede. There's a rumour he's coming back here.'

'Will he make trouble for you personally?'

'It is always possible,' said Anna. She was trembling now. 'Always possible. He certainly hates me. He does not know anything against me, against this house, we have always been careful. But now we must be particularly careful. His return here can do us no good.'

'Is he really as bad as all that?'

'Yes. Really so bad. He is a type, but as bad of the type as

343

you can imagine. And you do not know what some of these people can do.'

They were quiet for a little, sadness and fear hovering over their love.

'Anthony, my darling, it is time for sleep. I must leave you.'

'Do you remember I quoted from a poem of John Donne, soon after I first held you in my arms?'

'Of course I remember.'

'Sometimes, Anna, love, he put things better than anybody else. Here's something he said in a sermon. It's not a bad thought to take to bed.

> *'Every night's sleep is a Nunc Dimittis;*
> *then the Lord lets his servant depart in peace.*
> *The lying down is a valediction, a parting,*
> *a taking leave (shall I say so?) a shaking hands*
> *with God, and when thou shakest hands with God,*
> *let those hands be clean.'*

'And do you feel that, sweetheart? Do you feel your hands and my hands clean?'

'Very, very clean.'

344

PART VI

1945

Chapter 22

———————◆———————

'I WAS TO GIVE YOU a message of love and strength from Anna Langenbach, our beloved cousin,' said Colonel Kaspar von Arzfeld. 'She paid me a visit some days ago.'

He had travelled from home with considerable difficulty through the frozen landscape and shattered cities which constituted Germany in that January of 1945. Destruction was universal. Towns were reduced to deserts of rubble by the weight of Allied bombing. Movement by rail became daily less feasible as the air raids destroyed marshalling yards, rolling stock, stations, signal networks, and in many places picked up and tore into scorched pieces the rails themselves. People lived in cellars beneath the ruins, moving as little as possible, listening always for the shriek of sirens, the menacing roar of aircraft and gunfire, suffering increasingly in the towns from the shortage of all sorts of supplies which the destruction of transport had produced. From the beginning of the war food, in the German cities, had been difficult. Now there was everywhere the stench of hunger and death. Everywhere was grey, cold and empty of hope.

Through this Germany, heart loaded with misery, the old cavalry Colonel of Reserve made his laborious way to Berlin. He had, two weeks before, been curtly told that his post, a wartime post in the transportation section at the local Military District Headquarters, was to be abolished. He had not now even the distraction of a little unimportant duty to perform. In Berlin he reported to the governor of Plötzensee prison, noting with surprise the surly contempt apparently aroused by his name, the scant regard paid to his rank. He would be permitted, by the regulations, to have one half-hour visit to Captain von Arzfeld.

Frido had been arrested on 27th December. It was now 14th January. Kaspar looked at his son and exerted his

347

habitual self-discipline to keep his eyes and voice steady. The boy was pale – so pale that his father could not believe he was not seriously ill; but Frido smiled and said, 'I'm perfectly well!'

Deprived of both shoe-laces and braces he had perforce shuffled into the interview cell, holding up his trousers, his ordinary dignity under attack. The extraordinary thing was that, in spite of all, he seemed not only dignified, but composed and happy.

Happy! Kaspar tried, at first, to keep the conversation practical, to strike a note of robust optimism. It was, he assumed, best to imply that they were faced with some enormous mistake.

'You know when the – the hearing – will be?'

'Yes. I was told this morning. I am to face the judges – a People's Court you know, not a Court Martial – on 22nd January. In one week.'

'I do not know the procedure adopted,' said Kaspar, his voice old and, for all his efforts, quavering a little, 'I hope that a well-prepared defence –'

Frido looked at him with his serious and charming smile, a smile which immediately transported his father in space and time to the woods at Arzfeld and the childhood of his boys.

'Father, there is no defence to prepare. I intend, if permitted, to say certain things. That is all.'

'My son, under German law it is necessary to answer a charge and it is proper to put the circumstances in as favourable a light as possible. It is the business of a lawyer –'

'That applies to ordinary crime. I am to be accused of treason and conspiracy. I not only admit the factual truth of the accusation, I regard that treason and that conspiracy as evidence of my patriotism, my true love of Germany.'

Kaspar sat silent. There was no move from the guard in the interview cell, who stood like a statue, at a little distance. No doubt all this was reported. Frido was speaking softly but audibly. Now he was continuing.

'That is all I intend to say to them. Now speak to me about Arzfeld. It's been a hard winter so far, I imagine. Did we lose any trees in the November gales, I don't think you told me? Have you had a letter from Lise recently?'

348

Kaspar said in a low voice,

'Have you been treated correctly?'

'I've been interrogated, in the way that's now understood. Don't let's speak of it. It's over now – now the trial date's fixed. There's not long to go.'

'The trial!' said Kaspar. He could not take his mind to trial and aftermath. He gazed at his son's face. Frido said,

'The trial will, I expect, be swiftly followed by the penalty. It will be the same as for most of my friends. Better men than me.'

His father looked away, incapable of speaking.

'There's one thing I want to say, Father, one very important thing. Marcia Marvell – I want you to know that I love her and that I have written a letter to her, telling her I love her. I don't know what she feels in her heart but it would have been better, I think, to say nothing. It was thoughtless of me. She will suffer. I've had one letter back from her. I don't know what she really feels, but I – please do all you can.'

Kaspar nodded. He said,

'Lise has written everything about this to me.'

'Really?'

'Yes. The girls were afraid to write too much to you, afraid letters might harm you, compromise you. Because she's English. Of course it would have made no difference, not at all,' said Kaspar, glancing at the guard, 'but that's what the girls thought. And Lise told me you had written to Marcia. I know you love her. There is nothing to regret in that, my son.'

'Did Lise make any other comment?'

'She did,' said Kaspar slowly. 'She told me she knew, also, that Marcia loves you – has always, in her heart, loved you. And always will.'

By nature an uninventive man, Kaspar looked at Frido's expression and knew that his journey had been amply justified.

'I intend,' Kaspar said softly, 'to pay a visit to the girls. Very soon.' Frido nodded, and touched his father's hand.

Then they spoke for a little of small things, of home, of a relative here, a farm servant there. The guard looked at his watch and spoke. Kaspar rose. He said gently,

'You have chosen a hard road. God will sustain you.'

'I think it best to say goodbye, Father.'

Kaspar took his son's hand, holding it tight for several seconds. He looked away and moved to the cell door. There he paused, turned and looked very steadily at Frido, meeting his eyes.

'You thought at one time that Werner had a special place in my heart. But I have always loved you.'

'I know that.'

Colonel von Arzfeld slowly raised his hand in a gesture half salute, half farewell and turned away.

The Superintendent of the wards in which the girls wore themselves out day and night was a ferocious disciplinarian. In Sister Brigitta's eyes junior nurses could do little right. Marcia, less pliable in disposition than Lise, would often have been close to rebellion were it not for the knowledge that any adverse report on her would probably bring her nursing career – and her liberty – to an end. In all this she had the love and loyal support of Lise; and Marcia thought that no sister could have been more to her than Lise had become, more supportive, more selflessly comprehending. They shared all things.

They shared in particular, in that winter of 1944–45, two visitors. The first, on 17th December, was a Captain Hoffmann. According to protocol, he first reported to the Director of the Hospital, then to the Ward Superintendent. Thereafter, Lise and Marcia were grudgingly summoned.

Captain Hoffmann had a stiff, formal manner. He was, he said, a close colleague of Captain Frido von Arzfeld. He had business in these days before Christmas which brought him to this part of the front, to the village in which the hospital was. Captain von Arzfeld had, therefore, asked him to visit the hospital and to pay his respects to Fraülein von Arzfeld. He had also brought a letter. He handed the envelope to Lise.

'Also to Fraülein Marvell,' Hoffmann said, turning gravely to Marcia, 'and also a letter.' Saying that he would report both girls to be well – 'And hoping, one day, to see my brother in person!' exclaimed Lise – Hoffmann saluted and left, taking punctilious leave of a stern-faced Sister Brigitta. That evening Marcia read and re-read Frido's letter of 10th December. The girls shared a room in the nurses' hostel.

'Frido has written you a long letter,' said Lise gently. Her own communication from Frido had made sufficiently clear what that to Marcia must contain. Marcia lifted her eyes to Lise's and found that she only saw with difficulty through tears.

'Yes, as you say, it's a long letter, Lise.'

'I expect he's told you he loves you,' said Lise with blunt impatience. She knew that it was so. In one way she rejoiced that it was so. Marcia was so much a beloved sister that the idea of her one day becoming so in family relationship as well as in affection was most desirable. It was suitable. It was – tidy.

But with another part of herself Lise was less convinced that Marcia was suited to Frido, much though she loved them both. Frido was so essentially serious, while Marcia – hard though she worked, much though she had suffered – was apt to find huge numbers of things subjects for laughter which she freely indulged. That Frido was greatly in love with Marcia and had been for a long time Lise knew perfectly well. She said,

'Frido feels matters strongly. He always has.'

'Yes, I know.'

'And what do you, yourself, really feel?' For close though the girls were, they had never discussed Frido in these terms.

Marcia felt confused more than anything. She also experienced an untypical twinge of bitterness with life. 'God help me not to love anybody again while this damned war goes on,' she thought, 'I'm death to them!' Werner von Arzfeld lay in Poland. Toni Rudberg had not been heard of since Stalingrad – lucky, poor Toni, if he were simply dead she supposed. The thought of Toni stabbed her often. Now Frido was forcing her, again, to face emotions.

'It's hard to say what I feel, Lise. In one way I've always loved him. He reminds me of Werner, of course. And I know he's a – a wonderful person. And it's a marvellous compliment – to be told by somebody like your brother that he loves

351

one, like *both* your brothers, Lise, darling. But it's a great responsibility. One must be very sure, very truthful.'

Lise nodded agreement. She liked this way of defining the matter. Sure and truthful!

Marcia did not feel free to discuss, even with Lise, the other part of Frido's communication – Anna's secret, Anthony's part in all this. She had been entrusted with a confidence and, at least for the present, even Lise must remain outside the dangerous circle of those who shared it. The remarkable fact that Anthony was the father of Anna's son gave Marcia undiluted pleasure. From their first meeting she had loved and admired Anna, and – who could say? – when the hurricane sweeping over Europe ultimately lost its destructive force those two might come together again, peaceably, openly, honourably. It seemed highly improbable, but meanwhile the information brought Anthony nearer to her. She had always adored her brother and she loved the idea that he, too, had once been connected not only by passion but actually by fatherhood with this family to which she was bound by such extraordinarily compelling ties. It might, she thought, be reprehensible to think thus, but it was Marcia's way. She knew, too, that Anna, of all people, would have a child by a man only if she really loved him. And she felt delighted and, in her uncomplicated way, proud that her brother had, once upon a time, certainly won the love of so true and so beautiful a woman. She had once said to Anna, 'He loved you,' and Anna had sighed and shed some tears and pressed her hand. But they had exchanged no further confidences about Anthony. Something had seemed to tremble on Anna's tongue but she had not let it fall. Now Marcia knew what it was. She would treasure the secret. She would in due course write to Frido discreetly, gratefully, gently: a little noncomittally. It would be best to delay for a few days, to think about it, to choose the words with care. She wrote, in the event, on Christmas Day.

The girls' second private visitor to the hospital came a month later, on 16th January, 1945. This was none other than Kaspar von Arzfeld.

Kaspar had been treated with what he regarded as discourtesy at Plötzensee prison. To the Director of the Hospital,

352

however, and to Sister Brigitta – both Prussians of traditional instincts – he was a Colonel and a nobleman, and entitled to respect. Lise, that afternoon was summarily informed that she was to take the afternoon off – 'and Fraülein Marvell is to finish early, at five o'clock, so that she can join you. You have a visitor.' Pressure on the hospital was intense at that moment, but Sister Brigitta privately thought that both girls would be the better for a short break.

Kaspar, Lise with him, was awaiting her at the visitors' room in the hostel. When Marcia found them in the late afternoon, it was already dark outside. Kaspar had been provided with accommodation for the night. Marcia saw him with joy.

'Colonel von Arzfeld!' She moved forward to kiss him, a thing she had never done before. Then she saw his face, haggard, wretched. She also took in the fact that Lise had been crying.

He took Marcia's hands and held them between his own. He seemed unable to speak and looked as if with supplication at Lise. Lise said in a strangled sort of voice,

'Marcia, my father has news of Frido. Some weeks ago he was arrested. He is to appear before a court in Berlin.'

'Arrested? Appear before a court?'

'A People's Court,' said Kaspar, his voice unsteady, 'accused of treason. Accused of being involved in the attempt on the Führer's life last July.'

'But – we had messages from him – before Christmas – from a Captain Hoffmann.'

'He was arrested on 27th December. We did not hear for some time.'

The girls were silent, Lise's tears welling again.

'I have explained to Lise, dear little Marcia, that Frido intends to say nothing in his defence. In effect he will admit the charge – the facts. There can be only one penalty.' He managed a few sentences about his visit to the prison. Marcia could not take her eyes from Kaspar's face. Lise threw herself into his arms.

It was five days after this, on 21st January, that Anna came to

353

the attic in the evening, stood by Anthony and laid her cheek gently against his without a word.

'There's a new problem. My cousin, Kaspar von Arzfeld is coming to stay here for several weeks.'

'Soon?'

'Very soon. I have a letter from him. He has seen Frido.' Tears were running down Anna's cheeks but she mastered her voice.

'Frido is to go before a People's Court on 23rd January – Tuesday. He intends to admit – everything. There is not the slightest doubt what they will do to him.' She dropped her voice and muttered, broken, 'They will kill him. Like many others already.'

Anthony thought of the serious, intelligent face of Frido, bearing a little stiff, voice when arguing so calm, so reasonable, smile so affectionate, aura of simple goodness so extraordinarily touching. He could see Frido at Oxford; at Bargate; at Arzfeld. He was, he said to himself, thinking about an enemy officer – but he knew that he would feel the loss of Frido as sharply as any in the war. And it would, he supposed with an inward shudder, be a disgusting, a cruel death. There had been plenty of rumours current in Oflag XXXIII. There was something darkly mediaeval in the savagery with which German was pursuing German in these dreadful days.

Anna was still trembling, still pressing close against him.

'I have asked Cousin Kaspar to come here soon for a while. I have always loved him, and Lise, as you know, is far away. He must not be alone for too long at this time.'

'Of course not.' Anthony's mind was still following Frido – through echoing passages, towards what foul execution shed? Anna was murmuring with urgency.

'My darling, it would be impossible for Cousin Kaspar to be here, and to avoid picking up some hint about you. Of course, he, himself, would have no doubts about his duty. For him, whatever is going on, Germany is at war. But even if he discovered or guessed nothing he would be compromised if there were later suspicions or investigations. They would associate those suspicions with Frido's record. They would give Kaspar the benefit of no doubt.'

She seldom referred to her own risk. She must, Anthony

knew, be living all the time with the fear of arrest, questioning, torture, death.

'I could not have you both here at the same time,' she whispered, sadly but firmly. 'It would be too dangerous. For all of us. I'm sure of it.'

Anthony said, 'I'm fit to go. I'm a bit feeble and I'll go in short stretches. You can advise me on route and stops, the best way to plan it. I think it's mild, for January.' This last was certainly untrue. She put her arms round him. He smoothed her hair.

'My darling Anna, I'll get away safe, the war can't last long. I'll come for you, and we'll make a new life together, won't we? With Franzi?'

She didn't answer, but kissed him. Then they began talking of practical matters with great earnestness.

Hard, sickening work, and a general fear that overshadowed even their private horror, made the days race past for the two girls during that appalling winter.

All the nurses had heard the news of a Russian attack on 12th January. It was described as having been successfully beaten back with heavy losses and at first it had seemed far away, somewhere in central Poland, still that 'East Front' which, remote and barbaric, had so much dominated their imaginations since coming to work at the hospital. The hospital was pleasantly situated on the edge of a large village by the Oder river, a short distance north of Frankfurt-an-der-Oder and about ninety kilometres south-east of Berlin. It was not a military hospital although it had become customary to admit 'complicated' cases from the front, referred to the hospital Director by the military authorities.

Since 12th January, all had changed. Officers of the medical branch of the Wehrmacht had arrived with urgent demands. Every bed, the time of every doctor and every nurse, was to be made available for the wounded of Army Group A, now meeting the full fury of the greatest Russian offensive yet experienced in the war. Rumour spread like poison gas through the wards and corridors. It was whispered that the previous Saturday the enemy had first crossed the frontier into Silesia:

and that, further north, they had broken into East Prussia. The Red Army was on German soil! It was unbelievable! It was horrible! But, as one broken soldier after another found consolation in muttering for a few snatched, precious minutes to a nurse about his private nightmare, none could doubt any longer that it was true.

The population of the village had feared this for some time. Cowed, murmuring behind doors and by now sceptical of the Führer's promises, they had made their own deductions from the bland, official communiqués. Fighting around Warsaw, fighting east of the Masurian Lakes was one thing. Fighting the Bolsheviks who had crossed the Vistula and were tapping at the gates of Danzig was quite another. The people were gripped with terror, a terror which infected all within the hospital. Nobody had been allowed to leave the district – the Party's local leaders had strict instructions and these were as strictly enforced. There was to be no flight westward. German soil would be triumphantly defended. It was defeatist treachery to doubt it.

But now the Russians were in East Prussia and Silesia. One day, perhaps soon, they would be here.

The wounded Panzer Grenadier admitted on 20th January, was small and very young. He had a surname but the nurses immediately knew him as Willi. He whispered that he was seventeen years old, but Lise was confident that he had not yet seen his sixteenth birthday. He had a brown, country face, glistening brown eyes, a smile to delight, no legs and only one arm. And there were other injuries.

Willi caught Lise's hand with his remaining limb as she shifted his pillow. Despite wounds and weakness he had discovered her name and never failed to produce his smile for her. For him these were treasured moments.

'Fräulein Lise, what day is it?'

'It's Thursday, Willi, 25th January, 1945, to be exact.'

'Where is this hospital?' She told him. A Saxon himself, he knew the geography and understood her.

'When are we all to be taken to the west?'

'There are no plans that I know of to do that, Willi. You are safe here. We are a long way behind the front.'

Willi looked at her from his pillow. He had shed his smile.

'You must get away before they come, Fraülein Lise! They will come. We've got nothing to fight them with. They pour over us – tanks, guns, horses, men. Everything!'

'Hush, Willi, it's going to be all right –'

'No, you can't imagine! You know, we attacked, my company. It was a little counter-attack, the lieutenant told us we did it well, we surprised them, we took a village. A German village. The Ivans had been in it for twenty-four hours. There wasn't a soul alive. And my God, what they'd done to them! Children, the lot. And as for the women! My God, Fraülein Lise, whatever they order, you must get away!'

Lise gently detached her hand. 'And who would look after you, Willi? I think I'd better stay, to make sure you're good and get well.'

'Oh, I'm done for,' he said without emotion, 'but you – and the other, your friend, you must get away. Go secretly.' He was always on the edge of delirium.

'Fraülein Lise!'

'Now I must go, Willi. I'll be back later.'

'Fraülein Lise, your friend – she's not German, is she?'

'No, she's not German. Now settle down, Willi. I want you to sleep a little.'

Lise hastened away. From the doorway, the sharp voice of the matron cut through the ward.

'Fraülein von Arzfeld!'

Lise hurried to report.

'You are to go to the Superintendent's office immediately.'

Lise scuttled along the corridors.

A stranger, a grey man, stood in the Ward Superintendent's office. His face was colourless – not exactly white, thought Lise, but devoid of definable colour tones. Fleetingly, she wondered how one would paint it. It was not an old face, but the hair was sparse and grey. Outside, a bitter east wind was accompanied by flurries of snow and the man had not removed a grey raincoat. A grey, felt hat, with the damp of melted snow on the crown, stood on the Superintendent's table. The Superintendent murmured something and left the office. The grey man looked at Lise.

'You are Fraülein von Arzfeld?'

Lise nodded. She felt sick. She also felt fear but no surprise.

'My name is Müller. State Police.'

Lise supposed so, and said nothing. Müller opened a folder. Then he grunted and sat down in the Superintendent's chair, opening a notebook and taking a pencil from his pocket. His face was completely without expression. Lise remained standing in the middle of the room. Müller started writing.

'When did you last receive a letter from your brother, Frido von Arzfeld?'

'I have heard nothing from my brother since before Christmas. Just over a month ago.'

'A month ago,' said Müller, nodding and writing. 'And when did you last see him?' His inflexion seemed to imply that it was a matter of little importance. Lise was trembling, but fighting a fierce battle to conceal it.

'It was at Christmas, 1943. Over a year ago. Immediately before I came here.'

'We will talk about that again in a minute,' said Müller, in a bored and even tone, still contemplating his notebook rather than Lise. 'Now let us have one or two particulars about your friend – the young lady who came here with you and whom I shall be talking to later. It seems a strange story, does it not? A strange story indeed.'

Early that morning in Berlin, Horst Brauer surveyed himself in the long glass and approved of what he saw. He straightened his white tie a little, moved his white waistcoat fractionally, to ensure the buttons were exactly central. He settled his tailcoat so that it sat properly on his shoulders. Although cut to give plenty of freedom to the arms it could still appear smart and snug to the figure. Horst Brauer nodded at his reflection and took his top hat from a small polished table beside him. They were going to send a car, difficult though it often was for them. In the glass, Brauer could see his wife enter the room behind him. She smiled at him with an expression of humble and affectionate pride.

'You look really impressive, Horst, dear. I wish you always dressed here at home instead of – there. Then I could admire you more often. Oh dear, it's cold in here.'

Brauer ignored this and frowned.

'Ilse, it appears impossible to produce properly starched collars. This one is below the standard required of me and by me. Why is that?'

'Horst, my dear, it *is* very difficult. It's not easy to get the proper stuff. Everybody, of course, is having to make do with substitutes –'

'I am not everybody. I am an official of the State holding an extraordinary and delicate position. My appearance according to regulations is a symbol of the dignity of the State. Furthermore, it is because I have a right to expect that such things can be properly ordered that I, on a few occasions, bring my – my uniform – home. So that all can be attended to decently.'

'I've brushed your suit, Horst dear, and cleaned the trousers. I think they're spotless now. I know about the collar –'

He did not listen to her further mumblings. He was sure that with more energy and ingenuity these things could be better managed. He saw his wife's inadequacy reflected in the starched linen of other men. Even his detested assistant Fichter – a bungling lout with the bearing and manners of the provincial butcher he once had been – was sartorially impeccable. Ilse was bleating on about something else as she set his coffee before him.

'Last night's raid was really terrible, Frau Steiner told me. Thank Heaven we're some way out. It's the centre of Berlin that's been getting it worst. Oh, dear –'

Brauer also thought it providential that they lived in the outer southern suburbs but he did not care to imply that his life was of particular importance when measured against the sufferings of the Reich.

'Frau Steiner always exaggerates.'

'Will you be – late, Horst?'

'Certainly not.' He considered the day's business. Then he rose and peered out of the apartment window. The official car had not yet arrived. Brauer looked at the clock on the wall and frowned. His temper was always upset by the possibility of unpunctuality. His wife tried to distract him.

'There's one more awful story on the wireless this morning, Horst, about another man who's been betraying the Reich – caught preparing messages to be broadcast to our soldiers telling frightful lies about the Führer. The man on the wireless

359

said that everybody, not just the soldiers, should be aware and on their guard. What with that and all these other revelations –'

'There are traitors in every phase of history,' said Brauer grimly. 'Rats who gnaw at the supports of the house while the gale batters it from outside.' As if giving emphasis to his words, the freezing January east wind howled round the corner window of their sitting room.

'Yes, and it's so hard for one to credit it, this man was an officer – a German officer doing that! And with a famous old German name, too – I can't remember it. Then, last summer –'

Brauer looked at her contemptuously.

'If you saw as much as I do of the actions – and the deserved fates – of some of our "famous old German names", nothing would surprise you.' He finished his coffee and looked out of the window again. The official car, four minutes late, drew up at the street door of the apartment block, black and beetle-like against the snow. It would soon be dawn, and there was some grey light in the eastern sky already. Fires burning in the centre of the city illumined the northern horizon.

A few minutes later Brauer was being driven through the bleak, suburban streets. The driver was talking with resignation about the previous night's air raid. Brauer reflected that there were too many excuses made these days: failure of duty, inattention to detail – it was always blamed on an air raid. True, the city was devastated. Nothing was left of block after block but charred skeletons of buildings. In other whole quarters there wasn't a pane of glass. People huddled, shivering, where they still survived. For that one could thank not only enemy bombers with their indiscriminate fury, but those Germans who betrayed their own folk, soldiers, Führer. Brauer thought of Ilse's 'famous old German names' and snorted.

Nevertheless, life and business were, somehow, kept going. It was unpardonable to throw up one's hands, abandon standards, give in. It would be a pity, not a disaster, but most unfortunate, if he, Horst Brauer, were prevented by circumstances from the punctual discharge of his particular duties. There were six 'particular duties' today, 25th January. He looked at his watch. He had no confidence in the assistant executioner, Fichter. The man was awkward. Besides, there were so many new-fangled ideas thought up these days that a man had to have intelligence as well as strength and resolve. He looked at his watch again. The driver caught his eye in the mirror.

'We've got to go a long way round. They've blocked off the whole of Charlottenburg, the Heerstrasse's closed, the . . .'

'You know the possibilities,' said Brauer, 'and you know when I have to be at Plötzensee. Attend to it.' The driver said no more.

It was on 27th January that Lise caught Marcia's arm as they walked away from the hospital in the evening up the icy village street – caught her upper arm and held it, fingers pressing so hard that even through thickness of overcoat Marcia felt pain and looked at her in surprise. Lise was avoiding her face, controlling herself with the utmost difficulty. It had been an even harder day than usual. The broken fragments of men from the ever-nearing Eastern Front, bleeding remnants of so-called Armies outnumbered by more than twenty to one, had been pouring throughout the day into the hospital. The girls had been working well beyond even the extended stints which had now become normal. Eventually Sister Brigitta had said, grimly, 'Off you go, till five o'clock tomorrow morning. Have something to eat, sleep all you can.'

'There's so much to do – we –'

'Off you go,' said their superior, fixing Marcia in particular with a cold eye. 'It's an order. You will do no good working in your present state. You will make mistakes.'

They walked off through the snow. It was possible to hear the sound of gunfire if the wind was in the east, as it had been for most of the past two months: a cruel, incessant wind.

Lise said tonelessly, 'I've had word. They've done it.'

'Frido?'

'They've killed him. Executed him. Two days ago in Berlin.' She was trembling violently.

'The Director told me. He had received notification, to be communicated to me.'

Marcia put her arms around Lise standing in the snow, the evening air freezing about them.

'It was happening, it must have been happening when we were being interviewed by that pig –'

'Sh, sh!'

'By that pig, who wanted to know when we'd heard from him last and so forth. Who tried to frighten you, Marcia. About Frido.'

The member of the Gestapo, grey, bored, inscrutable, menacing, who had questioned Marcia two days earlier had, indeed, asked about 'her relations with Captain Frido von Arzfeld'. Marcia had referred to him as a dear friend, brother of the man she had been engaged to marry.

The grey man had looked at her. 'He has not spoken of marrying you himself?'

'No.' It was not important, Marcia thought, but Frido had taken trouble to send his letter of love privately, by Hoffmann's hand, and she saw no reason to betray it to a stranger.

'No!'

'Nor talked, written to you about political matters? About the progress of the war, perhaps?'

'Never!'

'Family matters, eh? You know that Captain von Arzfeld has been arrested on a very serious charge?'

'I do.' So the brute must have known, while he put that question, that Frido, trousers sagging, unshaven because deprived of a razor, Frido prison-pallid, followed only by greedy, hate-filled eyes, had been, perhaps at that very moment, pushed towards the executioner's sword, axe or noose in some bleak slaughter-shed.

The interrogation had continued.

'What is your reaction to his arrest?'

'His father, Colonel von Arzfeld, told us, told his sister and me. We are, naturally, deeply upset – horrified – that someone we – I include myself, as you know, in that family – loved and admired as a gallant officer should fall under such terrible suspicion. We find it difficult to believe. Incredible.'

The man was writing without looking up, as if Marcia's words were so predictable that he hardly needed to listen.

He murmured, 'Incredible, yes. You are English, Fraülein

362

Marvell. Yet you have not been interned. What do you think of that?'

'I am grateful. I have been able to train and to work as a nurse. It is work of humanity in which I deeply believe.'

'So in your own way you have been able to serve the Reich.'

'Exactly.'

The man finished writing. There was, Marcia had thought, nothing to damage Frido. The Gestapo man seemed to be of the same mind, since he changed the subject and in a slightly less disagreeable tone said,

'I believe you know Frau Anna Langenbach? Can you help me a little there, I wonder? You see, I have to investigate serious questions of legality and they have many aspects.'

'I don't understand.'

'Well, this is a friendly talk, Fraülein Marvell, so let me explain a little. You have a brother, Anthony Marvell. He is in the English Army?'

'You must understand, Herr –'

'Müller,'

'– Herr Müller, that I haven't seen my brother since before this war began, that I don't know if he's alive or dead. If he's alive and well, I presume he's in the Army, yes.'

'Did you know that he once had an intimate relationship, a sexual relationship, with Frau Anna Langenbach?'

'No – I – when do you mean? He never spoke to me of such a thing! Nor she!'

'But you both – you and your brother – knew the von Arzfelds and the Langenbachs before the War began between England and Germany, I think.'

'Certainly. But I don't know of the – matter you speak of. Frau Langenbach is a respected friend of mine.' Marcia did her best to sound outraged. A young, delicately-nurtured and defenceless girl to have such suggestions put to her by a strange man! Müller gave something like a grin.

'Well,' he said, 'if that's all, Fraülein Marvell, we'd better say goodbye for the time being. I hope you've not forgotten to tell me anything. And I hope everything you have told me is exactly true.'

And so, while this gruesome and inconclusive encounter had been played out, while Marcia had felt herself shaking with a fear she fought a brave, private battle to conceal, they had been doing Frido to death, hanging him from a noose like a carcase, or hacking him, head from body. She shuddered, hugging Lise close, heart beating violently, ghastly images before her eyes.

Chapter 23

———————◆———————

ON SUNDAY, 28TH JANUARY, Anna said as she brought Anthony his daily supplies, 'I'm going to church in Kranenberg. I'll be away two hours, no more.' Anthony was, they had agreed, to leave at the end of the next week. Every hour was precious.

'I'll be back by mid-day, my darling.' She whispered, 'I want to commit you to God's keeping in the place where I found you after so long.'

Anthony held her tight. He muttered,

'Frido?'

'We must think of him as dead.' She spoke flatly, releasing herself and turning her head away. 'I've no word yet from Kaspar. We must think of Frido as dead.'

The affairs of Party and State were at a critical stage in the Christmastide of 1944. Despite the angry pain that stabbed periodically at his heart, despite the consequential impatience to pursue the enemies of the Reich in Lower Saxony, it was not until 29th January, 1945 that Egon Schwede assumed his new responsibilities. These included a far-reaching mission to snuff out treachery and defeatism in an area which included his old home. He had been promoted. His rank was high in the home-based SS. He lost no time in enquiring about the situation in Kreis Kranenberg, which now incorporated Langenbach.

His heart beat a little faster when he called at the local Kranenberg Party Office, that office he had formerly occupied with such distinction, that office wherein he had once dreamed romantic, entrancing dreams, dreams cruelly shattered by that evil, unprincipled woman! He sat down heavily and stared at the man now filling what had once been his chair. The fellow was an outsider, from Hanover. He looked overweight, pudgy.

Schwede, wearing the uniform of *Obersturmbannführer SS*, expected and received deference. He fixed the present incumbent of NSDAP BURO Kranenberg with that eye which had brought sweat to the brow of many an inadequate Party official or backsliding citizen. They talked for a little, exchanging a few devoutly uttered sentiments of loyalty.

'What about the family at Langenbach? They were connected to some pretty unsound people, I remember.' Were there to be the slightest hint of a knowing look on the other's face when he spoke of Langenbach, Schwede thought, any remote indication that a sniggering tale about him, Schwede, had taken root in Kranenberg, then God help the fellow! But his stout companion looked serious and respectful.

'The old man died. His widow still lives there. Bedridden.'

'Anyone else?'

'Yes, the village school is housed in the Schloss now. An excellent woman, Maria Wendel, is in charge, a most loyal enthusiastic person, always prepared to do extra for the Party. Very hardworking. As a matter of fact, I've asked her and one or two others to join us at a small reception for you this evening, *Herr Obersturmbannführer*, I hope you don't mind. We wanted to celebrate your return to these parts with a small gathering, there are plenty who'd be most disappointed if they missed the chance to shake your hand again.'

Schwede acknowledged it. He had been touched at the invitation. And that evening toasts were drunk to Führer, Reich, Party, and, of course, to Victory: while the Red Army was already battering its way into East Prussia itself, while in the west the British and Americans were finally destroying the remnants of the German Ardennes offensive, and while, overhead, Allied bombers paid their terrible nightly visits to the towns and cities of western and central Germany.

Talk at the Party reception at Kranenberg for *Obersturmbannführer* Schwede, however, focused not on these calamities but on the weakness and folly of many of the German people themselves. Tales were exchanged in hushed tones of lack of enthusiasm, of obstruction of Party work: above all, of defeatism. Schwede found himself talking to a plain young woman with wire-framed spectacles, straight, dark hair and a narrow, uncompromising mouth. It was Fraülein Maria Wendel, the schoolmistress, the tenant of Schloss Langenbach.

Schwede knew in his guts how such a woman must hate Anna Langenbach, Anna the beautiful, the silk-skinned, the aloof, Anna the enchantress, the deceiver, Anna the viciously immoral!

'Well,' he said affably, 'how are things at Schloss Langenbach? You can talk frankly to me, I've known the family a long time. I don't expect it's always easy for you, holding your responsible position, in that atmosphere!'

Maria Wendel smiled at him. 'God, she's hideous!' he thought.

'Not always easy, Herr Schwede, you have expressed it perfectly. Of course, I won't say a word against young Frau Langenbach, she took the school in straight away when we were bombed, she's worked hard for the children in many ways. But there's a sense – I don't know how to put it –'

'A lack of inner sympathy?'

'Exactly! And Frau Anna Langenbach is very, shall we say, independent? Of course the old lady is – well, very old. But I don't personally like to see a woman assume so much of a man's role. I know Frau Anna has the responsibility – but her attitude, her way of life –'

'Way of life?'

'Yes, of course it means nothing, she simply isn't concerned. For instance, there's some Colonel, she says it's a cousin of hers, who's coming to stay with her next week. I don't say it's not correct, I believe he's not young, but a young widow in her situation, you understand me – you see the children take everything in, ask questions.'

Schwede looked at her attentively, encouragingly, and said nothing.

'Then yesterday, again it's nothing, the school is shut on Sunday, we never go there, it was Sunday. The place is locked up, only I and Frau Anna have keys. Well, yesterday, it's never happened before, I had to go to the Schloss. I wanted to change some of the children's lesson books before the week started and I only found out on Saturday that it hadn't been done. So I walked up to the Schloss.'

'You walked up to the Schloss,' said Schwede. 'So?' He held out his glass for an old waiter to refill.

'I knew Frau Anna wouldn't mind, as a matter of fact she was away, I saw the gardener and he told me she'd got the pony and trap and gone to church. I let myself in and went upstairs – the school rooms are on the first floor, you see – and coming round the corner of a passage I nearly bumped into a strange young man, believe it or not! Yet the house doors were locked. It frightened me. It might have been a criminal! But just before I came up to him – it was dark in the passage – he said "Anna!" So I supposed it was a friend. I said, "Excuse me" and he muttered something and walked on. Well, it's her business of course, not mine, but –'

'Did you speak of this encounter to Frau Langenbach?' enquired Schwede sternly.

'Yes, only this morning I mentioned it to her. I said I'd met a stranger in the Schloss and had quite a shock. She said, "Oh, that was a cousin of mine, visiting for the day. He left yesterday evening." And why not? It's just one never knows, with her, you understand me? It's nothing to do with me, I wasn't interested.'

Schwede considered her, silently.

'I said to Hans – that's the gardener – "I see Frau Anna had a young cousin calling on her yesterday!" And he said, "I don't know what you mean. Nobody's been here!" One never knows, you see! She's mysterious! But such a talented woman.'

Fraülein Wendel gave a tinkling, disagreeable laugh. Schwede said in a low voice,

'You are right to be vigilant,' and moved away. A young cousin indeed! And then a Colonel! So she was up to her tricks again, the whore, the adultress, the traitress! Traitress to her husband, to her German blood, to her country! There must be a settlement of accounts. As to exactly when and on what terms he, Schwede, would have a hand in the matter of deciding.

Next day he called at the local Police station. He had heard at the Party office that the Police were not what they had been. There was slackness. They complained of being understaffed. Ostensibly this was a courtesy call, but Schwede was alert for signs of indifference. He would know in what quarters to speak

368

a word which would send the officer in charge on a journey he wouldn't relish. He accepted a glass of beer and said conversationally,

'Any difficulties at Schloss Langenbach?'

'No, *Herr Obersturmbannführer*, none at all. They've got the village school there, you know, and the young Frau Langenbach seems to manage well, doing enough work for three women – and three men, for that matter!'

'The family have never shown much – much warmth toward the Party, you know,' said Schwede sorrowfully. His tone was moderate, judicious.

So that was it.

'I didn't know,' said the Police Lieutenant politely. 'There's never been any suspicion of wrong-doing, no breach of regulations over farm produce and so forth. And of course young Frau Langenbach is very popular here.'

'I dare say. Nevertheless it is possible the Schloss may be ordered to be searched.'

'Searched, *Herr Obersturmbannführer*? Why?'

'If there's an order it's to be searched, and police support is needed, that's enough for you.'

'Of course.'

'And not a word of this. I'm only warning you of a possibility.'

He got up to leave. He doubted if an ordinary search was the answer here, and anyway they'd got enough on Anna Langenbach for his purpose. Meanwhile, if any whisper reached her at the Schloss and she started to make some sort of nervous move – he couldn't imagine what – he'd have killed two birds with one stone. He'd have made that wretched bunch at Langenbach show their hands, and he'd have identified an indiscreet or disloyal Police officer. He was still undecided how to attack Anna most painfully. Through the child, probably.

The Police Lieutenant escorted him through the main office to the street door. Schwede's eye was caught by a list of unfamiliar names pinned to one of the walls amid a crowd of other notices. Against each name was a photograph.

'What's that? Usual wanted list?'

'No, it's the list of escaped prisoners of war – the ones

who've got out of camps in the last six months. The Armed Forces send the names to all Police Districts.'

'With photographs?'

'In most cases. We've never picked any up, although Oflag VI is only ten miles southwest of here, and a big Stalag's just east of Hanover. One must be vigilant.'

'What are the orders if one is caught?' asked Schwede. He was not particularly interested. His mind was still at Schloss Langenbach.

'Orders would be given for their collection by Military District Headquarters if it's a soldier, Luftwaffe command if an airman, and so forth. Of course, each of our Armed Forces looks after its own prisoners. Simultaneously, we'd notify all police stations so that the names could be removed from the lists. We've had no removals for a long time, unfortunately.'

'I take it Gau Headquarters would be informed at the same time?'

'Certainly, *Herr Obersturmbannführer.*'

'Well,' said Schwede, 'one must be vigilant. As you say.' He nodded without friendliness and moved to his car.

They had talked hurriedly, feverishly, on the Sunday evening.

'I will tell her you were a visiting cousin, she knows I have many relations. But the woman hates me. She knows you were in a locked house. She'll let her suspicions run loose.'

'Darling, I can never forgive myself –'

'It can't be helped. It happened. But she'll talk. My love, you must go tonight.' Kaspar was due to arrive on 5th February and Anthony's departure had been fixed for 3rd February. They had postponed the decision, the break. Love had struggled with prudence.

'You must go tonight!'

That Sunday night, 28th January, there was no moon. Anna let Anthony out of the back door of the Schloss. They held each other a last time in the darkness.

'I'll come back. I'll come back for you one day soon. I promise.'

'God keep you. I love you.'

Then, as they had agreed, Anthony walked not towards

Kranenberg but southward. He had his 'tally', his prisoner of war identification tag; and he had Jan Vogt's papers. Jan Vogt was still making for the Ruhr. Anthony's plan, endorsed by Anna, was much as before – to take slow, stopping trains westward. He had in his rucksack a makeshift sleeping bag, contrived by Anna with great ingenuity. He had talked to her at such length about conditions in Germany, he had become in a curious way so much a hidden part of the life of Schloss Langenbach, that he felt little anxiety about evading notice in the community. Knowledge in Oflag XXXIII had been good: improved by tutoring at Anna's hands, Anthony's sense of how to behave and what to expect was, he was sure, now excellent.

He felt greater anxiety about resisting cold. He knew that he was still weak, and soft from the enforced conditions of a fugitive's life. Escape in January was a different matter from the adventure he had shared with Robert in the autumn.

Anna knew the country perfectly, of course. She had investigated, and given him instructions how to find several barns as refuges which would see him through the first two days. The plan at first was to walk, by day, down tracks exactly described to him, not attempting to cover too much ground; and to sleep under cover by night. Then he should, on the fourth day, reach Wexter, a small railway station at sufficient distance from Kranenberg and Langenbach to invite no particular connection with them. From Wexter it should be possible to take a train north to Hanover, and from Hanover to board a succession of slow trains, changing as often as seemed prudent, by Osnabruck and Rheine towards northern Holland. Then real activity would start; and nothing could be planned in advance. They had decided, with little but guesswork about the war situation to guide them, that northern Holland offered the best chance.

Anthony trudged through the darkness, aiming to reach the first of Anna's sanctuaries in time to get some more rest before dawn and the day's march. She had found a good local map for him and he still had his escaper's compass from Oflag XXXIII. His thigh was sorer than he had expected once he began to walk any distance, to step or climb over obstacles, to stretch his legs. It was essential to put the first hours to good use, to put distance between himself and Langenbach.

371

Thereafter, Jan Vogt, even if detected, even if identified as Captain Anthony Marvell of the British Army, might have come from anywhere, have taken any route on the long march from Oflag XXXIII. He was setting off on Sunday night. He aimed to reach Wexter, to catch a train, on Wednesday or Thursday. It was necessary to remain alive and undetected from Sunday to Thursday, and to cover by farm roads and forest tracks a distance of just over thirty-five miles. They had agreed this ought to be within his powers. Mercifully, there was no snow on the ground. Walking should not be hard. The greatest hazard might lie in where to spend the third and fourth nights. If the weather became worse the temptation to seek refuge under cover, perhaps imprudently, would be strong. Anna had been realistic about this – 'There's no point in freezing to death to avoid capture, my darling!' But he knew that however brave her words and her spirit she longed for him to be undetected and far, far away.

Anthony found the eight or nine miles a day walking, which the plan involved, to be hard going. By evening each day he was exhausted. His body was inevitably soft. Nevertheless, he reached and identified the first two of what he thought of as 'Anna's barns'. On the third night he reckoned himself extraordinarily lucky. A woodman's hut in a forest had an unsecured door. There would be no visitors before morning, and the place was not only dry but had clearly been warmed by a forester's stove the previous day; and the warmth lingered. Anthony ate some of his provisions, tried not to think about the soreness of his thigh, and wondered when he would see Anna again. The first heart-quickening challenge of being again alone, walking, in a hostile world, had been succeeded by a greater sense of loneliness than he ever remembered. How extraordinary, how idyllic had been those weeks, cared for by Anna in a dusty attic, surrounded by improbable furniture, convalescent, confused and on the run, yet deeply, passionately in love! But as he reflected on this time he felt not only loneliness and deprivation but a certain peace. One could not be discontented if loved by such a woman.

It was almost warm in his sleeping bag in the forester's hut. The weather seemed to have become appreciably milder after the sun went down that Tuesday night. Anthony slept well.

At about four o'clock in the morning he was woken by a gentle, insistent sound.

It was snowing.

Anthony climbed out of his sleeping bag and looked outside the hut. Snow was already lying. If he moved while it was still coming down his footprints would soon be obliterated. The foresters would not be alerted to the fact of a stranger having used their hut, would not be able to follow up suspicions. Furthermore, the more snow that fell, the harder the going would become. He must move.

He shouldered his rucksack and stepped into the forest clearing. Snow was falling so thickly it got into his mouth and nostrils. It was hard to see anything, but a certain paleness of sky indicated a break in the trees and he thought he could identify from that the broad ride he hoped to follow. He had marked it before nightfall the previous evening. The difficulty was that this ride was likely to be used by foresters and their carts, and nobody could fail to be suspicious of a man lunatic enough to be walking alone in a forest in the middle of a snowstorm. Anthony walked for some time, making little distance in the deepening snow, wondering whether he might be found, a frozen corpse, when the snows melted in the spring.

After an hour the snow fall lessened and a few minutes later stopped. Anthony took advantage of the break to rest. He dumped his rucksack, sat on it under the friendly branch of a huge beech, got out his map, compass and torch, and considered his future.

The map seemed to indicate that there was a village about three miles to the south-west of where he thought he was sitting. He was fairly confident about his approximate position because although tracks were not marked on his map the forest was, and it was not large – apparently the spur of a larger *stadtforst* further south. The map might be out of date in this respect, because of cutting and planting, but Anthony could see no alternative to trusting it. He peered as closely as he could. If he walked westward he should reach a public road, a marked road running north and south, within about two miles, clear of the forest.

Anthony's plan, firmly recommended by Anna, had been to

use farm roads and forest tracks, to stay clear of even minor public roads unless in emergency. But according to the plan, too, he needed to move south some eight miles this day. He was unlikely to find another friendly hut, even were it safe to use one. The snow was lying thickly. He knew he wouldn't make it if he tried to walk down forest paths – but that he might, just, reach the public road itself provided that it existed and the map did not lie. This, Anthony thought, was an emergency! A flake fell, followed by another; it began to snow again.

Anthony picked himself up and set off along a track running roughly in the direction he wished. He could identify which was west and this track ran just north of west. The snow began falling more heavily. He must, he knew, move and keep moving. There should be about two hours to dawn.

It was at about nine o'clock the following morning, aching and stumbling, feeling little except exhaustion, that Anthony emerged from the westward rim of the forest. God knew, he thought, how he'd done it. He had fallen twenty times, slipped into the snow dead tired and only with appalling difficulty forced himself up and on again. His rucksack felt like a sack of coals, his clothing was soaked, his face was frozen, his leg hurt damnably. But he was, for better or worse, clear of the trees, standing in deep snow on a straight narrow road. The road was edged by a ditch and a line of telegraph poles. If he walked south he would ultimately, he supposed, identify for certain where he was. Then he could plan a move towards Wexter and its railway station, moving now by road. In this snow it seemed the best hope. Meanwhile he knew that he needed some sort of refuge, cover and rest. It might be for a short time only but he needed respite. He was all in, he thought, and started to walk heavily down the road to the south. The sky was very grey.

After about thirty minutes he saw the roofs of houses: steep roofs already heavily clad in snow, red brick houses with snow on every ledge and lintel. There might be, there must be a barn with an open or unlatched door. The huge barns which stood behind every substantial house in such villages would provide admirable cover – dryness, darkness, even hay on which to sleep. He dragged his legs towards the edge of the

374

village. The word 'barn' dominated his mind: he fixed on it, muttered it like an incantation. These barns were witnesses to an ancient system of husbandry, to communities of small farmers grouped for protection, for commerce, for society, for mutual assistance, each family going out from the village, tilling its own strip and growing, carting and storing its own produce. Anthony knew such barns. In weather like this families would be working in them, and as often as not the living rooms and a ladder to the upper floors opened off the barn itself. But Anthony would, he was sure, be lucky. He moved like a sleep-walker towards the village, now only a hundred yards away.

The first house – a house which acted, it seemed, like some sort of guardhouse to the village, a little detached from the rest – had exactly the sort of barn he envisaged. It extended from the back of the house, immense, beckoning. In front of the house an avenue of trees marked the beginning of the village street. Anthony, indifferent to all but physical discomfort and fatigue, supposed without concern that it was a pretty place. Amid the falling snowflakes it looked welcoming and romantic. Trying to look to right and left, to move with circumspection, Anthony walked towards the rear of the house, the end of the barn. It was all he could do to get one leg past the other, careless of whether he was trampling over garden, paddock or waste land. He could not believe he was as feeble as he had turned out to be. The hours of walking in deep snow had totally exhausted him. 'I'm a mess,' he thought, 'but after an hour or two in here, I'll be all right.'

There was a ditch, unperceived, and he fell into it heavily. He picked himself up, reached the massive door of the barn and pushed. It yielded. He pushed harder, and then fell on his face, rucksack hitting the back of his skull, as the door was opened suddenly from inside.

Anthony became aware of two skirts, two pairs of thick black stockings and worn brown shoes. He looked up and saw a stout, red-faced woman of middle-age in a shapeless coat with a handkerchief over her head. She was accompanied by an equally red-faced and only slightly less stout younger woman, similarly attired. Mother and daughter. They had to be. Anthony began to struggle to his feet to make an explanation.

Next moment he gave up the attempt with an agonized yelp as a pitchfork probed and menaced his neck.

'Lie still!' said the elder woman. '*Landstreicher*! Tramp! Thief!' She held the pitchfork like a reversed spear.

'I'm not a thief,' said Anthony, from the prone position, 'I was looking for shelter from the snow.'

'Well, who are you?'

Anthony indicated that he would like to rise but received a sharp reminder from the pitchfork and a forcefully enunciated '*Nein!*' from his hostess.

'I am a Dutch Engineer. I am travelling to the railway station at Wexter to catch a train, I'm on my way to the Ruhr, to Dortmund, to take up a new job in an engineering works there. I was walking to Wexter when the snow started. My name is Jan Vogt, a volunteer worker.'

'Heidi,' said the woman in a voice which sounded as if it was seldom disobeyed, 'go to the Police station and ask Herr Steipel to come here.'

'At once,' said the younger woman, disappearing into the interior. Anthony knew that he could not attempt flight. She would raise the hue and cry, in between spearing him to death with a pitchfork. In his feeble condition he had no hope of getting clear. Besides, how could escape help? He needed, at the moment, shelter to survive. The only hope was that Jan Vogt's papers would convince Herr Steipel.

Steipel took ten minutes to arrive. Anthony was aware of a long green coat, black boots and a rasping voice. He was however, permitted to stand, and then took in a Police shako, a dark green collar, a black leather belt and revolver holster. Out of all this Steipel looked at him without enthusiasm and silently took Jan Vogt's papers in his outstretched hand.

'Where have you come from?'

Anthony named a small place which he knew from the map lay some way to the east, but could credibly be served as a railway station by Wexter.

'From Klosterwebel. I'm trying to get to Wexter.'

'What were you doing in Klosterwebel?'

Anthony explained that he had been told to make his way to Dortmund from Silesia. Despairing, after some attempts, of moving by the main line railways from central Germany because of the weight of air attack on Leipzig and Berlin and the disruption of all services he had decided to try to move across country.

'I was told there would be a better chance if I could get to Kassel or Hanover, more chance of getting on to the Ruhr. I have to get there, for my job, *Herr Polizeileutnant.*' Anthony knew that he was flattering Steipel's rank.

'So why are you here, trying to get to Wexter?' asked Steipel incredulously. 'From Wexter trains go north or south. Where were you last in a train?'

'At Dessau. I couldn't get further west.'

'And you walked from Dessau to Klosterwebel? In January, Vogt? It must be nearly a hundred miles!'

'I got lifts on several farm carts, I've only taken five days and the weather's not been bad. But yesterday, I tried to take a short cut and got lost. Someone told me there's a railway station at Wexter, and I thought I'd try my luck by rail again. Then it started to snow.'

Steipel looked at him.

'I must make a report. At the Police station. Move!' He patted his holster and Anthony moved.

The Police station at Festerode was warm, and for that Anthony was grateful. His clothes were still sodden, there was no feeling in his facial muscles and he could only with difficulty move his fingers, but he was beginning to feel warmth. Steipel wrote at a desk while Anthony stood against a wall. After what seemed a long time Steipel looked up and said,

'It's my duty to search you.' At the same time he emptied Anthony's rucksack on to a table. Anthony watched him.

'To search you,' Steipel snapped again. 'Take off all your clothes. At once.'

Steipel was no genius but he had always been reported on as conscientious and thorough. He found Anthony's tally within three minutes. What was more creditable, he recognized it for what it was, although this was, in fact, his first escaped prisoner of war. He felt a glowing sense of personal achievement. A colleague stood guard over Anthony, naked, numbed and despairing. Steipel moved to the telephone.

'Nothing of particular interest, *Herr Obersturmbannführer.*'
Schwede spent most days travelling, rather than sitting at Gau
Headquarters. Petrol was damnably short but there was still
an adequate ration for really important Party work. Schwede
had always been active and inquisitive, a man who believed in
seeing things for himself. His visits, he grimly noted, were
already causing a stir. It was sadly true that even in the Party
idleness could take root unless a man of principle and energy
appeared, with a big boot and the strength to use it on a
subordinate's backside. Figuratively speaking, grinned
Schwede to himself: or generally so. He returned to the central
Gau office late on Wednesday, 31st January and looked in at
the Duty official's room.

'Nothing of interest, eh?'

'Local Police report. An escaped prisoner of war was recaptured at Festerode.'

'Festerode?'

'It's a small place. The local Police officer searched a fellow
pretending to be a volunteer worker, a Dutch engineer, and
found he was an escaped British officer! We've taken his name
off the list –' He nodded to a list on the wall, where a green
cross had just been pencilled across a name and photograph.
'He's been running since November!'

'Captain Anthony Marvell,' Schwede read aloud. Suddenly
his heart missed a beat. A phrase from a letter, an odious letter:
'Son of your own brother, Anthony Marvell.' It might be a common name in England, of course, but by God! He swung round.

'Where's this Englishman now?'

'He's in the Police Headquarters at Wexter, *Herr Obersturmbannführer.* He was taken there to await Army collection.
He'll go to whatever Oflag Military District Headquarters
order. Then –'

'Telephone Wexter now,' said Schwede quietly. 'This man
may be more interesting than an ordinary prisoner of war. Tell
them to hold him until I come. I'll be there in half an hour. I
want Pieck and Brockmann to come with me.' Pieck and
Brockmann were experienced Gestapo men. They were not
under Schwede's orders but already few people, from the
Gauleiter himself downwards, were disposed to argue with
him.

378

'Jawohl, Herr Obersturmbannführer.'
Schwede moved towards the door.

'One thing. Tell them to take a photograph of Marvell. At once. Develop it instantly.' He gave certain instructions.

The place of the wound on Anthony's thigh sent shock waves of pain through his body whenever it was touched. It had not taken Schwede long to discover this fact, which might easily save time and trouble. He made a sign to Pieck who started quietly beating Anthony again at exactly that point. Pieck used a length of rubber hose. He did not exert much strength. There was no need. Pieck was an artist in measuring the degree of force appropriate to the occasion. It wasn't in this case even necessary to lower the fellow's trousers he was so sensitive! Pieck swung the rubber hose accurately, timing exactly the interval between blows. Four seconds.

Anthony screamed once, then closed his teeth in a mighty effort of will. He saw bright lights, a mixture of yellow and white, before his eyes. Schwede watched with satisfaction.

'You realize you may have to face very serious charges – espionage and sabotage charges, completely outside conduct permitted to a prisoner of war? Even an escaped prisoner of war?'

Schwede, in fact, knew nothing which could support such charges. He wanted, however, to see Anthony squirm with fear. Best throw everything at him!

'You not only escaped – it is possible that you killed a German civilian and stole his clothing. Such offences are not to be tried by the Army. They are nothing to do with the Army.' All this, too, was invention. Schwede came to the heart of the matter.

'We know you were helped. Were hidden!'

In a sobbing voice he hardly knew came from his own lips Anthony heard himself say, it seemed for the hundredth time,

'I am a British officer. I have done only what is the duty of a soldier in any army, in any war. I escaped.' He was sitting on a small, hard chair, legs tied by the ankle, arms secured by the wrist behind the chair. The chair was set on the floor

379

of a large cell in Wexter Police station. Schwede told him, in a reasonable-sounding voice, that it was not the duty of German citizens to help such an escaper, and that to do so was a capital offence. He nodded to Pieck. Anthony could not hold back the screech that escaped as Pieck's rubber hose was plied again. Then he retched horribly. More rubber hose.

They had arranged for a telephone extension to be fitted up in the cell and now it rang. Schwede, sitting at a desk which had been placed in a corner, lifted the receiver and gestured to Pieck to desist. Pieck yawned. It had been a long day. Now it was turning into a long night,

As from a great distance Anthony heard Schwede's words –

'Yes, I have seen it, it is a good photograph. She is positive? Good.' Schwede replaced the instrument and looked grimly at Anthony.

'A loyal woman at Kranenberg, a Fraülein Wendel, has been interviewed at the local police station, Marvell. She has been shown your photograph, taken, developed and printed here. It was of superior quality to the photograph circulated by the army authorities after your escape.'

Schwede nodded his head several times. Nobody could have guessed the jealous images raised before his eyes by confirmation that this contemptible creature, this Anthony Marvell, was, indeed, the 'cousin' seen in the dark corridors of Schloss Langenbach by the searching eyes of Maria Wendel. This dark-haired, miserable youth, now yelling under Pieck's accurate strokes, had been hidden by that shameless woman, Anna Langenbach, hidden from the protectors of the Reich, hidden for weeks – and, without doubt, had been enjoying her body the whole time! Schwede choked.

'Fraülein Wendel has confirmed that she saw you in Schloss Langenbach a week ago. You have been hiding there, Marvell. You had better tell us all about it. Then we can discuss other things.'

Pieck watched Anthony's face carefully. This sort of business needed fine timing. Overdo it and you got nothing.

Anthony muttered, 'I've nothing to say.'

Pieck sighed. Schwede could contain himself no longer. He pushed his chair back from the desk violently, walked round to the chair and smashed his fist into Anthony's face three times. 'You swine!'

Anthony moaned. Blood ran down his left cheek from a cut eye and forehead. His head rolled sideways.

'You swine!'

'*Herr Obersturmbannführer,*' said Pieck reprovingly, 'that's not very scientific, if I may say so. That won't help.'

Anthony showed no signs of life, and Pieck said sadly, 'Now we'll have to bring him round.' He reached for a can of water.

At that moment the door opened and the local police officer came quickly in and reported to Schwede, talking fast –

'. . . asking for you, *Herr Obersturmbannführer.*'

Behind him Schwede could see, without pleasure, a figure in the uniform of a lieutenant-colonel of the Wehrmacht. A lieutenant-colonel who now pushed into the cell, looked sternly at Schwede and spoke. He spoke in a deep, resonant voice that seemed to come from far down in his throat. He looked to be about fifty. One empty sleeve was pinned across his tunic. The ribbon of the Iron Cross was at his button hole. He wore thick pebble glasses.

'My name is Bressler. I have responsibility in this area for all prisoners of war who fall to the jurisdiction of the Army. I am told you have a British officer here, Captain Marvell by name. Is this him?'

Schwede eyed Bressler with loathing. He said, 'Marvell is suspected of serious offences which may need to be subject to civil process. He was also assisted in his escape by certain Germans whose activities are to be investigated by State Security. Marvell's evidence will be relevant to these investigations.'

'And you were in the process of obtaining this evidence, I suppose.'

'I was, *Herr Oberstleutnant,*' said Schwede grimly. 'I was indeed.'

'Then you will, if you wish, apply to the Military authorities for permission to interview Marvell. He will now be taken to Oflag VI where he will be subject to military trial and punishment for escape: and for any misdemeanors and breaches of discipline connected with his escape.'

'*Will now be taken?*' snarled Schwede. 'I've not finished with him yet!'

Bressler had clearly anticipated this. He turned and snapped a command. Two soldiers entered the room, accompanied by two orderlies and a stretcher. Bressler had, it was plain, been promptly informed, and Anthony's condition exaggerated rather than understated. The soldiers stood rigidly, awaiting orders. They were armed. The local police lieutenant carefully avoided Schwede's eye.

'This is irregular,' said Schwede thickly. 'It will be reported.'

'I am acting in accordance with Army orders and recognized legitimate procedure,' said Bressler shortly. He did not look at Schwede again, and made a peremptory gesture. Anthony, barely conscious, was carried from the room. A military ambulance was waiting in the dark street where snow was falling again.

On 1st February, a message again came for Marcia during the morning.

'Marvell to the Superintendent's office, at once!'

It was Müller again. He looked more hostile and more animated. Marcia felt, as she had before, a strong sense of nausea.

'Fraülein Marvell, you'd best tell me the truth this time, all of it, and quickly. When I was here last week, you said you knew nothing of your brother's connection with Frau Anna Langenbach.'

'Yes.'

'That was a lie. You had been told of it in a letter, from Frido von Arzfeld, even if you hadn't known it before.'

'A private letter – a confidence – I didn't know whether to believe – perhaps a delusion – I couldn't –'

'Stop this fooling or you'll be sorry. My business is state security, and we're fighting a war. I want facts. You were told the Langenbach woman had a child by your brother. Did you know that your brother is a prisoner of war in Germany?'

'*In Germany?*' cried Marcia. She's genuine, I'd say, thought Müller, I'd back that squeak for sincerity.

'In Germany, where else? Furthermore, he at one time escaped from a prisoner of war camp. Now he may be faced with serious charges, as well as escaping.'

382

Marcia was silent. She was dumbfounded. Müller looked at her, a hard look.

'We caught him again, of course. Yesterday. And we reckon the Langenbach woman helped him – helped him, an enemy officer, hide from the Reich authorities. And you – you who are a friend of Anna Langenbach – are standing there telling me that this woman, this "respected friend", has been sheltering your precious brother and never got word to you about it? Your own brother? Is that what you're telling me, eh?' From habit, Müller's voice had risen to a shout and he had moved round the table and was standing very close to Marcia. Something in the way he was shouting, in his overt bullying, strengthened Marcia. She felt a glorious surge of anger and it exorcized fear for a moment.

'No, Herr Müller,' she said, 'that is not what I'm telling you. It is what you are telling me. I have said nothing, because I know nothing about it.'

Müller continued talking loudly and fast.

'You'd better tell me everything you know about Langenbach, there's an inquiry going on, it's a serious matter. It'll be best for your brother, I promise you. What's more, provided you tell me the truth there's no reason why you can't continue the good work you're doing for us.' His tone was suddenly reasonable.

'I know nothing, Herr Müller. Everything you have said has astonished me.'

'Nothing at all, is that it?' Müller looked at her lasciviously. Flushed, some brown locks escaping from her nurse's cap, eyes shining: she really was delicious. No wonder that traitor had fallen for her! Schwede was mad keen to get all the dirt he could on the Langenbach woman but he, Müller, doubted whether this little English piece could help much. She was obviously suffering from shock at hearing that her wretched brother was in custody, here in Germany! Müller wondered whether they had managed to get enough out of him – Schwede had sounded most peculiar when he'd telephoned that morning, he'd talked in a tone of excitement surely unwarranted by the tiny scale of the affair. What did one prisoner of war, one silly, disloyal woman who'd let her heart rule her head, produced a little bastard – what did it all add up to, even if she did have a cousin involved in the July business? Like a great many others, thought Müller, past caring much by now. He grunted, sat down again at Sister Brigitta's desk and opened another notebook.

'There's plenty to go on,' said Schwede. He was addressing the police officer in charge of Kranenberg. 'Plenty. I didn't need him to talk, his evidence could have added nothing to what I already knew. He was in Schloss Langenbach since November. Under your damned nose!'

The police officer in charge of Kranenberg looked respectful. There was no other way to look, and he put a lot into it.

'And now that place has got to be thoroughly searched. Turned inside out, you understand me! I intend to visit the family myself, once the search has started. And mind you question the servants, somebody must have felt suspicious, you can't keep a live man hidden for nearly two months without something showing!'

'*Herr Obersturmbannführer*, the only permanent servant is the gardener, Hans Treuerbach. Some women come and clean the schoolrooms, and a girl helps Frau Langenbach in the kitchen on a daily basis, but apart from that –'

'*Apart from that!* What the hell do you mean "Apart from that"? Take them to pieces, find out who heard what, and when! Do you want me to teach you your job? Somebody needs to.'

But only Hans, under a little pressure, conceded that he had 'spoken to Frau Anna about rats in the attic'.

'There was something up there, perhaps, but maybe it was only the wind. Frau Anna said it was the wind. I wasn't allowed to investigate.'

More pressure was applied. Hans recalled that the said rats had been heard 'about Christmas time'. The attics were turned inside out, furniture tested for finger prints, every corner was investigated. Meanwhile Anna Langenbach sat, her face impassive, her lips compressed, in a small room on the ground floor. With her was her ancient mother-in-law.

To them, after an hour, came Egon Schwede.

He addressed the old lady.

384

'Nobody regrets the necessity for this disturbance more than I, Frau Langenbach. Unfortunately we have proof that an enemy of the Reich, an escaped prisoner of war, has been sheltered for some weeks in your house. He was seen here, here in the Schloss, by Fraülein Wendel, the schoolteacher. She has recognized his photograph. He has now been recaptured.'

Anna did not look at Schwede. He noted with bitter regret that she was as lovely as ever. And here she was, facing a capital charge as she must know, and still behaving as if he was some unimportant lout who needn't even be noticed. He determined to play the same game. He would talk only to old Frau Langenbach, although he knew she was decrepit and unlikely to take in much, if anything. Usually bedridden, as he understood it, she was today sitting in an armchair with blankets wrapped round her.

Anna said quietly,

'They are saying there was some escaped prisoner of war hiding here, Mother. They are searching for evidence. They have found him somewhere else.'

'Yes,' said Schwede. 'They have found him somewhere else. And they have interrogated him. And they know that he has been living under your roof, here in the upper rooms of Schloss Langenbach.' He was sufficiently confident to be precise about the upper rooms and he thought he saw a gratifying flicker from Anna when he mentioned interrogation. 'Furthermore,' Schwede continued courteously, still addressing the old lady, 'when questioned about it, your daughter-in-law, last Monday, described a young stranger who was seen here as a cousin visiting for the day. No doubt she will explain to you the identity of this cousin visiting her for the day, who has now been identified by Fraülein Wendel, who saw him in this very house, as the escaped prisoner.'

'I don't understand,' said old Frau Langenbach weakly. 'Anna, what's this about a cousin?'

'There is confusion, Mother. You remember I told you my cousin Kaspar von Arzfeld is coming to stay here for a few days. There must have been a misunderstanding and –'

But Anna knew she had erred. The news that Wendel had identified Anthony, although she supposed she should have

385

anticipated it, had caught her unprepared. The introduction of Kaspar von Arzfeld's name, the suggestion that his imminent arrival might have been confused in the telling with Wendel's encounter with Anthony – this might be sufficient to blur the matter for an already muddled Frau Langenbach. It could not possibly convince anybody else. But what story could have done so?

Schwede was still speaking to Frau Langenbach, with every appearance of deference.

'I fear there was no confusion. Fraülein Wendel will testify as to what Frau Langenbach said to her, just as she will identify the young man seen in this house as the escaped prisoner now in our hands. The visit arranged for Colonel von Arzfeld will not now take place and has nothing to do with the matter.

'I must also tell you, with deep regret, *gnädige Frau Langenbach*, that this same escaped prisoner of war, this English officer, was, as it happens, well known to your daughter-in-law previously. We know that in the past there have been criminal relations between them. This distinguished family has been cruelly deceived.'

He saw with grim pleasure that he had struck home. Anna must have known that the game was up in respect of the concealment of the enemy, Marvell. She must know that was a hanging matter, with no possible mercy to be expected. She had not flinched so far, the bitch. But she could not have known – indeed, only those who had had the luck to read young von Arzfeld's letter to the sister could have known – that her own wretched misdoings, her immorality, her lies were now also on the table. It wasn't necessary, of course, but it was, Schwede reflected with satisfaction, justice that her sins had all been brought home. He had watched her face as he spoke. He knew that he had won. He rose and spoke formally and politely.

'Arrangements will be made by the Kreis authorities for your own well-being, Frau Langenbach. Frau Anna Langenbach will be accompanying a police officer from this place. She will not be returning.'

The old lady stared at him. She had taken in more than he – or Anna – suspected. She said only one word, softly,

'Franzi?'

'The boy will be taken care of,' Schwede said smoothly. 'Arrangements have been made.'

Many hundred miles to the east another interview was that day being conducted, another duel fought, another defiance organized against powerful odds.

'Why do you not join your friends in the fight against Fascism? They are being very cooperative, very wise. They understand what is truly good for your country.'

'They must do what they think right, Colonel. So must I.'

The Russian Colonel's tone was wheedling, his voice soft. He smiled often and looked at his stubby fingers. He had the air of a man with all the time in the world. He spoke excellent German.

'Rudberg, you are, perhaps, being arrogant in believing you are an infallible judge of what is right – when so many think differently. Perhaps they have more understanding of the facts, the situation. May this not be so?'

The strongly constructed wooden hut in which the interview was taking place was warm – indeed, the contrast in temperature with the bitter cold outside was grotesque. They were, Toni Rudberg knew, about two hundred miles south-east of Moscow. To be warm was extraordinary, and for this reason he was not unhappy that the session should continue for some time. He knew the arguments which would be deployed, the alternating cajolery and menace. He gave the impression of considering the Colonel's last words. He knew this particular Colonel. There had been many such occasions. Some of his colleagues were so obviously longing to shoot you that it seemed control might snap if another minute elapsed. One had to be careful with those. This one, clearly, was immensely bored. He must regard interviews of this kind as providing not unwelcome relief to the monotony of winter. Most of them, quite simply, drank.

'I am sorry if I appear arrogant, Colonel. I do not know how a man can act rightly except by trying to obey his own conscience.'

'What you call conscience,' said the Colonel agreeably, 'is simply a matter of how your reactions have been conditioned

387

by your upbringing, your training. It is, therefore, capable of itself being developed. Changed. To suppose that conscience is anything else is a bourgeois illusion.'

Toni said nothing but registered interest. He knew that a significant number of German officer prisoners had decided that their lives would be a good deal more comfortable – and probably longer – if their consciences were developed in the way recommended. There were some famous names among them, too, and by all accounts they were leading lives of ease. No doubt a good many – probably most – were simply determined to survive and, like Toni, were clear that Hitler was not going to last long. Others might have persuaded themselves that the future really did belong to Communism – and that anyway, as Bismarck had said, 'Germany should have no enemies to the east.' They had come, these gentlemen of the 'Free German Officers League', of the 'National Committee', and tried to make others see matters as they did. Toni, sceptical about most things, was unsure exactly why he found the idea of joining them so repellent. It certainly wasn't because of his oath to the Führer. The Colonel pursued the subject.

'Your comrades have spoken to you?'

'Some of them have done so, Colonel, as you know.' Toni suddenly felt faint. Warmth had at first seemed delightful. Now it seemed to have produced a reaction, a sort of shock. He knew that hunger, cold and absence of communication had produced a weakened body and jangling nerves. Still, he had survived so far. Two years of captivity. Two years alone.

'Your comrades made no impression on you?'

It had been incredible to hear their voices, to speak to other human beings again. It had been distasteful to hear what they had to say.

'I was interested, of course.'

The Colonel changed his tack. His voice became harsher.

'The Soviet forces are about to conquer Fascism. This is February, 1945. The Red Army has already entered Germany. It can only now be a question of a few months before your country will be liberated.'

Toni looked attentive. He had no idea of whether there was a shred of truth in any of this. He wished he was not so close to retching.

'When that liberation takes place – and it has started – the Soviet Union will recognize its friends among the Germans. There will be some who will be rewarded for their friendship, who will enjoy positions of responsibility. Others –' The Colonel laughed, as if in high amusement. He looked at Toni with quizzical enjoyment. 'Don't you think that's something to reflect upon? You were a Major, after all. You know about responsibility.'

'Perhaps so,' agreed Toni. The Colonel suddenly seemed indistinct and remote. Toni felt sweat on his face, and put everything he could still command into remaining upright.

'Pray God,' he was conscious of thinking, 'that he doesn't light a cigarette.'

The Colonel lit a cigarette, reeking, pungent. He opened a new line of persuasion. He seemed to consider, as if puzzled.

'Do you like solitary confinement, Rudberg? You know it's been ordered for you so-called General Staff Officers. And there are no instructions to alter this – whatever the world situation. It will simply continue. Would you not prefer different treatment?' Toni tried to make out the outlines of the Colonel's face. It was becoming blurred again.

'There are courses of instruction,' said the Colonel. 'There is an anti-Fascist school. You could study. You would find it very interesting.'

Toni collapsed at that moment. He fell heavily to the floor of the wooden hut. A handful of snow was slapped in his face to revive him and he soon found himself again plodding feebly under escort towards the compound holding his own cell, through deep snow with aching limbs unaccustomed to movement, face exposed to the icy malice of the east wind.

Chapter 24

———————◆———————

'I'M DELIGHTED – what wonderful news, Mrs Marvell.'

It was a poor telephone line and necessary to shout most sentences twice. Robert Anderson was, indeed, delighted. The Marvells had received a letter from Anthony. It was the last day of February. The letter had arrived with commendable speed, dated 19th of the month.

'Of course he can't say much but at least it means that he's alive, he's in a camp somewhere. As you know, dear Robert, when you got back and came here and told us all about it at the beginning of January we couldn't help fearing that something ghastly had happened to him after you parted.'

'I know. And you know how much I hated leaving him.'

'Thank Heavens you *did* leave him! Still, it's been a bad two months! I expect the dear boy gave himself up and was put in punishment cells, as you told us would happen. And couldn't write! Brutes, aren't they! But still, he's alive, and it won't be long now, we're sure of it. We'll tell you if we hear again.'

'Please do. I'm going back to the other side again quite soon, you know.'

'My dear, *not* going back already!'

'I want to. Apparently they need people with legal training to join the War Crimes Commission, which will be functioning in the occupied territory once we move into Germany.'

'It doesn't sound a pleasant job, Robert.'

'Pleasant – no, certainly not. But I think it may be worth doing. I've had five weeks' leave, you know, and I'm disgustingly fit again.' He arranged to spend a night at Bargate the following weekend.

That Saturday, after dinner in their small sitting room upstairs (Bargate had been abandoned by Americans but was still for the most part under dust sheets) John Marvell said,

'Well, Robert, so you're going to be one of our avenging angels!'

Robert did not particularly relish the description.

'I hope it's going to be better than vengeance. Crimes have been committed – horrible crimes. I don't think that's in dispute.'

'Probably not,' said John, 'but I doubt if the victors are the best people to try the perpetrators. When one thinks about the Russian front – about what the Soviets have done to people in their power – one's gorge rises at the idea of them sitting in judgement on anyone. For them, if not for us, it will be a matter of simple revenge.'

Robert thought it best to change the subject. His somewhat Puritan temperament was disturbed by the feeling that moral fervour might seem close to humbug in John Marvell's eyes. He said, with some diffidence,

'I suppose you've heard nothing of your daughter? Of Marcia? I know what a worry it's been, the whole thing.' Robert had met Marcia often in the old days, Oxford days, London days. He found her fascinating. How long ago it seemed!

Hilda stitched away at her needlework. John said, 'Yes, a worry all the time, naturally. But she'll survive. I've always had complete faith that she'll survive. Marcia will have done right in her own eyes, however hard it has been, and will be, to understand it.'

Hilda said, 'And now Anthony's survived, too. We're very lucky, in a way.'

Oflag VI prisoners' trek to the east began on the last day of February, 1945, the day Anthony's letter reached Bargate. There was no formal warning beyond the announcement that all prisoners would parade next day, with their authorized belongings for 'a routine move'. Some of this move would be performed on foot, most by train. Enquiries of the camp guards – with whom, as in Oflag XXXIII, relationships had been established varying from tolerant detestation to corrupt geniality – produced no information. They had, it was clear, none to give, were ignorant and fearful of their own future. It seemed

391

that most if not all of the staff was to accompany the prisoners. It also seemed that, at any rate as an Officers' Prison Camp, Oflag VI was closing down and reopening, name, staff and all, in a new place. This was a migration.

'Our chaps will be across the Rhine in a few weeks and here soon after,' said one of Anthony's messmates confidently. As in all camps there were plenty of illicit wireless sets and news on the progress of the war was as good as Allied communiqués permitted. The prisoners were comfortably aware that they were significantly better informed than their captors. They did not, however, know what their captors planned for them. 'Are we going east, Fritz?' Every guard was bombarded with the same question that day. The answer, invariably was a sour shrug of the shoulders. Yet where else could they go? The Russian offensive seemed to have come to a halt in East Prussia, in Silesia, on the Austrian border. Presumably the next heave would take it to Berlin, to the Elbe, to the heart of Europe. Meanwhile, within the shrinking confines of the Reich, there was more room to the east than in the west. But not much.

'They'll want to keep us as bargaining counters as long as possible,' said Matheson, a lugubrious Scot from Dornoch who played a useful part in camp life, being so pessimistic in all circumstances that his fellow prisoners found it essential to contradict him by voicing exaggerated hopes and thus actually sometimes felt them.

'They'll not want us to be liberated if they can hang on to us,' Matheson said sadly. 'We're cards in their hand. We'll be going east.'

'How strong a card in Hitler's hand do you reckon you are, Jock? Mightn't he have other preoccupations, with half Germany lost and the rest going shortly?' But they knew he must be right. They could not be sent west, with the Allies now closing up to the Rhine: while in the south it sounded as if the Americans had already punched a hole into the Palatinate, and presumably would soon be advancing on Bavaria. To the east the move must surely be: although by now it could not possibly be for far.

And the journey, in bitter March weather, turned out to be to a camp in Saxony, a pleasant enough place when the weather improved, secluded in woods on the borders of Silesia. The prisoners marched for fourteen painful miles and were then packed into an inadequate number of bitterly cold railway carriages for a journey which took fourteen hours to cover, Anthony reckoned, only some two hundred miles. The new camp was now to be given the same title as the old, 'Oflag VI', although it already existed as a temporary officers' camp and was overcrowded, swelled by intakes from other camps, evacuated like themselves before the advancing tide of Germany's foes. Colonel Bressler, moving with them, was Commandant.

Food, like space, was desperately short – a consequence, all recognized, of the breakdown of the transportation services of the Reich. Red Cross parcels, those blessed alleviators of hunger, had now, it seemed, ceased to arrive. The end, they all knew, could not be far away but they did not know in what shape they would be when it came. The camp took familiar form – the same regular rows of wooden huts, the same German guard compound, the same inner and outer perimeter wires, the same watch towers. But here was no talk of escape – that was all done with. Nerves were increasingly frayed as hunger bit, as men became more querulous, as all waited for others to exert themselves and finish the war.

When first brought back to Oflag VI Anthony had been sentenced to six weeks in the punishment cells. His punishment was at first mitigated by admission to the camp hospital, to recover from the attentions of Pieck and Schwede, and from a reopened thigh wound. Then the sentence was held in suspension for the move to Saxony. On arrival there he was interviewed by Bressler and told his sentence would again be suspended.

'Any indiscipline, any reports of improper behaviour, Captain Marvell, and you will immediately be confined – to carry out the full period of your punishment, added to any further sentence which it might be my duty to impose.'

Bressler had looked at Anthony over the top of his spectacles. His voice, as ever, seemed to boom from somewhere half-way down his chest. Behind the pebble glasses Anthony fancied he saw a glint of amusement. Who would be imprisoning whom at the end of Anthony's nominal sentence? Anthony doubted whether Bressler had the slightest illusions. He looked at the Commandant with respect and liking. The man had saved him.

The weeks dragged on, weeks of boredom mingled with rumour, but marked for all by hunger, with the feebleness and irritation it engendered. Small jealousies and resentments had always loomed large in prison. Now they threatened to become insupportable.

Meanwhile more evident daily was the terror of the German guards as news – filtered news, censored, born of rumour, but vivid and gathered with fearful eagerness – reached them of a renewed Soviet offensive.

'These lads are scared stiff of the Russkies,' said Matheson with relish. 'They know what's coming to them!'

Fritz – at least one of the guards was called or nicknamed Fritz in every camp – was a local man, a Saxon. Fritz was also loquacious and well-informed – a Hermann, thought Anthony, with something like nostalgia for Oflag XXXIII and its well-ordered, decently nourished existence. Fritz took grisly pleasure in relating to the prisoners the stories rife in Saxony as the rumours from the Front grew ever worse and the population of the neighbouring villages shivered and waited. They waited with mounting panic for the Red Army to break through the fragile screen of the Wehrmacht: a screen assisted, at its last gasp, by *Volksgrenadier* formations, groups of the elderly and the very young, enrolled under threat of instant execution, pitifully equipped with an armband and a rifle, shown on maps at the Führer's Headquarters as battalions and divisions. All knew that a mass flight westward was the only way to avoid a frightful fate: but any movement of the population had been expressly forbidden, and Party officials had been armed with draconian powers to prevent it. In the neighbourhood of Oflag VI, Fritz told them, stories were rife of what would happen when the Red Army arrived. Despite the regulations some refugees had slipped westward and the tales they told made folk shudder.

'Ten, twenty, thirty fellows will rape a woman. Then they'll shoot her if she's no good for any more. Or, if it's a Panzer unit, they often loop a rope round her, attach it to a tank and drive along with her bumping behind until she's finished. It seems they like that, it amuses them.'

'What about the men, Fritz?'

Fritz, with a certain show of delicacy, said that men – young men, boys – were also sexually assaulted and murdered if the inclination took their enemies which it often did.

'And anyone else is likely to be shot. Straight away. And of course it's not only the girls that are treated like that. It's old women, children, the lot.'

'Well, Fritz,' someone remarked, 'look what you did to them!'

But, in fact, the prisoners in Oflag VI were shaken by what they heard. Fritz would grunt and shrug his shoulders. 'Who had done what, and when?' he said to himself, uneasy and uncertain. Anthony listened to Fritz's tales, thought about the fate of Europe and the end of the war as sharply as any of them. Every reflection, general or personal, now sickened him.

He tried to accustom his mind to the worst on the subject of Anna. He told himself every day that she must have been executed – executed because of his own errors. Those brutes would have grabbed her immediately they knew he had been at Schloss Langenbach. It was his foolishness that had betrayed her. He felt little elation at the prospect of liberation, and small concern at the imminence, it seemed, of Allied victory. *They* would not have been scrupulous about getting proof of Anna's involvement. *They* would not have been slow in inflicting the penalty. No Allied advance would be likely to help Anna. Fritz told them that the Anglo-American air raids were worse than ever, turning whole cities into deserts. No air raid was likely to liberate Anna. It might be merciful if she died in one, but it was unlikely. From every direction death and horror threatened each of the people he loved, or had already overtaken them.

'Marvell's pretty odd, these days, he's got worse,' his companions would murmur to each other. Anthony had no close friends from earlier times in Oflag VI. He made no attempt to discover congenial spirits. His remoteness was resented here and there. 'Toffee-nosed bugger' one or two muttered. But the prisoners had other concerns. They were, on the whole, tolerant.

'Marvell had a bad time after recapture, I gather. He was wounded in an air raid when on the run, lay up for a long while, then got knocked about by Gestapo thugs. He doesn't want to talk about it.'

He didn't want to talk about it. It was not important to anybody. There were, in this camp, no plans for escape, no long-term studies, projects or entertainments for which a man might expect to be enlisted. Everybody was waiting, bored, discontented, anxious for whatever the ultimate defeat of Germany might bring. One solitary, more or less, made little difference.

The third week in April arrived. The German camp staff appeared to have fewer illusions even than the prisoners.

'We could walk out of this place at any time,' said Matheson, shaking his head. 'But I'm not sure exactly where we'd go.'

Curiously, Red Cross parcels had started again to appear and the prisoners' health and spirits quickly recovered in consequence. But deprived for many years of responsibility, the prisoners needed orders to be given and decisions to be taken by others. Deep in their hearts, while all longed for liberty, some feared it a little too. Every day, now, they could hear the roll of artillery in the east, continuous, ever louder, ever nearer.

It was on 18th April that Lise was summoned to Ward Reception to find the Ward Superintendent, Sister Brigitta, at the centre of a peculiar scene. They had for some days heard unceasing gun fire to the east and the atmosphere throughout the hospital was tense. Sister Brigitta was facing a small man in Party uniform with a wizened face and pince nez. They were looking at each other with unflinching hostility. In the corridor, audience of what appeared a confrontation, were four dirty, ragged bundles, just identifiable as human beings. Two elderly folk, almost certainly male and female, were standing, wrapped in coats and scarves, faces barely emergent. There was something in their posture that was supplicant and fearful. On the floor were two different bundles, recognizable, Lise thought, as young women. Presumably, gaining entry by subterfuge or determination, the elders had carried the younger pair into the hospital: although a civil establishment, the hospital had been ordered for several weeks to admit only military casualties. The four bundles were covered with dust.

'I suppose they've come in a farm cart,' thought Lise. She saw the eyes of one of the girls fixed on her. They looked mad.

The wizened Party official was speaking. He had a thin, precise voice.

'I am empowered to remind you that all places at this hospital are reserved for the military and that no treatment is to be given to civilians, whatever their condition. That is an order throughout this district, which has for several weeks been designated a war zone.'

Sister Brigitta said,

'We have treated very large numbers of wounded soldiers here. We have also, by our Director's order, continued to treat others who have nowhere else to go, especially –'

'Your Director's order is improper. I hereby declare it superceded.'

'– Especially where the injuries are attributable to the actions of the enemy. As in this case, I believe, Herr Schlitter.'

'The Gau authority, which I represent,' said Schlitter, 'has been charged with enforcing regulations. In this case the regulation is being disobeyed. On a routine visit to this hospital I observed these people entering. They have no claim to be treated here.'

Sister Brigitta eyed him. 'In default of an order from my own Director, Herr Schlitter, I have both a moral and a professional duty to these people and I intend to discharge it. I–'

At this point one of the elderly bundles, certainly male because standing cap in hand, coughed apologetically and spoke.

'It's our granddaughters you see, we –'

'Shut up!' said Schlitter, his thin voice rising. The old man flinched and bowed. Sister Brigitta raised her hand with immense authority.

'On the contrary, I know this man's explanation will resolve matters. Continue!'

Caught, unenviably, between two such persons, and avoiding Schlitter's eye, the old man continued,

'It's our granddaughters. We were in the farm when an Ivan

397

patrol arrived. Then a few hours later they left and some of
our boys turned up. The farm's where the fighting is now. We
stayed in the cellar, we didn't know where to go or what to
do. Last night we hitched the horse to the cart and moved
here. But when the Ivans came they caught the girls, you see.'

One of the girls started to speak. Her grandmother tried to
hush her.

'Sh, sh!'

The girl jabbered incomprehensibly, her voice rising to a
screech like a parrot. Her eyes were transfixed with terror.
Schlitter started to talk, but Sister Brigitta gestured to the old
man to continue. Schlitter looked baleful.

'It's not only – you know – it's their breasts as well, you
see,' said the old man deferentially. 'They would just go on at
them, they bit the nipples off, you see, as well as everything
else they did to them. And we couldn't stop the bleeding
though it's better than it was. There and, you know –'

'We'll do what we can,' said Sister Brigitta briskly. 'Fraülein
Arzfeld,' she snapped some orders to Lise. To Schlitter she
said, 'These girls have been injured by the enemy, as much as
any soldier and worse than many.'

'They are not military personnel. I shall make an immediate
report!'

Sister Brigitta took no further notice of him and he withdrew,
announcing that he intended immediately to see the Hospital
Director. The old couple stood huddled in the corridor, itself
an overflow ward, until Sister Brigitta hustled them away. Lise
wondered fleetingly where they had left the cart and whether
Schlitter would arrest them, out of sheer malevolence, when
they left the hospital – if, indeed, he could effectively do so
since there seemed to have been no police in the village for
some time. She took gentle charge of the two girls and established that each, with suitable encouragement, was able to
walk.

That night the gunfire in the east sounded louder and more
menacing. Lise told Marcia of the peasants' arrival and of
the encounter between Schlitter and the Ward Superintendent.

'We've had some like that,' said Marcia, shaken. 'But I
didn't deal with them myself. Lise, I suppose that's what's

coming, is it? Of course, we've been told all the time, but now it's only a few miles away!'

'Perhaps they'll respect a hospital.'

But they had both heard stories. There had been the tale of a hospital run by an Abbey, somewhere in Silesia. One of their own nurses claimed that a sister of hers had been on the nursing staff there, had hidden and ultimately escaped. The Abbey had been occupied by the Russians, it was said. Red Army soldiers had murdered every human being, doctors, monks, patients, and, of course, nurses. Their colleague's sister had allegedly witnessed the Russians' arrival.

'They were like mad, wicked children. They smashed everything, furniture, glasses, medical equipment. The surgical spirit they drank. They played games with everything, threw it about, took it to pieces, the way a spoilt, destructive youngster treats a toy. The people they treated like insects to be squashed. They threw the patients out of the upper windows, roaring with laughter all the time!'

'Was anybody spared?' Lise asked. 'No,' the nurse had answered, 'nobody. Nobody at all.'

Three days later the Hospital Director assembled all the staff and spoke briefly and without evasion.

'We have to make difficult choices. It is not possible to obtain directions which are practicable to obey. I have certain responsibilities and I must now make decisions.

'You all know the stories of what can be expected from the Russian Army, even in a hospital. Unfortunately, I believe these stories to be true. I do not expect they are true of everywhere, all the time, but I fear they are sufficiently true to mean you are all at grave risk. The front is now under ten miles from here.' He spoke against a rumble of gunfire. It was not German gunfire. German detachments had been drifting back through the village for the last two days. The wards, of course, were as full as ever and the nurses were worked off their feet.

'I have asked for military transport to evacuate the hospital. I have received none. I have, however, spoken to the local Wehrmacht Commander. He has agreed to requisition a certain number of farm carts. In them we must try to load as many as possible of our patients who cannot walk. Every person who can walk, even slowly, must walk. There are no riding horses left in the neighbourhood. There are no motor cars, and if there were there is no fuel for them. Five columns will leave, starting tonight.' He gave details.

'I wish to say one more thing. In ordinary circumstances it would be the first duty of all of us, at whatever personal risk, to remain with our patients, to care for them to the end. Circumstances today are not ordinary. I hereby declare,' the Director said, standing ramrod-straight, and frowning, 'that I regard it as consistent with the sense of duty of every female member of the hospital, of every nurse, to move independently at any time, if thereby she sees a better chance to escape. And, of course, return to her duty in more favourable circumstances. I cannot protect you as I should. You must do your best to protect yourselves. Your capture,' said the Director carefully, 'will not help your patients. Thank you.'

His last words were accompanied by a number of explosions, sounding nearer than before. It was being whispered that somewhere, both north and south of them, Russian armies had already penetrated west of where they were; and that in the north a mighty Soviet push was being mounted towards Berlin itself.

That night five pathetic little columns, carts, bicycles, limping men and bravely marching nurses started the painful move westward. In spite of the Director's pessimism three motor vans had been produced from somewhere, burning wooden fuel in remarkable contraptions fitted to the roofs, but somehow gaining from it sufficient power to move. Lise and Marcia moved with Sister Brigitta: two ancient ward orderlies, two dozen patients on foot and seven more loaded on carts which they all took turns to drag. They were under the nominal control of one of the doctors. Doctor Winckelmann was plump and elderly. Marcia thought that the journey was going to be as hard on him as on any of them.

They moved in darkness. The April nights were still cold. They had their route. Doctor Winckelmann spoke with a little assumed authority at their first halt, soon after dawn.

'We are behind German lines. We should now have six hours' rest. The patients require it.'

But it was to Sister Brigitta that the party looked for discipline and guidance. Untiring, driven by an iron sense of duty supported by an equally iron constitution, this remarkable woman steered the little party westward. Progress had been very slow. Now she spoke.

'Herr Winckelmann, I do not believe that we are, strictly speaking, behind German lines. It does not seem to me that there is anything which can precisely be called a German line.'

It was true that the roads had been cluttered with columns of mixed character, a few motor vehicles, exhausted horses and even more exhausted men: and every enquiry about the enemy had been received with shrugs. They were, they uneasily felt, not moving covered by the Wehrmacht so much as fleeing with it.

'I believe,' said Sister Brigitta flatly, 'that we should try to get back as soon as possible not to where the Director told us he hopes to re-open our hospital, south of Brandenburg, but west of the Elbe. That is over seventy miles.'

'Sister Brigitta, we have no authority –'

'The Director did not know the circumstances we would find on the roads. It has been obvious throughout these last hours. We must keep moving westward. We must move at least to the west of the Elbe. We cannot stop except when absolutely necessary. If we are overrun we know what will happen. We cannot defend ourselves. There will be no mercy.'

She spoke dispassionately. All knew that she had little fear for herself. The wounded men, limbs aching, nodded. Fear lends strength. They muttered among themselves. The Elbe, as Sister Brigitta had said, was probably seventy miles away but east of it they could all scent the imminence of death, at best.

And so the little column became not a party 'redeploying to a new location' as Doctor Winckelmann importantly expressed it to various military police encountered on the way, but a group of refugees seeking personal safety and bent on escaping not only the enemy but the harsh measures of their own side taken against all, even at this last, terrible hour, who were less than absolutely obedient to authority. They moved as best they

401

could and rested only when they could go no further. The
sounds of battle, heavy gunfire, now rumbled on every horizon.
And by night, every horizon was red with fire.

On the sixth day, Sister Brigitta said,

'One more good march and a night's sleep and we'll see the
Elbe!'

'What happens the far side? How do we get across? There'll
be check points on every bridge, if it's not blown. Where are
the Americans?'

Nobody chose to discuss these questions, muttered without
great concern. To keep going westward was to them the road
to salvation and it was best to think no further. They knew
that if they could reach territory which the Anglo-Americans
would no doubt soon overrun they might – they just might –
survive. Marcia's heart beat faster at the thought.

'We must cross the Elbe,' said Sister Brigitta, 'somehow.'
It had been a shorter journey than they had first calculated,
agonizing though they had found it.

But late on the afternoon of the sixth day, as they moved
along a small road running northwestward, they encountered
a disturbing sight. A gaggle of country people, wagons piled
high with possessions, fear rising from them like gases from a
manure cart, met them coming the other way; moving not west
but southeastward. A few words showed why. These refugees
were trying to escape from the menace nearest to them, and
Russian troops were already approaching their village from the
south-west, while to the north more were, at that moment,
moving rapidly toward the Elbe itself with nothing in their
path. So the refugees said, desperate, incoherent, as they
crowded round the little hospital column, each with new tales
of horror spread like singed paper caught on the wind, tales of
terror, burning villages, raped farmsteads, everywhere
corpses, corpses. The eyes of the children were bright with
fear and fatigue.

East of the great river, it now seemed that there were few
pockets of territory to which the Red Army had not penetrated.

'They are all around us,' said Lise to Marcia. 'All around
us.' They pushed on for a few miles and that night Sister
Brigitta held conference in a low voice with Doctor Winckelmann. Thereafter she summoned the nurses.

402

'We're going to try to get the wounded, the ones that can't walk, into villages. They'll have to make out they're sick members of the population. Everybody else will try his luck in getting away individually. We'll divide bandages and medicaments between them, give them all we can. You girls stick together, hide, try to get west. You can do no more for these fellows.'

Marcia took Lise's hand.

'We'll start right away. Now.'

'You'll start after we've done the evening dressings, given the patients as good a send off as we can manage,' said the Ward Superintendent implacably. 'Not before.'

'And you, Sister Brigitta,' said Lise timidly. 'What will you do?'

They were standing in a clearing in a small wood. They had, as usual, hitched up as cover some tarpaulins carried on the carts. It was raining lightly but less cold than previously. There was already a touch of spring in the air.

'Oh, me,' said the gruff Prussian with something nearer a smile than Marcia had ever seen on her face. 'I'll stay with old Winckelmann. We'll manage somehow. He'd be utterly lost without me!'

As they got ready to move off by themselves, Lise took Marcia's hand and shook her head with great sadness. She whispered, even now haunted by the universal fear of the penalties of disloyalty,

'Ah, Marcia, this is the end for Germany, you know. Of course these people have brought it on all our heads, they are evil, they deserve it. But I can't help – although I hate them, I can't help suffering deep at the heart for Germany. *You* can't feel that, in a way you must feel happy. I can understand that. The Germans have been beaten! But it's different for me, to say "The Germans have been beaten."'

'But dearest Lise,' said Marcia, with a small touch of her old irrepressible self, 'dearest Lise, to tell you the honest truth it has never – never, ever, ever – occurred to me that they wouldn't be!'

Anna Langenbach moved slowly and aimlessly along the

inner perimeter wire of the camp. For the hundredth time she wondered why she had not already been tried and condemned by some sort of court. She was under no illusions about the penalty for her offence – a penalty it would carry in any country, she acknowledged, with the extraordinary, fair-minded detachment which made such a mark on all who knew her. But it had not yet happened. She lived every day with death, but yet she lived. Every morning she imagined that there would be a harsh cry, 'Prisoner Langenbach!' And she would be summoned, a charge read, a perfunctory enquiry as to whether she had anything to say – and then? To kneel in a ditch perhaps, to receive a bullet in the back of the neck? To be strung up, ankles bound, on some rough gallows? It could not go on long. Every hour she died.

And yet she was still alive. After her arrest she was told she would 'in due course' face criminal charges. Meanwhile she was to be confined, and would 'probably face further interrogation'. That had been in February. And since that February day, that day of agony when she had tried to say goodbye to Franzi, had seen him pushed away from her with a surly policeman's hand on his shoulder, watched him looking back at her, trying to break free, starting to cry – since that day, now seventy-eight days and seventy-seven nights ago, she had indeed been confined. Confined for the most part in this terrible place. And she had indeed been interrogated, as they had promised she would be.

The confinement was worse than the interrogation. The camp was a place of internment, not for those awaiting trial. Her proper place, she supposed grimly, was a prison – in theory, at least, a prison for those under examination rather than for the condemned. But after a few days, and without explanation, she had been moved under the care of a sour-faced wardress by a train from Kranenberg – her own Kranenberg! By an irony the local prison was served from Kranenberg station. And from Kranenberg she had been taken northward, crammed into a horse-wagon with many others. Ultimately, she had reached the camp. At no time had anybody told her what was happening, what would happen, what had been decided. Once she tried to ask one of the camp guards.

404

'I believe my case is being investigated. Can you please tell me –'

She was almost stunned by the flat of a hand once, twice, thrice across the face. The woman yelled –

'Shut up!'

Anna turned away. Another inmate had been watching.

'You asked for it! They aren't allowed to talk to us.'

'I only wished to find out what is happening to me, I've not been condemned, I'm awaiting trial.'

'Well, who has been condemned?' said the woman with a snarl. 'Do you think we're all criminals here? We're here without explanation, just like you.'

Anna realized that her situation was a matter of indifference to her fellows in the camp. Their concern was, somehow, to remain alive. This had now gone on for ten weeks. It was late April, 1945.

On arrival she had been given a striped prison suit to wear. Her head was shaved and she was ordered to scrub herself with carbolic soap in cold water. Shivering, she was then pushed into a hut where sixty other inmates existed from day to day, fearful, foul-smelling and enfeebled. And, above all, famished. In some camps, the prisoners told each other, there was work – you were made to work until you dropped, and then beaten until they tired or you died. In some camps you hadn't a chance, nobody ever reappeared. This was an easy place. No work. You were left alone. The only difficulty was that everybody, quite quickly, was starving to death.

For as the weeks had passed, as Anna drew on her reserves of spirit to believe that all might one day be well with Franzi, even with Anthony, hoping nothing for herself, she realized that the most immediate enemy was hunger. It might, she thought, be best to try to die from starvation, since death must anyway be imminent. But she could not do it. She could not abandon the will to live, the struggle to exist for a further day, week, month, futile though the struggle might be. Supplies of food, cruelly inadequate as they had always been, were now barely reaching the camp at all. The guards looked well fed but the inmates (and she reckoned there must be several thousand of them, for the place stretched as far as the eye could see) were receiving only a tiny share of an evil-smelling hogswill every day. And for that tiny share they had to fight at the trough like beasts. In this part of the camp only women were confined, and Anna realized, with sickened pity, why so many of these women lay like skeletons in corners. They had, quite simply, been beaten in the fight for food.

At first Anna – strong and well-nourished by the standards of wartime – had instinctively tried to help some emaciated creature. She was roughly disabused.

'Don't try that! You can't keep them alive. Let them go.'

It was a large, gaunt woman speaking, a virago with a grim, ravaged face. Somehow this woman had retained strength. Her name was Ilse Meier. Anna looked at her steadily.

'Can one believe that? Believe that one shouldn't try to help?'

'Of course one can. One must. If any of us get out of this place it'll be because we're more determined and a bit stronger than the others. You're strong. You've got a good body. You might survive. They're giving us rations now for about one-fifth of the people here. That means four-fifths will die. It's just a question of when.'

Indeed, large numbers were already dying. By the middle of April Anna had herself taken part in over twenty different burial parties. These consisted of gangs of prisoners ordered to drag corpses to a large open pit, a mass grave. At first, efforts had been made to cover it, and some lime had been spread. Now the numbers made this impracticable. The grave was open. The stench was foul. At first, Anna had been horribly sick at burial duty. Now she acknowledged it as part of existence. The dead could not lie in the huts. It had to be done.

There was no ordinary work carried out by the camp inmates. Camp routine was almost non-existent, except for the morning roll-call, hideous travesty of a ceremony, where rank on rank of skeleton-like, pyjama-clad figures stood in all weathers to be ineptly counted by the guards, stood for hours until they fainted – or, on several memorable occasions, actually died – on the parade itself. Apart from roll-call there was feeding time. And, for the rest, there was monotony and despair. At first, Anna's old impatience flickered at the idiocy of it all. What did it concern the authorities who had created this hell, whether a few more wretches had died in the night? To what was the number relevant, the subject of such protracted counting and calculation, when only one person in five could be fed? There was no attempt that Anna could see to separate the prisoners by category or account for them. They formed one large, shapeless, suffering mass of sick humanity, unrecognizable as individuals, rough order kept by wardresses armed with long whips. Only death could bring release, or so it seemed for most of the time.

Only once was Anna reminded that she was a person, Anna Langenbach. Ironically, the occasion was her recent interrogation. She had already been in the place ten weeks, and she was very feeble. A wardress yelled her name on roll-call one morning, and she found herself being pushed along the central roadway which ran through an inner perimeter wire to the administrative compound of the camp. It was, she calculated, 21st April.

A man was sitting at a desk in the wooden hut. She stood in front of him, shaven-headed, pallid, legs threatening to give beneath her, hating the smell she exuded like them all. From somewhere she tried to summon the strength to face this man. She had prayed a great deal in the camp. She prayed now.

'Lord, help me to find courage, to remain devoted to truth, to remember that they are all – the interned, the guards, this man sitting at this desk here – all are loved by You.'

The man looked at her as at some mildly repellent animal.

'Your name is Langenbach. Your case is to come before a People's Court.'

Anna heard herself saying, 'I wish to ask why, if I am not yet tried or condemned, I am confined in this place.'

The man looked at her as if the question were self-evidently absurd as well as insolent.

'You are interned here because you have, on a previous occasion, acted with criminal disregard for the fundamental laws of the Reich. You falsified the fact about the true paternity of your child. For that you have deserved internment.'

Anna had always expected this. She said,

'You have no proof whatever to support such an allegation.'

She had always been determined to protect Franzi from – from

407

what? She had confided in nobody except – once – dearest Frido.

'No proof whatever!' she said firmly.

The man at the desk grunted. To tell the truth, he said to himself, this accusation didn't rest on firm ground. The only evidence came from the remarks of a self-confessed and now executed traitor in a pretty wild letter. The man had clearly been unstable, anyway; and you could hardly invent a more poisoned source. In enquiries around Langenbach he'd met astonishment –

'The little Langenbach? That's right, his father was a Luftwaffe officer, killed before he was born.'

'The widow was heart-broken. No, I've never heard anything against Frau Anna, to tell you the truth.'

He had bullied, suggested, but been met by a wall of loyalty to Anna Langenbach and belief in her. Even when he'd broached the subject of the 'very serious charges' he'd found sheer incomprehension.

'It's hard to believe Frau Anna would help an enemy of Germany! Perhaps there was a mistake, she didn't know who he was!'

Idiots! But on the question of paternity he was less sure. He continued,

'Furthermore, serious charges of treason, of helping the enemy, are still being investigated. When they are ready they will be preferred against you. You may be sure of that.'

'When will that be?'

'In due course,' said the man indifferently. He shuffled some papers and said,

'Meanwhile, there are various points on which I require answers. The English prisoner you are alleged to have helped escape, Marvell – he has a sister. You know her.'

Anna nodded.

'I want to know whether you communicated with her and told her that her brother was hiding at Schloss Langenbach.'

Anna's limbs ached horribly. '*Mein Herr*,' she said softly, 'I have not seen Fraülein Marvell for a year, at least. I have written no letter to her in that time. And I supposed that this man's alleged hiding in my home was to be the subject of an accusation. I can, in that case, hardly be expected to admit now that it took place.'

For Anna, useless though the attempt presumably was, had decided that she would do her damndest to brazen matters out if she ever came to trial. She would say that she had known nothing of anybody breaking in and hiding at the Schloss. She would say that Fraülein Wendel must have misunderstood her. She hoped for nothing, but she would go down fighting. She would certainly not admit the matter in response to irrelevant suggestions about Marcia. If this man lost his temper at her defiance, beat her, killed her, so be it.

Then the questions had come thick and fast, put to her with angry, bored impatience. Anna looked at him and knew that in his eyes she was an object, a number, an obscenely clad, noisome, female creature who could at any time be snuffed out at the whim of the Camp Commandant for some fancied act of insubordination, who had no right whatever to life and who yet was wasting time, wasting his, the interrogator's valuable time because she faced serious charges and serious charges, affecting security, had to be dealt with scrupulously, exhaustively, according to exact procedure. Anna could see all this in his face as he snapped, shouted, yawned. He did not strike her. The questions did not bother her. She guessed – rightly – that they were directed at implicating the von Arzfeld family, including Marcia, with anti-State conspiratorial activities, as evidenced by her own actions and Frido's. No other member of the family was remotely concerned with her own conduct, nor, she suspected, with Frido's. But she guessed – again rightly – that the attempt to involve them was the reason for postponement of her own trial. The German authorities were pursuing every lead, scouring the shrinking Reich for the smallest stain of treason until the very end. After an hour he let her go.

When she shuffled back to the women's camp she saw Ilse Meier.

'Did they beat you?'

'No. Just questions. And there's no point. They'll hang or shoot me when they want to. They go on probing and investigating for all the world as if they had time, as if it mattered. And we'll all die soon, anyway.'

409

There had been another burial party the evening before. A few tears of exhaustion rolled down Anna's cheeks. They came rarely. Ilse Meier looked at her with something more like animation than Anna had seen in weeks.

'Hold on! We've got to hold on! Do you know what – I got it from the Sow!'

The Sow was a wardress of huge dimensions, less energetic than most, with whom Ilse seemed to have established some sort of rapport. When unobserved by colleagues the Sow could sometimes be seen speaking to her with something not far fom normality.

'I got it from the Sow. The British are already across the Weser! A few more weeks – perhaps a few more days – and they'll be here! And then this stinking hole will be cleared, and if any of us are alive we'll get out.'

The prisoners had no access to information about the war. Engrossed as they were in the fierce business of surviving from a dawn to a dusk they were only sluggishly aware that a war was being fought – and on German soil.

'Across the Weser,' hissed Ilse Meier, 'and it's 21st April. My mother's birthday! And they're not far from my home. And not many kilometres from here.'

'*They'll* come for me soon, now, Ilse –'

'If they come for you we'll hide you, pretend you died, pretend you're in the cess pit with the rest. Hold on, Anna Langenbach!'

Anna looked at her. For the first time since February and arrest, for the first time in that vile place, she felt a tiny spark of hope.

'Hold on, Anna Langenbach! Hold on!'

Chapter 25

———————◆———————

THE GENERAL'S OFFICE, sumptuous with dark nineteenth-century panelling and heavy furniture, had been the study of a rich German industrialist. Senior members of the staff occupied spacious premises in adjoining rooms. Only a short driveway separated the house – the Villa, as all knew it – from the factory itself. The factory had, remarkably, escaped Allied bombing. It was now the temporary home of Divisional Headquarters, whose vehicles were parked in orderly rows on the tarmac in front of the factory gate, camouflaged nets folded away since 8th May, 1945, paint now being applied liberally to coachwork, to Headquarters sign boards, to twin flagpoles on which Union Jack and Divisional Ensign fluttered in triumph. German forces in the west had surrendered to Field-Marshal Montgomery on Lüneburg Heath. There had been seven weeks of nominal peace in Europe. The Army was sprucing itself up. Long years of drabness were now behind it. The victors reckoned they had the right, and no small opportunity, to cut a dash.

The factory manager – the proprietor, owner of the General's study, was not in evidence – had, from the first day, assured Divisional Headquarters of all possible co-operation. As if by magic, everything the Staff demanded appeared, every task commissioned was instantly performed. Timber, expert carpenters, workmen skilled at every sort of construction or repair reported immediately the factory manager gave the word. He had quickly made himself indispensable: the ubiquitous, indispensable Herr Hanke.

'He's a good chap, is Hanke,' said the General's Aide-de-Camp to nobody in particular, after Herr Hanke had appeared with two charming watercolours of wildfowl which he suggested the General might like hung in his office: the General was reputed to be keen on ornithology. Hanke was assiduous

411

in such thoughtful gestures. He studied the tastes and foibles of the British intruders with a lover's eye, an eye which missed nothing.

'Hanke's a splendid man,' said the ADC. 'He'll get one anything. He was anti-Nazi, apparently, so he's very cheerful now. I suspect most of the stuff he produces for us he simply takes from old Party members, tells them to hand over or else! It's best not to enquire too closely. He certainly delivers the goods!' And Herr Hanke, who had always managed the factory under the 'Herr Direktor' with unobtrusive efficiency and had never played a prominent part in political life, had indeed destroyed his Party card without a second of regret on 3rd May. 'That's over,' he said to himself, '*Alles Vorbei*! And there were many of them I never liked.'

Hanke had, moreover, a close cousin, a woman who had worked at the local Party office for years, a secretary of long standing. He sought her on that same 3rd May when the British Army were already surging through the neighbourhood, when nearby towns and villages were already crowded with strange, khaki uniforms, when rumours already abounded of capitulation. Hanke found his cousin, a conscientious spinster, a devotee of the National Socialist ideal, a believer: she was in tears.

'Friedrich, it's over. It's the worst day in the history of the world. What can we do?'

Hanke immediately told his cousin Hannelore what to do. She was aghast.

'I can't – the Party leadership – it would be destroying years of work –'

'There is no Party leadership. You should now – *now* Hannelore, do you hear me? – at once, destroy the records and the membership lists. It's not a great deal of paper. It can be done.'

'They're irreplaceable!'

'I hope so. Are they duplicated?'

'In Berlin,' said Hannelore. Hanke reckoned that anything in Berlin stood a fair chance of being destroyed itself, by now. Anyway, the list of Party members in Kreis Klempen was unlikely to be of urgent interest to the conquerors of Berlin. Hanke told himself that he had never, at any time, done anything which could be challenged in law or morality, but it was an excellent opportunity to expunge 'complications'.

'You must do what I propose immediately.'

'Oh, Friedrich, it's like sacrilege, my own work –'

'Don't be a fool. There's nobody here but you. If you can't do it, give them to me. I'll get rid of them.'

Accustomed to authority from childhood, always a little in awe of bustling, competent Cousin Friedrich, she had submitted. It might, Hanke reflected, save a lot of trouble. In this he was right.

'Hanke will get one anything,' the General's ADC said daily. 'He's a splendid man!' The General had already become agreeably used to the possibility of making lavish demands for his office and quarters. He had developed a taste for saying to the ADC –

'Try to get some –'

The ADC would look blank.

'You know – I'm sure they're obtainable. Get hold of Hanke, he'll know. I'd like them by Thursday.'

And Hanke would know. In those few weeks which had elapsed since the end of the War in Europe, those weeks and months before the Army began its shrinkage to a peacetime shape and function, before it reverted to more regular, more conventional, more restrained and inhibited ways of life, there was a flowering, a triumph, a vulgar exuberance. This was victory. In shattered towns, in villages packed with desperate refugees from East Prussia and Pomerania, the vanquished – yellow of skin, thin, hungry, lethargic – looked on, expressionless. In the countryside the farmers and their people concentrated again on the possibilities of the harvest.

The General's duties were various. He was responsible for a large tract of Germany in which a British Control Commission was busy trying to recreate something of the fabric of government, handicapped by the laudable injunction against employing ex-Nazis – who, inevitably, comprised the ablest administrators. He had the tedious task of clearing up what had until recently been a battlefield: unexploded mines, ammunition of all sorts, the litter of a victorious as well as a defeated army that disfigured the landscape. He had a host of duties associated with 'security': the war was only recently won, the victors

413

could still hardly accustom themselves to the fact, and no risks could be taken with dissident elements of the population if they existed. Then there were the non-Germans. He had three camps, housing between them seven thousand 'Displaced Persons' – the human flotsam of war. Human flotsam, produced by German conquest, German forced labour and, latterly, German retreat: human flotsam from every tribe in Europe, Poles, Latts, Serbs, Slovenes, Croats, Ukrainians – flotsam that had to be sorted, categorized, interviewed, despatched (if possible) to whatever authorities were established in its country of origin. In many cases this human flotsam was reluctant – reluctant to the point of suicide – to return to wherever the Allied authorities benevolently decreed.

'They're afraid, sir,' the General's staff told him, 'afraid to go back to the Communists, afraid of the Russians. They won't go unless at the point of a gun. And often not then.'

The General sighed over the refractoriness of humanity, leaves blown untidily over the map of Europe by the gales of war.

The General had, as well, to discharge the ordinary military business of his Division. He had to ensure that the Division was fit to do whatever the future required of it amid the somewhat distracting atmosphere of peace, the temptations of conquest after the tensions of battle. He had to live, also, with a certain amount of anxiety as to whether he would be commanding his Division very long. A temporary Major-General, his rank in the Army was only that of Lieutenant-Colonel. War and a huge expansion had brought rapid advancement to young men like him. Soon, after Japan had been beaten, there would be contraction, reversion to a peace establishment, reduction in rank . . . He turned his mind to more immediate matters.

The General rang the bell on his desk and the Deputy Assistant Adjutant-General came in. The morning, the first in the office for three days, was to be devoted to administrative and disciplinary matters. It was 27th June.

'This is rather a nuisance, this Marvell case,' said the General, opening the folder handed to him, 'but I've had a word with the Corps Commander personally. He's happy that I deal with it myself. Nobody wants it to go to Court Martial:

that would be ridiculous. I'll make it clear to Marvell he won't get another chance. I take it he's here?'

On 19th May a small boat sank within twenty yards of the west bank of the Elbe. Shortly after seven o'clock in the morning two dripping figures emerged from the river and collapsed on a small strand of river beach.

'Oh, my God!' said Marcia twenty minutes later. 'I never thought that boat would get more than half-way.' The boat had been a miracle, a last hope, found abandoned on the east bank, overturned, clearly unsound. They had taken two discarded slats of timber from a ruined house to use as paddles. They had launched it and paddled out into the strong north-flowing current. The wind was in the east, and helped them. Marcia said,

'It'll drift us over to the west bank if we can keep afloat.'

Dawn was just breaking. Hearts in mouths the girls had reached midstream

'How far could you swim, Lise?' Neither of them was a powerful swimmer and the current was strong. The Elbe is wide.

'Keep paddling, Lise!'

Then the boat had swamped. They had swum, struggled, clothes dragging them down, swallowing great quantities of Elbe water, sure that they were drowning. Suddenly Marcia found blessed stones beneath her feet, slipped, swallowed more water, somehow slithered to the bank. Lise, a little stronger, was just ahead. They lay, retching and gasping. Sun, merciful spring sun, began to warm them. It promised to be a dry day.

One hour later the girls walked into a farmhouse. Around them flat, featureless country extended to a low line of wooded hills on the western horizon. They believed that in this part of Germany there were no Russian troops west of the river. The immediate terror, the threat of rape, mutilation, murder which had hung over them for weeks as they struggled westward – this terror was, perhaps, over. They were not sure. Fear had become part of life. But as they first spied the farm from a little distance and saw a young woman come out of the house to hang clothes on a line they sensed something which might be safety.

At the farmhouse an older woman, suspicious, listened to their explanations. There were no men around.

'We've escaped from the east. We got across in a boat. It's sunk.'

The woman nodded slowly. In spite of her bedraggled appearance Lise spoke with a certain authority. At the farm they had by now seen a good many refugees. The state of some of them beggared description. This one seemed to have got away with it, skin and confidence unimpaired.

'You'd better take your clothes off and dry in here for a bit. Where are you trying to get to? There are soldiers everywhere – Americans, English. It's best for girls like you to be careful. We've not got much food, but there's some coffee –

'Is the war over?'

'Yes, thank God!' said the woman. 'Ten days ago it must have been. But only He knows what will become of us all now.'

Three hours later the girls were feeling something like life in their limbs, sitting in the kitchen, huddled in blankets. Their clothes were wrung out and drying in the fresh May breeze outside. Lise had no idea beyond somehow getting to Arzfeld. She had no money and nothing she could use as money. She was still in a state of shock, overwhelmed with relief at having apparently escaped from that zone where the Red Army was bloodily rampaging. Lise sipped her mug of *ersatz* coffee and tried to think coherently. She asked the farm woman about their whereabouts and found she was failing to take in the answers. The names of places meant nothing to her. Half of her mind was still alert for the sounds of vehicles driving up, of drunken shouts, excited cries, presages of a sickening fate.

Marcia was silent, deep in her own thoughts.

There was the sound of vehicles driving up. There were shouts. Lise went rigid.

Marcia jumped up and ran to the window.

'My God, soldiers!'

'What sort?' hissed Lise.

'Well, not Russians, anyway!'

416

The bang on the door was peremptory and the farm woman answered it. A figure stood in the doorway, blocking the light. He was wearing a steel helmet and a short khaki jacket, ending at the waist. Several others appeared behind him. In the lane by the farm gate were two armoured cars. The figure in the doorway began shouting.

'Hey, any men here? German soldiers? *Deutsche Soldaten*, huh? *Verstehen?*' His manner was rough and suspicious but he did not induce fear. The farm woman looked nervous and resigned but there was no panic in the air, no stench of terror. She shook her head.

'Best have a look around, Lieutenant,' said the soldier standing immediately behind him. He had seen Marcia and Lise and liked what he saw.

'That's right. Sergeant Fox, get the vehicles turned round. We'll have a good look round. There's Heinie soldiers dressed as farm boys in every barn from here to the Rhine. Out of the way, mother!'

Marcia had wrapped the blanket round her as securely as she could. Her hair was still damp. There was colour again in her cheeks. She got up from the kitchen chair and marched up to the lieutenant.

'Are you an American officer?'

He looked at her with surprise, and a good deal of appreciation.

'That's right, sister. Out of the way, now.'

'Could you please help me,' said Marcia. 'I am British. I am a refugee and I urgently need to make contact with the British authorities. Please tell me how I can do so. This girl with me is a brave, anti-Nazi German who has saved my life. We need help.'

Anthony spent 19th May in London. He had been flown to England two days after the German capitulation. The liberation of Oflag VI had been an extraordinary episode. First there had been the arrival of the Russians. The prisoners had for several days found themselves free to come and go as they wished. The guards simply disappeared. They did not remain to meet their own end at Russian hands. They were not, as in some

417

places, overpowered by their prisoners and incarcerated in their turn. They disappeared. They were no longer there.

'Strictly speaking,' observed Anthony to his messmates, 'they've deserted.' Bressler kept to his own quarters.

The prisoners made up parties to investigate what was happening in the neighbourhood. The war seemed to be pretty well over. The wireless was listened to now without hindrance and news bulletins were posted by the prisoners themselves. Visits were paid to several villages already over-run by the Red Army. The visitors returned much shaken. 'Not that I've got much sympathy for them,' someone would say, 'but Fritz was certainly right. The stories weren't exaggerated. Not good when you actually see it. Not good at all.'

Then, on the second day of this extraordinary period of suspense, a vehicle had arrived with a British officer – a British officer who knew about them and who had instructions. There was, they learned with joy, to be no delay in their repatriation. Agreement had been reached with the Russians. Some of the camps over-run in Poland and East Prussia would take longer to clear: the Russians, it was said, were 'being a bit difficult'. But in their case Anthony and his fellow captives were within a short distance of American lines. Transfer points had been agreed, transport was made lavishly available and hurriedly converted bomber aircraft flew them to England. On 10th May Anthony, for the first time since October, 1942, was in his mother's arms.

Spring came warm and early that year in England. John and Hilda had slightly extended their living quarters: they were using the inner hall again. The heart of the house was beating. Anthony found that he could sleep, and for days did nothing else.

It was just ten days later that John Marvell said, 'I suppose they'll give you quite a decent stretch of leave? Any idea what the future's likely to be after that?'

Although it was a warm day the inner hall needed life restoring to it and Hilda had lit a fire, which smoked atrociously. The smell was delicious: there had never been a shortage of firewood at Bargate. Anthony gazed at the fire.

'Yes, a decent stretch of leave, I hope,' said his father again.

Anthony said abruptly –

'I'm going back to Germany next week. I'm going to report to the Battalion.'

Anthony's old battalion from North Africa had invaded Sicily and then been withdrawn from the Mediterranean to take part in the campaign in North West Europe. They were now somewhere in central Germany, part of the 'British Liberation Army': exactly where, Anthony knew not.

'Good Heavens, old boy, do they want you back that quickly?'

'I've talked to the Depot. It's all fixed up.' He had telephoned from London on the previous day. By good fortune the Depot Commander was a friend.

'Yes, Anthony, some replacements are going, other chaps coming home. Yes, I *could* fix it, they want Captains. I'll have to send a personal signal to Colonel Harry – you know Harry White's commanding?'

Another friend.

'Yes. Please do, Oliver.'

'But, Anthony, my dear old boy, why? You're due for a month's leave.'

'Please do this for me, Oliver. I'll explain some other time.'

'The problem is *moving* you! You can imagine the queues – both ways!'

Anthony had walked down Pall Mall. To his delight a familiar, tall, languid figure lowered itself down the steps of a club.

'Charles!'

Charles Oliphant said, 'Well, well! I'm glad you're alive. There was a rumour the serious Anderson got away and you were knocked on the head.'

They chatted happily. Oliphant had, he said, been free for three months.

'Charles, how on earth –'

'Well, you see, I got away.'

'*You* got away! You never seemed even mildly interested in anything so energetic!'

'Quite. The Germans thought so too, I fancy. I got to Sweden. Out of camp in a laundry basket, that *very* old trick, and absolutely beastly I may tell you. Then to Lubeck where I struck lucky.'

419

Oliphant still conveyed the impression of having lifted no finger. Anthony gazed at him and admired.

'I'm back in Germany now. I've taken on the job of looking after a *very* senior General. He's not as bad as he looks and I go around explaining him away to people. He's touchingly grateful. It gets me a lot of travel and he's got unlimited use of an aeroplane. We're flying back there next week, 24th.'

Anthony looked at him.

'Charles, is there a spare seat? Could your General take me over?'

'My dear boy, nothing easier. He's most obliging. He even flew my young brother, Robin, home last week for twenty-four hours in London, on some spurious excuse – my baby brother is a troop leader in my Regiment over there. Of course he'll make no difficulties over you. But, my dear fellow, why on earth do you want to go back to the bloody place? You must be owed ages of leave. And, as you know, the authorities are sure we're all psychiatric cases, we old prisoners, so why not exploit the fact and have a holiday?' But it was not Oliphant's way to intrude with personal questions. He guessed Anthony had reasons of his own. The flight was arranged.

And so, that evening at Bargate, Anthony said, 'I'm going back next week.' He went on as naturally as he could, 'There's bound to be news of Marcia any day now. Over there I might be able to help. I'm sure there'll be pretty regular leave so I'll be home again soon. And I want to see the Regiment again.'

'Old boy, you'll only have been home a fortnight.' But they said no more. John had spoken very recently to an old friend in the Foreign Office and they had been promised information about Marcia immediately it was to hand. The case of Miss Marvell was well-known. People were kind but it was made clear that the office had other concerns as well.

That night when they had gone to bed Hilda said,

'They're mad to let him return to any sort of duty. Behind that quietness his nerves are jangling, he's in a terrible state. I can't get near him.'

Anthony had talked briefly and uninformatively of his escape experiences. The Marvells had asked little, wanting nothing but to give him peace, decent food, normality, affection. Anthony had said,

'I was lucky. I was sheltered for a while in the house of a brave, anti-Nazi family. Then, when I was recaptured after trying to get west from there, I was beaten up by some Gestapo thug. It didn't go on long.'

They guessed – they knew – that there was far more to tell, and that he would tell it, if ever, when he chose. But they longed for time.

If even half the statements about Tissendorf camp were true, Robert Anderson reflected, they still composed a dreadful indictment. From a handful of the survivors, carefully nursed back to something like health, he had now spent a good many hours extracting a dossier of evidence. These were the fit ones, the lucky ones, those quick to recuperate. Evidence had started to be taken as soon as possible; it was still only 19th May. Many others would take weeks or months: or more. But from these lucky ones, their memories fresh, their hatred raw, he had composed a record in some detail of the lives of the inmates of Tissendorf. To each witness he had explained that the authorities had no wish to put additional strain on those who had already suffered much –

'But you will understand, it is necessary to bring the guilty to justice. For that we need evidence, while recollections are still fresh.'

They were eager to provide it. Some of the recollections he recorded were not so much fresh as foul. He wrote page after page not only about human cruelty and human suffering but about human degradation. He wrote about murder. He wrote about sickness and famine until he could smell the stench of bodies as he wrote. He wrote about cannibalism. It was, several prisoners explained without emotion, important to prevent some of the harder cases killing for food.

'They had become beasts, you see,' one witness said to him quietly. 'It's not very deep, the veneer which separates us from brutes. Civilization. Religion. Break it down and we become creatures without souls, capable of anything. Anything.'

He looked very old and wise, pallid skeleton though he was.

'What is your age?' asked Robert, writing.

'Twenty-six.'

He took down similar stories, similar sentiments from many.

'They had become beasts, you see.'

'Did the guards know of this? Was it realised? Did they feel responsible for the depths to which their treatment had pushed their prisoners?'

The witnesses were curiously indifferent about their guards, although some particularly vindictive warders or wardresses were described, with their habits, in fearful detail. But the horrors of the place, in the later stages, had principally derived from famine.

'They didn't feed us. They let us die, scavenge, become like beasts. Like I've told you.'

Then, as many attested, came the unbelievable moment when the guards disappeared. The word went round that the British Army was near, that the prisoners could make the camp their own, that the kitchens and food stores could be stormed.

'We couldn't get out. The gates were still barred. But we could go anywhere within the camp. Everyone knew where the food store was. Thousands rushed at it – of course many were trampled and didn't get up, it was inevitable. There was no order. It was anarchy. But the storeroom doors were broken down.'

'What happened then?'

A pause, always. The next part of the story was repeated so often it had to be true.

'*They* came back.'

'They?'

'SS. They meant to defend the camp, you see. The Commandant, the guards, had been ready to hand it over, ask the Allies to send in food supplies. But then *they* came back. And of course they found a mob, they found chaos. It was just when the food store was being looted. Some people bolted, some went mad and tried to go for the SS themselves, a whole mob went for them with their bare hands, imagine! Screaming like wildcats!'

'And then?'

422

'The SS opened fire. It went on and on. You never heard such noise. Screeching, shouting. Most of us got behind huts and lay on the ground. There was blood everywhere. And smoke. You saw some people staggering about, then collapsing, still holding loaves of bread they'd looted and with a leg or arm hanging by a skin, ripped off by bullets. I'd been in that hell over a year but we'd seen nothing like that afternoon.'

Robert wrote it down. The identity of the SS Unit and its commander had been established.

'Did any of the prisoners try to establish contact with the SS? Try to co-operate in getting some sort of order?'

'Co-operate, *Herr Hauptmann*? I don't understand. It wasn't possible. They were shooting, you see.'

But one woman, thin like the rest, a scarecrow, but eyes shining fiercely from a gaunt, lined face said in her evidence,

'Yes, of course it should have been done. The SS were frightened. The prisoners were a mob, out of their minds. It should have been possible for somebody to talk to the SS, get the prisoners moving into another part of camp, give an undertaking they could keep the food they had, calm things down. What happened was the worst thing of all. Chaos, followed by mass murder. You see, the prisoners were in a huddle, they couldn't get away.'

Robert wrote busily. He checked her name.

'Frau Meier, was there any –'

'Fraülein Meier.'

'Fraülein Meier, was there any attempt of the kind you've described?'

'Yes, one. One brave woman walked towards the SS, absolutely calm. She was calling out, calming the prisoners near her. She had such presence, it was having some effect. She had no fear. And amid all that, that –'

Robert nodded, face grave.

'All that filth and panic and screaming and shouting and death, she had dignity. She walked towards the SS and called out. I heard her. I was lying on the ground. I heard her. She called out,

'"Please stop shooting. I am sure we can all help each other." It was simple, but it made sense.'

'There was no response? They kept on shooting?'

423

'No, there was a command shouted, I remember it. She'd made an impression. They stopped shooting. The screams went on because people were bleeding, wounded, dying but the shooting stopped. Then there was a sort of commotion in another part of the crowd and another surge towards the SS. Mad! You see there weren't many SS. Maybe about thirty. They were frightened, I could see it. Then it was their turn to panic. They started shooting again.'

'And this woman?'

'She shouted at the officer, "Stop firing!" It was like an order! She had real authority, you see. And for a moment I almost thought he'd obey. Then I expect he felt ashamed, felt he'd almost shown weakness, hesitated – and on a prisoner's order! And a woman's! He shot her. With his pistol. I saw it.'

'Was this woman a foreigner? A Jewess? What?'

'No, she was German. I knew her quite well. There was nobody like her.'

'A German anti-Nazi?'

'Was she? I imagine so,' said Fraülein Meier with a shrug. 'We didn't talk politics in Tissendorf! Her name was Langenbach. Anna Langenbach.'

Lieutenant Robin Oliphant drove up to the farm, an attractive, mellow building with rose-coloured brick supporting massive timbers. Two huge barns, set at right angles, formed with the dwelling house three sides of a square. Robin climbed down from his scout car and stood, admiring. These places gave a superb impression of being built to last. He had orders, ten days after the capitulation as it now was, to search such farms on a random basis. Not much had been found and by now, 19th May, he doubted whether much would. Every member of the Wehrmacht had to be corralled into a Prison of War Camp, investigated and retained to await the pleasure of the victorious Powers. It was thought that a good many had slipped away before the final surrender ten days before, contrived to melt into the countryside; but so far Robin had found no traces of it. He banged on the door of the farmhouse and asked the usual peremptory questions.

The farmer was a hard-faced man of over sixty. He stood in

the doorway shaking his head, his equally hard-faced wife at his elbow.

'We need more men but we've nobody. We're doing all the work.'

He seemed deliberately to be misunderstanding Robin's questions, assuming that the enquiries were concerned with whether there was enough labour to work the farm rather than the hunt for illegally concealed German soldiers.

'Are the barns empty?'

'We're storing apples and there are my carts. The beasts are all out.'

Robin turned on his heel. His troop sergeant, Sergeant Tompkins, had been moving round the buildings while Robin stood at the farm door. Now he called,

'Mr Oliphant, sir! Are we going to search?'

'Certainly we are. I just wanted to give them the chance to admit it, if there are people here who shouldn't be.'

'There's somebody in here, sir!' Sergeant Tompkins was standing by the huge door of the nearest barn. Robin shot a look at the farmer and his wife, moved to the barn door and listened.

Voices. A gabble of shrill sounds. The door was bolted.

Robin shouted to the farmer who was watching, not moving.

'Kommen sie hier!'

The man moved over sulkily. He said, 'It's the refugee children.'

Robin spoke and understood a certain amount of German.

'Refugee children?'

'We were asked to take some in. For humanity.'

'Open up.'

Slowly, he did so. Robin moved into the barn. At first the darkness after the strong sunlight blinded him. He was conscious of movement, of chattering. Then he saw shapes, small, scampering, huddling away in the corner farthest from the door.

'Christ!' said Sergeant Tompkins softly.

About twenty children of ages which might range from four to eight, were cowering as far from Robin as they could. As his eyes grew accustomed to the light he could see that most were naked, while a few wore scraps of clothing. The air was foul. The barn, it was clear, was used for every purpose. In the middle of the floor was a large, old-fashioned trough with vestiges of some swill in it.

Robin walked towards the little group and spoke gently. They looked at him, absolutely silent.

'Can you understand me? We'll help you, I promise.'

They gazed, disbelieving, frightened of the unknown. He awkwardly raised his hand, with some inner reservation, seeking to pat the head of the nearest small figure, to establish some sort of kindly credentials. He felt black anger when the little creature shrank away, obviously fearing a blow. He could now see that these children were not only naked but filthy, their hair caked with dirt, their bodies streaked with their own excrement. On several small bodies he recognized weals and what looked like dried blood. These were animals, unloved and unvalued animals, jostling to eat on all fours from a trough, beaten, degraded, wretched and afraid. He went outside the barn.

'Sergeant Tompkins, we're going to see that all these children are got away. I'll talk to squadron Headquarters on the radio. There is an organization already working on things like this.'

To the farmer he said, in passable German,

'You and your wife are under arrest. *Verhaftet.*'

'Why?' said the man, astonished. 'We did what they told us, sheltered them, fed them. We got paid little enough for each, for our trouble, I can tell you. It was worth nothing to us.'

'Where are the families of these children?'

'How can we know? They told us they're children of people in the camps – you know! The camps.' He spoke with hesitation. He was unused to speaking freely of such things. His wife joined in.

'That's right. They're all children of people in prison or in camps, so they've no families, nobody to look after them.'

'And you've been looking after them,' said Robin, voice trembling.

'Yes. And we've got a list of them.' The woman darted back into the farmhouse and reappeared with a paper.

426

'I've kept it up to date. They're all there. Twenty-three. You can count.'

She looked pleased. Robin glanced without interest at the list, his nausea mixed with angry compassion. The woman had scrawled name after name with a mauve pencil on a dirty piece of lined paper, as each poor little inmate had been brought to that cruel place.

'Schmidt K., Velten K., Langenbach F., Milch O., . . .'

'You will be held responsible for the way you have treated these children,' Robin said, hoping he was right. Sergeant Tompkins said,

'Just leave the barn open for now, sir?'

'I think,' said Robin, 'that it might be better to burn it down. We must see to moving these children. That will take time. Then it will be better to burn it down.'

'My dear Anthony, you seem to be in trouble, you old ass.' It was 20th June.

Robert wore his customary frown and Anthony hoped that his friend's duties in connection with war crimes were not making him self-righteous. Robert always had firm convictions, but humour had generally saved him from pomposity. And Anthony was grateful for the visit which Robert had contrived to pay. Robert had heard that his friend was in trouble, that he had been placed in close arrest and then released, but released as one to face a charge, trial by Court Martial or some other form of military justice. He had immediately managed to drive to Anthony's battalion and was relieved to find him accessible to friends. They had a splendid reunion.

But Anthony did not show himself keen to discuss his own case. He said, briefly,

'Yes, I'm for it. I'm going before the Divisional Commander next Tuesday.'

'Hm! I suppose you just boiled over?' Robert had heard something of what was alleged.

'Yes, I think you can say that. And I'm glad of it.'

'Oh dear,' thought Robert. 'He's defiant, he's sure he's right about something, he's going to do himself harm.'

Anthony said nothing more, and Robert changed the subject

for a little. He would return to it but he could see Anthony was in a difficult mood.

They had already reminisced gleefully, caught up with each other's news, re-lived the days of their escape from Oflag XXXIII. They had not seen each other since parting in rain and distress on a train at Kranenberg. Robert was now working exceptionally hard, he said. He had a grim look about him.

'One of the smaller fry against whom we've got a case is a brute you must have suffered from in the later stages. He was Commandant of your camp. Bressler.'

'Bressler?' said Anthony, unsmiling. 'Of course. He saved me.'

'Well, he didn't save others, it appears.'

'Robert,' said Anthony with urgency, 'if Bressler is to be accused of anything, I insist on giving evidence on his behalf. The man rescued me from the Gestapo.' He told Robert the story in greater detail. Robert nodded with a touch of impatience.

'Where there's something to be said for any of these people it will be said, you know. But I hope you're not going to turn into too much of a crusader for unpopular causes, Anthony. There's no need to get over-excited about it.'

'On the contrary,' said Anthony. 'I suspect there's every need.'

Robert looked at him. 'If you read, day after day, the horrors I have read: if you took down, day after day, the evidence I take down – you might be rather less, shall we say, sensitive? A month ago, for instance, I took depositions from people who were in a camp not all that far from here, a place called Tissendorf. The things they told me were fresh in their memories. They didn't exaggerate, they told me the same things, their stories tallied. And, of course, that was nothing to what went on in these death camps in the east. In the east, factories were built near the camps, near an inexhaustible source of labour, you see. So many days or weeks could be extracted from the fit ones. Then they'd die – of disease or ill-treatment and there'd be plenty to replace them.'

Anthony was silent. Robert said quietly,

'And because there were so many deaths, so many corpses, such a problem of disposal, the Nazis built their big idea on it

428

– which was to use these places, also, in order simply to kill hundreds and thousands of people. They arrived only to die. It was murder at once or murder after a short period of work. Murder on a vast scale, an unimaginable scale. Hundreds of thousands. Perhaps millions. Their plan was to dispose of all European Jews, you see. But it wasn't, of course, only Jews.'

Anthony looked at him. He had no illusions, he thought, about the Nazis but he had always ascribed to wartime propaganda a good deal of the stories of the concentration camps. But Robert was collecting evidence. Robert was speaking from knowledge. Anthony thought of Bressler. He thought of Frido, of old Kaspar, of Lise. He thought of Anna. Could people of the same race as they, do things like this?

'You should,' said Robert remorselessly, 'see the photographs I've seen, read the depositions I've read. In these places people starved, were flogged, clubbed to death for the merest trifle. Where they weren't murdered at once as a matter of policy, that is.'

'Do you think many people in Germany knew? Apart from those actually involved?'

'That,' said Robert, 'we don't know. And perhaps we never will know. Fully.'

'Robert, you mentioned a camp called Tissendorf.'

'Yes. The Tissendorf unfortunates suffered from callousness rather than premeditated murder. Nevertheless, it showed one vividly the level to which people were reduced. And there was killing as well as dying there too.'

'Please tell me everything you can about it.' And Robert did.

They sat for a while, silent. ('My father,' Lise had said, 'says she was taken to a place called Tissendorf. That is what people whispered.') Robert supposed Anthony was worried at his predicament. Who wouldn't be? He'd been an ass. But Robert had come to perform an additional duty.

'Listen, old boy, I see a lot of papers in my job. I want to talk to you about your sister, Marcia. I've seen something that concerns her.'

Anthony's mind seemed elsewhere. 'Marcia? She's got home all right – went back about the time I came out again. Rather absurd, because I told my parents one of the reasons for pulling

429

strings to get back here was to find if I could help her! I've not seen her. I had a long letter. She had an extraordinary war! She ended up with the Americans. She says they were wonderful to her.'

'I dare say. She was processed quickly but of course it's not yet complete.'

'What do you mean "processed"? She was repatriated. She's at home now. At Bargate.'

'And subject to further enquiries. You see, Marcia wasn't interned.'

'I know. I know the whole story. She wrote it all to me, pages of it.' And, thought Anthony with a bitter pang, I had news of her before that. He remembered Anna, naked, lovely, lying in his arms in a dusty attic at Schloss Langenbach, talking of Marcia, stroking his hair, saying, 'I love your little sister. Everybody loves her.' Yes, he'd had news of Marcia all right. And in her letter Marcia had written one paragraph he carried everywhere, every hour, in his head,

'Ant, darling, I know Anna Langenbach's little boy is your son. Frido, beloved Frido, wrote this to me, before he was arrested. Anna had confided in him and he didn't want to be the only person to know in case something happened to him – and to Anna – and my God, it has, hasn't it? So I know that much, and I'm glad, darling Ant, because she was the most marvellous person I've ever known. But nobody else knows – unless Anna's told them. I didn't even tell Lise. But oh, darling, can anything be done to find out what's happened to them?'

'Marcia wrote it all fully, very interesting,' said Anthony steadily. He had received Marcia's letter on 1st June, two days after his visit to Arzfeld. Not that it would have made any difference. He added,

'She was lucky to get away from the Red Army, unraped, unmurdered. Very lucky. She was caught in the east you know, in the last days of the war.'

'Quite. Well, I'm glad she's safe, of course. But – and I'm sure you and your family fully understand this – she is, inevitably, being investigated.'

'Investigated? For what?'

Robert looked at him, his frown expressing a little irritation. Anthony was being obtuse.

430

'Anthony, people who – er, gave comfort, help, to the enemy in this war are liable to be tried for treason. Some will undoubtedly be hanged. You probably know that trials on a big scale are going on in France, of collaborators with the Germans. There've been a considerable number of executions already.'

To his annoyance, Anthony laughed.

'Are you suggesting a British judge is going to condemn Marcia to death for nursing? Is that the point we've reached?'

'Of course not. But her actions – her attitude – are bound to be investigated. It's not entirely plain sailing. I'd better tell you – in fact it's one reason I wanted to see you – I've seen a file on her. There's an immense amount of collation going on. We've got all the Gestapo records, they were most meticulous people, very thorough. Indexes and cross-references immaculate. Marcia was on a Gestapo index.'

'I would imagine so. She was, to them, an enemy alien. Presumably, she was only at liberty on sufferance. What's odd about that?'

'Marcia was interviewed by the Gestapo several times. At an interview in January this year, Anthony, she said – and it was recorded – "In my own way I have been able to serve the Reich." That's going to take a good deal of explaining, you know.'

'I hardly believe the note of a Gestapo interrogator will be preferred to my sister's explanations.' Anthony spoke coldly.

Robert sighed. He wished to help Marcia but it was discouraging that her own brother was so difficult to persuade of the need. He said,

'I think it's all going quite well. Probably best not to get your parents too worried if you mention it to them. I've seen a note on the file – "A frightened as well as a silly girl. I doubt if this should go to prosecution." So I *hope* Marcia's not in bad trouble. But she's got some explaining to do.'

Anthony looked at him thoughtfully. 'I understand, Robert. And I'm grateful for your visit – very. You've told me some pretty dreadful things. I hope you – we – don't get infected. I hope we don't catch the awful virus of supposing that because some evil things have been done, everybody we've fought against is evil.'

'Of course not.' Robert sounded impatient again.

'Or that only our enemies are capable of evil. You've got a sword of righteousness in your hand, it seems to me. It needs to be a double-edged sword, doesn't it?'

They said goodbye, affectionate and cool.

'I know perfectly well, Marvell,' said the General, 'that you had a bad time as a prisoner. It's for that reason you have been treated with a good deal of consideration. None of your experiences in the least excuse your behaviour. As I understand it, you admit the facts specified in this charge, and you understand that the charge is a serious one, and that the facts add up to a serious case of insubordination?'

'I do, sir.'

'On 30th May, you said to Brigadier Pringle, "You are an ignorant and stupid little man"?'

'I did.'

'Do you wish to tell me why?'

'Why I said it, sir?'

'Why you said it.'

'Because he is. Brigadier Pringle ordered me to be arrested when he observed me talking to a German. I tried to explain the circumstances to him. He appeared incapable of imagining that what I told him could be true, or, if true, that it could be relevant.'

'You are aware of the orders forbidding fraternization with the German population?'

'Certainly. But in this case the young lady in question, whom I knew well before the war, was my sister's closest friend. She escaped from the Russians, she reached her home, and it was important to me to learn something about my sister. I made a visit to her home when nearby –'

'It is alleged,' said the General, 'that you took a military vehicle on an unauthorized journey when you were *not* nearby: that you, unexpectedly I presume, found Brigadier Pringle's mission established in this house, Arzfeld: and that you did not report yourself, but sought out this young woman. It says here you were seen kissing her.'

'That is correct.'

432

'That you talked at length to her.'

'That is correct.'

'About your sister, you say.'

'Yes, sir.' But here Anthony was being less than exact.

'Lise, dear Lise,' Anthony had said, not trusting his voice, knowing that he had no right to hope, 'Lise, your cousin, Anna Langenbach. Does anybody know what has happened to her?' They were in the scullery off the kitchen at Arzfeld, used, by permission, for the family's needs. 'Your cousin, Anna,' Anthony said, 'she helped me, you know. Saved me. Does anybody know anything?'

He did not know how much Lise was aware of his own feelings where Anna was concerned. Lise seemed to be avoiding his eye. Their conversation was wholly unnatural. A British officer, member of an occupying Army, was talking (illegally) to a German girl about her (anti-Nazi?) cousin's fate. His lover, his beloved. He had first seen Lise, so pale, so exhausted-looking, outside the kitchen door, had embraced her spontaneously, taken her arm, steered her towards some sort of privacy. Anthony's driver looked on, bored, speculative.

Lise had said quietly, speaking as if embarrassed,

'They arrested her. My father says she was taken to a place called Tissendorf. Nobody mentioned it, of course, but that is what people whispered. We are sure she is dead.' She said it flatly, not looking at him. Then she started to cry, to cry for Anna, for herself, for Frido, for all of them. He put his arm around her, wishing his own tears could come as easily, give him relief. Lise said, gulping,

'They killed Frido, too.'

Anthony knew it. 'I was at Langenbach, Lise, hidden at Langenbach for weeks. During last winter. Anna –' He couldn't go on. Lise watched his face, drying her tears. She whispered,

'You have seen Marcia?'

'No. She's in England. I expect a letter.'

'Give her my love,' said Lise, 'if I'm allowed to send it under your rules.' He ignored the sharpness, the bitterness. He spoke shakily.

'Lise, what about Franzi – Anna's little boy?'

'Nobody knows. They took him away. You must understand

nobody knows anything yet in this country. There's no feeling, no communication. We're lifeless. Germany is a corpse.'

Then Brigadier Pringle had arrived.

The General considered the folder in front of him and turned a page.

'When Brigadier Pringle pointed out to you your breach of orders, you abused him.'

'No, sir. I explained – I began trying to explain – the circumstances. He then told me he didn't care a bugger – his words, sir – whether the girl knew my sister or anything about her. She was a German and I was to clear off immediately. A report would be made on me. I couldn't do that, sir. I had to find out from this young lady –'

'Fräulein von Arzfeld,' said the General, reading.

'Yes, sir. She had, or might have information which was of great importance to me. I'm afraid I lost my temper and told Brigadier Pringle what I thought of him and his attitude.'

'Additionally, Brigadier Pringle's statement runs:

'Captain Marvell also attempted to interfere with the apprehension of an officer of the Wehrmacht who was concealing his military status and living on the same premises.'

Is that true?'

'That, sir, refers to Colonel von Arzfeld. A civilian for many years but, I believe, a Colonel of the Reserve who may have been called up for a wartime job. By a coincidence he was being taken off just as I arrived at Arzfeld. I explained it was an absurd mistake to treat him as a member of the German Armed Forces. He left the German Army, wounded, after the First World War. I may say that his son was executed for playing a part in the plot to kill Hitler.'

'That has nothing to do with the matter,' said the General. 'That's for others to sift, do you understand? In the meantime, there are orders about all – *all* – ex-members of the German Army and it's not for you to start questioning them, still less interfering with your superior officer's execution of them. Did you know this von Arzfeld before, or something? You seem rather mixed up with these people.'

434

'Yes, sir,' said Anthony, 'I knew him. And a – a member of his family – saved my life – at great personal risk – when I escaped from prison camp.'

'That, too,' said the General, 'has little to do with the matter. Now, you'd better understand one or two things very clearly . . .'

'There's a great deal of work to do, Comrade Müller,' said the People's Police Major heavily, 'a great deal of work. There's a huge task of record building and collation. There's been an inevitable but undesirable break in continuity. Our work needs continuity.'

East of the Elbe river, in Prussia, Saxony, Thuringia, Silesia, Germans were being entrusted where possible with domestic security, as the Red Army concentrated its troops and as Communist Party authorities started to organize: organize reliable elements: organize for permanence: organize for a new and dominant role.

'Security information needs continuity. We all know that.'

'Exactly, Comrade,' said Müller respectfully.

'I'm glad you reported promptly for re-education. We're shorthanded. The people round here will need a lot of watching. It's going to take a long time to eradicate Fascist tendencies. We're going to need vigilance for years. And we lack experienced men, men who not only understand police work, political work, but who know this neighbourhood, know Saxony.'

'May I make a suggestion, Comrade Major?'

'You may.'

'I have an acquaintance who's anxious to return to this part of Germany. He's very experienced and reliable. He would have risen higher in the Service but he was suspect – you see he always felt uneasy, felt in his heart that we, the Party, represent the future.'

'Where is he now?'

'He's in the west. He's unhappy there. There's apparently a rumour they're going to persecute him. Probably Fascist elements are after him. The British are hand in glove with the

Fascists, of course. He'd like to work for us. He's a first-class man. His name's Egon Schwede.'

'Could we get him? There are procedures –'

'Yes,' said Müller confidently, 'I've been into it. I think we could.'

'You will,' said the General, 'be severely reprimanded. I am also recommending that you be posted to another part of the world immediately. You may regard yourself as treated with wholly exceptional leniency. Any further insolence, disobedience or nonsense of this or any other kind and you will have finally shown yourself as unfit to serve, and will undoubtedly be tried by Court Martial. Meanwhile, I don't care who helped you or didn't help you, I don't care what are your private views on the rights and wrongs of individual cases. You are here to enforce the regulations of an Army of occupation, not to question them.'

He nodded curtly. The Deputy Assistant Adjutant-General opened the office door. Anthony saluted, turned about and marched from the room.

PART VII

1958

Chapter 26

———————————◆———————————

'MY DARLING SISTER, it was a long time ago. A long, long time ago.'

Marcia's mind went back to Werner, to riding with Werner through sun-speckled woods, to finding herself breathless, naked on the green, green grass in Werner's arms. She found herself thinking of Werner quite often these days although she had some difficulty in exactly remembering his face. Lise had showed her a photograph last year, in 1957.

'You must have it.'

'No – that's not how I remember him! That looks a boy – charming, but a boy!'

Yet the photograph, Lise said, had been taken in the same summer that Marcia had first met him. Werner had been twenty-five, self-possessed, mature. Marcia had been nine-teen. 'Now I'm nearly forty,' she thought. 'The twenty-five year-olds are certainly boys to me now!'

She and Anthony were walking slowly through the garden at Bargate, back to the house, back to dinner. They were walking along the length of the herbaceous border: del-phiniums, peonies, cranebill, late irises, veronica, white daisies with huge orange centres – June was a glorious month and seven o'clock on a fine June evening England's most agreeable hour.

Hilda had died in 1953. Under sixty years old, worried about her husband's health, she herself had died suddenly, unexpectedly, leaving her family bereft and almost outraged. They depended upon her hugely. Before she died, she had done much to restore her beloved garden from the ravages of war.

John Marvell lived quietly in a house several sizes too big for him. To his continuing surprise his farms were infinitely more prosperous than before the war. It was, he told himself, natural, inevitable, but he could not entirely get used to it. Land, before 1939, had been a most unproductive investment. Farmers had been a depressed class, paying uneconomic rents to impecunious landowners. Farms had been hard, often impossible, to let. John Marvell had taken the management of the three largest farms into his own hands, installed an expert young manager and found himself making a remarkable amount of money. Land was expected to go ever higher in price.

John was sixty-eight years old, fitter than he had been for several years and very lonely. He had suffered from acute depression in the latter years of the war, despairing of ever seeing Anthony or Marcia again, wretched at the course of the world, exhausted, melancholic. He was quickly cured of this by his childrens' return, then shattered again by his wife's death. He could not get used to living without Hilda. John was lonely and Bargate was too large. At times he would exclaim –

'It's crazy, one old man living in a house this size!'

But he loved Bargate. He could not bear to contemplate leaving it, no longer hearing the familiar clank of particular doors shutting, sounds he would have recognized if recorded and played to him, blindfolded, anywhere in the world. He loathed the idea of sniffing no more the wood smoke from the logs burning in the inner hall, smelling no more the strong scent of the honeysuckle outside the libary window. He still, conscientiously, carried out his duties in the county. People said,

'John Marvell's well-named – he's really splendid. Such a charming person, takes on anything, never says "no". Sad for him in that great house on his own.' For Bargate, previously considered a country house of modest size, now had the name of an unmanageable place, as perceptions of scale shrank all over England.

John, despite his loneliness, was not ill-content. He was in the place he loved. His two children had survived the war, and visited him often. He was esteemed by his neighbours and unostentatiously prosperous. 'I'm a lucky man, undeservedly lucky,' he said humbly to himself, and he had a well-merited name for helping the less fortunate in a hundred unrecorded ways. Only one – or, he conceded inwardly, one and a half – flies could be found in John's ointment. The first was Anthony's failure to marry.

John would dearly have loved a daughter-in-law. He would have hoped for grandchildren, and Bargate, even in these reduced days, would have been a fine place for them to visit, perhaps even to grow up. Anthony loved Bargate, and John had made over to him most of the land, but he doubted if his son would ever live in the house. He certainly would not do so alone. Bargate needed children, women, voices, confusion. Still, it might happen. Anthony might yet settle down. He was only forty-two, after all: or was it forty-three?

John knew in his heart that it was not Anthony's age but his attitude which gave little hope in the matter of 'settling down'. Yet Anthony was successful. Called to the Bar late because of war service, he had soon given up practice and joined an industrial company, helped by contacts made (oddly enough) in Oflag XXXIII. Anthony had prospered. He lived comfortably in London. He came home most weekends. Sometimes John would say with forced jocularity –

'You ought to find a nice wife, old boy! You're leaving it a bit late! You ought to start a family here and move me out, you know! You can do that at any time, as I've always told you.'

Anthony would shake his head, smiling, 'Perhaps one day, Father.' Non-committal. A quiet, strong man now, with the spontaneous movement of youth seldom in evidence, his smile was as it always had been, but a great deal less frequent. John knew his son liked women. Sometimes he would bring friends for weekends and John longed for Hilda's shrewd eye, percipient comment. She would have said at once,

'There's nothing there. Nothing whatever between them. No spark.'

Or one day, perhaps –

'Yes, I think he's rather smitten.'

John, by contrast, felt unobservant, baffled. The same friends seldom came more than once or twice. Anthony always seemed happiest when the only other weekend guest was Marcia: and, of course, Robert.

For the other half-fly in the ointment was Robert Anderson.

441

Or, John confessed to himself with irritated fairness, it was Marcia's relationship with Robert, her husband.

Marcia had married Robert Anderson in 1946. He had been a staunch friend and supporter throughout that painful time when Marcia had been many times questioned over her activities during the war. Robert had become a frequent visitor to Bargate. He had, or so it seemed, re-established his close friendship with Anthony with whom he had shared so much. Robert was well-informed on the whole business – the whole wretched business, John said angrily to himself – of war-crimes, treason trials and so forth.

Marcia, anyway, had emerged unscathed from what John called 'all that nonsense'. And Robert, although he had played no direct part, had been a sensible adviser, strong, honourable, calm. Hilda and John had watched, with anxiety, how obviously he was falling in love with Marcia. Marcia herself had been uncommunicative for a long time after her return to England. She had, John said fairly, 'been through it'. Hilda did not dissent. About Robert, Hilda observed –

'He's head over heels in love with her. She's not in the least in love with him. She feels he's a rock – something strong and immovable. She thinks she needs that.'

'He's a handsome rock!'

'That has little to do with it. He's been a sort of saviour in her eyes. It might work. She might come to love him. I doubt it.'

John accepted Hilda's assessment. He always did. They were, therefore, unsure how much rejoicing was appropriate when Marcia announced that she intended to become Mrs Anderson 'quickly and quietly'. Hilda's doubts were not dispelled by Marcia's remarking,

'Darling Robert, I know him so well. We can say anything to each other. Such a relief. And he's clever, much cleverer than people think. Also such a relief. One doesn't have to say things twice.'

Like Anthony, Robert had been called to the Bar after leaving the Army and taking his final examinations. Unlike Anthony he had continued to practise, and with surprising speed built up a considerable reputation, principally in civil cases. He, too, was prosperous. When he married Marcia in 1946 he had been poor.

'They'll have to scrape,' Hilda said, unworried. She recognized Robert's determination. Half-Scots, half-American, there was a dourness in him, a hard taste for achievement. But now, with no Hilda to share his worries, John felt uneasy. Marcia was surprisingly thoughtful as far as John was concerned – an excellent, kind, daughter, he said to himself. But she seemed to talk little to Robert when they were both at Bargate. She seldom spoke of him when he wasn't there. Sometimes a light remark jarred on her father. He had said, not for the first time,

'I wonder when Anthony is going to find a nice girl and marry her?'

'Oh, he'll stay single if you ask me! Dear, sensible, Ant!'

Robert himself behaved with politeness towards John – a politeness tinged at times with a certain fretful impatience. Once John heard Robert say to Marcia,

'It can't go on! It's a lunatic way to live these days! One old man – he needs to spend thousands on the roof alone!'

John had been sitting, unobserved, in the darkness of a corner in the inner hall. Marcia had murmured something, cool, unsmiling. She had seen John. And John was unsurprised, unresentful that Robert found irritating his father-in-law's way of life and domestic economy. 'He's quite right,' he said to himself, equably. The farms appeared to keep bankruptcy comfortably at bay for the time being. Meanwhile, whatever lay between him and Robert it was not affection. He esteemed his son-in-law, as others did. But Marcia had no child.

'Yes, of course, it all started a long time ago, when we went to Arzfeld together. Now Ant, I want to talk to you seriously. We've got time.'

Anthony had arrived from London only twenty minutes before. Robert and Marcia had driven down an hour earlier. It was Friday. A tranquil, summer weekend stretched ahead of them.

'Robert's probably impatient –'

'Robert will be perfectly all right. I want to talk to you about Lise von Arzfeld.'

Anthony halted and looked at his sister hard.

'Are you going to start telling me, once again, that I ought to marry Lise von Arzfeld? Because I don't intend to.'

'No, it's far too late for that. Anyway, she'll never marry now. But it's not just Lise I want to talk about.'

Anthony believed it. From the moment of Marcia's return from Germany in 1945 she had been the one person he could talk to about Anna. Marcia had known and loved Anna. Marcia knew of his own love for Anna. Marcia certainly sympathized with him, even, it might be, understood his inability to feel anything profound for any other woman. But now the years had passed, now he did not choose to talk to Marcia about these things, and when she spoke of Lise the shadow of Anna, the shadow of their recollections of Anna lay between them, moved silently with them as they strolled in the evening through the gardens of Bargate.

Anthony knew, too, that Marcia was strongly affected by the fact that Franzi was his son. She had been faithful to her promise to guard this secret. She had never told Lise – she paid a visit to Lise at least every other year. It was inconceivable ('Why?' he would say to himself with a stab of concern: but it was so) that she should tell Robert. To all the world but Anthony and Marcia, Franzi was the son and heir of Kurt Langenbach, Luftwaffe hero, master-elect of broad lands in Lower Saxony.

Lise had taken Franzi to her heart when the confused, frightened little boy was recovered from horrible surroundings in 1945. Kaspar von Arzfeld was Anna's closest cousin. Old Frau Langenbach died that April, one month before the capitulation, died in confusion and discomfort, moved from her home to an institution, deprived of any she knew or loved. Cousin Lise had taken Franzi to Arzfeld, brought him up, looked after him, loved him. Marcia, therefore, had seen a good deal of Franzi. On several occasions she had reassured Anthony.

'He knows Kurt Langenbach, his hero-father, was the best aviator Germany ever produced. He knows his mother was murdered by wicked Nazis. He loves his cousin Lise. And his old cousin Kaspar.'

'I don't know what I want.'

444

'You must leave it like that now. One day, when he's old enough to take it, he deserves the truth. But not yet. After all, he's inheriting a good deal at Langenbach.'

Anthony had digested all this. He had little idea how the inheritance laws had been constituted by the newly-fledged Federal Republic.

'He'll inherit Arzfeld, too, one day, I suppose,' thought Anthony. 'Who else? Unless Lise leaves it to some charity.' And he thought what it might be like to have Franzi inheriting Bargate instead. He had paid two visits to Arzfeld, the last four years ago. Lise told Franzi to call him '"Uncle Anton", as a great friend of your mother'. Had she said it with a twist of meaning? He fancied not. Lise knew how he had been sheltered by Anna, knew – without resentment – that he had been the cause of Anna's condemnation, her death: but no more, he thought, no more.

Franzi had been uninterested, a strong, handsome fifteen-year-old when last sighted. Each Christmas Anthony sent him carefully chosen and expensive presents. He received letters of gratitude composed with equal care.

'It's not just Lise I want to talk about,' Marcia said. She looked at Anthony with determination. She felt this was not going to be easy.

'I've had a letter. Lise's coming to England. I could never get her to do so before.'

'Well, that's splendid.'

'I want to get her to Bargate.'

'Of course, she must come to Bargate. Father will enjoy it when he gets used to the idea. We'll talk to him this evening.'

'She's coming with Franzi.'

'I see,' said Anthony. He saw.

'Lise thinks it will be a good holiday, a new experience for Franzi, before he goes to Marburg University. He speaks good English. I saw him the year before last, as you know.'

'He always did speak passable English. Most impressive. German education.'

'He's seldom been away from Germany. He was seventeen

445

when I saw him last. He's charming – a little spoilt, but charming. And very good looking.'

'When, exactly, does Lise plan to come?'

'In July. I've got the dates. They're going to drive. Franzi will drive her most of the time, I expect. He's at the fast car stage.'

They strolled on in silence.

'It's the fortnight you said you plan to be here yourself,' said Marcia abruptly.

It couldn't be! Or, to be more exact, it could only be if Marcia had so fixed it. There was always summer work to be done on the farms and Anthony had, as usual, arranged leave from his employers to see to it personally. Marcia was watching him. She said,

'They won't get in the way. I've fixed Mrs Trapsell who'll come in every day. Franzi will enjoy helping, I'm sure. He's been brought up to farming, he'll be interested to see the difference between England and home.'

'I doubt it. Anyway, Lise will need to be looked after –'

'I'll look after Lise. I look forward to it. She'll spend some time in London with us. I'm afraid Robert won't like that –'

'Does he resent Lise?'

'Yes, she's a bit of my life where he doesn't belong. A bit of which he doesn't much approve.' Anthony moved the conversation back. He was by now used, with some sadness, to the fact that Marcia and Robert shared little. He felt a certain sense of responsibility. Yet he, himself, found Robert much less sympathetic than in the old days. He said,

'Franzi will want to see London. He won't want to sit here.'

'It will do Lise good to be without him for a bit. If he wants to go to London you can show him things.'

'Marcia, I have these weeks in July off because I'll be very busy at Bargate. I don't have to tell you that.'

'And I don't have to tell you,' said Marcia, 'that this is your son. That he's nineteen, and here's what I have to say to you, very important, I *think* it's the right time to tell him the truth: him and Lise, so she can help. There are such things as natural feelings aren't there?'

A long, pacing silence.

'Marcia, natural feelings or no, I don't think I can – tell

446

him. It would – it might – destroy his peace of mind, his sense of identity. For what? To get a little emotional satisfaction for myself? To clear the account?'

Marcia looked at him. 'Something about truth? Something about love?'

Anthony had never heard or seen her so serious. He was shaken. He said,

'My God, Marcia, I don't know how I'd do it.'

Marcia murmured,

'Well, you're the person who would best know how Anna would see it. I rather thought, darling Ant, that the two of you shared something worth acknowledging, perpetually. Isn't that right?'

They neared the house.

'Ant, you're trembling.' She was holding his arm tight. 'After all these years, fourteen years, you call it a long time but you're trembling!'

'Well, why not?' He pulled his arm away, his voice unsteady too. How could even Marcia understand what once had been?

'Why can't it thunder and get it over? It's ghastly weather, July at its worst. What an awful evening to have to dress up and go out to dinner.'

'They're your friends, not mine. And it would be just as sticky if we stayed here. Anyway, we'll probably get a good dinner. Anthony says the Prendergasts live very well.'

'I'm sure of it,' said Robert Anderson. 'Peter Prendergast would be a mean man if he didn't. He's made that company from nothing and he's made it huge. But I never relished acting for them. He's a shallow, disagreeable man, for all his business acumen. I've never envied Anthony working for him.'

Marcia recognized the evening as one which Robert had decided not to enjoy. There were many such. They had few serious rows. They simply liked different things and agreed on few subjects. Once she had found this stimulating.

'Robert contradicts me, flatly, it's splendid. He makes me think.'

Now she admitted dully to herself that their minds, their sensibilities were out of harmony. Marcia found it difficult to

447

make conversation without Robert regarding it, all too patently, as inaccurate, misguided, or merely silly. And Robert no doubt found his own remarks treated with similar irritation or incomprehension. People, too, they had difficulty in sharing. Even Anthony, once so close a friend as well as so beloved a brother, could be a subject for disagreement. They were not, she knew well, really disagreeing about other things, other people. Behind every chilly or barbed exchange they were, painfully, saying things, hurt, hurting things about themselves.

Any reference to Marcia's life in Germany, to her buried wartime years, brought irritated reactions from Robert which aroused exaggerated responses in her. She had only to mention Arzfeld, for instance,

'I suppose they shut their eyes to what was going on, like most people, quick to denounce it afterwards. Or they were just frightened –'

'No, it wasn't exactly like that.' Kaspar's grave, hopeless face. Frido's angry stories. No, it wasn't exactly like that.

'Of course it must have been pretty demoralizing to live in an atmosphere where an indiscreet word could land you in a camp or worse. We can't imagine it.' Robert was trying to be fair, judicious.

'You shouldn't exaggerate, Robert. It was wartime, after all. People in every country accept that you have to be discreet, loyal, keep your mouth shut, in wartime.'

'Not much like that here. But you wouldn't know.'

'Really? What about people who were interned? What about a woman I heard of who was sentenced to five years' penal servitude here for saying Hitler was a good leader, better than Churchill?'

'Well, it was a monstrous sentiment. Silly sentence, monstrous sentiment.'

Marcia sighed.

Marcia was just forty years old, and as she sat at her dressing table, touched her neck and ears with scent and looked into the glass, she knew that she was still lovely. Her skin was as it had been at twenty, her figure only a little fuller, her eyes as bright. 'But I laugh less,' she thought. 'I suppose that's middle age. And I *feel* much less. Maturity? Boredom?' They were well off now. Robert was successful. He worked exceptionally hard. Their flat, on the second floor of an Eaton Square house, was charming.

'Is Anthony going to be there, do you know?' Robert called from his dressing room. 'He introduced us to the Prendergasts in the first place. I've only had business dealings with the man.'

'No, Ant's taking several weeks off at Bargate.'

'Playing at farming for a little.'

Marcia ignored this. 'What exactly does Prendergast do? I mean, what does his company do?'

'My dear girl, he's only head of the biggest heavy engineering business this country possesses. He operates world-wide. He's England's answer to Krupp – or what Krupp once most lamentably was. Krupp, Schneider – Creusot, you name it!'

Marcia felt incapable of naming it.

'Surely you're ready? We ought to go.'

Mrs Peter Prendergast had indicated that it was a large party. She had also conveyed, without saying anything to which exception could be taken, that there would be dis-tinguished people present – a good deal more distinguished than the Robert Andersons. A postcard had requested – and assumed – their acceptance.

'What she means,' said Robert, frowning, as they drove the short distance to the Prendergast house, 'is that they'll all be richer. That is the only Prendergast yardstick of distinction.' He looked at Marcia and said, without any change to his serious, ironic tone,

'One thing's certain. You'll be the prettiest woman there. You look lovely, Marcia.' She smiled, politely rather than with tenderness or gratitude. She said,

'I rather liked Peter Prendergast the only time I met him. He's got animal attraction. Magnetism.' Marcia knew as she said it, that Robert would feel a critical implication behind the words, imputation that her husband lacked these qualities. She gave an inward sigh. Had the needle been deliberate? She hardly knew. A few minutes later they moved together into the Prendergasts' drawing room.

Marcia felt eyes turning to her, frankly admiring, or surrep-titious or lascivious. She knew she still had power. There were few faces she knew in the room, and those few met at impersonal occasions, attended as Robert's wife. She found herself talking without animation to a flabby-faced man who was determined to take her upper arm to emphasize a point. Two dry martinis ahead he would be difficult to shake clear. Dinner was announced with commendable speed. Sixteen at dinner she reckoned, looking quickly at the table as they moved towards it – sixteen, and everything done very well. Would it be fun to be Prendergast? Suddenly, and as disconcertingly often these days, Marcia felt lonely.

Peter Prendergast called out to them as they edged into the dining room. He had a commanding voice.

'We're one short to start with, I'm afraid. We've got a guest flying in from Frankfurt and I've just had word his flight was delayed by two hours. The brave chap's coming straight here. He'll be with us soon!'

Marcia heard a man murmur something and Prendergast answer, 'That's right! Over here for this two-day get-together!'

'They all know each other,' thought Marcia. 'They do business with each other, make money from each other, think in the same phrases as each other. And the women are as interested in it as their men. Except me.' She told herself not to be sanctimonious and turned to her neighbour on the right, a grey-haired, pale man, who eyed her with appreciation. He was, however, almost immediately captured by Mrs Prendergast on whose left he sat. To Marcia's left was an empty chair, the guest from Frankfurt presumably. She felt happy at the prospect of a little peace from pointless conversation, filling the air, passing the time. Prendergast food, probably excellent, would best be enjoyed without the distraction of a neighbour. Marcia felt unslighted, content. Long might it continue. Long might Herr Rumpelmayer or whoever it was, be delayed in the endless passages of London Airport.

Marcia finished her pâté de foie gras with enjoyment. Trying to catch Robert's eye, she succeeded. He flashed at her a smile so spontaneous and so young that the clouds of sad years parted a little and she smiled back. It hadn't worked – but it was sad it hadn't worked.

Then there was a disturbance behind her chair, Prendergast up from his seat, moving about, talking rather loudly. The table shone, polished mahogany reflecting silver, glass, candles, faces rosy, unnaturally charming in the candlelight. Behind the row of diners was darkness. Marcia was aware of the empty chair beside her pulled out, then filled by a stranger.

Peter Prendergast's voice said, 'Bless you for arriving, despite the difficulties. Introductions later. We'll have a long talk after dinner. This is Mrs –' Marcia heard him hesitate, 'Mrs Anderson. Mrs Anderson, Count Toni Rudberg.'

Ten long minutes went by, a sick sensation in Marcia's stomach. She drank some wine and felt worse. As Toni sat down, Marcia's grey neighbour on the other side claimed her attention. She heard Toni exchanging agreeable nothings about the vagaries of air travel with the lady on his left. A little more wine. Better. Was nobody talking? The room seemed silent.

Marcia heard Toni say, softly, 'Mrs Anderson, did I hear?'

'Yes, Count Rudberg. Why are you alive? Nobody told me.'

'I did not feel I had the right to notify people widely. Not until I again got accustomed to life. I returned from the dead. In 1955. Adenauer did a deal with Stalin and got us survivors home. We had no expectations, no hopes, no skills. Germany was recovering. They told us we'd missed the worst.'

'Nothing, I imagine, to what you'd had.'

'Who can compare these things? Marcia, you again! Do you live in London?'

'Let's talk about what you're doing now, and, if you can bear it, what happened to you then. Not about me.'

Marcia hoped she looked calm, interested, perhaps entertained. Inwardly she was shattered. She looked at Toni, carefully not meeting his eyes, inspecting him, a casual, passing glance. His hair was white. She remembered that he was born in 1909 and that his birthday was in the summer. Apart from the hair, he looked extraordinarily unchanged. There were lines on the brown face, lines at the corner of the mouth, an expression of seriousness. She guessed that he often wore spectacles now. There was less easy assurance, perhaps. But he was amazing! She heard herself saying – softly –

'You were twelve years there? Twelve years a prisoner?'

'Just under thirteen. The first eight in Solitary, as I was in a special category. General Staff.'

451

'*Eight years in solitary confinement!* Toni! Did they do that to everyone like you?'

'No. Some were shot, of course. Some were persuaded to join various curious organizations, to produce pro-Soviet propaganda for German soldiers. They had rather comfortable lives in consequence. Privileged.'

'Did you feel tempted?'

'To be more comfortable, to save my life, my health, my sanity – yes, of course. But they were opportunists – or simpletons. I knew that ordinary German soldiers would despise them. With reason.'

'What happened to people like that?' He shrugged his shoulders. Across the table Marcia heard a man call out to her right-hand neighbour some fierce opinions about General de Gaulle who had, the previous month, been voted into office in France. She helped herself to a dish. Toni said without great interest,

'Some are in positions of authority in the East. They've seen the Communist light. Even a few rigorously educated Prussian noblemen have seen the Communist light, been converted, become enthusiasts. Moral seriousness is a dreadful thing.'

This was more like the old Toni.

'And what do *you* do, now, Toni?' Something strange had been teasing her and she identified it. 'Toni! Your English! It's perfect! It – it never used to be.'

He laughed. 'I've worked very hard. You see I'm a business man now. I have to go to and from America all the time. One can't do business in Britain or America except in English and I've learned and learned. Do I talk American?'

'A little. Nicely.'

'And now I'm going to be coming and going to England all the time. This is my fourth visit. But they've only been for a few days each. I like your country very much!'

'How did you get your job, Toni?'

'Through a man I was with in prison.'

'Like Anthony!'

'Anthony?'

'My brother. He was a prisoner in Germany.'

'Ah!' Toni did some digesting and remembering. Had there not been a story? He looked full at Marcia.

452

'Marcia, I always wondered on my short visits where you were, whether you survived the war, what had happened. I longed to discover but I feared as well. So I did nothing. Now I meet you – in a tycoon's house. Do you say "tycoon" here?'

'We certainly do.'

'Is your husband a tycoon?'

'No, he's a very clever lawyer. That's him, opposite. He's done business for our host at times. He's an intelligent and charming man.'

'I'm sure of it. Have you now any contact with the von Arzfeld family?'

'I see Lise at least every other year. She's coming over here later this month. How long will you be in England?'

'This time only three days. I shall be coming here regularly after next month. In September I will be here. Perhaps for quite a long time. May I telephone?'

'In September?'

'No, Marcia, not in September. Tomorrow. Or the next day. Or the day after.'

'I'd like you to meet Robert. My husband.'

'Of course. Now I know your name I can discover your address, your telephone number. You live in London? There is a book.'

Marcia nodded.

'There are a lot of people called R. Anderson in London, Toni!'

'I will telephone them all.'

'We should love to see you,' said Marcia primly, pretending to look away. 'And after dinner I must bring you and Robert together. Have you a wife?'

'No wife.'

She looked full at him.

Toni said quietly, 'Oh Marcia! What a different world it was when the wind separated us, when great gusts of it blew us apart!'

Marcia said, also very quietly, 'A different world. A terrible world. I can't look back at some of it without horror. But oh, Toni! I felt alive!'

Toni nodded, still looking at her, holding her eyes, very grave.

453

Marcia murmured,'Don't telephone, Toni. Please. Get in touch if you're here in September.'

'You are sometimes free at lunchtime?'

'I am always free at lunchtime.'

Marcia made a strong, physical effort and turned to her neglected neighbour on the other side.

'I didn't meet that German who came in late and sat next to you. He's very thick with Peter Prendergast.'

'He's an Austrian. His name's Toni Rudberg. I knew him long ago.'

'You looked as if you found plenty to talk about.'

'Well, there were people we both knew and so forth –'

'He looked a bit smooth.'

'He was thirteen years a prisoner of war in Russia. If that leaves a man smooth I would think it quite an achievement.'

'Hmm! I suppose you knew him quite well?'

'Yes, he's a sort of cousin of the von Arzfelds, you see. A family connection of some kind, anyway.'

'Something from your long-buried past, my dear.'

'Yes. Something from my past. My long-ago, deep-buried past.'

Chapter 27

———◆———

'I'VE MANAGED to drag you round the farms but you've spent half the week going to London in that car of yours – London, London, London! In July! It's absurd – hot, crowded, sticky and absurd!'

'A great city, Uncle Anton! I couldn't come for just three weeks to England and not see something of London.'

'Well, today you can have a change. I'll show you some of the country, something of Sussex.'

Lise and Franzi had been in England for two weeks. They had arrived at Bargate, Franzi at the wheel of a smart Mercedes, an expensive car for a nineteen-year-old, Anthony had observed without enthusiasm. From the first, Franzi had impressed the Marvell household and everyone else with his good looks, his excellent manners and his unforced charm. When they had first arrived – Anthony had made sure that he was down from London, Marcia was due at the weekend – Franzi had at first hovered in the background while Lise, a little embarrassed, hesitant, came to kiss Anthony, to greet John. Then Franzi had moved forward and bowed, his formality belied by merry, blue eyes full of intelligence and laughter: Anna's eyes.

John Marvell, as forecast, had taken the visit happily from the first. He had been mildly curious to meet Lise, companion of Marcia's extraordinary, ambivalent war years, referred to now so seldom. He liked her immediately. She looked older than he expected, much older than Marcia, he thought, although he knew they were about the same age. Lise's fair hair was bound back with severity at the nape of her neck. She had a reflective, almost nun-like look about her, and when her shyness was past, her gentle composure made the same restrained impression. She might have looked different to his eyes, John thought, had he known her as a girl, known her and thus seen her as Marcia and no doubt Anthony saw her.

But Lise was an easy, charming guest and, truth to tell, John found a little new company stimulating.

Marcia had descended on Bargate on their first weekend, and on the Monday had carried Lise to London 'for a few days'.

'We'll have a lovely time,' Marcia said. 'Robert's had to go to Belfast, on some case. You can leave Franzi here. We'll be alone together, quite like old times. We'll go sightseeing! And the flat's cool!'

Franzi was very tall. Anthony had prepared himself for the transition from boyhood but still received a shock. He had not seen Franzi for four years. The boy was strikingly, agonizingly, Anna's son. He had that particularly direct, concentrated look that brought Anna herself into the room in a way to stop the breath. He had, Anthony recognized at once, a most enjoyable sense of humour. He radiated health and vigour, and his smile was enchanting. At the first opportunity Anthony drew Lise aside.

'Franzi does you great credit!'

He said it with mixed feelings. It would be delightful, even if surreptitiously, to take a jot of credit for such a son. His own nervous unease at being confronted, cornered, had entirely dissolved in the warmth of Franzi's personality. He found himself chuckling with pleasure at Franzi's remarks, looking forward to his first appearance at breakfast, to his coming into a room.

And Franzi, too, seemed to find Anthony's company agreeable. He had not, as Anthony gibed, been 'dragged' round the farms but had shown interest and enthusiasm when Anthony told him about the systems at Bargate. Anthony had pretended to grumble at Franzi's determination to see London –

'And you a countryman!'

But at such moments he recognized in himself, behind the badinage, a cold touch of unhappiness, of deprivation. For some hours he was going to miss Franzi. Franzi, however, returned from his jaunts to the metropolis in fine fettle. He had made English friends skiing in the previous winter and had renewed the acquaintance. He had apparently found open hospitality. The Wrench family, with offspring of Franzi's age, lived in London. Julius Wrench's name was well-known in the City. Anthony saw that the world of high-powered business with which Wrench was involved held fascination for Franzi. Franzi was enchanted by the idea of America. He had little in common with the uncertain, sometimes idealistic, often tortured young men of Anthony's own generation – Frido von Arzfeld, Robert Anderson, even Anthony himself.

Anthony told himself that Franzi 'had too much money for a young man'. But he showed none of the ostentation of a self-consciously rich young man. He seemed to have nothing of a playboy in the making. Nevertheless – 'He takes things for granted,' Anthony thought, trying to find Franzi flawed, as if to dim the splendour of his son and thus protect himself from its radiation. And there was that Mercedes! Anthony spoke casually to Lise,

'Franzi seems very keen on his University future. I imagine he'll be much more financially secure than most of his contemporaries there. That can create problems.'

'Franzi is very sensible, very serious. I don't think he will become lazy just because he has some money.'

'No, I don't expect so – but it can happen.'

Lise clearly did not regard the risk as high. She said, 'My father is very fond of Franzi. He wants Arzfeld to go to him one day.'

'I see. I suppose Franzi has also inherited from his grandfather Langenbach?'

Anthony disliked saying it. But Lise had already spoken of Anna to him, in discussing Franzi. He himself found it difficult to mention her name, to keep his voice steady, even after all these years.

'Yes, that is so. But most things at Langenbach have been sold you know. It was difficult. There were all sorts of legal problems. The Nazis, in the last months of the war, started a process to confiscate the estate.'

'Why? Because of Anna? It wasn't hers – or was it?'

'It was not clear.'

Did he fancy it, or was Lise a little embarrassed. She went on, 'Anyway, that hadn't got far, fortunately. But there have been a lot of complications on the Langenbach side. Schloss Langenbach is now a private school, you know, a school for children who are, what do you say, backward?'

457

And the attics? The narrow stair on which the longed-for footfall could only be Anna's? For what were they now used?

'Most things there are sold. Franzi will never live at Langenbach,' said Lise. 'It has given him some money. Not to use all by himself yet, of course.'

'We say – "In Trust".'

'Yes. But you are right, for a young man he has a good deal. And Arzfeld one day, perhaps, if such places can be kept still by a family. I think that's difficult everywhere.'

'Very difficult.'

Anthony was thinking of Franzi's inheritance. He knew all about his childhood, about a little boy dragged from his mother, beaten and starved. The wheel had certainly come full circle. Hesitantly he asked,

'Does Franzi remember his mother?'

'Certainly. You must speak to him of her. He loves to hear others talk of her.'

Lise said this so easily that Anthony could not believe she thought the subject delicate. He felt the need to be sure. He said – carefully – 'He's like his mother. Very von Arzfeld, you know. I can see it. I expect your father can.'

'Yes,' said Lise seriously. 'I think so too. Sometimes I think I see a little Langenbach in him. But not so often. Not nearly so often.'

Marcia had looked thoughtfully at Anthony as soon as they found themselves together after her arrival.

'How are you doing, Ant?'

She used the inelegant, once-irritating pet name much less now. He liked it.

'He's a charming boy.'

'And you're going to tell him, aren't you?'

'Marcia, I long to, in many ways. But is it really right? Isn't it, perhaps, self-indulgent, on my part?'

'I'm interested that you feel it might be. You weren't keen on the idea when last we talked.'

'I'm keen on it now.'

'Well, as you know, I think you should. And I'll tell Lise. Then she can help cope with him. She's pretty sensible, you know. She's much tougher than she looks. I'll tell her when we're in London together, if you like. I'd better wait until I hear from you that you've had your heart-to-heart with Franzi.'

'That would be best,' said Anthony, a sick yet excited sensation predominant. 'Yes, that would be best.'

'I'll cope with Lise, she'll be all right. Give me time. She's devoted to the boy, she's bound to feel deeply concerned, confused. Give me time.'

'Don't you think that Lise may have always suspected something?'

'No, I don't. And I'd know. Ant, I realize it's going to be a hard task telling him. But I think it's right. Be gentle. Be humble.'

'How could one be otherwise?'

'And be loving.'

'Yes,' said Anthony. He suddenly found a constriction in his throat. 'Yes, that too.'

And Marcia carried Lise off. With only mild curiosity Anthony heard Marcia say as they got into the car, 'A *very* odd thing happened the other day, Lise, love. You'll never guess who turned up –'

He turned away. They shared many memories, those two. He had his own.

'I'll show you some of Sussex,' said Anthony. It was a hot day.

'Can we go in my car, Uncle Anton? You've not been in it yet!'

'We'll go by lanes, small roads. You'll have to drive slowly and you'll hate every minute of it. You'll be itching for an *autobahn*, yearning for speed!'

'I expect so, Uncle Anton!'

'It's extraordinary,' thought Anthony, 'how easy I feel with him, how I love his company, how I have known him, in my heart, for ever.' He looked sideways at Franzi as they drove towards the white wooden gates opening from Bargate drive on to the narrow lane which led to the Flintdown road. 'Yes,' Anthony thought, 'I know him all right.' And the slender hand resting on the steering wheel was Anna's hand. 'Damn it, it's the sheer *love* in the boy,' thought Anthony. 'He's Anna's son, every inch of him.'

'And mine. And mine.'

'I'll open the gate.'

'No, I know it, I'll do it, Uncle Anton.' Franzi was already out of the driving seat, coping with the awkward gate catch, jumping in again, driving on.

'Hang on, we must shut it behind us. Cattle. Stop again. That's why it was more sensible to let your passenger do it.'

'Sorry, Uncle Anton. German officiousness!'

'We're making a cattle grid there, this autumn. And keep in to the left of the road, for God's sake!'

Anthony loved the excuse to chide, to mock, to exercise, in appearance, a little affectionate tutelage. They drove southward in companionable silence towards the line of the Downs. For twenty minutes Anthony uttered nothing but a few crisp directions.

'When you top the next rise you'll see the Channel. It's a wonderful viewpoint.'

They stopped and got out of the car, strolling for a little, sitting while Anthony pointed out landmarks. There was everywhere an enormous peace.

'Your country is very beautiful, Uncle Anton.'

'Yes, it is, isn't it.'

'I like to practise my English. But you still speak beautiful German, Uncle Anton, I like hearing it. Which shall we talk?'

'Let's talk both, just as we find it most easy, depending on what we want to say.'

When they got back into the car there was suddenly something awkward between them, as if each recognized that there had to be a change of style in their conversation, that it had to become more personal. The atmosphere had changed and Anthony knew that Franzi felt it just as he did, though nothing had been said. Where there had been ease now there was tension. They drove slowly westward, keeping to small roads, towards the border of West Sussex. Anthony felt himself impelled by some force outside himself when he heard his own voice saying –

'How well do you remember your mother, Franzi?'

'Better than people might suppose. I was five years old, you know, when they – took her away. Took me away.'

'I know. I know what happened.'

'It was the most terrible thing. I don't think anything that happens in life can be as terrible as that.'

He talked for a little, without strain. Anthony discovered that they had never told Franzi much about Anna's death, insofar as details were known. The boy was anxious to learn. Hints and guesses can fester more than the most brutal facts. He listened with gratitude while Anthony, painfully, carefully, told him all he knew.

'They told you that I saw a good deal of your mother at that time? That she hid me, an escaped enemy prisoner of war, at Langenbach, nursed me, saved my life?'

'Yes, Cousin Lise told me the story. It's amazing. I can never understand it fully. I mean, it's a romantic story, Uncle Anton, but it must have seemed, even to my mother, an extraordinary thing to do. I know she hated the Nazis and so forth, but after all there was a war and you were, were –'

'An enemy. Yes.'

'I can see even Cousin Kaspar von Arzfeld finds it hard to understand. And he loved my mother. And nobody could hate the Nazis more than him. They killed his son.'

'Certainly. But I'm sure he finds it hard to accept, as you say. It was – what your mother did was – the action of a very brave, remarkable woman, you see. A person whose moral sense was much higher than –'

Anthony could not find the right words. It would be misleading to say 'than patriotism'. Anna's patriotism was profound.

'Than that of other people,' Franzi supplied.

One could settle for that.

'I suppose war turns everybody's moral ideas a bit upside down, Uncle.'

'There's an English saying "All's fair in love and war". It's not true. Cruelty and injustice remain cruelty and injustice whether or not you're fighting for your life, or however strong your passions. Decency and mercy are noble whatever flag you're fighting under.'

'Human qualities more important than causes.'

'Causes matter too, Franzi. Causes matter too.'

They started speaking of Frido. Franzi knew the story well.

'Cousin Lise adored her brother.'

'So did everybody, rightly so. I'm glad to have the chance

461

to tell you how he looked to me, a comparative stranger, an enemy as it turned out.'

He talked, finding himself remembering with greater vividness all the time. Franzi nodded, fascinated, his slender fingers moving as his hand rested on the steering wheel, as if he were fingering a clarinet.

'The fact that I knew some of your people so – so well – helped me through what I think of as the first gateway to wisdom.'

'Which is –?'

Anthony tried to speak casually, to avoid sententiousness.

'To put oneself in another's place. To ask "How would I have behaved?" To avoid being self-righteous, sanctimonious, *scheinheilig*. To condemn evil, but to remember that the evil-doers are themselves what I suppose religious people would call the wandering, alienated children of God.'

He said it as lightly as he could. He didn't know if Franzi believed in God.

'Not easy, Uncle Anton.'

'Not easy at all. The Nazi period was an aberration.'

Franzi said, 'Germans could be found to do these things. I have read books, Uncle Anton, some people say they're exaggerated but I don't think so, books by survivors. Of the camps. The stories – not only the mass murders, but the obscenities, the humiliations, the things human beings were made to do so that their masters could laugh!' He paused, rather breathless, remembering.

'Horrible, Franzi, horrible, I know. And everywhere, regrettably, people can be found to whom tasks of the utmost beastliness become matters of routine, reward, promotion. Sensibilities get dulled quickly, Franzi, and some people start with precious few. And don't forget that more camp guards than not were non-German – Poles, Russians, Latvians, and so forth. No race has a monopoly of brutality, Franzi.'

After a little Anthony said, 'People are capable of all manner of disgusting behaviour when they are taught to regard other human beings as mere objects.'

'And the Jews, for instance, were objects.'

'Yes – threatening, malevolent objects for whom no humiliation could be too extreme, no policy too inhuman – because, you see, they were less than human, outside the ordinary limits. Words didn't apply any more.'

He knew that he had to turn back from the relief afforded by history, world politics, back even from philosophy and morality, painfully back to themselves, to Anthony and Franzi. After a little he said,

'Your mother's action in saving me led to her arrest and her death, Franzi. You would have the right to hate me for that.'

Franzi's slim hands were tighter on the wheel than they had been. He said,

'Yes, I realize that. But I don't hate you, Uncle Anton. I don't quite understand it, but I'm sure my mother did what she felt she had to do. That she could do no other.'

'What do you remember most about her? Describe it to me.'

'Something gentle, very strong at the same time. Perhaps all mothers are like that.'

'No, not all. Go on.'

'When I was unhappy, upset about something, frightened, she only had to speak a word, touch me once, let me feel the skin of her hand against my cheek. Very soft, dry, cool –'

'Yes,' said Anthony. 'Soft. Dry. Cool. Yes.'

'Then I was peaceful. It was like being blessed.'

'Go on.'

Franzi seemed to have run out of recollections. Anthony said,

'Her voice? What do you remember about her voice?' Franzi nodded, eyes on the Sussex road, absorbed.

'Her voice. Always seeming about to smile. But that's wrong, isn't it? A voice laughs, it doesn't smile.'

'No, your mother's voice smiled, you put it quite right.'

'And everything – everything expressed very definitely. Strongly – kindly but strongly. I can't think of her voice saying anything boring, or stupid, or cruel.'

'Never. Franzi, your memory is absolutely correct. Can you remember what she looked like?'

'A pale face. Brown hair. Tall – but I suppose everyone seemed tall to me. She used to take my hands and I would climb up her with my feet, as if she were a tree. I loved looking at her face. Something was always happening to it. It was never still. Like the voice – never dull. Alive. Am I right?'

463

'Entirely right. Franzi, did your cousin Lise tell you that I – I and my sister Marcia, whom you know so well – first met your mother before the war began? We visited Arzfeld, you see.'

'And my mother was there?'

'No – we broke down in a car, Marcia wasn't there. It was near Langenbach. Your mother rescued us. She always rescued people. And she drove us back to Arzfeld. Then I – I met her in London, when she used to visit her grandmother. As you know, you've got English blood, an English great-grand-mother.'

Anthony tried to keep his voice conversational, as if at the level of social reminiscence. It was, he knew with self-contempt, an effort both absurd and unsuccessful. Franzi, however, seemed preoccupied with something else. He was frowning slightly. The afternoon was momentarily less brilliant. A small black cloud had drifted across from France to mask the sun. Still cowardly, Anthony felt the need to lighten the atmosphere, to remind them both of banality, weather, routes, traffic, people.

'Next week these roads will be much more crowded. They have a big race meeting, horse racing – at a beautiful place near here, called Goodwood. At the end of July.'

They drove on in silence for a while. Franzi said ruminatively,

'So you first met my mother before the war, at Langenbach, Uncle Anton! Then you met my father?'

'No,' said Anthony. 'He was away. In Spain. Your grand-parents, the Langenbachs were there, of course.'

Suddenly he knew, with complete assurance, that he loved Franzi, loved him as he had only once felt love for anybody, loved him deeply, proudly, painfully. It was at the same time natural and profoundly disturbing. The realization made him catch his breath. 'Something about love!' Marcia had said. Yes, indeed, a thousand times! It seemed as if the small cold lump in the heart which had been there so long, an irremovable part of him, was there no longer and he felt warm, transformed. He looked at Franzi. Yes, he thought, illuminated, astonished, I love him. He is my son, and I thank God for him and I love him with all my heart. It is right that he is with me now. It is right that he should hear me.

Franzi looked straight ahead, absorbed, still frowning a little. Then he turned his head, looked full into Anthony's eyes for a second, and smiled.

'Uncle –'

'For God's sake – *Get over to the left!*'

Franzi jerked the wheel and wrenched the car over to the left. Absence of traffic on the small country lane had led him momentarily to forget where he should be holding the car. It was, however, uncertain that he could have averted the accident, for the heavy, square, blue van belonging to an electrical components company was driving too fast down the crown of the narrow lane towards them, swinging too fast and too wide round the narrowing bend, bound for collision. As it was, the van caught the right-hand passenger side of the Mercedes like a sharp, merciless, slicing knife.

The ambulance took only twenty minutes to come. The spot was remote, no telephone near, the van driver and Franzi both shattered but without serious physical injury. A considerate householder, home three hundred yards away, heard the crash, drove to the scene, raced back, telephoned. By then, however, Anthony was dead.

Chapter 28

———————◆———————

'I DID NOT BELIEVE you would come. I did not dare hope you would come.'

He spoke the words softly. He had been sitting at the table for twenty minutes. He had posted the note in good time. She must have received it.

> 'I shall be at "L'Alouette" restaurant in Walton St from a quarter to one next Thursday, 9th September. I shall live only in the hope that you will lunch with me there.'

He wished to give her no difficulty or embarrassment about reply. With a humility which he had never evinced in earlier days he had simply made himself available, left the invitation like a sigh, a whisper in her ears, resigned to being taken for granted, spurned, or simply ignored. It had not been difficult to find her address. 'I shall live only in the hope that you will lunch with me there.' And for twenty minutes, feeling like a boy of eighteen, who waits nervous, sick at heart, thinking it impossible a woman can take him seriously, he sat in the restaurant called 'L'Alouette'. One o'clock struck on the church tower in Pont St.

There was another movement at the swing doors. It was a small place. Every time the doors opened a slight draught, not unpleasant, brushed the tables. From his position at the far end of the narrow room he could see the street doors open, shut again. It happened every thirty seconds from the moment of his settling at this table. Every thirty seconds another sickening, deadening disappointment.

'An aperitif, sir?'

'I'll wait. My guest will be here soon.'

Badgered by the waiter again, needing distraction, he ordered a drink at one o'clock.

'My guest seems to be a bit late. I'd like a whisky.'

466

'A scotch, sir? With soda water?'

'With nothing.

He waited what seemed an age but was in fact one minute for the whisky, sipped it without taste or pleasure. He saw his reflection in the clear, brown liquid as he put the glass down. 'Since when has whisky been reflective, Narcissus?' – feeling an idiot, though nobody could have detected his thoughts, he had momentarily ignored the fact that the restaurant table mat was a circle of polished metal and had shown him his face through the whisky at the base of the glass. 'Not much to lunch with!' He had been surprised to see how distraught he had looked in that twisted reflection. The swing doors again, an infuriating sound, the draught of air, the renewal of tension. He carefully refrained from looking up. He'd order a solitary lunch and eat it, nauseated by it; he'd order it at one-fifteen.

'Sorry I'm a bit late.'

He could not look up at first, his heart was thumping so hard he needed a second for self-collection. There was no doubt of it. He rose stiffly to his feet. She was wearing a light grey dress, bare arms, a red belt, red handbag. Eyes as he remembered, mouth as he remembered. Voice a little deeper than he remembered, although it had always been deep, full-throated.

'I did not believe you would come.'

'Well, I don't suppose I should have, should I?' said Marcia. 'But here I am.'

'I was distressed to hear about your brother. Truly distressed.'

It had taken about ten minutes to cover the preliminaries, set up transmission posts, establish communication. Ten minutes, with the heart of each beating fast.

'It's been ghastly. We were very close.'

'I know that.'

'Poor, darling old Ant,' she blinked back tears. 'Of course, you know he was once in love with Anna Langenbach? With the woman you wanted to marry, Toni!'

Toni looked at his plate, unsmiling, and then looked up, looked Marcia full in the face.

467

'Yes, I did want that. It was a piece of selfish foolishness. I thought you and I had no future.'

'Well, I suppose we didn't really. And Anna had a pretty good future!'

'Everything seemed possible. She was attractive, we got on. And yes, of course I was influenced by the fact that she was a woman – let's say a woman of property. Does one say that?'

'It has a nice, old-fashioned ring. And you were a nice, old-fashioned boy, weren't you!'

Toni didn't smile.

'For two reasons it was criminal folly. First, because I didn't in the least love her, delightful, lovely woman though she was. Second because I loved you.'

Marcia nibbled at a *Noisette d'agneau* with little appetite. Toni continued, almost inaudibly –

'Yes, I loved you. But I didn't reckon, at the time, that I loved you so much that nothing else could ever be a substitute for it. I thought I might – how would you put it? – get you out of my system. By the means of an elegant, charming, desirable alternative.'

'And couldn't you?'

'You know I couldn't.'

'I minded, Toni.'

He sighed.

'Anna soon made me stop my nonsense as far as she was concerned. She would never have cared a rap for me. And at heart, of course, I felt nothing, nothing of any real depth for her. I just wanted a wife – a decorative, desirable, prosperous wife. With you it was different.'

'And so?'

'And so, you see, you stayed in my system. For long, long years of solitude, fear, hunger, despair, you stayed in my system. I don't like that expression. Is it correct?'

'I'm not sure it is, Toni, dear. One gets someone out of one's system, but, odd though it seems, I'm not sure one gets someone in.'

'So what's the right expression?'

Marcia ignored this. Remembering, cloudy-eyed, she said –

'You said to me, "We should thank God for what we've had together and not expect anything from the future.' You were pushing me away, Toni. I was an embarrassment. And you wanted to pursue Anna unembarrassed.'

'Marcia –'

'Didn't you, Toni?'

Toni gazed at her with a steadiness very different from the dancing vivacity which his eyes had held in the old days when they encountered the eyes of a woman.

'Yes. You are right.'

Marcia smiled gratefully.

'I'm *so* glad to hear you say that, Toni.'

He was puzzled. 'How – glad?'

'Because, you see, it's honest. There's no love without honesty, Toni. To feel something *really*, is so burning, so important that it just can't exist with lies or double talk. One can't use that word, love, except with total, total –'

'Surrender,' suggested Toni, almost inaudibly. Astonishingly, he found tears were pricking at his eyelids.

'Well, sincerity, anyway. At least I can't. But not everybody's capable of it. Perhaps they're happier if they aren't.'

Toni was silent.

'It hurt never to hear from you, Toni, to have Kaspar von Arzfeld read aloud from a letter to him – and never a word to me. To hear you mentioned – Oh Toni! I can feel it still! Of course I knew you had made the break. But I can feel it still.'

Toni bowed his head.

Marcia said – 'Anthony. Anna Langenbach.'

'Ah, yes. I have heard the stories. She protected him, an escaped prisoner of war. That was very dangerous and she paid for it, poor, beautiful Anna. They were lovers, I suppose?'

'Yes, they were.'

'I hope he was worthy of her, I expect he was, your poor brother. If he was like you he must have been worthy of her.'

'I don't know about that. But I know they loved each other deeply. It's an extraordinary story. Anthony escaped from a Prisoner of War Camp with Robert. With my husband.'

'Robert. Your husband.'

'Did I tell you, when we met in July, how Ant got stranded and how Robert got back to England?'

'No. And I do not in the least wish to hear about it.'

Marcia avoided his eye.

469

'How long are you in England this time, Toni?'

'That depends. Marcia, do you love your husband?'

She looked at him. He looked at her seriously, sternly, without affectation. It was a different face from that she remembered. She was suddenly aware of nobody else in the room. There appeared to be silence all around them, empty tables, the rest of the world withdrawn to a respectful distance having for the moment no part to play. There was just Toni, the other side of his untasted *Escalope de veau Marsala*, his eyes holding hers. Marcia found that both her hands were on the table cloth and were touching both of his.

'Oh Toni,' said Marcia, 'no, I don't. Not the least little bit.'

'Is it possible, Toni, that a feeling like this can last between two people who don't see each other for fifteen years? It's a dream isn't it?

'Yes, it is possible. No, it is not a dream. Have I shocked you with the suddenness of this? I've been thinking of it, of you, every hour since we met in July, you know.'

'No. No shock.'

'You understand that I mean it – more than anything, ever?'

'Yes. I think I do. I think I believe you. I will let you have my answer tomorrow. I won't keep you waiting. I won't leave you in doubt.'

'I am forty-nine, Marcia. And you know what happened to thirteen of my years.'

'I'm forty. And you know what happened to some of mine.'

'Marcia, once in the war they came to me with hints about you, about the undesirability of an officer of my position being involved with an English girl. I explained to them that I probably wouldn't see you again, so they let me alone. I denied you, Marcia. The cock crew for me. Imagine!'

'I'm imagining.'

'I have deserved nothing. But still I ask you to believe me now.'

'Perhaps I do.'

'Marcia, do you remember –'

'Smell of apples, Toni, in a bedroom in that little *Gasthof* near Arzfeld. Large, ancient fourposter bed. Hard, ancient mattress.'

'Vienna. That winter of 1939. Marcia, you wore a cossack hat, a fur hat, long boots. I had never seen such a sparkle as there was in your eyes, standing in the snow, laughing.'

'It was my first real laughter since Werner was killed. You brought me to life again. I was living a half-life. Werner was gone, your kind Rudberg cousins treated me as if I was a convalescent, I knew I'd been an idiot to stay in Austria, an enemy alien, God knew what would happen. Then you happened.'

'You were lovely, adorable, you touched my heart as no other woman had. I didn't like that. I liked being free, selfish, untied. You stole my freedom though I didn't realize it at the time. You're a thief. I've never regained my freedom, Marcia. But now I don't want to.'

'You said to me, Toni, "When you laugh, it's like water rippling over stones in the sunlight." Do you remember saying that? It wasn't very good but I was touched that you were attempting poetic expression, touched by the effort! Do you remember?'

'Yes. It was actually at Arzfeld, a hot day, the woods green, cool and inviting. You wore a yellow dress. Your neck and arms were pale brown against it.

'I so longed for the hours to pass, for the evening.'

'So did I.'

'If we . . . Your father would, I suppose, be upset. These things disturb the pattern of family life, make it uncomfortable. I've never met him but I know you love him. I understand that aspect.'

'How patient, how objective you are, Count Rudberg! Where's that impetuosity I recall?'

'Still there. But I prefer to say these things than to wait for you to say them.'

'My father's a darling. He's been shattered – utterly shattered – by Ant's, by Anthony's –' she looked away for a moment.

'I certainly don't wish to hurt him. But if I were to become happy he'd be happy himself. He'd mutter a little at first. He's

471

conventional, principled. His own marriage was very happy. But by now he doesn't feel affection for Robert although he respects him, he's sad we're like we are. And he's disappointed not to have grandchildren, I know that.'

'Ah –'

'I'm forty, Toni. Forty-one next birthday.'

They laughed at each other.

'Do you remember –'

'Polite conversation at Arzfeld –'

'You explaining you were there because your friend Captain Berckheim had a sister nearby and had persuaded you to spend a few days in the neighbourhood, to see the country! Did Berckheim actually exist?'

'Certainly he existed. And his sister. They had their uses. Berckheim made my presence less obviously deliberate, when all I wanted was to see you.'

'What happened to Berckheim?'

'Killed on the Leningrad front.'

'They were terrible days, Toni. Terrible, exciting days. But I look back, too, to so much sweetness. Like an enchanting melody, seductive, almost forgotten, suddenly heard again. And there's been such discordance since – in my own life, I mean.'

'Do you remember –'

'Does the cause for which you fought bother you, Toni?'

'Does it bother you, Marcia?'

'A bit, yes. One knew so little at the time. Frido, of course. Whispers, frowns, shakings of the head by dear old conservatives like Kaspar von Arzfeld. But now one reads – Awful!'

'Yes, of course. Well, I'll be honest with you, I wasn't bothered about that, I didn't concern myself with politics, I thought the Nazis were a loud, vulgar lot but they had a lot of popular support and you need popular support in a war.'

'Which they had started.'

'I suppose so. I didn't think of that much, either. I was a soldier. It was a challenge. I frankly enjoyed it. Most people in most countries prefer to think their Government has an overwhelming case once a war starts, isn't that so?'

'I dare say. But didn't you know of dreadful things being done – on the Eastern Front, I'm not talking about the camps –'

'Yes. I did. But there were so many beastly things going on there, such horrors being suffered as well as inflicted that I didn't fuss too much. I wasn't personally involved, you see. And I had a job to do, I was incredibly busy: and pretty busy just keeping alive, a lot of the time.'

He saw her eyes still clouded and touched her arm with the tips of his fingers.

'It wasn't good, Marcia, I know that. Not good at all, any of it. Maybe a price will go on being paid for a long time. I think I've paid my share of that price. Don't you?'

'My God, Toni, the things people have done to each other in our time!'

'And are likely to continue to do, Marcia. By other names, to other sorts of people, in different uniforms, uttering different cries.'

Toni could not, Marcia thought, have expressed this sombre reflection in the old days except in a light, sardonic tone, with a smile and a shrug and a call, nevertheless, to love and forget. Now there was nothing of mockery behind the sad, ordinary words. He sounded not bitter but sorrowful.

'I suppose we're survivors, aren't we, Toni?'

'Perhaps we are. Natural survivors. More wine?'

'Yes please. Sooner or later I'll have to think what to do with Bargate, you know. My home. Now Anthony's gone, it will come to me – unless Father turns me from his door for ever. Which he won't. I mean which he wouldn't.'

'I see.'

Marcia giggled.

'Oh Toni – if I agree to – to what you want, and I've not said I will, just think, you'll have your wish, you'll be what you schemed to be, married to a woman of property.'

'Will he be utterly destroyed?'

'Robert? No, I don't think so. He'll be impatient that I could be so foolish. He's a nice man, really – intolerant but nice. For a long time I used to tell myself awful things about him. I used to pretend that he had all sorts of unpleasant

473

characteristics. Then I realized that it's silly – and dishonest – to persuade yourself someone is awful just because you don't love them. It's not a crime, to be unloved. The crime was mine, to marry him.'

Marcia was graver than at any time in the last hour. 'Yes,' she said, 'the crime was mine. But I don't think I can go on paying the penalty for ever. I'm not sure, but I don't think so.'

'Yet his pride – his pride as a man, that will be hit hard, won't it?'

'He doesn't feel in that sort of way. Perhaps I'd have cared for him more if he did. He's reasonable, impatient, articulate. He was in love with me, whatever that meant. Even at the beginning it didn't mean much. Not what I'd call a consuming flame! An obsession, perhaps. He wanted me badly. He disapproved of me. He wanted to possess and reform an object of which he disapproved. Which he, nevertheless, desired.'

'He sounds very different from me.'

'He is. But he used to be amusing, attractive once. And intelligent. Anthony and he were devoted to each other when they were younger, and he could always make me laugh. Still – Toni, I've not said I'll do it yet. I've not taken the decision. And what do you really want – that I get a divorce? Marry you?'

'Exactly. Exactly that.'

'You're a Catholic. Doesn't that complicate things?'

'Yes. There will be complications. We shall master them. I know perfectly well that you are meant to be with me always. It is God's will, I am sure of it.'

'It doesn't sound exactly orthodox if I may say so.'

'I am not exactly orthodox. But I spent thirteen years in a Russian prison and even I, selfish, frivolous, undeserving Rudberg, have thought about such things. And believe.'

Marcia sighed. She said,

'I'm not ruthless enough – perhaps I'm not ruthless enough for happiness. At sudden moments I remember how delightful Robert could be – can be: how kind and helpful he was to me when I was in trouble. I've said he won't be destroyed – he won't! But I don't want to undervalue him, run him down. It's just that we aren't making each other happy and I don't

474

think we ever can. Love's gone, Toni. On my side it was never there. Wicked of me – but should one live with a mistake like that, or give two people another chance?'

Long ago, Toni would have listened to this with calculating approval. He would have said to himself complacently that the woman was coming round easily, that, like all women, she was making a last effort at squaring the circle, having it both ways, easing her conscience: but that 'all would be well', he'd have his way. Now he recognized that he didn't feel in the least like that. He found himself loving Marcia the more for what he thought was genuine consideration. Yes, this Robert whom he did not know was a man, a person, he was not evil, he was not cruel, he was not nobody. He deserved decency. Toni knew he could not express this in a way to convince. Marcia no doubt remembered only the old Rudberg, determined to flatter, nod, sigh, smile, have his way with a girl. He took her hand and said,

'I understand you perfectly. You are right to feel as you do. I could not love you if you felt otherwise.'

Marcia looked at him with some surprise. Then it was her turn again to feel tears forcing their way to her eyes.

'So. You will answer me tomorrow!'

'Within twenty-four hours. Just a little thinking to be done. No confidences. No confessions. No girlish heart-to-hearts, no asking of advice. Just a little hard thinking.' 'Even praying,' Marcia nearly added, but she was not sure.

'Twenty-four hours is one thousand four hundred and forty minutes. You have already used the first. I shall think of you in each of them, willing you, willing you, willing you to reach the answer I desire. More than anything, ever. And I love you.' They were standing on the pavement. Marcia sang softly –

> *'Ich liebe dich,*
> *So wie du mich –'*

'Ah, if you meant that –'

She laughed. 'Goodbye, Toni. No, don't touch me. Stay here. I'll tell you my answer tomorrow. I'll leave you now.'

As long ago, he whispered,

475

'I am very, very loving of you, Marcia.'

'No, Toni, that's still not entirely right.' There was a catch in her voice. She walked away, very fast. As Toni turned back into the restaurant to settle accounts, murmur thanks, collect his hat, he felt a humble, magical assurance that he need not unduly doubt what her answer would be.